A FISTFUL OF FIRE

A MADISON FOX ADVENTURE - BOOK TWO

REBECCA CHASTAIN

This book is a work of fiction. Names, characters, dialogue, places, and incidents either are drawn from the author's imagination or are used fictitiously. Any resemblance to actual persons, living or dead, business establishments, locales, or events is entirely coincidental. Any resemblance to an actual cat is 100 percent intentional and approved by Mack Fu, who shamelessly insisted on being immortalized in the pages of this novel.

A FISTFUL OF FIRE

Copyright © 2015 by Rebecca Chastain
Cover design by Yocla Designs
Book layout by Deranged Doctor Design

www.rebeccachastain.com

All rights reserved. In accordance with the US Copyright Act of 1976, scanning, uploading, and electronic sharing of any part of this book without permission of the author constitute unlawful piracy and theft of the author's intellectual property. No part of this book may be used or reproduced in any manner whatsoever without written permission, except in the case of brief quotations embodied in critical articles and reviews. If you would like to use material from this book (other than for review purposes), prior written permission must be obtained from the publisher. Please do not participate in or encourage piracy of copyrighted materials in violation of the author's rights.

Mind Your Muse Books
PO Box 374
Rocklin, CA 95677

ISBN: 978-0-9906031-5-3

1st Edition

Also by Rebecca Chastain

Madison Fox, Illuminant Enforcer
A Fistful of Evil
A Fistful of Fire

Gargoyle Guardian Chronicles
Magic of the Gargoyles
Curse of the Gargoyles
Secret of the Gargoyles

Tiny Glitches
(paranormal romance)

Never miss any novel news:
Sign up for Rebecca's newsletter to receive emails
regarding future releases and behind-the-scenes information at
www.rebeccachastain.com/newsletter

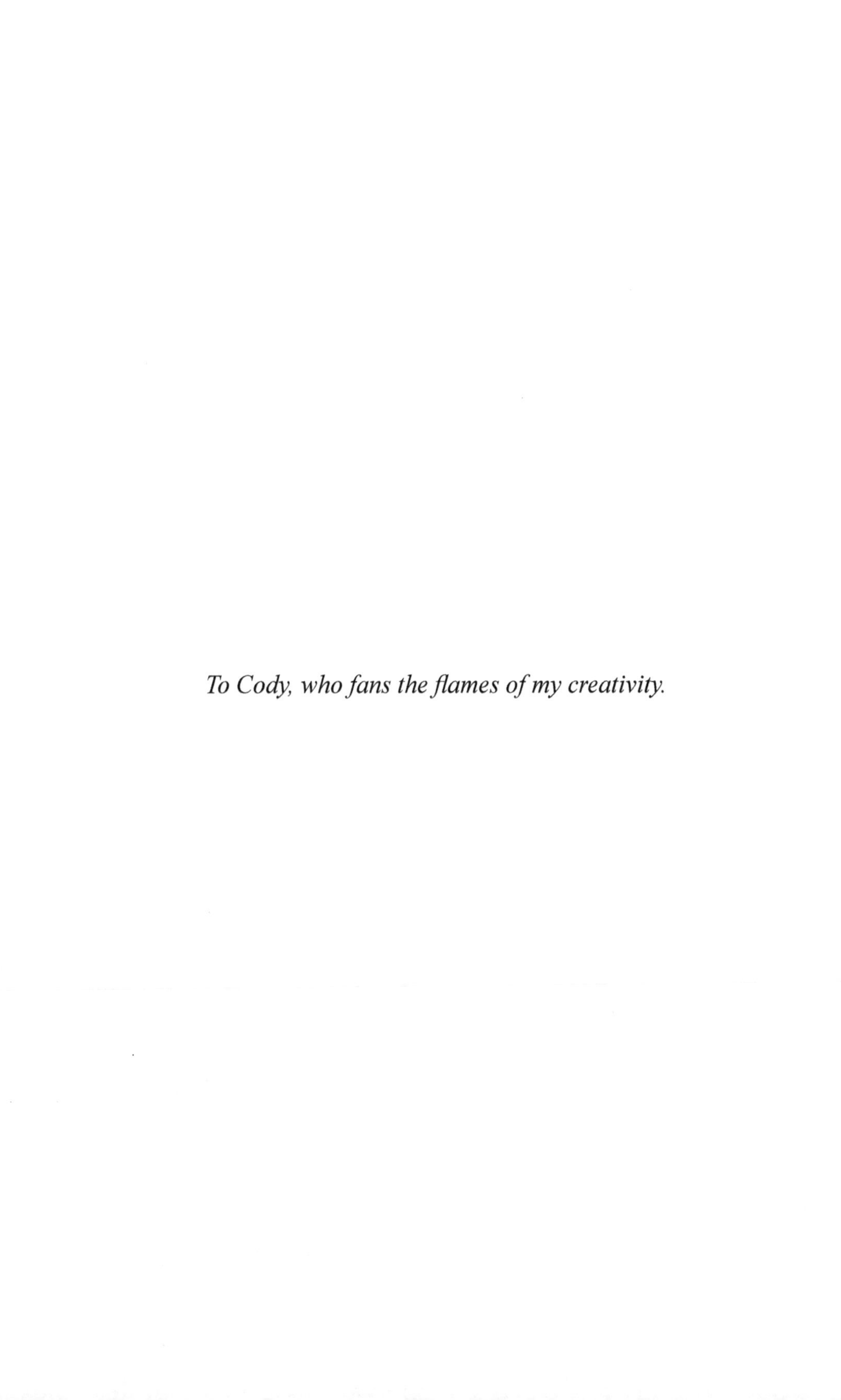

To Cody, who fans the flames of my creativity.

1

A Man Can Work from Sun to Sun, but a Woman's Work Is Never Done

AN INKY PUDDLE OF *ATRUM* pooled in front of a storage closet beside the hotel elevators. Six fist-size imps bopped around in the *atrum*, their primordial ooze. In the time it took me to pull my collapsible wand of petrified wood from my back pocket and extend it, a chinchilla-shaped bubble swelled in the *atrum*, growing glassy ebony eyes, a mouthful of needle-like teeth, and tiny feet. Soundlessly, it sprang an inch into the air, disconnecting from the puddle and becoming a seventh fully formed imp.

I pushed *lux lucis* into the wand, filling the entire length with the white energy. The imps turned, attention snagged by the bright waving light. As one, they opened jaws as tall as their bodies, revealing rows of sharp black teeth and proving they were little more than brainless mouths. I slashed the thin wood through their insubstantial bodies, and the imps exploded into harmless black glitter. By the time the disintegrated *atrum* sifted to the floor, the flecks were as gray as the carpet.

I smiled and pressed the tip of the wand into my palm, collapsing the hollow segments like an old radio antenna until it was short enough to return to the back pocket of my jeans.

A few days ago, this hotel had been coated top to bottom with *atrum*, thanks to a video game convention and the mobs of gamer geeks overflowing the event floor. Okay, technically, the nerd herd hadn't been responsible for the evil, but they'd disseminated it as unwitting hosts. The real evil had been a demon camping in their midst, taking advantage of my newbie enforcer status and weak control of my region. Besting it had nearly killed me, but survival had firmed my resolve to stick to my new career path.

I'd been running cleanup here at ground zero and throughout my region ever since. Eventually I'd catch up and catch my breath.

I crouched next to the empty black puddle. *Atrum* was the insidious source from which basic evil creatures spawned and on which more complex evil creatures thrived. I found it repulsive and took great delight in destroying it. Though this patch was only two feet across, left alone, the *atrum* would continue to spawn imps and taint any people who stepped through it.

I gathered *lux lucis* in my palm. My soul glowed a soft butter white, but as the *lux lucis* collected in my hand, it brightened like a fluorescent light warming up. If I were using normal sight, a light as bright as my hand would have left a stain on my retina and cast shadows around my feet. But I wasn't using normal sight; I was viewing the world in Primordium, and no matter how bright the *lux lucis*, it never cast a shadow. I liked to think of Primordium as soul sight, because Primordium afforded me a black-and-white morality-based view of the world. Living things fell in two categories: white and good, like plants and animals, and black and bad, like imps and their more intelligent cohorts, vervet. It sounded simplistic until humans were thrown into the mix. Normal people's souls were a patchwork of stains representing a gray scale of unethical decisions.

The pure white souls of enforcers, mine included, were an exception and a necessity. My job was to fight evil, and my soul was my weapon.

I focused on my hand. Moving my body's *lux lucis* was a relatively new experience for me. Shoving my soul's energy into my pet wood wand or straight into an evil creature I could do without thinking, but manipulating the energy took more concentration.

I pushed *lux lucis* along the top of my hand to my fingertips, then pulled it back down my palm to my wrist, repeating the loop again and again until a seamless cycle of light zipped around my hand. I waited until the crest of *lux lucis* reached my fingertips, then gave it a flip. *Lux lucis* jumped from my fingers to the carpet and rolled through the smear of black *atrum*. White energy ate through dark, leaving the carpet a clean, inanimate gray.

Standing, I brushed my hands together with satisfaction and examined the hallway. Though I knew the carpet's floral print swirled with pastel colors and the paintings nailed to the beige walls displayed jarringly colorful interpretations of the Sacramento Valley, in Primordium the walls, paintings, and carpet were all the same inanimate charcoal gray. Indirect illumination gave depth to the hall, but trying to determine the light's source would give me a headache.

I mentally checked the floor off my list of areas to clean and turned to the elevator. An onyx shadow oozed through the seam between the door and the floor, fleshing out into a monkey's paw tipped with lion claws. A second arm joined the first. Claws sank into the carpet and heaved, pulling the entire body through the paper-thin opening. It puffed into the shape of a vervet, and I shifted my weight to the balls of my feet.

Black as a demon's soul from the tip of its scorpion tail to the crown of its spiked primate head and coated with the scales of a diseased fish, the vervet was a compact nightmare. I preferred imps. Both creatures spawned from *atrum*, but at least imps looked like chinchilla fluff balls. Plus, imps lacked any semblance of a brain.

The vervet spotted me and grinned, exposing jagged teeth long enough to spear my arm clean through. I lunged for it, missing when it sprang to the wall.

A door halfway down the hall opened, and a trio of middle-aged women exited their room, laughing and chatting. The vervet swung to look at them, hunger sparking in its dark eyes. I made another grab for it, but it leapt to the ceiling, then the opposite wall. A few more jumps widened the gap between us, then it galloped along the vertical surface as if gravity didn't exist, its long black talons leaving no marks in the plaster. While I was still reaching for my wand, the vervet pounced on the nylon-clad calf of the lead lady, sinking a mouthful of fangs into her soul. Flecks of *atrum* replaced her soul's *lux lucis*, one swallow at a time. Oblivious, the woman rifled through her purse.

The vervet clawed up her body to her stomach, each talon depositing a prick of *atrum* to tarnish her soul. Twisting, it took a bite from her companion's chest. Whatever the host said made the women toss their heads back with fresh mirth. The vervet clambered over them, eating up the joy brightening their souls.

The juxtaposition of the women's clueless happiness with the spawn of evil snacking on them twisted my stomach. Narrowing my sights on the vervet, I charged.

When the trio spotted me barreling toward them, they finally reacted, first with scowls at my audacity to run in the hallway, then with widening eyes when they spied the petrified wood I brandished fully extended. My badass enforcer vibe, which came across as loony-bin crazy to norms, plastered them against the wall.

When I was within arm's reach of the vervet—and the woman it clung to—I made a grab for it. The vervet rocketed into the air and swung down the hallway, teeth wide in a silent laugh. The woman jerked and yelled, thinking I'd tried to punch her.

"Sorry!" I stumbled but didn't slow.

"I'm reporting you to the manager!" one of the women shouted after me.

My shoulders hunched. This was exactly the kind of attention I was supposed to avoid. My job was strictly undercover. Getting arrested tended to hamper an enforcer's ability to defend her region.

Finding the balance between doing my job and keeping a low profile was a struggle. I couldn't let the vervet feast on the women. *Atrum* corrupted. In people who earned their *atrum* through immoral acts, it created a feedback loop, maintaining a person's immoral nature—or enhancing it. For innocents like those women, it was possible they might shrug off planted *atrum* and restore their souls to their natural states, but it was just as likely the *atrum* would take root, influencing the women to make vile decisions that would spread evil further. Leaving the vervet on the trio could have resulted in a cascade of larger problems.

Plus, it galled me to see good people corrupted. If my tactics had been less than circumspect, so be it.

The hallway cut left at ninety degrees, and the vervet hurled out of sight. I slowed, clutching a cramp in my side. I'd been over this hotel a hundred times in the last two and a half days, and I knew that only ten or fifteen rooms lay beyond the bend before the hallway dead-ended. The vervet was trapped.

I rounded the corner at a jog. A maid's cart cozied up to a doorway near the end of the hall, the maid absent. The vervet cannonballed into a stack of towels, then collapsed on its back. Lifting one arm, it extended a single dark digit—the middle one of three—sitting up enough to bare a cluttered row of sharp ebony teeth in a grin.

I lowered the pet wood to my side but held myself ready to strike.

"Back at you." I flipped it off with a sweet smile of my own.

A young maid stepped out of the adjacent room into the crosshairs of my crude gesture. She gasped, crossed herself, and scuttled backward into the room, slamming the door before the vervet could react. A good thing, too. With her light gray soul, she was prime vervet-snack material.

Abashed, I tucked my offending hand behind my back. Frightening the staff would win me no points with my boss. I needed to finish this quickly before she called her manager.

"Hold still and let me kill you, you stupid little bugger."

The lock slammed home against the other side of the door. Okay. Time to disappear before she called the *cops*.

I charged the vervet. It bounced to the ceiling at the last minute, but I anticipated the move. Slicing through the air with the wand, I cleaved the vervet in two, pulsing *lux lucis* into the mutated creature. It exploded. Harmless graying particles floated around my head and shoulders. Grimacing, I ducked aside, surreptitiously wiping my hair. I waited until I reached the empty stairwell before doing a heebie-jeebies dance. When my phone belted out "Hail to the Chief" from my back pocket, I jumped and swallowed a startled shriek.

I pulled my metallic-green cell phone from my pocket. It was my first cell phone ever, newly purchased for this job, and I'd named it Medusa. A week of being on call twenty-four-seven combined with a job that had no defined work hours, and my ardor for the new technology had cooled considerably. I swiped the screen and said hello to my boss.

"Come to the office," Mr. Pitt said instead of a greeting.

"I've got the top two floors left."

"They'll wait." The line went dead.

"Keep up the good work, Madison," I said on his behalf, pocketing Medusa. "You're the best."

Grumpy was Mr. Pitt's default, or it had been since he'd hired me. He'd wanted a fully trained illuminant enforcer. When my predecessor transferred to another region and no experienced enforcers applied for the job, he'd been forced to accept me. Since I'd spent the first twenty-five years of my life unaware that my ability to see souls was a weapon for fighting evil, I had a lot of catching up to do.

Mr. Pitt had hired Doris, a retired enforcer, to give me some last-minute training, and we squeezed in one packed night of lessons before she left for a family vacation. My boss and I both would have preferred I spend more time learning the ropes before jumping into field work, but the appearance of a demon in our region had necessitated immediate action. A week later, demon vanquished and region almost clean, I felt I deserved a pat on the back, if not a Medal of Valor. Apparently Mr. Pitt needed more proof of my competence than mere survival.

I clattered down the stairs and exited through the quiet lobby. With luck, whatever Mr. Pitt wanted wouldn't take too much time. I was on a deadline. Tonight I had a date with Dr. Alex Love, the hottest vet in the state.

My stomach flip-flopped as I slid behind the wheel of my Civic and started the car. I'd lusted after the man for three years, and tonight I'd see if reality lived up to my fantasies. And I had plenty of fantasies, several of which I indulged in during the short drive to my office.

Cold November air slapped me back to the present when I slid out of my car a few minutes later. I tried to box up my excitement, but I ruined it by checking the time. Only six hours and fourteen minutes until my date.

I jogged across the parking lot and darted through the glass doors into the heated interior of the two-story office building. Rubbing the chill out of my arms, I walked through the building's lobby, past the restrooms and elevator, and down a hushed hall. As always, murmured confidential conversations and muted keyboard clacks emanated from the mortgage company, but the temp agency bustled with a louder, no-nonsense air. Passing *that* door made me smile. My aimless temp days had ended when Mr. Pitt offered me this job. Now I saved the world—or my portion of it—and got paid to do it.

Tucked at the end of the hallway, my region's headquarters were humble and serene. No one would suspect Illumination Studios was anything other than the tiny bumper sticker company it claimed to be. If my job had entailed working within its confines, I would have been fitted for a straitjacket after three days.

Of course, the fact that I *liked* sprinting through the suburban neighborhoods of Roseville, California, engaging in skirmishes with evil creatures others couldn't see, might mean I was already insane.

"Good morning, Sharon," I sang.

The receptionist tracked my entrance with hard brown eyes, the rest of her body statue still at her tall wooden desk. Behind her, soft white lights glistened on the metallic letters of our fake company, but the same warm glow fell flat across Sharon's shoulders, shadowing her eyes and thin mouth. I'd met tortoises with more expressive faces—and who were more cheerful.

Focusing on keeping my shoulders relaxed under the receptionist's inscrutable stare, I strode past the glass-walled conference room—and stuttered to a halt.

Rows of empty, slender spray-topped glass vials lined the long conference table. Rose stood near one end, clutching a bottle in her hands, eyes closed. The Latina's long dark hair was slicked back in a simple ponytail and she was barefoot. More shocking, she wore jeans and a men's T-shirt two sizes too big. Since when did Rose swap out her figure-flattering dresses for clothes that could have come from my closet?

I backpedaled to the open doorway, waiting until she opened her eyes before I stepped in.

"Good morning."

She squinted at me, then gestured me to her side. "I could use some of that bounce right now."

"Bounce?" I eased closer, keeping myself and my purse well clear of the table. I wasn't a complete klutz, but I didn't want to take any chances with vials set up like fragile dominoes.

"Perky morning cheer. You've got it in spades."

"It's date day." I tried not to picture Alex topless, but the image refused to be ignored. Only six hours and eleven minutes.

"Honey, I can't wait until you finally jump his bones." She fanned herself. "I'm getting dizzy off your horny fumes."

"Excuse me for getting a little excited."

"Excited? Don't try to lie to an empath. That's lust, plain and simple. I felt you coming from the parking lot."

I blushed. She had to be exaggerating. "Fine. I'm lusty. But it's *Dr.*

Love. Even his name sounds sexy."

"So does Dr. Bigdick."

"Hmm, that doesn't have quite the same ring. Dr. Love is a name you could marry into."

"Madison Love? It sounds like a Playboy Bunny's name."

"A happily married Playboy Bunny's name, and better than Madison Bigdick."

Rose snorted. "It can't be just a name thing. How long's it been?"

"Since I've had a date? Not long."

Rose let one sculpted eyebrow call me on my lie.

"Okay, okay. Maybe it's been a while."

Rose crossed her arms.

"Fine. It's been a long time. Ages. Forever. I can't even remember what a penis looks like."

Rose burst out laughing, and I grinned.

"Hang on. This is good stuff." She set down the vial she'd been holding, then picked up the next one and closed her eyes. I waited, curiosity growing. Rose cracked an eye to glare at me. "No fidgeting."

"What are you doing?"

"Making sure we stay in business another season. Now hush."

I closed my mouth. What was that supposed to mean?

Rose sighed. "Think about that date or get out of the room. Anticipation and lust I can work with; curiosity is just mucking things up."

I frowned.

"Irritation doesn't work for me, either. Shoo." Rose waved a hand at me without opening her eyes. I backed carefully out of the room, waiting until safely outside the glass before sticking my tongue out at her. She smiled without looking.

"That's a load of carob chips, and you know it!" Mr. Pitt bellowed from his office. I ducked into my cubicle. The blinds on the glass front of Mr. Pitt's office were drawn, making it impossible to see who received his reaming. For once, it wasn't me.

"Of course Isabel would prefer—" Pause. "This is damn high and—" Pause. No other voices came from his office. He was on the phone. "Don't quote me the rules, Liam," Mr. Pitt shouted. "Fine. No, that won't work— Fine. Tonight."

The bang of the phone slamming into the cradle made me jump, and I dropped into my chair.

"MadiSON!" Mr. Pitt bellowed.

Oh joy. What have I done now?

2

YOUR IGNORANCE IS THEIR POWER

Y ES, MR. PITT?" I PAUSED in the doorway of his office. While he was *Mr. Pitt* to me, my boss's nameplate said *Brad Pitt*, a grossly unfair coincidence given my boss's fleshy red lips, protruding hazel eyes, and a shiny bald crown rimmed with a nest of short gray hair. About the only thing he had in common with the actor who had been named *People*'s Sexiest Man Alive was his age.

At this moment, his face glowed a shade usually seen on the skin of beets. I had a fleeting concern for his blood pressure, and a more lasting concern for myself. *Please don't let him have heard I was terrorizing hotel guests and staff. Let his irritation be focused on a new horribly evil creature that has taken a liking to our region.*

I crossed my fingers behind my back.

"Sit."

Of the two leather chairs across from his desk, I chose the one closest to the door and perched on the edge, rehearsing an apology.

Mr. Pitt stared at the laminated map of our region on his wall, his jaw clenching and relaxing. The hotel and a few other areas were marked with red dots. Trouble was brewing in our region. So long as it didn't interfere with tonight's date, I'd be happy with a change of scenery. The hotel cleanup was gratifying but repetitive.

"You haven't been here long enough to learn the rhythms of this region," Mr. Pitt said. "You'll have to take my word that there's been unusual activity this year. Ours isn't the only region affected. Isabel's,

Liam's, Margaret's, even Kathleen's and Ron's have been hit hard."

I let out my breath. This wasn't about my tactics at the hotel. Mr. Pitt had also answered one of my questions about the heated conversation I'd just overheard: Liam, fellow recipient of Mr. Pitt's vitriol, was a warden. That made him Mr. Pitt's counterpart of another nearby region and boss of his own illuminant enforcer. What had he done to earn Mr. Pitt's wrath?

"Jacob's needed this year and can't be tied up."

"Who is Jacob?"

"He's the enforcer of Roseville—everything west of the freeway," Mr. Pitt clarified when I started to protest.

"Oh." My region's western edge followed the line of I-80, which bisected the city. Of the two sides of Roseville, mine was the smaller by more than half.

"Roseville has the ninth largest sales of any city in California, and a majority of those are due to the Galleria," Mr. Pitt said.

I blinked at the non sequitur. "The mall?"

"Half of Sacramento and people as far away as Colfax and Grass Valley shop there, especially this time of year. The Galleria is a large responsibility, and it takes a lot of time during the holidays."

"The mall does?"

"Yes, Madison. The mall!" Mr. Pitt swiped a hand over his face, then gripped his armrests. "Which is why I'm assigning you to take over cito duty this year."

My good mood took a punch to the stomach. "What is cito duty and what does it have to do with the mall?" I didn't like how much he'd built this up. Mr. Pitt didn't explain assignments. He delivered them like whip cracks, fast and expecting me to jump.

"Right. Of course you don't know. The mall swarms with citos this time of year. You'll be there to stay on top of things and prevent an outbreak."

I skipped over the obvious question to the most important one. "Do you mean full-time?"

"Yes. It will be good for you."

Crap. Whatever cito duty was, it was going to suck.

"What about the hotel?"

"After you finish up today, Joy and Will should be able to handle it." Joy and Will were Illuminea, supposedly born out of *lux lucis*, though they looked completely human. They behaved like pacifist enforcers: Where I enjoyed killing evil creatures, the Illuminea refused to fight, and they restricted their *lux lucis* use to positively influencing people. I wasn't sure how spreading goodwill was going to eliminate the hotel's residual evil, but that wasn't my main concern.

"And the rest of my—our—region?"

"Jacob, Rafi, and Summer will look in on things. I'll talk with Margaret about borrowing her enforcer, too, if it comes to that."

"Wait. You're going to stick me in Jacob's region doing something at the mall, which, again, is in his region, and you're going to bring him and other enforcers in to do my job? That doesn't sound right."

Mr. Pitt's jaw bounced.

"I'm sure I can do more good in my position." Alarm bells clanged in my head. Why was I being relegated to this mall task? Why wasn't *I* needed in *my* region, especially if there was an uncharacteristic amount of evil?

"You don't know enough to know where you can do the most good." Mr. Pitt planted his hands on his desk and glared.

"All the more reason I should continue to work in my region." I leaned forward. "At least let me work with these other enforcers. I'm sure I could learn a lot from them."

"That's out of the question." Mr. Pitt's expression closed.

"Why? What's wrong with the other enforcers?"

"Nothing. It's a warden thing. Trust me, I've worked long and hard to shape this region. When Doris returns, you'll get plenty more training. For now, the mall is a good compromise. It's important work."

So important that Jacob couldn't be "tied up" with it? "But—"

"Enough with the hangdog expression, Madison. Think of this as a rite of passage, something all enforcers have to do."

"Is it?"

"Sure. Check in here Friday at five thirty to pick up spray."

"Five thirty, as in a.m.?" I squeaked.

Mr. Pitt smiled wanly. "Considering the mall will be open from six p.m. Thanksgiving day straight through to Friday, I think I'm being generous."

"Um, yes. Thank you." I fidgeted in my seat, then finally asked the question I dreaded. "And citos are?"

"They're— Ah, you have it! Everything you need to know is in the handbook." Mr. Pitt gestured to someone in the doorway.

I turned and all thoughts ground to a standstill. Niko Demitrius stood with one shoulder resting against the doorway. He held up a tattered booklet in one hand, but I doubt I would have noticed it if Mr. Pitt hadn't mentioned it. A few days' acquaintance wasn't enough time to inure me to Niko's aura of competence paired with physical perfection, but at least I didn't gape as I soaked in his handsome profile.

I stood and fussed unnecessarily with the hem of my sweater. The last time I'd seen Niko, I'd been a mess, strung out on adrenaline and shock after killing a demon. Even so, I'd felt like a real enforcer and basked in Niko's respect. Yet only three days later, Niko was here to witness Mr. Pitt shuffling me aside because I wasn't good enough to deal with the "unusual activity" in my own region. The only thing that would make this situation more embarrassing would be if Niko remembered I'd set Justin Timberlake's "SexyBack" as my ringtone for him.

"As ordered, one enforcer handbook," Niko said. Mr. Pitt scurried around his desk, and I stepped between the two leather chairs to make room for him. It was that or move closer to Niko, and my face already felt sunburned from our current proximity.

Mr. Pitt accepted the book as if it were a fragile holy object, frowning and muttering to himself. I pretended to cough, and pressed my cool fingers to my cheeks, willing the blush to fade.

I peeked at Niko again. In the office's harsh fluorescent lights, his creamy shirt made his dark skin glow. He crossed his arms, and the movement pulled the shirt tight against his well-rounded biceps and flat pecs.

Realizing my peek had become a stare, I shifted my gaze to Niko's face. He grinned at me, perfect white teeth gleaming.

Where was a sinkhole when I needed one?

"Everything you need to know is in here," Mr. Pitt said. He set the book in my hands. Despite its leather binding, it weighed no more than a small paperback.

"Everything?"

"Yep. Are you feeling okay, Madison? This would be the worst possible time to get sick." Mr. Pitt stepped close to get a good look at my flushed face. I waved him back.

"I feel fine. If that's all, I'll just . . ." I flapped a hand toward the door.

Mr. Pitt glanced to Niko, then back at me. His concerned expression cleared, and he rolled his eyes. "Back to work," he agreed.

I squeezed between the back side of the leather chair and the glass wall. Niko stepped into the office to give me room to pass.

"Nice seeing you," I mumbled. Once through the doorway, I took a deep breath to expel tension, only to inhale Niko's delicious roasted-cinnamon scent. Rushing the few yards to my cubicle, I collapsed into my chair and closed my eyes. That could have been worse. I could have tripped. Or drooled.

After five deep breaths, my brain finally came back online. Niko was an optivus aegis, an illuminant enforcer on steroids whose territory included all of Northern California. He worked where he was most needed, which is why he'd been here when the demon had set up shop in my region. If he was still in the area, it must be due to the unwarranted levels of evil Mr. Pitt mentioned.

And, holy crap, how had I missed the fact that I was going to be stuck at the mall on *Black Friday*?

I flopped the handbook onto my desk, then laid my head down on top of my crossed arms. I would have guessed the mall on the largest shopping day of the year would be a hub of evil, not where Mr. Pitt would stick his least favorite—and only—enforcer to get her out of the way.

"I'll be there," Niko said, his voice clear as he exited Mr. Pitt's office.

I snapped upright, smoothed my hair with one hand, and rummaged blindly in my purse. Just a busy professional here. I tried to look casual when I glanced up to say good-bye. I was pretty sure the imprint of my sweater's weave was pressed into my forehead.

"Can I talk with you?" Niko asked.

"Of course."

"In private?"

I wiped damp palms down my thighs. "Okay."

Niko grabbed his leather coat from the chair in the cubicle adjoining mine and headed toward the rear exit. I followed.

The back door let out onto a small patio tucked between matching two-story office buildings. Cold wind cut through my fleece sweater and shook the bare branches of sweet gum trees spaced around the terrace. I wrapped my arms around myself. Niko shrugged into his jacket and let the door shut behind us. We had the patio-turned-wind-tunnel to ourselves.

Niko stalked to the edge of the patio. I followed on an invisible leash. Beyond the concrete, the hillside dropped steeply, giving us a view of the top of an office building below us and the barren branches of the tree-lined Douglas Boulevard beyond. Small evergreen shrubbery fenced the terrace. I kept my distance, having had the misfortune of seeing a spider the size of my palm in those bushes once.

A swath of leaves faded from green to brown and twirled to the ground when Niko ran his fingertips along the straight line of the nearest trimmed hedge. I blinked to Primordium. Bright midday sunlight dimmed to a subtle, directionless light, and the colors of the world washed to gray scale. Niko's bright soul drew my eyes like a beacon. Compared to his, my soul looked as weak as melted butter. Niko's contained the strength of an ancient tree, solid and confident. I wtasn't above a twinge of jealousy.

An arctic gust cleared my head, and I forced myself to be analytical. I'd looked at Niko in Primordium only a few times, but now I thought I detected an uncharacteristic dimness to his impressive soul.

"What's going on?" I pulled a hand from my armpit to point at his fingers, which he'd moved to rest on a tree trunk. *Lux lucis* seeped from the tree into Niko, recharging his soul. Unlike the more fragile leaves of the hedge, the tree gave its energy without suffering any visible loss of life. I blinked to normal vision to avoid becoming mesmerized by the swirl of *lux lucis*.

"I ran into some trouble on the way here. But that's not what I want to talk about."

"Oh?" Shifting to the side, I used Niko's six-foot frame to block the wind.

"The local wardens are holding an emergency strategy meeting tonight to discuss the unusual concentration of evil in this area. Many enforcers are going, and I think you should, too."

"Tonight?" Any remaining fog of lust whisked away at his words. Fantasizing about Niko was fun, and based on my body's reactions, I bet the man kicked off some impressive pheromones, but that was just lust. Tonight I had a chance with a man I had more than a physical attraction to. "No. I can't. I have a date."

Niko straightened and slid his hands into his pockets. He frowned, and for once his smoldering look had no effect on me. "Reschedule. Brad could really use your support."

"I know the feeling. I've cleaned up the region, done my job. Where's my support? What do I get? Cito duty, which I suspect is awful."

"It is."

"Thanks. No. I think I'll keep my date."

Niko waited, silent and patient. I glared at him.

"You're serious, aren't you?" I pictured Dr. Love's—*Alex's*—face. His smiling blue eyes with soft crinkles in the corners. His perpetually tousled brown hair that I'd been dreaming of running my hands through since we first met. His shy smile when he asked me out. Anticipation of this date had been my shining carrot dangling at the end of a grueling week.

"If this meeting's so important, why didn't Mr. Pitt tell me about it?"

"It's not mandatory for enforcers to attend."

"So I could ask Mr. Pitt about it on Friday?" Hope blossomed afresh.

"We need trained, engaged enforcers right now, ones conversant with what's happening in and around their regions. Enforcers who put their education and region above their social calendars."

I flinched. That was low. I *did* want to learn, but not at the expense of my personal happiness.

"Jacob has experience and an interest in his region. That's why he's being given more responsibility and you're being put in the mall."

I wanted to scream. I yearned for tonight's date with a feeling akin to homesickness. It had been years since my last serious relationship, and the romantic encounters since weren't worth noting. In Alex, I saw a potential for happiness and true connection. I didn't want to ruin my chance before the first date.

I shifted to my toes and back down, shivering against the endless breeze. Tonight's meeting might be a complete waste of my time. What did it matter if I was there? Apparently I'd be working in the mall, not addressing whatever evil plagued my region.

The beginning of a headache tapped against the inside of my forehead. I'd been playing catch-up since the day I'd been hired, and I wasn't foolish enough to think I'd come close to learning all the skills needed to perform—and survive—as an enforcer. I knew I should seize every opportunity to learn, which meant attending a meeting that would give me firsthand knowledge of the current threat. Plus, who knew what else I would learn. Maybe something to counter the perpetual "you don't know enough" argument.

"Mr. Pitt would be happy if I went?" I wasn't going to cancel my date *and* piss off my boss just because Niko said it was a good idea.

"Yes."

"Why does Mr. Pitt need my support?"

"Does that mean you're going?"

My chest hurt, and I rubbed my breastbone. My neck was stiff when I nodded. *This had better make Mr. Pitt happy.*

"Good. I'll pick you up at your place at six and fill you in on the way."

My brain crossed wires, making it sound like I had just agreed to a date with Niko. Worse, I'd betrayed Alex, swapping him with Niko. I opened my mouth to protest, but Niko was already striding away. He stopped and spun on the ball of a foot.

"Treat that handbook like gold. You don't even want to know how much Brad paid for it." He spun back toward the parking lot, whistling as he walked. I recognized the tune instantly: "SexyBack."

Blinking back tears of frustration heaped on embarrassment, I stomped back into the office. Tonight's date was ruined, but that didn't mean my entire shot with Alex was sabotaged.

I crossed my fingers that I was right.

3

LATE BUT WORTH THE WAIT

BY THE TIME I REACHED my desk, my eyes were dry and I'd unclenched a jaw gritted tight with cold and frustration. I yanked my jacket from my chair, stuffed the handbook in my purse, and stalked out through the back. I really needed to slam something, but the door's self-closing glider hinge eased it back to the frame with an aggravating soft whoosh of air.

I held myself together until I'd slid into the driver's seat of my Civic and closed the door. Then I screamed, stomped my feet, slammed my hands on the steering wheel, and embraced a hissy fit that could have taught two-year-olds everywhere a thing or two. When I finished, I brushed my hair out of my face and took a few deep breaths before opening my eyes.

A woman sat in a maroon Mercedes parked in front of me, a water bottle poised in front of her open mouth. She averted huge eyes and fumbled with her door handle. In seconds, she scurried across the pavement on pencil-thin high heels toward the office building.

Sighing, I fished my cell phone out of my purse. There was nothing for it but to call Alex and pray like crazy he didn't think I was flaky and would still want to go on a date with me.

My stomach roiled. This was going to look awful. I was canceling only five hours and forty-two minutes before our date. I *was* a flake. Why would Alex want to take another chance on me?

I tucked Medusa in my pants' pocket and got out of my car. I paced behind the Civic's bumper, working through what to say. Everything sounded lame. Everything *was* lame.

"Stupid meeting. Stupid me for prioritizing work above Alex. Stupid

Niko for making it impossible for me to say no." I circled around those thoughts a time or two, savoring my frustration before acknowledging its pointlessness.

I will *get information in this meeting. It will be useful and good for my career.*

For Niko's sake, it better be.

Rubbing my nauseous stomach, I dialed the Love and Caring Veterinary Clinic. The receptionist put me on hold when I asked for Dr. Love. A moment later, his smooth, deep voice greeted me.

"Hi, uh, Alex. It's Madison."

"Hi, Madison." I could hear the smile in his voice and grinned in response. "You're not canceling on me, are you?" He was teasing. My heart plummeted.

"Um."

"Oh. You are." The smile was gone.

Crap. Make this right, Dice, I pep-talked myself, using my best friend Bridget's nickname for me for extra luck. I resumed pacing, my steps quick and sharp. "I am, but I don't want to. God, if it was up to me, we'd already be on our date." I smacked myself in the forehead. Now I sounded too eager. "It's just this meeting came up at work at the last minute. There are some problems with our . . . production, and we need to address it before Black Friday." It was the truth, but so carefully bent it felt like a lie.

"I see."

No. Not with that tone of voice, you don't. "The meeting doesn't matter," I hurried on. "The important thing is I was really, really looking forward to tonight, and I can't even express how *bummed* I am that I need to postpone it."

"Oh?"

Was that hope in his voice? Or was I hearing what I wanted? "I feel awful for calling you at the last minute like this. Can we move tonight to another night?"

"It sounds like you're going to be very busy." He was giving me a way out. Oh, yes, there was hope! It was coated with a healthy dose of caution, but that was understandable. Butterflies boxed in my stomach. I about-faced and paced the other direction, running my shaking free hand through my hair. If I could say the right thing, I could make this right, right now.

"I have been counting the hours until tonight since you asked me out," I confessed. "I have talked about it with my friends until they were sick of hearing about it."

That earned me a chuckle. "You really do have a meeting, don't you?"

"*Yes*. I tried to get out of it, but I'm so new here, no one is cutting me any slack."

"What time is it?"

"Six o'clock." I hadn't asked what time the meeting was, but that was the time I'd agreed to Niko picking me up. My stomach twisted at the datelike image that evoked.

"Figures. Do you want to meet afterward?"

I froze, everything inside me screaming yes, but I forced myself to think before I spoke. "I want to, but I'm not sure when the meeting will end, and I don't want to call you later, canceling again."

"Ah, good point." He sounded disappointed. Was that a good thing? "We were crazy to try to plan anything so close to Thanksgiving anyway. When should we reschedule?"

I pumped my fist—a move I'd never done before, and I was thankful no one saw me do it now.

I had no idea what my schedule at the mall would be, or even what I'd be doing. However, I didn't want to push our date out too far. There was only so long Alex could be expected to wait for me. "What about Sunday evening?"

"Sunday. Hmm, let me check." I heard a few clicks of a keyboard. "That works for me."

I danced in place.

"Great! And, Alex? I'm really looking forward to our date," I said, infusing my voice with unedited earnestness.

"Hey, Madison?"

"Yeah?"

"So am I."

When we hung up, my whoop of joy echoed off the buildings and made the smokers near the lobby jump and stare. I didn't care. I still had a date with Dr. Love!

I slid back behind the wheel and did a seated Snoopy dance. I'd made it work. I'd saved my date and I was going to learn more about my region, all while getting on Mr. Pitt's good side.

I turned on the car and headed back to the hotel.

Just four days until my date. I'd survive.

At the hotel, I swept through the upper two floors, unearthing and exterminating a nest of imps and a half dozen vervet that had escaped my first dozen passes. Cleaning up after a demon was worse than taking a demon head-on.

My gut constricted, calling me on my lie. Confronting a demon had been the most terrifying experience of my entire life. It was idiotic to claim being bored was worse than being scared witless. I'd taken the job believing the most deadly weapon I needed was the charmingly nicknamed pet wood, or petrified wood wand. After I'd almost died as a result of my ignorance, Niko had loaned me his knife. I hadn't left home without its comforting weight in my purse since, especially not after killing the demon. I hated the knife, but I hated being vulnerable more.

Since I hadn't thought I'd see Niko again so soon, I hadn't felt much urgency to rush out and spend my hard-earned money on a knife of my own. But with Niko back in town, it'd be unprofessional to keep his knife.

Motivated to maintain possession of something sharp and deadly at all times, I rushed through my final sweep of the hotel and wrapped up with enough time to stop by Accessories and More for a replacement knife before getting ready for tonight's meeting.

Twenty minutes later I sat trapped on Douglas Boulevard when it abruptly turned into a parking lot just beyond the last crossroad. At the edge of Roseville's city limits, the boulevard squeezed down to two lanes each way and typically jumped from forty miles per hour to sixty. Large swaths of undeveloped tree-filled land swept up one side of the road, a long wall of a subdivision barricaded the other, and the landscaped median made U-turns impossible.

The reason for today's standstill fast became apparent: Against the sky's cerulean backdrop, smoke billowed in an angry column close enough to smell through my heater vents. Two fire engines barreled down the shoulder, kicking up gravel against the side of my Civic, sirens deafening through my rolled-up windows.

The Cadillac in front of me crept forward, and I eased up to it again. Inch by inch, we crawled around the bend. Flashing lights and temporary barricades came into view, snaking the backlog through the turn lane and up the opposite side of the road, the two lanes temporarily divided by orange cones. Traffic oozed in both directions under the watchful eye of fluorescent-vested police.

It was impossible not to be a looky-loo. The fire raged through a roadside Christmas tree stand. Rows of display trees ready for tomorrow's sales burned from crown to base like gigantic candles, but it was the bound trees stacked like a bonfire that shot flames higher than the fire trucks. Passing by, even with a median, two lanes, and an extra twenty feet of open space between me and the fire, muted warmth pressed against my right side. I breathed a sigh of relief when I crept past the final fire truck.

With the show behind us, traffic picked up. A mile later, when cones and flares directed us back to our own side, the road opened up before me. Jacob might have the larger portion of Roseville under his enforcer domain, but my region included the drastically more expensive suburb of Granite Bay, a sprawl of expensive, spacious housing divisions and horse properties stretching from Roseville's eastern city limits to the shores of Folsom Lake. Out here, stoplights were a rarity, and few people bothered to notice the speed limit. I surged back to freeway speeds with the rest of the cars around me and rocketed to Accessories and More.

The convenience store crouched in a battered parking lot at the edge of my region. A dozen neon signs behind the window's iron bars invited customers inside, but I was the only taker. Sharing a barren lot with a liquor store and situated off the lake access road, Accessories and More catered more to visiting boaters than it did to the wealthy locals, with everything from car oil and cell phones to Doritos and highlighters. It also had a glass-front counter where pet wood wands lay alongside a variety of weapons for enforcers and violent normal folks.

"Wow. She still lives and breathes," Muhamad said in a stage whisper to his business partner, Musad. Or maybe it was Musad who spoke. I couldn't tell the twins apart.

"Look—all of her limbs are still attached, too, Muhamad," Musad said, confirming I'd guessed correctly.

"Hardy-har-har. You know, some might not think it's wise to mock the woman who watches over the region they work in."

"Meh," Musad said.

"You're going to have to try harder to scare us."

"I only have a week's experience." I wriggled my fingers at them like a witch in a B flick.

Both men's heads fell back in identical laughter. Watching them clasp their belts beneath small beer bellies in the exact same gesture was like watching a man beside a mirror. The only difference between them was the colors of their shirts.

"Oh, good one, Madison Fox," Muhamad said when he caught his breath.

"Well played, young enforcer. What can we do for you today?"

I pulled Niko's knife from my purse. I'd had to buy a bigger purse once I started carrying it around. With an eight-inch blade and another five inches for a hilt, the sucker had stuck out of my previous bag like a red flag. I unsheathed the knife and laid it on the glass counter. The wide double-edged blade shone a flat gray, the hilt a flat black. Even in Primordium, the knife looked plain. Invisible in either sight was a bone shaft running the length of the blade. Left to its own nature, *lux lucis* flowed through living creatures and plants. The second-best conduit was a previously living substance. Hence my extend-O wand made of petrified wood. Regular wood would have worked, too, but the hollowed, expandable-collapsible wands only came in petrified versions for structural strength. In the blade, the bone acted as the conduit for *lux lucis*.

"Whoa!" Musad backed up, hands raised. "This is all you, Muhamad."

"What's a tiny woman like you doing with this half-pint sword?" Muhamad asked. His gaze flicked to the door.

"Niko loaned it to me."

"Ah."

Musad stepped back up to the counter. "Ah."

"I need a knife just like this."

"No."

"What?"

"First, this isn't a knife. It's a dagger. Second, it's too much blade for you. Third, you've got it stuffed in your purse, where Niko carries it strapped to his belt. Did you know it's illegal to carry a blade this length concealed in California?"

I shook my head. I'd ranked it as "more deadly than pet wood" and had tried not to think too much about it.

"Why didn't you mention this last time you saw me with the knife?" I'd dropped into the shop to replace my pet wood the day after Niko had given me the blade. My original wand hadn't survived its first encounter with a demon.

"Call me a sucker. I wanted to see you live through your first week."

"I'm touched."

"These you can conceal." Muhamad ignored my sarcasm and pointed through the glass at a fan of folding knives and tiny blades.

"They're all so small."

Musad snorted. Muhamad opened the back of the case and pulled out a silver-handled folding knife, unfolded it until it locked open, and laid it on the glass. "Give it a try."

With a short three-inch blade, the knife was featherlight. Unlike Niko's dagger, the blade held an edge on only one side. *Lux lucis* slid easily into the blade but backed up into my palm just as fast. The weak bone shaft could barely hold enough *lux lucis* to disintegrate an imp. I set the knife down before I burned it out. If I was committing to carrying a knife, I wanted something stronger than pet wood.

"Keep in mind knives are not meant to hold *lux lucis*. They are designed to be conduits once you've stuck the knife in something."

"I know." I wiped my hand on my leg. "Got one stronger than a needle?"

"Try out this Bowie." Muhamad reached into the case and pulled out a black knife a smidgen longer and wider than the folding knife, but solid. The back side was curved and sharp from halfway up the blade to the tip, and *lux lucis* fell into the blade almost as fast as it did Niko's dagger.

"This is more like it."

The brothers shared a look, and Musad slipped from behind the counter.

"Why don't you put this monster away and we'll pretend we never saw you carrying it," Muhamad said.

I set down the Bowie and hefted Niko's dagger into my purse. It took some wedging, but I got it to the bottom and settled my pet wood, handbook, and wallet on top.

"A purse is a clumsy place for a weapon," Musad said, coming up beside me. He set a leather case on the counter next to the knife, then slid the Bowie into the sheath. A small snap locked the blade inside. "This attaches to your belt for a horizontal carry. On you, I think the small of your back." He held the blade up to me, measuring it against my body.

"No way. It would scare people." It scared me. The odds of accidentally cutting myself on a knife in my purse were low. If I strapped one to me, I'd be lucky to have all my fingers by the end of the week.

"Good thing evil creatures politely wait for you to scrounge up your weapon before they attack," Muhamad said.

"If I may." Musad lifted the hem of my sweater with his thumb and forefinger, pressed the flat sheath to my hip, then lowered the fabric over the knife. "Voilà. Problem solved."

Goose bumps spread across my stomach from the touch of the cool leather. Musad pulled his hand back.

"When you don't wear it, you can stuff it in that piece of luggage you're carting around," Muhamad said. "It's legally concealable."

I liked the sound of that. If I were honest with myself, I'd brushed aside qualms about the clumsy location of Niko's knife more than once. Plus, I would be able to downgrade to a normal-size purse again. "I'll take it."

Both men were all smiles as Musad swiped my credit card. The smell of melting plastic must have been in my head. The tiny Bowie was cheaper than a knife the size of Niko's, but not by much.

The column of smoke from the Christmas tree stand rose black against the red-tinged sunset. As I headed back into Roseville, bumper-to-bumper traffic clogged Douglas all the way from the lake, so I took a left on Auburn Folsom Road and opted for a more circuitous route home. Half the population had the same idea. By the time I pulled under my apartment carport, I had twenty minutes to spare. I ran for the stairs.

Mr. Bond greeted me with a yowl. I pushed the door shut and bent in half, panting from jogging up two flights. The obese Siamese mutt twined between my legs, tromping on my toes and meowing very pointed, crisp words.

"I think I'm glad I can't understand you." He chirped in agreement. Straightening, I tossed my purse onto the dining table, hit the play button on my answering machine, and fed Mr. Bond. He quieted in time for me to hear Bridget's dramatic whisper.

"Your mission, whether or not you choose to accept it, is to ascertain Dr. Love's kissing skill." My best friend was almost as excited about my date as I was—or had been. The reminder I wouldn't be getting up close and personal with Alex's lips tonight put a slump in my shoulders.

I toed my tennis shoes off and pulled my sweater over my head as the answering machine beeped to the next message.

"Hey, honey, it's me," Mom said. "I wanted to remind you to bring potato salad and gravy tomorrow."

Crap. In the excitement of the previous week, I'd forgotten that I'd promised to contribute to Mom's Thanksgiving meal. I opened my pantry cupboard, but no potatoes had miraculously translocated to my bare shelf.

"Oh, and there were two fires this afternoon off Highway Sixty-Five," she continued. "I'm sure it'll all be cleared up tomorrow, but just in case, take the Lincoln Newcastle Highway. See you tomorrow. Watch out for the pyro."

Was he going to jump out of the bushes at me? Even if he did, there wasn't much I could do. Whoever the firebug was, his type of sickness was a problem for ordinary police.

Mom made some baby noises at Mr. Bond before hanging up. I eyed my cat. He was up to his eyebrows in his food bowl, oblivious to the world.

"I hope you got that the first time, because I'm not playing it again." His tail twitched.

The third message was Dad, whispering. "I told your mom I'd go with her to the gym this morning, and I didn't. Now she's threatening to not make pumpkin pie. You'd better bring a backup one just in case." I could hear Mom call to Dad in the background, then the sound of tools banging. "I'm in my office!" Dad yelled. Quieter, he said, "And bring extra whipped cream."

"Oscar, who are you on the phone with?" Mom asked, louder now. The message ended with a clatter.

I suspected I wasn't going to make it through Thanksgiving with my sanity intact.

A shiver reminded me I stood in only a bra and pants, with Niko due to arrive any minute. Snatching up the phone, I headed for my closet. I might not be going on a date tonight, but I was going to meet other illuminant enforcers. I still wanted to dress to impress, or at least to make a good impression.

Halfway to my bedroom, my stomach growled. I turned back to the kitchen. The fridge contained exactly four things: a box of leftover pizza, a half-empty bottle of Gewürztraminer, a bag of salad mix, and strawberry jam. No yogurt.

In an effort to increase my strength as an enforcer, I'd been trying to eat food containing *lux lucis*. Recharging by absorbing energy from plants was convenient and necessary, but Niko had told me a few days ago that ingesting *lux lucis* would improve my base level of energy. I'd yet to see a difference. Plus, the options for *lux lucis* food were limited to fermented food with live bacteria or food freshly picked, such as fruits and vegetables. Cooking killed *lux lucis*. That left raw foods, and even salads took time to prepare. Which is why I'd eaten more yogurts in the last week than I had in the six months prior while the ingredients of the salad bag had rotted into slimy green soup.

I chewed methodically through one cold meat-and-vegetable-loaded slice of pizza, then washed my hands and dialed Bridget to deliver my bad news. I thumbed through my wardrobe while the phone rang. Everything I owned fell into two categories: comfortable and practical or impractical and sexy. The impractical clothes were all shoved to the back, virtually unworn. All except the orange and cream dress I had set aside for tonight's thwarted date.

I sighed as Bridget picked up.

"Is this a prank call?" she demanded, though I knew she had caller ID. Traffic sounds hummed in the background.

"What are you wearing?" I panted into the phone.

"About five pounds too many. Some clients sent in chocolates today. Swiss chocolates."

"I'm jealous."

"I've gotta say, I expected a lot more squealing."

"I would if I were still going on a date."

"What!"

"I had to postpone. Something's going on in the region, and there's a big meeting tonight. Niko said I should attend."

Bridget was the only person I'd ever told about my ability to see souls, and when I became an enforcer, she was the first to know. Despite my implausible explanations of Primordium and evil creatures invisible to her, she never once doubted me. Everyone needed a friend like Bridget.

"Ooooh, Niko said you should go, and poor Dr. Love gets tossed to the curb."

"It wasn't like that." If my tone was a tad defensive, Bridget didn't comment.

"Sure, sure. Will Mr. Dark and Deadly himself be there?"

"Yep."

"Take a picture for me. I want to see what he looks like. Topless, preferably."

"I'll see what I can do, Digit." Bridget had met Niko once, but she didn't remember, and I wanted to keep it that way.

"Was Dr. Love okay with rescheduling?"

"Yeah. But I wanted a date tonight, not Sunday," I whined.

"Oh, you poor thing. You have to wait a couple more days, and in the meantime, you get to hang out with a man who, and I'm quoting you, 'can make a woman's hoo-ha tingle just by thinking of her.'"

"I never said that!"

"It's in the subtext every time you mention Niko. Seriously, though, what's the meeting about? Who's going to be there?"

"Other wardens, maybe a few enforcers." Some of my thwarted-date blues eased at the thought of meeting some other people in my line of work.

"Sounds interesting. Take notes; I want to hear about everything tomorrow."

We said good-bye so she could go into her yoga class and I could finish getting dressed. Mr. Bond darted through my closet, skidded across my bill-strewn desk, scattering papers to the floor, and sprinted back to the front room and his scratching post.

"You know you're not a kitten, right?" I shouted after my tank-size beast. I picked up the papers without looking at them too closely. I didn't want to get distracted by bills right now.

I burrowed to the back of my closet for my gray interview slacks and paired them with an emerald boat-neck sweater that complemented my eyes. The combination was professional and attractive, and hopefully dressy enough for the meeting. Just in case, I dabbed on some mascara, then checked myself in the mirror. There wasn't time to do anything special with my hair other than brush it. I needed a trim.

Mr. Bond galloped by again, nearly knocking me down as we passed in the hall. This time he paused in the bedroom to sharpen his claws on my mattress. I raced after him to scold him, and he darted to the front room, instigating a game of chase. I obliged. The poor cat really needed more attention than I'd given him lately.

In between tossing tiny fake mice up and down the short hall, I scarfed down another slice of cold pizza. The microwave clock read 6:02 when it occurred to me Niko was actually going to see my apartment in all its mail-cluttered, shoe-scattered, plant-filled jungle glory. I raced to the middle of my front room and froze. Where to start?

A sharp three-beat knock rattled my door.

"One moment," I called. I scooped two pairs of shoes and a pile of mail into my arms and ran them to my bedroom. Slipping into some short black kitten heels, I raced back to the front room, only to dart back to the bathroom mirror to fluff my hair and check my teeth. I gave Mr. Bond a rushed pet as I passed him in the hallway, shrugged on my coat, and snatched up my purse.

Taking a deep breath, I opened the door. Niko filled my doorway, and my heart pattered. The date-with-Niko fantasy I'd done such a good job of suppressing swamped my brain cells.

$$4$$

If You're Not Outraged, You're Not Paying Attention

M Y GAZE DIPPED TO NIKO'S smooth lips. "Hello," I croaked. I didn't invite Niko in, but he stood too close for me to exit without stepping into his arms. "I'm ready to go." I urged him back, intent on maintaining the illusion of being an organized, tidy individual.

Mr. Bond pushed between my legs, and I tightened my calves around my cat to prevent him from escaping. "Nope. You're not going anywhere." I bent and scooped Mr. Bond up. He meowed pitifully. I swung around to drop him back into the front room, thought better of a move that would put my butt in Niko's face, and backed up beside the open door.

Niko took the opening as an invitation and stepped inside, shutting the door behind him. With a sigh, I set Mr. Bond down. He rushed Niko. The optivus aegis offered his hand to my curious beast. Mr. Bond sniffed his fingertips and allowed himself to be petted.

"This is Mr. Bond."

Niko straightened, his vigilant gaze skimming over my dining room, which was lined with bookcases draped with a dozen golden pothos plants, their long strands half concealing the books on the shelves. The front room held sturdier plants stuffed in every nook available and lined up on either side of the TV. The flotsam of life and cat toys littered the floor. Niko looked amused, but I wasn't sure if it was due to my messiness, the indoor jungle, or my cat, who had flopped across Niko's right foot and was rubbing his face back and forth across the leather surface.

Way to play it cool, Mr. Bond.

"Nice cat. He's rather large."

"That's how I like my men," I quipped. Heat flooded my face. Mr. Bond shot me a look I swore told me I was an idiot. Then he swam his body across the floor to Niko's other shoe.

Niko laughed and bent to gently extricate his foot. I glanced heavenward and asked for help to stop acting like a complete idiot around Niko. If this was how my ancestors responded to sexy men, it was a wonder we'd ever propagated.

I followed Niko outside and gently shut the door in Mr. Bond's face, telling him to be good. I locked up while Niko blew fur off his hands. Clumps of fluffy dark hair floated away on the chilly breeze. I opened my mouth to apologize for my cat's indiscriminate shedding, but Niko was already jogging down the stairs.

Shadows coated the apartment walkways and the children's jungle gym squatting in front of my building. I blinked to Primordium for easier navigation and a better view. The moldy-smelling lawn dotted with dog-poop land mines transformed into undulating blades of light carpeting the hillside. Beyond the manicured landscape lay the reason I rented a third-floor apartment: Lining the protected wetland stream, majestic oak and cotton trees provided a year-round source of beauty. Right now, their long branches were bare of all but a few stubborn leaves, and in the daylight, they looked dormant, possibly dead. I knew better. In Primordium, they glowed a healthy, immutable white, their limbs a vast, intricate fractal against the dark sky.

Beyond the oaks, the marshland gleamed with *lux lucis*. Blackberry brambles, water grasses, cattails, and dense bushes overlapped white upon white. I'd toured a dozen apartment complexes in Roseville, and none came close to having to a view like this.

"I can see why you chose your place," Niko said.

His words so closely mirrored my thoughts, my gut clenched in momentary panic that he could read my mind. A quick glance reassured me he was admiring the greenbelt.

"I think I have the best apartment in the complex."

"I've always been fond of this region of California."

For the first time, it occurred to me to wonder where Niko lived. Since his territory as optivus aegis included most of Northern California, did he live near its center in Redding, or somewhere more coveted like Napa Valley? I was trying to decide whether Niko would fit better in a tiny cabin in the woods or a sleek modern loft in Sacramento when the anomalous glowing interior of a car caught my eye. Cars were inanimate and therefore should be gray in Primordium.

I stepped closer. The driver's seat and center console glistened with a soft layer of *lux lucis*, as did the steering wheel.

"It's the leather," Niko said, popping open the driver's door. "I spend a lot of time driving."

I blinked and straightened. In normal vision, Niko's BMW was solid black, the interior a tanned leather. Right. Previously living materials held *lux lucis* better than any other medium. Niko used a lot of *lux lucis*, and his soul was one of the strongest I'd seen. It stood to reason some of his good energy would rub off on his environment.

It was unnerving how he'd known exactly what I was thinking. Again.

I slid into the passenger seat and thumped my ginormous purse onto the floorboard. Now would be a good time to give Niko back his dagger. Only, he turned the ignition over before I could speak, and the gentle wave of heat from the vents wafted his spicy cinnamon and coffee scent across my cold cheeks. The car's interior lights dimmed. I pulled on my seat belt. Anything I said would turn awkward. It was the Law of Madison in Niko's Presence. So I savored the soft hum and whine of the engine as he backed out of the parking spot and eased toward the exit across a gauntlet of speed bumps, waiting for Niko to speak first.

I lasted until we exited the complex and headed south on Sierra College Boulevard. I lived outside the southern border of my region, and we should have been driving in the opposite direction. "Where are we going?"

"Liam's office. He's got the largest region in the affected area."

I waited for Niko to elaborate. The silence stretched, long and tense for those of us with unchecked curiosity and escalating anticipation. After a few miles, we left Roseville behind and entered Orangevale. No gap existed between the cities, but the farther we drove into Orangevale, the more obvious the change. Roseville had pockets of million-dollar homes and mini-malls with art galleries and wine bars; Orangevale had pockets of poverty-level apartments and run-down strip malls. The landscaped median shrank and disappeared. Homes crept closer to the road.

"There's a lot you don't know, Madison."

"I believe that's been mentioned."

Niko shot me a sharp glance. "About Brad. Many people in the CIA would like to see your warden removed from his position."

I gaped at Niko. He wasn't referring to the CIA most people knew. He was talking about the Collaborative Illumination Alliance, the organization we all worked for. I'd been ready for a lecture on my inexperience, or maybe instructions for whatever I'd be doing at the mall, not a statement of my boss's unpopularity. The most intelligent response I could muster was, "Huh?"

"Brad made some bad decisions in the past."

"What sort of bad decisions?" I braced myself as we took a sharp turn off Hazel, mentally bracing myself for Niko's next words, too.

"The kind that brought him in front of a Triumvirate hearing."

I'd never heard of a Triumvirate, but a hearing couldn't have been a good thing.

"Afterward, Brad was demoted to this tiny region. There are those who believe he's not fit to work as a warden at all. You're not helping, either."

"Excuse me?"

"You have next to no training, yet you're the sole enforcer in his region. Since your job posting ran for months with no other takers, hiring you for the role of an enforcer despite your lack of experience isn't the issue so much as Brad refusing all offers for you to train under local enforcers."

There had been offers? I'd assumed when Mr. Pitt had said training with other enforcers was out of the question, he'd meant they hadn't been open to the idea. "Why would he refuse?"

"Because the ranking enforcer's warden calls the shots. Whoever you worked under would be following their warden's orders, even if you guys were in your region. If Brad conceded control of his region to another warden, no matter how temporarily, it would be that much easier to convince the Triumvirate he was superfluous."

"Hang on. People think Mr. Pitt is an unfit warden because he hired me, an untrained enforcer, but he can't get me more training because if he does, he'll be kicked out?"

"Essentially, yes."

"That's not fair."

Niko didn't respond.

"What about you? Could you train me?" I suspected he could teach me one thing a day for a year and still have unshared expertise left over.

He shook his head. "It's not a good use of my time."

"Ouch."

"The things I'm doing are well above your skill level." His dark gaze swept my face, then returned to the road. "You need someone to teach you the basics."

"Sure. Of course." It might have been true, but it didn't give me the warm fuzzies to be dismissed as inferior. "That's why Doris is training me. Or will be."

"She didn't give you a bad start. You survived a demon."

"Good point."

"If you hadn't, Brad's fate would already be sealed. For whatever reason, he's investing heavily in you—it's why he maxed himself out buying you the handbook."

I slumped back in my seat, mind spinning. I had no idea why Mr. Pitt would put so much faith in me. If anyone had asked, I would have said Mr. Pitt would prefer anyone *but* me as his enforcer.

Maybe he was trying to force the CIA to fire him, but it didn't make sense. If that was his strategy, why buy me the expensive handbook? I'd shoved the book into my purse earlier today and completely forgotten about it. Nothing about it made it look worth a penny, let alone the fortune Niko implied. Maybe every word was a gem of wisdom.

Which still didn't explain Mr. Pitt's action. Or why other people thought he shouldn't be a warden.

"Is he a bad warden?" I'd met only one warden in my life. Maybe Mr. Pitt was awful. Maybe other wardens didn't yell at their enforcers.

"Depends on who you ask."

"I'm asking you, Niko." I let exasperation seep into my tone.

"And I'm telling you to make up your own mind."

I crossed my arms. "Thanks. That's helpful." When Niko said

nothing, and his serious profile gave even less away, I turned to face forward. I couldn't tell if he was warning me to be wary of Mr. Pitt or of the people who disliked him. "What would happen to me if Mr. Pitt got booted?"

"His region's so small, it'd be split between Liam, Isabel, and Margaret. You'd have to find a new region and work under another enforcer until you were more competent. There are a few openings in Southern California, a few more on the East Coast. You wouldn't be without options."

Niko's confidence that I'd be demoted hardly registered. I didn't want to relocate, no matter how much I liked or was suited for the position of illuminant enforcer. I'd built a life I liked *here*. All my friends and family were here. Yet, if Mr. Pitt lost his job, mine would disappear, too. How unfair!

"All this stems from something in Mr. Pitt's past?"

"Yes."

"And you won't tell me what it is?"

"It's not for me to explain."

Convenient. "Then why bother to tell me?"

Niko waited silently, and the answer hit me a few seconds later.

"There will be people, wardens, at this meeting who want Mr. Pitt removed." Niko's smile was my confirmation. "Do all the wardens think Mr. Pitt is inept?"

"Most do."

"All the wardens who would get his region?"

"Not all." Niko's approving glance warmed me.

From what I understood, Mr. Pitt needed to have a clean region now more than ever to prove he was worthy of keeping his region and his job. The last thing he needed was to shuffle his enforcer off to the mall and leave his region vulnerable to a takeover. I said as much to Niko.

He shook his head. "If Brad hadn't agreed to the arrangement, we might be headed to a retirement party now."

My mall assignment hadn't been Mr. Pitt's idea? That explained the hostile phone call I'd overheard earlier.

"At least with this compromise, he retains some control over you and Rose," Niko continued. "She's the best empath in the state, and she'll keep you guys in business through the cito season. And you might be working outside of Brad's jurisdiction, but you'll still be answering to him."

"Let's say I believe Mr. Pitt is a good warden. What can I do so he and I both keep our jobs?"

"Exactly what Brad says."

Niko turned into the lot of a beige two-story office building. A cluster of cars was parked near the entrance, but Niko chose a spot several rows back.

I fidgeted with my purse strap and let out a slow breath. "And if I agree with the other wardens?" It didn't make me a traitor to ask.

"Then you should talk with a warden you trust. Or I can put you in touch with an inspector."

"What's an inspector?"

"Inspectors are the internal affairs agents for the CIA."

My stomach sloshed with a pizza-topped acidic pool of anxiety. Why hadn't I stuck with my original plan? I could be sitting across a table from Alex right now, oblivious to inter-regional political undercurrents and my fragile job security.

"No one in there is your enemy," Niko said. He'd twisted to look at me, and I studied his face for clues. He wouldn't have warned me about Mr. Pitt's questionable reputation and shaky hold on our region unless he believed in Mr. Pitt, right? Or was he warning me because he didn't want to see me hurt by Mr. Pitt's downfall? Why wouldn't he just say what he thought?

"They want what's best for their regions," Niko continued. "They fight evil, like you. Give them a chance."

"Even though they want to take my region and my job?"

"No one has it out for you. They're simply not sure you have the skills you need. That's very different."

It sounded the same to me. I followed Niko into the building, feeling like an unloved stepchild.

Illumination Studios and the front for Liam's region—Searchlight Polling—shared similarities. Both were in office buildings, for example. Both had conference rooms, receptionist desks, and bland carpeting. But saying they were *similar* was like saying my apartment was similar to Gwyneth Paltrow's mansion.

With an open floor plan sprawling across the entire second floor,

floor-to-ceiling windows occupying three sides, metallic sculptures hanging from the ceiling, and almost a dozen desks, Searchlight Polling looked like a well-funded start-up. In comparison, Illumination Studios looked like a cramped chunk of warehouse outfitted by a third-rate call center's knockoff furniture.

Even the conference room outshone ours, with a sleek oval table ringed by chairs, adorned by a halo of lights, and flanked by sliding redwood panels for doors. Several people already sat around the table, and I recognized Mr. Pitt's short, round form. He looked hunched and small, the top of his head a shiny dome under the lights.

Niko skirted the conference room and led the way past high-end computers atop spacious desks to a break room straight out of a Hilton lobby. Plush chairs circled a small coffee table in one corner; in the other, a large rustic-chic wooden table with bench seats served as an area for lunches. A long counter stretched the back wall, with cupboards and a sink, a fancy coffee machine, and an industrial refrigerator. Even with six people milling in front of what looked like a catered spread, the room felt spacious. Illumination Studios had a mini-fridge, a wobbly round plastic-topped table, three chairs, and barely enough room for those three chairs to be occupied at the same time.

I was the enforcer from the ghetto. Good to know.

"Niko!" The enthusiastic greeting came from a sandy-haired man in tight khakis and a long-sleeve T-shirt printed with an eight-bit image of a princess. His eyes bounced to me, full of curiosity.

"Hi, Jacob." Niko shook Jacob's hand. "Madison, this is Jacob, enforcer of West Roseville."

"I have you to thank for sparing me from cito duty," Jacob said, all white teeth and sparkling brown eyes.

Right. This was the enforcer too valuable to be burdened with the mall this year. If Jacob was old enough to drink, it was by months. I suspected he'd cultivated the short beard defining the line of his jaw in an attempt to add a few years. I shook his hand. His grip was tight and enthusiastic. I wanted to dislike him on principle, if only for the implication that I was lesser than him. But his smile contained no gloating, and my censure withered before it could take root.

"You were smart to come," a woman with a soft Southern accent and gorgeous olive-black skin said. Niko introduced her as Sheila, a warden-in-training under Liam. I hid my surprised that she wasn't a full warden, despite being middle-aged. Everyone seemed to think twenty-five made me a late-bloomer enforcer, but wardens must be different.

"About time you met real wardens," Sheila said.

"Sheila . . ."

"What?" Sheila met Niko's reproachful expression with defiance. "Now isn't the time to be in the dark, even if Brad would prefer to keep her there."

"I'm always eager to learn," I said, asserting myself back into the conversation. "My boss knows that."

"You hear that, Niko? She's eager to learn. She believes Brad will do something about it."

"He has. I've trained with Doris, and I have a handbook. I've taken out a demon." I closed my mouth. My defense sounded pathetic and boastful all at once.

"Bless your heart." Sheila patted my shoulder. I slid my fists into my jacket pockets. Niko said nothing, and Jacob examined his shoes.

"It was good to meet you. I hope you pay attention." Sheila left the break room, a limp in her stride.

"We're all on the same side?" I hissed at Niko.

"And everyone has their own opinion," he said.

The rest of the introductions went smoother. The other two wardens-in-training were polar opposites: Ashley, a petite blonde in pink who looked like she belonged on a professional cheerleading squad, and Dominic, who radiated hipster from his stretched lobes and black-and-white scarf to his maroon corduroy pants, frayed from the heels of his loafers. Along with Jacob, they drew Niko aside, all three hanging on the optivus aegis's words.

I got a "hey" from Claire, the sole enforcer-in-training at the meeting. The lackluster greeting came with a perfected look of disdain, though for my wardrobe rather than my status as Mr. Pitt's enforcer. Or maybe for both. I brushed off Claire's hostility easier than Sheila's. Still a teen, Claire could have walked out of the cast of *Gossip Girl* in her Catholic high school uniform and camera-ready makeup. Everything about her screamed "popular girl," and I'd stopped caring about the opinion of people like her long before I left high school.

Aside from Jacob, two other enforcers were in attendance, both refreshingly polite. Rafi was naturally tan, with a day-old beard and deep-set dark eyes. He excused himself to talk with Dominic, both men gravitating back toward Niko. The optivus aegis chatted with everyone, appearing oblivious to blatant and subtle idolization. If possible, it made me like Niko more.

Summer, the enforcer of Citrus Heights, resisted Niko's allure and waited with me while I selected a pile of organic raw cookies and poured myself a green tea. People who could see in Primordium and work with *lux lucis* were rare—before today, I'd known only six people, including myself, with these characteristics. Four, if I counted only the humans. I marveled at being in the presence of so many people who shared my secret world.

"It's nice to meet the enforcer sharing my border," she said. Next to her Native American cheekbones and willowy limbs, I felt boxy and plain.

"I hear you're new, like, brand-new," Summer said. "Sit by me, and I'll fill you in if you have any questions."

"Thanks. I'll try not to abuse your offer."

Summer laughed, and for the first time since I greeted Niko on my doorstep, my shoulders relaxed.

Eight chairs ringed the conference table, though it could easily fit more. The rest of the chairs lined the walls, like theater seating. Or in this case, segregated seating. All the wardens and wardens-in-training sat at the table, as did Niko. The rest of us sat in the back.

"What's with the seating arrangement?" I asked Summer.

"Standard procedure. It's a strategy meeting. They're the planners." She gestured to the wardens already seated around the table. "We're the doers."

It sounded like the kind of elitist thinking to be expected from people who judged enforcers before meeting them.

Okay, I was feeling a tad defensive.

Mr. Pitt glanced up from the paper he held, and his bushy eyebrows climbed his forehead. I grinned and waved with the fingers gripping my teacup. Mr. Pitt closed his mouth. He looked for Niko, who gave him a slight nod before turning back to his conversation with Jacob and Sheila. Mr. Pitt rose and gestured to me.

"I'd like to introduce my enforcer," Mr. Pitt said, interrupting the other wardens' conversations at the table.

"Madison, this is Kathleen Fairchild, Isabel Dulat, Ronald Stevenson, and Liam Wu."

I set down my cup next to my chair and stepped up to the table to shake everyone's hand. I had the novel experience of feeling small compared to another woman: Topping six feet, Kathleen sprang from Amazonian stock, all of her solid yet fit. Even her hair was big, the gray-streaked brown mane billowing around her head and shoulders. She shook my hand, then turned immediately back to the paperwork spread before her.

"Ah, the brave soul taking charge of my region's mall," Isabel said. "I appreciate your sense of teamwork. We need those with the most skill on the front lines right now, not stuck in one place. If this madness continues, I'll be running Jacob ragged."

Isabel was Kathleen's opposite in nearly every way: petite, plump, with short walnut-brown hair, and tiny cold hands. If I'd seen her on the street, I would have guessed her to be a middle school teacher. In other words, she looked nice even as she delivered the backhanded compliment. My smile turned brittle, and I kept my teeth locked.

"Ron," Ronald corrected as I shook his large hand. "It's good to see a new face." Despite looking like a linebacker gone soft, his grip was gentle. I liked him immediately, and not entirely because he didn't add a disparaging comment.

I finally reached Liam, the object of my curiosity. This was his office and his region, not to mention half the people in the room worked under him. The powerful warden was the oldest at the table and as short as Isabel, with a mostly gray buzz cut and fine lines creasing his tan face. Serious dark eyes beneath heavy epicanthic folds watched me impassively. It occurred to me that Liam, like the other wardens, was judging my soul.

"Welcome, Madison. I hope you find this meeting informative." His grip stopped just short of breaking my fingers.

"I'm sure I will."

Rafi pulled an extra chair into the room. After discreetly flexing my fingers, I returned to my seat next to Summer. Rafi sat to Summer's right, and Claire flounced to the seat beside him.

Conversations died as Liam called the meeting together, and Jacob strode to the remaining chair against the wall. Claire set her phone in her lap, eyes on Liam, but her fingers didn't stop moving. I tried to imagine what a blind text from me would look like. A senseless autocorrect mess, I was sure.

While no one was paying attention to me, I blinked to Primordium.

We were a fine-looking group. Not a jot of black to be found on anyone's soul in the conference room, let alone softer gray stains. The differences between enforcer souls were in varying degrees of strength, rather than color, with Niko at the top of the pack and Claire near the bottom. However, defining a distinction between Jacob, Rafi, and Summer was more challenging. I peeked at the creamy-white glow of my hand. I couldn't tell how I stacked up against these trained professionals, but I suspected it wasn't a flattering comparison.

When I looked at Mr. Pitt, I forgot any feelings of inadequacy. Mr. Pitt's soul nearly vibrated with strength, but its shape had me blinking and twisting to get a better look. His soul didn't hold to his body like an enforcer's soul or even a normal person's soul. It protruded at weird angles, shifting around him as he moved.

Had it always been that way? I scanned my memory, only to realize I'd never looked at Mr. Pitt in Primordium. In my preoccupation with all the evil accumulating outside the office, I hadn't thought to examine the people within the safe confines of our headquarters. What else had I missed?

I jerked my attention to another warden. Kathleen's soul had the same aura of strength and peculiar shape. Bouncing my gaze between the two wardens, I decided it wasn't the same bizarre configuration. Kathleen's soul appeared more like a cube with a nose, while Mr. Pitt's looked closer to an irregular trapezoid. The other wardens' souls were similarly misshapen. The souls of Ashley, Sheila, and Dominic closely resembled Liam's, and I wondered if something in their training shaped their souls.

I leaned in to ask Summer about the wardens' souls but realized that not only would her answer be longer than she could whisper while her boss talked, but it was also something I should have already noticed and figured out. I glanced down at my purse and the handbook hidden within its depths. Now wasn't the time to pull it out, either. I added *wardens' souls* to the list of topics I'd be looking up later tonight and tried to concentrate on the meeting.

"Thank you for attending," Liam said to Niko. "I know you've spent a disproportionate amount of time in Brad's region lately."

I bristled, and Mr. Pitt's expression smoothed to bland indifference.

"I think you're all getting sick of seeing me in your regions," Niko said. His smile elicited strained chuckles from the other wardens.

"Yes, I'd be more than happy to not see you in an official capacity in my region for years to come, as soon as we get to the bottom of this." Liam tapped a few keys on a laptop in front of him. A projection of his desktop appeared on the blank wall at the end of the room. Rafi dimmed the lights, then resumed his seat. "We've all noticed an increase in evil, some of us more than others, especially in the last month or so. Based on the information you all provided, I've created a time lapse map showing the most recent flare-ups. From this, hopefully we can discern a pattern and devise a plan."

A map of Roseville and the surrounding cities appeared on the screen, with a little *October 15* date stamp. Solid red lines sectioned off each warden's region. Within each, dotted red lines delineated enforcer territories. Mesmerized, I soaked it in. I'd been too busy with my own problems to give much thought to anything beyond my region's borders. Seen on this scale, my region looked puny. While the Folsom region to the east also had only one full enforcer for the entire region, it encompassed twice the square miles of mine. Liam's region, with three separate enforcer territories, covered half the map, and Isabel's almost as much. When I saw her region extended to Lincoln and my parents' community, I leaned close to Summer.

"Who's the enforcer in Lincoln?" I asked, hoping it was Rafi. I wasn't above asking for a little preferential treatment for my family.

"Grace Patterson," Summer whispered. "She didn't come tonight. Too busy with the fires."

The fires? As in the ones my mom had warned me about in her message? A dozen questions jumped to the tip of my tongue, but the images on the screen forestalled them.

Patches of black appeared across the map, growing or shrinking and disappearing as the date changed. It took less than two minutes for the time lapse to reach today's date. Then it looped. I couldn't tear my gaze from my region. Each day the flickers of black cropped up in new places and disappeared until my hire date. Then the black splotches spread and bled for several long days, first at ground zero of the demon's appearance, then all across my region, spilling over into Jacob's territory and flowing down into Summer's. I squirmed in my chair, no longer needing the hot tea for warmth. In a wave, the black patches receded to sporadic outcroppings.

Thanks to Niko, I knew that many—possibly all—wardens in this room believed I shouldn't be responsible for a region. Seeing the raw data wasn't doing me, or Mr. Pitt, any favors.

I stuffed a lemon macaroon into my mouth to disguise my nervousness. Tart citrus jolted my taste buds. The map cycled through the last month again. I forced myself to watch the rest of it. While no other region experienced the same steady black buildup as mine had, the frequency and size of the black patches all over the map increased in the last few weeks.

"Whose region is above mine?" I asked Summer.

"Margaret McTavish's. I don't know why she's not here."

"Where do Kathleen and Ron fit?"

"Kathleen is Folsom. Ron is North Highlands and Antelope."

Which placed Ron's region south of Jacob's and, based on the dotted lines, it had two enforcers.

"Rafi?" I asked.

Hearing his name, the rugged Iranian enforcer flashed me a smile. I smiled back and looked away.

"Orangevale." Which meant Rafi's region bordered mine to the south, though not as much as Summer's region.

The black sprawl from ground zero swelled to fill the map again. I slid lower in my chair. Here was the big picture, the view Mr. Pitt saw daily from his office while I hunted imps and vervet. Unfortunately, it was impossible to miss that my tiny region had suffered a disproportionate concentration of evil compared to all other regions. It was as if there were a magnet for evil located at the heart of my region.

I swallowed a gulp of lukewarm tea. Was I the problem?

Focused on ground zero, I didn't notice the rest of my region until the fifth time through. Dark patches had cropped up and disappeared deeper in my region over the last two days. Patches Mr. Pitt hadn't mentioned to me. Niko's need to recharge today took on new significance. He'd been cleaning up evil on my behalf. No wonder the wardens didn't think I could handle my region!

"What about the prajurit?" Kathleen asked. "Has anyone seen them?"

"Not for weeks," Ron said.

"Longer," Mr. Pitt said.

Liam shook his head. "I spoke with a queen almost two months ago. What about you, Niko?"

"I've been checking when I can. There's a hive in Woodland and another south of Sacramento."

"Have they heard where the hives around here have gone?" Ashley asked.

"Not even so much as a rumor."

"Has everyone checked old hives?" Isabel asked.

"I knew of two," Rafi said, causing all heads at the table to turn toward him. "Both hives were abandoned. It's like the prajurit flew out and simply never returned."

"I found the same," Jacob said.

"This makes no sense," Isabel said.

I couldn't agree more. What exactly were prajurit? They had hives and could fly. Were they bees of some sort?

"It does explain the salamanders, with the prajurit absent," Dominic said.

There were nods all around the table, everyone's expression grim. I glanced at Summer.

"Salamanders?" I asked.

Her eyebrows shot up. "You don't know? All the fires lately have been set by salamanders."

The explanation covered about as much as a fingerprint on a windshield. My knowledge of salamanders could be summed up in a single memory of a black-and-white picture in biology class of a man standing with a full-grown three-inch salamander in his palm and a four-foot-long salamander of a different species at his feet. Only myth connected salamanders to fire. Of course, a week ago I would have said demons were mythological creatures.

I pictured giant human-size salamanders walking upright around Roseville, using lighters to set dry grasses ablaze. I added a backward-facing baseball cap and tutu to my imaginary salamander, completing the absurd image.

"Normally the prajurit kill salamanders before they're fully developed," Summer added, again giving me enough information to evoke a dozen more questions.

"I've added in the recent fires," Liam said. "Those in orange are questionably connected to salamanders."

The map reset showing a larger radius, and in this time lapse, patches of red and orange scattered, spread, and disappeared. The date stamp started in late August and continued through today. There were more fires than I remembered, but it'd been an exceptionally active fire season. California's drought had transformed the countryside into one giant tinderbox, and even the smallest fires had often swelled out of hand. The majority of red notations marched up the I-80 corridor to the north, from Newcastle to Weimar, where grass fires started near the freeway had engulfed patches of open land and threatened homes. Up until this moment, I had believed the news reports blaming the fires on lit cigarettes flicked from cars.

Larger fires spread across the map in the foothills, bringing back memories of hot September days when the skies of Roseville had been a toxic haze. The red and orange patches grew and shrank and shifted like a current across the map. New splotches appeared in October, smaller and seemingly at random. November was the same, though for the first time the fires moved from the countryside into areas with denser population. A few fires popped up in Folsom, a few in Fair Oaks. These flashed on and off the map, small and quickly extinguished. A couple appeared in West Roseville, then hopscotched up Highway 65 to Lincoln, ending with the fires my mom had mentioned, all in red. Definitely started by salamanders, according to Liam. I almost missed the small orange dot on Douglas Boulevard from today's Christmas tree fire.

"How can you tell when it's a salamander fire?" I asked Summer, hoping I sounded halfway intelligent.

"You either see the salamander," she whispered, "or, in the bigger fires, you find a nest."

"There's no other sign?"

"Maybe if you determine the fire's origin, but a fire intentionally started always has lots of *atrum*, salamander or no."

Liam combined the two time lapses, showing the last month. Even with the fires happening mostly in other regions, my region looked like the epicenter.

"When all is laid out on a single map, it's clear the bulk of evil is centered here." Liam clicked a few buttons on his keyboard, and all instances of evil and fires over the last month appeared simultaneously on one static map. A bright yellow line circled my region. Within its confines, solid black swallowed the map.

No one looked at me, but I felt the weight of their regard nonetheless. Color climbed Mr. Pitt's neck. "Up until today, my region's been fire-free," he said.

"What an odd coincidence," Isabel said, dismissing him. "We need to know what's behind this if we're going to fight it. Any theories?"

"When I was younger, I worked a region with mind-jacks," Ron said. "When we broke them, they swarmed, and it looked a lot like this."

Mind-jacks? I didn't ask. The room was too quiet.

Kathleen gave herself a shake. "No. Even swarming, they would have left a pattern, or at least a trail," she said. "This appears to originate and be contained to our regions."

"Has anyone considered it could be as simple as a vacuum?" Sheila asked. "Where there is weakness, evil moves in. Obviously, there's a vacuum of strength, and the rest of this could be the ripples."

"Yet, I've held my region for years," Mr. Pitt said, meeting Sheila's gaze calmly. "Up until recently, there hasn't been a problem."

"You've had trained enforcers before now," Liam said.

I struggled not to fidget. They couldn't seriously be blaming all the evil obscuring the map on *me*, could they?

"Jacob had little more experience than Madison when he hired out with me," Mr. Pitt said.

I started. Jacob had been Mr. Pitt's enforcer at one time? When had he switched to Isabel's region, and why?

"A region needs stability, and you've had a problem retaining enforcers over the years," Isabel said.

He had? What did those enforcers know that I didn't? Did it have something to do with Mr. Pitt's mysterious and secretive past?

"The demon obviously saw weakness when your region changed enforcer hands yet again. Who knows how long it'd been waiting to move in," Liam said.

"It's just as likely the demon sensed the general weakness in all your regions," Niko said.

"It didn't pick our regions," Liam said.

I waited for my boss to defend himself or me. His face got redder, but he said nothing. No one expressly blamed me, though no one held back an opinion of my ignorance and inexperience. I bit my tongue to keep quiet. My earlier conversation with Sheila had proved how silly I sounded when I tried to defend myself. Summer, Rafi, and Jacob didn't meet my gaze. Claire smiled. It was the kind of smile a man might have thought was sweet but set the hairs on the back of my neck standing. Frowning, I pulled my spine straighter and focused on Liam.

"Now's not the time to have an untrained enforcer in the field," Liam said. "Madison's lack of experience is a liability, which you know, Brad, or you wouldn't have agreed to put her on cito duty. But this isn't just about Madison. We need strong wardens as much as strong enforcers until we figure out this little mystery." Liam let the statement hang alongside the evil-smeared map, with its bright yellow bull's-eye on my region. "Jacob, Claire, Summer, and Rafi will rotate through Brad's region. Unless anyone has any objections, I'll coordinate, since my enforcers will be picking up the bulk of the excess work. Isabel, I'll limit Jacob's involvement as much as possible. Claire, I know we're working around your school schedule. I'll coordinate with Kathleen to ensure we're not overextending you. Brad, you can report problems to me, and I'll pass it along accordingly. Ron, we'll keep your enforcers in reserve."

Isabel and Kathleen nodded, avoiding eye contact with Mr. Pitt. A moment later, Ron nodded. The muscles in Mr. Pitt's temples bunched, but his pink face remained placid. Liam had rendered him powerless, an employee of another warden rather than the ruler of his own region.

I finally saw what Mr. Pitt must have known since this morning: The meeting was a ruse. Liam getting the other wardens to agree to him taking control of *all* enforcer activity in Mr. Pitt's region had been his true purpose all along. Niko had said this was the best compromise Mr. Pitt could make, but it seemed like a defeat to me. If me being trained by an outside enforcer would have put our region in the hands of a different warden, making Mr. Pitt vulnerable, this maneuver seemed akin to severing Mr. Pitt's femoral artery. He might still be in charge of me, but what was the point if neither of us had a region to defend?

"Madison," Liam said, turning to me with an indulgent smile, "whatever time you have after the mall, you're more than welcome to pursue evil in your region. Just be sure to check in with me so we're not doubling up on personnel."

How could Mr. Pitt sit there and agree? And how could I not? I was doing my best to be a good enforcer, which according to Niko meant doing as Mr. Pitt instructed—if Mr. Pitt could be trusted.

I sat quiet, gagged with indecision and doubt.

5

Don't Judge a Book by Its Cover

I T'S GOING TO BE A rough couple of weeks," Liam said, meeting the eyes of the wardens and enforcers, "but I'm sure we'll be back within normal operating parameters by the new year."

By the new year? I slumped in my seat. I'd be trapped working a mall in Jacob's region for over a month?

Niko assigned himself the task of meeting with the local prajurit who could be found. Liam devised a reporting system to keep his map up to date and accessible by all wardens. How better for everyone to watch Liam prove himself a more effective warden of my region than Mr. Pitt? Yet hoping for him to fail was hoping for evil to flourish. What if Liam *was* the better warden? Didn't the people of Roseville deserve to have the best leader at the helm?

The meeting broke up with the wardens touting the importance of carrying "live water." I kept quiet and added the term to my list of questions for the handbook. Liam used my inexperience as an excuse to subvert Mr. Pitt's authority. I didn't want to add to Liam's cause by voicing stupid questions now, even to Summer.

Why couldn't the escalating evil involve imps or vervet, or even demons? Those I knew about and could be helpful fighting.

Summer invited me to walk out with her, and Rafi lingered while she collected her purse. "I found this great new Thai restaurant we should all try," she said, including me as easily as her longtime coworker. "It's actually close to your region, Madison, on Sunrise. We should have lunch once things settle a bit."

"I'd like that." It would be nice to have an enforcer friend or two. Bridget was wonderful, and I could share everything with her, but it would be great to commiserate and talk shop with a fellow enforcer. Plus, I might pick up some tips from Summer. "Tell me truthfully, is this mall thing going to be bad?"

"Bad?" Rafi glanced at Summer. "Boring, maybe, but not bad."

"Yeah, monotonous but not stressful," Summer agreed.

"Don't worry, Madison. They'll be assigning you demons again soon, I'm sure," Rafi teased.

My purse snagged on a chair and the handbook tipped out and flopped across my toes. By the time I untangled the strap, chastising myself for my usual grace, Rafi had picked the book up for me.

"Hey, Madison," Jacob called, coming up behind us. "Brad said you'll be at the mall early on Friday. Let's swap digits so we can meet up and I can show you the cito ropes. Not much to it, really. Just point, shoot, and watch 'em disappear. Whoa, is that a handbook?" Jacob grabbed the book from Rafi and ran his thumbs along the pages, ruffling the tattered ends. "You guys ever seen one of these before?" he asked Rafi and Summer.

"Nope," Summer said, taking the book so she could inspect it.

"Once," Rafi said.

"Is it true they're all crazy?"

"The one I met was. Like a crow in a coin shop. It couldn't follow a thought to the end of a sentence."

"I've always heard they were flighty." Summer handed me the book. "Though I'm sure there's bits of wisdom in there. Let us know if it says anything useful."

"Flighty? We're talking about a book, right?" I asked.

"Well, a handbook," Summer said. The silence lasted a beat too long. "Haven't you opened it yet?"

I frowned. "I just got it a few hours ago."

"Yeah, there's no rush," Jacob said. "Gimme your phone. I'll enter my number."

I handed over Medusa, still feeling like I was missing the joke and pretty sure it meant I was the butt of it.

"Take a look," Summer said.

I opened the book. The first page was blank. So was the next. I flipped through. Every single page was blank. "Wha—"

"In Primordium," Rafi said.

I blinked. The leather binding glowed white. As did the pages. Whoever had used it before me must have spent a lot of time with it for that much *lux lucis* to still be coating the interior. I fanned the pages again. They were still blank. Frowning, I flipped to the front.

As I watched, bold cursive scrawled the words, *Hi, Madison Amelia Fox.* The text was standard black on white, appearing from nothing across the page.

Atrum printed on *lux lucis*? I ran my fingers over the text, pushing a little *lux lucis* into the page. The words didn't change, and the page didn't get noticeably brighter. The *lux lucis* simply absorbed.

No, the text wasn't *atrum*. Despite being black in Primordium, the words couldn't be formed of evil energy. If they had been, the book's surplus of *lux lucis* would have erased it immediately. More important, books didn't write their own text.

This was impossible.

Jacob burst out laughing, covering his mouth with the back of his open fist. He snapped a picture with his phone. "Your face! Priceless."

Summer and Rafi grinned.

"Are you guys playing a trick on me?"

Summer shook her head. "Does it recognize you?"

I turned the book for her to see.

"Oh, good. At least you got one with some situational awareness. I've heard that's rare."

Jacob simmered down to a chuckle and finished entering his number into Medusa. He held out my phone, and I closed the handbook to accept it. "I hope that thing's helpful. Brad's a good starter warden, but old school. Anyway, see you way too early on Friday. Thanks again for taking the citos off my hands." He left with a jaunty wave.

I frowned at his back. *Starter warden?*

"I don't know how he has so much energy," Summer said. "After the last week, I'm beat, and it's not just from the demon smut that spilled over from your region, Madison. Things really are a lot worse than normal."

I blinked. Summer didn't sound upset, but I heard an accusation buried in her comment. Was I being too sensitive?

"The wunderkind didn't have a slew of wraiths flare up at a high school," Rafi said.

"Wunderkind?" I echoed.

Summer smiled. "Jacob's always been quick, and he got strong fast. I think Isabel is grooming him to become an optivus aegis."

"I'm sure he's regretting his reputation," Rafi said. "The wardens work him twice as hard as the rest of us. He's the first enforcer everyone calls when they need backup—except Brad."

"What's Mr. Pitt got against him?"

"Jacob left your region pretty fast for Isabel's. I think there was . . . tension between Brad and Jacob. They weren't a good fit." Summer poked my shoulder. "What's with 'Mr. Pitt'? He doesn't make you call him that, does he?"

I shook my head. "I never thought about it. He's just Mr. Pitt."

That wasn't the full truth. I hadn't needed Niko or anyone else at this meeting to point out my inadequacies as an enforcer. I'd known from the start I had the ability but not the experience to do my job, and despite giving Mr. Pitt a dozen reasons to fire me before I proved myself with the demon, he'd kept me on. I'd hoped a little formality would smooth over my blunders. Plus, now *Brad* sounded weird when I said it.

"I'm sure that'll pass," Summer said. "You know, it's probably a good thing you're getting some mall time this year. It's going to be dull after your first week, but they can't all be demons, right? Anyway, the only way to get promoted to a region with more responsibility is through experience, and every species encountered helps, even citos."

Her assumption that I would want to ditch my current region notwithstanding, it was a nice sentiment, even if it was mostly a lie to spare my feelings. Any experience I gained fighting the evil plaguing my region would be more valuable than facing down a single species at the mall. Since I didn't have a choice in the matter, and I didn't want to whine, I exchanged numbers with Summer and Rafi, then walked alone to Niko's car. The BMW's lights flashed as I neared. Glancing over my shoulder, I saw Niko near the entrance, talking with Isabel and Liam.

A bright orange Fiat gunned down the aisle toward the exit. With the sunroof open and the interior lit by overhead fluorescent lamps, I couldn't mistake Mr. Pitt's shiny dome behind the wheel. I would have recognized his fierce froggy scowl anywhere.

"I second that sentiment," I said, sliding into the BMW. A familiar feeling of impending doom settled on my shoulders. Across the lot, Liam smiled and shook hands with Isabel and Niko. I expected to hear him whistle as he sauntered to his Audi.

I plopped my purse onto the floor and glanced around. Niko was still chatting near the entrance, and no one was looking my way. I cracked open the handbook.

My personalized greeting was absent. In its place, the first page read, *I'm not flighty or crazy.*

I slammed the book shut and shoved it in my purse.

A patter against the windshield brought my head up. Fat drops flattened against the pane. Niko jogged across the parking lot, swiping drops from his shaved head. When he slid into the driver's seat, he brought with him the ozone-laden scent of the forefront of a storm, wet pavement, and his own signature deliciousness. I took a deep breath, then swallowed hard. The heater vents whirred to life, pushing the heady fragrance against my face, and my seat belt proved especially difficult to latch, despite a lifetime's practice.

"What do you want to know?" Niko asked. I cracked my window for some fresh air. Niko waited, car idling, watching me.

"What are prajer eats?" I blurted.

"Prajurit," Niko said, then spelled it. He put a hand behind my seat and turned to look behind him as he backed out of the space. "They're a who, not a what. Basically a small but fierce humanlike winged species we have an alliance with. Each hive is led by a queen, not unlike bees. Don't ever make the comparison to their faces, though."

"By small, you mean . . ."

"I've never met a queen over six inches tall. Most of her warriors are shorter, some no taller than four inches."

I checked his profile to see if he was joking. In the dim lights from the dash, he looked completely serious. "Fairies."

"You'd lose an eye if they ever heard you call them that."

I powered my window closed and drummed my fingers against my leg. I didn't need fresh air to distract me: The absurdity of this conversation did a fine job. I reviewed everything said about the prajurit in the meeting. It matched what Niko said. He'd never joked with me about the job before, either. Which meant little fairy people existed.

Just when I thought this job couldn't get any weirder, too.

There's a lot you don't know, I told myself in my best sarcastic mockery of Mr. Pitt. Glancing at the handbook where it poked from my purse, I decided I'd rather get my answers from Niko.

"And they've disappeared?" I asked.

"Around here they have. There used to be a hive on the northern edge of your region and several others up the hill. If they were still around, we wouldn't have this salamander problem."

I skipped over questions about the salamanders. One new species at a time, please. "Has this ever happened before? Maybe they moved or, er, migrated?"

"Prajurit are territorial to a fault. They move only when necessity dictates or a young queen starts a new hive. They don't abandon territory."

"Not even because of the increased evil?"

"They don't back down from a fight."

They sounded like my kind of (miniature, winged) people. I'd met enforcers, wardens, an empath, and Illuminea since discovering our clandestine CIA. Of those, only enforcers fought evil. Wardens monitored and ordered and strategized, leaving the actual combat to enforcers. Empaths, or maybe only Rose, since she was the sole empath I knew, could not see in Primordium or use *lux lucis*, so fighting *atrum* was out of the question. Illuminea were passive; they influenced people to make better decisions and spread *lux lucis* wherever they went, but they didn't engage in combat.

Yet, how helpful would a fairy-size person be, especially since anything larger than the smallest evil imp would dwarf them? How much *lux lucis* could their bodies store and expend in a fight? I opened my mouth to ask, but Niko beat me.

"Did you learn anything at the meeting?"

"Liam's got it out for Mr. Pitt."

Niko made a noncommittal sound. "He and Brad have their differences, but don't let that blind you. Liam is very good at his job. Only the best wardens are selected to teach others."

"And to take over neighboring regions? How is this arrangement any different than me training under another enforcer? Liam has all the power. The way he set things up made Mr. Pitt a figurehead."

"Don't count Brad out. And remember, you're not tied to Brad's fate. Keep your nose down, do the work, make a good impression with the other wardens. They'll see you have potential."

That word always sounded like an insult: *potential.*

Niko turned into the entrance of my apartment complex and eased over the speed bumps. I wanted to ask him again if he thought Mr. Pitt should be forced out of his job, but I knew he wouldn't answer. I wished it were easier to tell which way he leaned. I desperately wanted to keep my job. I didn't want to have to move, and if I were being honest with myself, it rankled to be expected to take a demotion if I was forced to work somewhere else. I'd been given the title of enforcer, not enforcer-in-training. I wanted to keep it. But if Mr. Pitt were unfit to manage the region, I'd be dooming myself—and all the innocent people living in this region—by trusting him.

I realized Niko had parked and was waiting for me to get out. Flustered, I fumbled with my seat belt, then remembered his knife. I hauled my gigantic purse onto my lap and dug out Niko's dagger.

"Should I be worried?" Niko glanced at the sheathed weapon. In the yellow light illuminating the parking lot, I thought I caught the hint of a teasing smile.

"Thank you for loaning me your dagger. It was very helpful." The smooth hilt brought back an unpleasant memory. I shifted the knife to my opposite hand and thrust it toward Niko. "I won't be needing it anymore."

His smile disappeared. "Okay, now I'm worried." He accepted the dagger and laid it across his legs. "You can't survive with pet wood as your only weapon."

"I know. But did you know it's illegal for me to carry that around in my purse?"

"Yes."

I opened and closed my mouth. "Then why did you let me!"

"Which is worse, breaking the law or being killed?"

"How about neither." I didn't check the irritation in my tone. Rifling through my purse, I pulled out the slender Bowie knife, still in its sheath. "See, perfectly legal to carry in a purse."

"And so quickly retrieved," Niko said.

"It attaches to a belt."

"I don't think you quite grasp the concept of a belt, if you've got it stored in there, too," Niko said, eyeing my purse.

"I just got this today. I don't have a belt."

"You'll get one?"

"Friday. I'll be at the mall anyway."

"Okay." He gripped the Bowie's handle, testing it. "Good decision. This is a nice size for you."

"Thanks."

I took a deep breath, savoring the rich spicy scent of Niko's cologne. Rain strummed the roof and pattered against the windows, emphasizing the warm seclusion of the car. Maybe it said something about me, but being in a shadowy parked car at night with a gorgeous man brought up all kinds of interesting ideas.

I looked away from Niko. We both held knives; there was nothing sexy about this scene. It was beyond time for me to go.

"Thank you for taking me to the meeting." I shoved the Bowie back into my purse and popped open the door. Cool air rushed in, along with a smattering of raindrops. "And for your knife last week."

"It's yours anytime you need it."

"Thanks, but it's so big, I honestly don't know what to do with it."

Dear God, I was staring at his crotch. I sprang from the car, my blush hot enough to heat my eyeballs. "Have a good Thanksgiving," I said, without leaning down; then I closed the door softly and tipped my face up to the rain. Soothing drops splashed my cheeks.

Sophisticated, professional, collected. Words Niko would never use to describe me.

Realizing the BMW hadn't moved, I guessed he was waiting until I reached my door before leaving. How very old-fashioned. And annoying.

I trotted up the grassy hill, seeking the fastest way out of his line of sight. The thought of him staring at my backside made me nervous, even if he meant nothing by it. *Please let my butt look good in these pants.* The parking lot lights weren't flattering, but maybe they'd cast a good shadow.

Halfway up the hill, something chilly touched my butt. I glanced down. "Oh, frick!" The sprinklers were on. Under the disguise of rain, and in my own embarrassed haste, I hadn't heard their telltale hiss.

Everything from my crotch down was soaked. I ran the last few steps to the sidewalk, cussing the whole way. It looked like I'd peed my pants. *Way to be classy, Dice.* I peeked over my shoulder, praying Niko had miraculously missed the show. He hadn't. In the faint light of his car's dash, I could see the white of his grin.

"Bastard," I said through clenched teeth, and tossed him a jaunty wave. Pretending my pants weren't glued to me, I darted up the stairs. Behind me, his car engine revved as he backed out.

Mr. Bond came bounding out of the bedroom, blinking against the bright light of the front room lamp when I stepped inside my apartment.

"I just made an ass of myself." Mr. Bond sniffed my dripping pants and batted at the stream of water trickling toward his paw, springing backward when he made contact. I tossed my purse aside, kicked off my shoes, and peeled my pants down chilled thighs. Mr. Bond raced ahead of me to the bathroom, where I wrung my pants out in the tub with his acute supervision before hopping into the shower. Mr. Bond waited impatiently by his food dish when I emerged several minutes later, the heat of the water having soothed away the sting of embarrassment.

I slipped on flannel pants and a well-worn Race for the Cure T-shirt I'd picked up at a charity event years earlier. Then I blinked to Primordium, swapping my front room's bright full-spectrum glow for mysterious, directionless illumination. The colorful spines filling my bookcases, the bright blue ceramic bowl holding my car keys, and the jet-black frame of my TV all became the same shade of gray. In this sight, nothing truly black existed in my apartment, thanks to *atrum* never having a chance to get a foothold. I soaked in the peace of my sanctuary before gathering *lux lucis* in my palms and heading for the sliding glass window.

Pressing my hands to the frame, I pushed *lux lucis* onto the wood. It clung there, bright against a wall of gray. Smoothing my hands along the paint, I applied a thin layer of *lux lucis* to the entire door frame, creating a ward along the door's seal. It was Wednesday, so I recharged using the thick-trunked Massangeana by the TV, then repeated the ward around the front door.

While no *atrum* creatures specifically hunted me—or so I liked to believe in order to sleep at night—placing simple wards over all entrances to my home kept me safe from casual invasion. That I knew of, my wards had never been tested, so I operated on faith. I'd like to keep it that way, too.

Mr. Bond trotted beside me into the bedroom and sat in the middle of the floor while I took *lux lucis* from a rubber tree before warding the window. His meows grew louder and more insistent as I worked, but I ignored him until after I'd recharged at yet another plant. Before I'd become an enforcer, I'd adorned my apartment with a handful of plants. Now that they'd become an energy source, I crammed plants in wherever they fit and pampered them all. If I didn't recharge, my body would do it passively while I slept. Plants were the first victims. Anything small and helpless, like a certain obese Siamese, would suffer next.

Nightly ritual complete and fully recharged, I appeased Mr. Bond with some dry food, then collapsed into my gray recliner, with the foot rest kicked up. I eyed the clock on the DVD player. It wasn't even ten o'clock. If my evening had gone according to plan, I still would have been out with Alex. Perhaps savoring a kiss or two.

Please don't let me have built this up too much. After all, Alex *was* still single. Maybe he lived with an ex-wife. Or had a gambling problem. Or didn't like to read fiction. I shuddered.

Mr. Bond circled my purse and stuffed his head inside, proving he hadn't been hungry so much as worried he'd never get fed again, since he'd hardly taken two bites before abandoning his full food dish to search through my belongings. With his head deep in my purse, his right paw scrabbled on the outside, trying to touch whatever he saw inside.

He pulled his head out, circled my purse again, and stuck a paw in, then removed the paw to submerge his head, paw batting uselessly against the outside. I giggled.

"What'd you find there, buddy?" His responding meow was muffled. I pushed the footrest closed, startling him out of my purse. He raced for the bedroom, tail flagpole straight. Seconds later, he galloped back to scratch on his post. I opened my purse to see what had set him off.

The handbook lay crumpled under the knife. I cringed, remembering Niko's admonishment to treat the book like gold. Pulling it out, I smoothed the cover. Mr. Bond trotted over. I held the book for him to sniff. He pressed his cheek to the leather, hooking his upper lip on the cover. His fascination with rubbing his top canines on my books had dented more than one cover.

"No fangs on this one." I pulled the book away, and Mr. Bond took a swipe at my hand.

"Hey!" He tore off, this time to the kitchen, where he rumpled the throw rug, flopped to his side, and pummeled the wadded fabric with his back legs. "You're being weird." Like he'd had catnip. Or not enough attention. Familiar guilt welled up. I'd been extra busy since I'd become an enforcer, and I hadn't spent as much time with him as he deserved. Apparently he'd decided to lash out.

I threw a fake mouse to him, and he batted it around the kitchen like a hockey puck. I returned to the chair and curled up in it, studying the handbook. Scuff marks and scratches marred the supple leather cover, and beneath a layer of grime, faint bands of color wove across the surface. No title or author's name graced the cover or spine. The back was a replica of the front and equally as abused. At one time, the handbook must have been beautiful. I opened it across my lap and blinked to Primordium.

I AM NOT A TOY! Don't let that clawed brute near me again! scrawled across the front page.

"Mr. Bond is harmless." The book, however, was creepy. I pulled a dinged TV tray table closer and set the book on top of it, then wiped my hands on my legs. Steeling myself for the surreal experience, I settled in for a conversation with a book. "So what exactly are you?"

The words disappeared; then new text wrote itself across the blank page. *I'm a book. You're going to need a lot of help if you couldn't figure that one out.*

Oh, goodie. It knew sarcasm. "What can you teach me? Do you know anything about being an enforcer?"

Normal books know more about being an illuminant enforcer than you do.

Another critic. Lucky me.

Bored with his mouse, Mr. Bond jumped onto my lap. In Primordium, his plump body glistened with *lux lucis*. I slid my fingers through his fur and consciously calmed my annoyance.

Unerringly, Mr. Bond zeroed in on the book, stretching his neck out to giraffe lengths to sniff it from my lap. When he shifted to bat it, I snatched the book out of his reach. He mewled. I nudged him from my lap. Mr. Bond landed on the floor with a thump and sulked to lie across my shoes. I laid the book down again and wiped my fingers on the arms of the chair. The handbook might look like a normal, if *lux lucis*–suffused book, but somewhere in it or on it lurked a brain, and the idea of putting my fingertips on it turned my stomach.

I told you that thing is dangerous, scrawled across the page in the book's distinctive printing. Or was it handwriting?

"That *thing* is my cat, and he's just curious."

I believe there's a saying that applies here: There's more than one way to skin a cat.

"I think you were looking for 'curiosity killed the cat.'"

No. I had it right.

I glared at the book. Being a book, it merely lay there. This was foolish.

"So, O great and wise book, teach me something useful."

Of their own accord, the pages fluttered. I jerked back and eyed the book in disbelief. Had it just *sighed* at me?

"Am I annoying you?" I didn't quite get the full load of sarcasm behind the question from my position huddled at the back of my chair. If it could move its own pages, what else could it do? *It's a book, Dice. Get a grip.*

I am a book, Madison.

The words on the page so closely echoed my thoughts I stilled like a bunny in headlights, breath held.

Can you hear me? I thought.

The words continued to scrawl across the page without pause. If the book could hear my thoughts, it didn't respond to them.

You know we're not just shelving decoration, right?

I leaned closer in case it was nearsighted and gave it my best scowl. The novelty of talking to a book had dissipated.

When have you ever found all a book's answers on the first page?

Oh. It had a point.

I flipped to the next page. It was blank. So was the next. Trying not to think about what I was touching, I picked up the book and thumbed through it. I was about to accuse it of being as blank as it had been at Liam's office when I came across an entry.

HOUND was written in bold letters. Beneath it lay a small block of text in a precise font.

Dogs converted to evil by excessive atrum. *Semiharmful. Avoid being bitten.*

Scoffing, I flipped a few more pages before finding the next entry.

IMP. Name derived from human mythology and misplaced on these small collections of live atrum. *Herd animals. They gravitate toward greater evil. Mostly harmless unless left unattended.*

A final entry capped off the book's useless bestiary.

VERVET. Previously called simia *before early American enforcers adopted the French vernacular. Four-legged, scorpion-tailed, semi-intelligent. Pranksters. Mostly harmless. Avoid being bitten.*

"This is helpful? What about which weapons work best or how to kill each creature? You don't even mention a net for hounds. I know more than this already. What imbecile put this book together?" So much for Mr. Pitt's expensive training tool. Maybe Mr. Pitt *was* slipping as a warden.

I returned to the first page, now blank.

Then, it scribbled faster than I could keep up with: *That hurt. Just because I'm paper, doesn't mean I don't have feelings. You'd best keep that in mind as well as the fact that*—it switched to all caps to fill the rest of the page—*YOU'RE JUST AN ENFORCER.* The angry words pulsed before fading into the white page like ink drying into invisibility. In normal-size font, and at a calm, deliberate speed, it wrote, *I am a creature of infinite wisdom. I know what you need to learn, when you need to learn it.* The font size bumped up several points. *You're not ready for further instruction.* These words remained prominent on the page.

"I'm more than ready—"

Tiny writing scrawled across the bottom. *All apologies must be heartfelt to be considered.*

"You've got to be kidding me!" Let it be noted the that time was exactly 10:29 on the Wednesday before Thanksgiving when I officially lost my sanity. I was yelling at a book.

"What about prajurit? What about salamanders? What about wardens' souls? Citos? The history of enforcers? The science behind *lux lucis*? Anything?" I thumbed roughly through the book, but even the three entries it had previously revealed were now missing.

"Fine. I don't need more useless crap in my life. I'm going to bed."

Mr. Bond leapt for the TV tray when I stood. It wobbled precariously when he landed, knocking the book to the floor. He dove off the tray, officially toppling it, and pounced on the book, throwing his substantial weight against its cover and grinding his entire side into the book.

"At least one of us likes it." I reached for the book; Mr. Bond swiped at me. "Okay. That's it; no more book for you. Even if it deserves a few claw marks in it, you're not behaving very nicely."

I distracted Mr. Bond with a tossed mouse, then snatched up the book, stuffing it back in my purse. Mr. Bond raced to my side like I had a treat.

"This is too bizarre." I crammed my purse into my filing cabinet and shut it. Mr. Bond sat in front of the drawer as patiently as he might have sat in front of a mole hole. "Good luck with that one. Let me know if it gets out."

I tossed in my flannel sheets, unable to quiet my thoughts. A sentient book sounded fun in principle until it turned out to be a total pain. Rather than instructional, the handbook appeared designed to sabotage any chance of my success. At a time when I needed knowledge, it gave me halfhearted, misleading information about creatures already familiar to me. In the meantime, I'd been shuffled off to the mall so "real" enforcers could face the mysterious upsurge of evil without me bungling the process. Mr. Pitt might have worded it differently, and Summer might have sugarcoated it, but I understood the real sentiment behind my new responsibilities.

Every time I circled back to my banishment, it stung my pride and spiked my anger.

Just be a good little enforcer and do as you're told, I taunted myself. Well, I'd been told to keep my region free of evil, and that's what I'd do. I wouldn't ask for permission, either.

When I woke the next morning, I dressed for my parents' get-together, then drove down Douglas in the opposite direction. Five minutes later, I reached my destination and hunted down Bill, owner and mourner of the cremated tree stand.

"This is our biggest sales day of the year. We're pulling in another truck, but it's going to be a tight year for us now."

Between the roar of steady traffic down Douglas behind us and the hammering of new temporary fences to hold the forthcoming trees, I had to lean close to hear the soft-spoken man.

"Are there any suspects?" I asked, breath misting in the cool air.

Bill had been reluctant to talk to me until I told him I was doing a community-outreach piece on him. It wasn't my fault he mistook my careful wording to mean I was a reporter. It saved time and meant he didn't dismiss me as crazy—two positives.

"Not that they told me."

"That's frustrating."

"You're telling me. If I could get my hands on the imbecile responsible . . ." Bill's hands clenched to fists.

"Mind if I take a look?" I gestured toward the muddy patch of ash beyond their new fence lines.

"Aren't you a little overdressed?"

"Overdressed and underwarm. But when the boss gives me an assignment, I go." I wouldn't have time to change before going to my parents', so I stood next to the blustery road on this chilly fall morning in a cocktail-length teal and black dress and an even shorter black peacoat. Between the bottom of the dress's fluttering hem and my leather boots stretched a good foot and a half of exposed blotchy-white skin coated with heavy goose bumps.

"I don't know what you expect to see, but go ahead."

In a way, Bill had been fortunate. The area designated for the Christmas tree stand—and for all manner of other roadside vendors throughout the year—was large. Even factoring in parking, the dirt plot provided ample room for Bill's new sales lot, without infringing on the charred remnants of his burned trees.

I traversed the puddle-strewn lot with care, trying to look graceful while mincing. Heavy fire trucks had left channels in the soft dirt, which had filled with rainwater and sooty runoff overnight. I hopped the last of these narrow ponds and paused a few feet from the ash heap. Rummaging through my purse, I pulled out my pet wood for one hand and my knife for the other. After a quick check to make sure Bill wasn't going to protest—he was too busy painting a bold new sign—I tiptoed closer to the waterlogged ashes.

I blinked to Primordium and let out a tight breath.

No human-size salamander waited to bathe me in flames. There weren't even vervet. In fact, despite the monochrome of Primordium, the *atrum* residue made the extinguished fire look a lot like it did in normal sight: a black smear over an otherwise forgettable patch of dirt. This, I could handle.

Before I got to work, I surveyed the gray landscape around the charred patch. This much *atrum* was bound to have spawned imps. None lurked on the ground, but I wasn't surprised to find a handful feeding off Bill's staff. Unfortunately, imploding an imp attached to a person was nearly impossible without (1) invading the individual's personal space and (2) looking like a deranged nutter grabbing at empty air. They'd have to wait.

I slid the pet wood and sheathed knife into my peacoat pockets, measured the distance to the edge of the *atrum* pool, and blinked back to normal sight so I could walk through the mess without falling on my face. Five steps later, I blinked back to Primordium and put my experience cleaning up the hotel to practice. With a little concentration, I looped *lux lucis* around my hand, adding more energy gradually until my control started to wobble. Then I crouched and touched my hand to the *atrum*.

Lux lucis rolled from my fingertips and kept going, eating through the evil energy and leaving a giant shell of clean ground. Gritty ash and mud stuck to my palm when I stood; otherwise I would have planted my hands on my hips with pride. This was how a real enforcer took care of her region. I hid my smile after noticing the scowls Bill's crew directed at me. Attempting to explain that my pleasure came from exterminating evil would have made matters worse, so I kept my back to the men and my grin to myself.

I repeated the process three more times, blinking to normal vision each time I moved to a new location, before I attracted the imps' attention. I'd expected nothing less. The brainless bundles of *atrum* had a fatal attraction to *lux lucis*. With my clean hand, I pulled my pet wood from my pocket and flicked my wrist. A quick press of *lux lucis* filled the extended wand with deadly energy.

The first imp bounced up to me on tiny feet, its round little body similar enough to a chinchilla's to qualify as cute—until it opened its maw and exposed a double stack of teeth, like a tiny round shark's mouth. I poked through its insubstantial body with the tip of the pet wood and pulsed a little extra *lux lucis* down the wand. The petite evil fluff exploded into a glitter of *atrum*.

Despite having witnessed their herdmate's fate, the remaining imps hopped toward me, eager to snack on my delicious, untainted soul. One by one, I extinguished them, keeping my flourishes to a minimum; then I swept the final swath of *atrum* with a sluggish roll of *lux lucis*.

None of the imps had been larger than a grapefruit, but combined with all the energy I'd exerted to clean up the *atrum* puddle, my vision darkened when I straightened. I braced myself on the pet wood—and stumbled when it collapsed beneath my weight.

I blinked to normal sight. Mud and ash coated my boots to the ankle, and my right hand matched. Miraculously, the hem of my skirt remained clean. I wobbled to my car, tossing Bill a parting wave and smile. After laying down a reusable grocery bag to protect my carpet and scraping as much gunk as possible from my palm with a handy twig, I collapsed into my car. Grabbing a Chipotle napkin from my glove box, I wrapped it around my dirty hand and put my car in gear.

I suffered no more fatigue than I had after cleansing a few hotel floors. If that's all cleaning up after salamanders took, I was more than capable. Sticking me in the mall was the wrong decision. It was *my* job to protect the people of Roseville, not Jacob's or Summer's or Rafi's, even if they were stronger and more experienced enforcers. It was possible the citizens of Roseville might have preferred another enforcer if they understood the amount of evil lurking in their backyard, but they didn't understand and they didn't have a choice, did they? They had me; I was more than good enough, and I would do whatever it took to keep my position.

Gosh, is this how dictators think of themselves?

I drove two blocks, pulled into the library's empty parking lot, and stumbled to the nearest tree. *Lux lucis* gushed into me from its trunk. I savored the feeling for a count of five before moving on to the next tree, spreading the energy drain among several sturdy crimson maples.

All flesh between my ankles and hips was numb by the time I jogged, fully charged, back to my car. I used a few more napkins to clean the bulk of the mud and ash from my boots and hand. I would have done a more thorough job, but a glance at the clock had me peeling out from the lot. I was late, and I still needed to pick up food.

6

My Family Tree Is Full of Nuts

THREE MONTHS AGO, AFTER YEARS of coercion, cajoling, and out-and-out begging for me to return to Berkeley where I'd grown up, my parents retired, sold my childhood home, and relocated a mere twenty minutes from me in an active-living retirement community in Lincoln. With flabbergasting ease, they embraced their new life, hosting parties, participating in badminton tournaments, and taking art and dance classes. There was even talk of buying a golf cart to putt around with other cart aficionados in the sprawling community. Drumming my fingernails on the steering wheel, I crept along behind one such couple in a lemon-yellow golf cart and worried about the negative influence of retirement on my parents' decision-making abilities.

Mom was waiting on the front porch when I pulled into their driveway, though for the cotton-top couple in the golf cart, not me. She hustled to the cart, a box of brown sugar in hand, and tossed me a wave. With hair dyed a few shades lighter than mine and far better styled, trendy glasses, and a few extra pounds rounding out her frame, retirement looked good on Mom. I eyed the only other car in the driveway, a silver Prius, with unjustified malice. Trust Bridget to beat me to my own parents' house, emphasizing my tardiness with her punctuality.

"Couldn't you be late once in your life?" I asked Bridget when she opened the Civic's passenger door to grab my groceries.

"But then who would have painted the face of the man driving Oscar's newest model train?" she asked.

"Oh no. Dad's made another toy train scene?" I let myself into the house, holding the door for Bridget.

"Honestly, I can't tell if it's the same one as last time I was here," she whispered as she passed me.

"Check out those tiny hands, Son," Dad said, greeting me with his favorite truncation of my name. He lifted Bridget's free hand to display her dainty fingers against his blunt digits. "The Union Pacific just acquired the most handsome conductor on rails. Come see."

I dutifully followed Dad to his office, where a gigantic circular toy train set sprawled across a worktable. A miniature landscape enveloped the tracks, complete with plastic trees, an acrylic glaze river, a tiny handcrafted cabin, and a baking soda–dusted mountain tunnel. My unfortunate familiarity with my dad's train obsession meant I knew with one glance that this model was all new. While I obediently examined Bridget's fine facial-painting skills on the fingernail-size human figure seated in the caboose, I wondered how heavily trains had factored into my parents' retirement relocation. Dad was a nut about trains. Roseville was a railroad town. Add in Mom's social nature and refusal to live trackside, as Dad would prefer, and this community less than a half hour from Roseville's rail yard fit in their ideal-home Goldilocks zone.

My proximity had probably only been a bonus.

Mom came back inside and whisked us all into the kitchen to set the table, arrange the flowers, and pen the place cards. I protested over the place cards, since a whopping ten people—all local family—would be attending.

"When you host, we'll do things your way," Mom said. I shut up and transferred my store-bought potato salad to one of Mom's crystal serving trays without protest.

As soon as we could, Bridget and I slipped into the backyard, champagne glasses in hand.

"How was it?" Bridget asked.

"How was what?"

"The warden meeting, silly."

"Shh. Keep your voice down." I glanced at the cracked kitchen window and nudged Bridget farther around the side of the house. I'd mentioned my ability to see souls to my parents once as a teen, and they'd sent me to a psychologist. If they heard me talking about killing evil creatures, they'd organize a drug-addiction intervention. Bridget, however, found the whole secretive world fascinating, like a TV show she was peripherally involved in.

"Is everyone a Calvin Klein model in their spare time?"

"Sadly, no. Most are pretty average, though Rafi . . ." I paused to take a sip of champagne.

Bridget pounced. "Who's Rafi? Is he a warden?"

"He's an enforcer in Orangevale." With her red hair, porcelain skin, and sharp intellect, Bridget attracted men like catnip called to cats. She remained single because she was a workaholic, picky to a fault, and insisted any man she dated pass my soul inspection. Most didn't make the cut. If I hooked Bridget up with an enforcer, I'd know for a fact she was dating a good guy. So would she. Plus, enforcers worked weird hours, so he would understand her long days.

"Enforcer is good. No, enforcer is *great*. What's he like?"

"Scruffy, though you'd call it manly. Yea tall"—I gestured above our heads—"with a soft Middle Eastern accent. Dark, intense eyes. Lashes for miles. Early to mid thirties. He seemed nice, but we talked for only a minute or two."

"Sounds nummy. Anyone else I should know about?"

"Not as date material." I described the other enforcers and wardens in broad strokes. While I talked, I blinked to Primordium. The meeting and its purpose of ferreting out a pattern behind the evil uptick seemed surreal while standing in my parents' backyard, but I'd be remiss to not guarantee their safety. Thanks to an expensive landscaper and my mom's continued diligence, the enclosed space could have been photographed for *Sunset* magazine, with its vine-covered archway, winding brick path, small water fountain, and perfectly pruned shrubbery and flower beds. It looked just as good in Primordium, and a quick scan confirmed the area was clear of any traces of *atrum*.

"So was the meeting worth postponing with Dr. Love?" Bridget asked, putting a pant into Alex's name.

I checked the back window again and shushed Bridget. "It was but it wasn't. I learned some important stuff." I decided on the spot not to tell Bridget about the increased evil. It didn't seem fair to concern her over something she could do nothing about. I added too much melodrama to my next words to compensate. "Like the other wardens want to force

Mr. Pitt out of his position and disband my region."

"What? That's outrageous! On what grounds?" She slugged back her champagne, and I could see her lawyer brain engage.

"Something happened in Mr. Pitt's past, and he got booted to my small region. They think he's making bad decisions, like hiring me as his enforcer."

"They're lucky to have you!"

"I think so, too. Trust me. And if Mr. Pitt is booted, I'll have to transfer if I want to remain an enforcer, and I do. Niko says the closest openings are in Southern California."

"But that's so far."

"It's that or the East Coast."

"Well, that's not going to work. What are you going to do?"

"Not much. As of tomorrow, I'm working in the mall—don't ask me doing what, because I still don't know—and other enforcers will be splitting the duties of my region, with everyone reporting to Liam."

"So they're hamstringing Mr. Pitt. Does he see what's going on?"

"Yes. Not that he's doing anything about it."

"Maybe he needs outside counsel."

"Are you going to storm into my office, briefcase blazing, and tell him how to do his job?" I asked.

She glared at me. Her support made me smile, but I really didn't want the lawyer lecture I saw brewing.

Bridget threw up her hands. "I don't want you to move."

"Me, neither." Since we both were shivering and our champagne glasses were empty, we ducked back inside.

"What'd you bring today?" I asked.

"Shrimp and pea risotto and cranberry-pistachio biscotti."

"Homemade?" She nodded. "Could you make me look any worse?"

She smiled smugly, then shrugged. "It's the least I could do for your parents inviting me over four years in a row."

"Are you kidding? Mom forgets which of us is hers half the time."

Thanksgiving dinner was a cozy affair. My mom's sister Evelyn brought homemade biscuits, and her boyfriend, Milton, provided three bottles of Mt. Vernon Zinfandel, earning him my seal of approval. My cousin Megan's two kids were young enough to still think hanging with adults was cool but old enough to entertain themselves at the kid table.

Not even Megan's husband, David, spoiled the easygoing atmosphere, despite lingering tension between us from my stint as an atrocious used-car saleswoman at the lot he owned. But as pleasant as the scene looked, it was a smoke screen for the main event: the interrogation.

It began shortly after all dishes had been passed around, along with the expected compliments for each one.

"Tell us about your new job, Madison," Megan suggested.

I'd practiced for this one. "It's at Illumination Studios. The company makes bumper stickers. My official job title is sales associate. It's a glorified title for a little bit of everything."

"The way the economy's going, I hope you guys can keep afloat," Milton said. Bald, in steel-toed boots and a black shirt adorned with flames, Milton looked like a badass biker gone soft. Probably because he was one. "A lot of small businesses are closing shop lately."

After last night's meeting, my paranoia made his comment sound like a veiled threat. I blinked and examined his soul. It glowed gray, without black streaks, but without any traces of white, either. He was neutral, as could be expected of a man his age. His neutrality also guaranteed he wasn't a member of the CIA or involved with the imminent takeover of my region.

"I'm sure we'll be fine," I said.

I forced myself to examine everyone around the table. It was a bit like looking through their belongings without asking, but if anyone had brought in evil, I needed to know. My family was a clean group, though Megan had a few dark patches I wished I could ask her about. The last time I'd looked at my parents' souls had been over ten years ago. It pleased me to see they looked pretty much the same—light gray, with traces of white. I didn't bother to look at Bridget. She'd made me examine her multiple times, especially after tough cases, and she always looked the same: sort of like a Dalmatian, only with gray spots instead of black.

I blinked back to normal sight with a sigh of relief.

"Are you going to be working at any more *Star Trek* conferences?"

"You mean video game conventions?" I asked. Mom nodded. Apparently the concept of *if you've seen one nerd, you've seen them all* ran in the family. "That was hopefully a one-time deal," I said, speaking of both the convention and the demon who'd inhabited it.

Seeing the interrogators gearing up for a whole new slew of questions, I gave Bridget our *I need rescuing* signal. Like a gallant friend on a white steed, she rode to my rescue.

"I'm more interested in her smokin' hot coworker," Bridget said.

"Oh?" Aunt Evelyn asked.

"Oh?" Dad growled.

"Um, you know, for myself. Not for Madison. She's got the date with her vet."

Every eye at the table jerked to me—even Megan's kids turned to stare with open mouths. I glared at Bridget. She mouthed, *"I'm sorry,"* but the damage was done.

"Aren't most vets a little old for you?" Aunt Evelyn asked innocently.

"Depends on the war." Milton waved his turkey-laden fork in a sweeping gesture. "We've had nonstop wars since Vietnam. It's all those damn Bushes in the White House getting rich off good ol' American blood."

"Oh, don't get him started on the presidents," Evelyn admonished us, like we had any say in the matter.

"Republicans love war. You don't see them out on the front lines, though. If I could get a minute with a Bush, I'd tell him—"

"Not a veteran. A veterinarian. An animal doctor," Bridget clarified over Milton's ongoing rant.

"Oh," Evelyn said.

"—and he can eat my shorts while he's down there!" Milton concluded with a fierce jab of his fork into his plate. Peas and risotto sprayed across the table in front of him.

"This is the first I've heard of a date," Dad said. He pretended to be oblivious to Evelyn's frantic whispered conversation with her boyfriend.

"Oh, an animal doctor." Milton's blush spread across his pale, bald head.

"There's nothing to tell." I forked a bite and avoided eye contact.

"What's his name?" Mom asked.

I shot Bridget another glare. She compressed her lips to hide her smile.

"Alex Love," I said.

"How long have you known him?"

"He's Mr. Bond's doctor, Mom. I've known him as long as I've had

Mr. Bond. Really, there's nothing to tell because I haven't had a date yet." *Oh, hell.* Mom had that look in her eye. The one that said she was already picking out yarn to knit baby socks for my unborn twins. "Did Bridget tell you she had a case where her client was a woman accused of sexual harassment by her husband?"

"You can do that?" Megan asked, awed.

"More proof the system is flawed," Milton said. "Did you win?"

Unfortunately, Mom didn't fall for my diversionary ploy. While everyone else hung on the bizarre details of Bridget's case, Mom leaned over and whispered, "We'll talk later, dear."

I groaned and dug into my meal. If Mom decided to launch a full-scale interrogation into my love life, I was going to need my strength—and some ninja skills—to avoid it.

Eventually the conversation turned to the recent fires plaguing the state, and I kept my mouth shut there, too. The evil-world connection to the fires was another detail I'd avoided telling Bridget. I hated secrecy between us, and I considered pulling her aside to fill her in but decided against it for the same reason as before: Bridget couldn't do anything but worry about crazed evil fire-breathing salamanders, and I couldn't even reassure her I would protect her. Damn Mr. Pitt for rolling over and letting Liam commandeer our region.

After the second helping of dessert and some general good-natured groaning, Megan's family left, and Bridget and I headed out a few minutes later. Mom and Dad walked us to the door.

"Your cranberry-pistachio bits of heaven were wonderful," Dad said, giving Bridget a hug. "Don't be a stranger," he said to me.

"Evelyn had the wonderful idea of us all going to the mall tomorrow," Mom said.

My stomach flip-flopped. "Tomorrow? Black Friday? You don't want to be out in those crowds." Not with me there, doing whatever hunting citos involved.

"Of course I do. Think of all the sales!"

"Count me out," Dad said, retreating to the kitchen.

"I can't. Holly is in town tomorrow. We were all going to hang out," Bridget said, including me in the gesture.

Holly was a college friend. She'd taken up permanent residence in Davis after we'd graduated, so her driving forty minutes to be "in town" wasn't a big deal. I appreciated Bridget giving me the out, but I couldn't take it. I knew my luck: If I told my mom I was busy, even in a mall filled to capacity, we'd run into each other and my lie would be exposed.

"There'll be plenty of time for Holly after we're done shopping. What do you say, Madison? Are you up for a little fun with your aunt and me? I promise not to ask about Alex tomorrow."

I wasn't going to get a better offer. "Deal. I'll pick you two up here tomorrow. How about six?"

"We'll be ready. Have a good night. Drive safe."

"Pushover," Bridget said once Mom closed the door.

"What else was I supposed to do?"

She shrugged. "Tell me how it goes."

"A little something like this." I mimed shooting myself in both feet and collapsed dramatically against my car.

"It won't be that bad." Bridget laughed.

"Famous last words."

I changed out of my good clothes when I got home and flopped into my chair to savor my turkey-induced food coma. After a few minutes of channel surfing, I turned off the TV and tugged the handbook out of my purse, along with leather polish I'd purchased that morning with the food. After the way I'd reacted last night, I realized I probably did have some apologizing to do. Plus, maybe the handbook would be more useful if I could get on its good side. If not, I wouldn't have to open it again and I could stuff it on some shelf to be forgotten until the next new enforcer came along.

Mr. Bond leapt to my lap to investigate. I allowed him to sniff the polish jar, but I held the book out of his reach. Once he sprawled comfortably across my lap, with clumps of fur stuck to the fleece sweater I'd changed into, I turned my attention to the book and blinked.

The majority of the first page, which I considered its face, remained blank except for the small-print disclaimer at the bottom: *All apologies must be heartfelt to be considered.*

"I'm very sorry for being so harsh." Mr. Bond started purring, assuming I was talking to him. "I hope you will accept my humble and *heartfelt* apology."

I gently closed the book, blinked back to normal vision, and opened the jar of polish. Mr. Bond got one whiff of the potent contents and pushed off my stomach to jump to the floor. Resettling myself, I took out the provided cloth and rubbed polish into the cover. Scuff marks and scratches buffed out, and the soft leather soaked in the polish, darkening to a healthy tan. Previously indistinct green and blue ribbons of color twined across the cover in a simple but beautiful pattern. After using a separate rag to wipe off the excess polish, I laid the book on the table. *This had better have worked.*

I opened the book and blinked.

Apology accepted, was penned neatly across the top of the page.

"Do *you* have anything else to say?"

No.

"Are you certain you don't wish to apologize to me?"

The page went blank. I waited. I'd been thinking this over as I drove home. If I accepted that a book could talk, think, hear me, and have emotions, I needed to treat it like I would a person. I wanted more than to assuage its hurt pride; I wanted a working relationship, and for that, we needed some mutual respect. I was willing to give the book the benefit of the doubt, despite how useless it'd been last night. I needed to see if it was willing to reciprocate.

I held my silence like a parent waiting for a child to confess.

I apologize for my rudeness. The words flashed across the page and disappeared nearly as fast. I hid my triumphant grin.

"Do you have a name?"

The edges of the pages curled. I jerked back, then turned the motion into wiping lingering polish off my hands. If it could see me, I didn't want the book to know it had scared me.

Lord Valentinus Aurelius.

"Really?"

It has a nice ring, doesn't it?

"Is that your real name?"

Will you call me that?

I considered the fragile ego I was dealing with and my desire to learn more to prove my usefulness to the wardens.

"Let's drop the 'lord.' I'll call you Valentine, unless you'd like to be called Aurelius more."

Valentine is fine.

"You totally made it up, didn't you?"

Maybe. They're both good, strong Latin names, even if you did anglicize Valentinus. Plus, Marcus Aurelius was one of my favorite enforcers.

I let that absorb a moment, opening and closing my mouth over several questions that could lead this conversation seriously astray.

"Okay, Valentine, I need to become a top-notch enforcer as of yesterday if Mr. Pitt and I are going to keep our region. Oh, wait, you don't know. Mr. Pitt is—"

The only warden with a brain, though you wouldn't know it the way the others work to deface him.

At least I knew where Valentine fell in the whole fire-or-keep Mr. Pitt debate. "How do you know that?"

I'm paper, not platinum.

Was that a book joke?

"Then you know I need all the help I can get." As we'd talked, or as I'd talked and he had written, the previous words had faded away, so each new line he spoke—wrote, agh, whatever!—was the only text on the page.

You've got to give a little to get a little.

"What do have in mind?"

First of all, I'm not a wallet. I don't belong stuffed in a purse. How am I supposed to observe anything from in there?

"You, uh, observe? You don't osmose or something?"

I look. See. Examine. Watch. Note. Take a gander at.

"Okay, okay. I get it. Where exactly do you see from?" If squishy, moist eyeballs were going to appear somewhere on the book, I didn't want my fingers anywhere near them.

Everywhere.

"That's helpful."

Valentine fluttered a page-ruffle sigh. *I see like you feel. If your hand is covered in a glove, it doesn't matter what you touch—all you're really feeling is the glove. When you stuff me into the bottom of your purse, it doesn't matter where you take me, all I see are tampons and gum wrappers.*

"How do you purpose I carry you?"

In your hand.

"That's going to get a bit cumbersome."

Do you have a better idea?

"Let me think about it. In the meantime, what can you tell me about salamanders? And prajurit?"

No more black pit?

"I promise. I won't leave you in my purse."

Fine. It's there.

"Where?"

Turn a page.

"Why don't you tell me here?"

Because if I wanted to have everything printed on one page, I'd be a piece of paper, not a book.

"Zero to grumpy in no time flat," I muttered, and thumbed through the pages. Again, nearly all were blank. I finally came across one with text.

PRAJURIT BERSAYAP.

This entry had a pencil sketch of a thin couple, both clad extravagantly in heavily decorated long-sleeve tops so tight they might have been tattoos if not for small flares of fabric near the shoulders and elbows. The waist and hems of their dark, flared pantaloons were similarly adorned, ending just below the knees. Cloth bindings wrapped their feet and ankles. Both held crossbows and wore slender swords nearly as long as their arms. The woman had the surreal beauty of a Barbie doll, only refined and exaggerated, with an eye-to-face ratio usually reserved for kittens, a full bow mouth, and a chin delicate enough to appear sharp. The man could have been her masculine twin. I stared the longest at their two sets of round wings and the extra segment of their bodies extending from their behinds like bees' abdomens.

Niko's words came back to me: *Each hive is led by a queen, not unlike bees. Don't ever make the comparison to their faces, though.* I had a hard time picturing meeting a tiny winged humanlike creature at all, let alone conversing with one.

I'd spent most of my life knowing I could see souls. I'd had only a handful of days to acclimate to the existence of pure evil creatures and my ability to kill them. It had taken a bit of mental adjustment, but in many ways, it had been a logical step: *See souls. Protect souls.* The prajurit didn't fit. They looked like they belonged in a Disney movie, not in this world.

I read Valentine's description.

Aka "winged warrior." Typically four to six inches in height, with an average flight speed of fifteen to twenty miles per hour. The prajurit live in a monarchical hive community, led by a queen. Though allies of the CIA, the prajurit do not recognize CIA-delineated regions, and instead patrol areas designated and controlled by the reigning queen. Prajurit are fiercely territorial; they protect their land and air from all forms of atrum *as well as from neighboring clans. Feuds and bloody takeovers are common. Origin: Indonesia.*

I studied the picture again, then turned back to the first page. "Are they visible only in Primordium?"

Hardly.

"Then why haven't I seen them before? Or other people, for that matter?"

They're skilled.

I drummed my fingers on my knee. Valentine's intentionally obtuse answer irritated me. I wanted to call him on it, but as long as he was giving me *some* information, I didn't want to chance sending him back into a pout. "If the prajurit were still around, how would I work with them?"

As your warden saw fit.

"Come on. That's a Niko answer."

He's a wise man.

"He is, which is why he said I should learn everything I can from you."

Valentine paused before writing, *Prajurit and wardens work together, so Brad would coordinate with the queen or queens in your region.*

"Okay." Now I was getting somewhere. I would now know what prajurit looked like if I ever came across one. I suspected Valentine could share a great deal more about the prajurit with me, but since they weren't the pressing problem, I didn't push. Instead, I asked about salamanders and flipped through the otherwise blank book until I came to their entry. The sketch of the salamander looked exactly like its normal-world counterpart, only pure black.

A few inches to a few feet large. Salamanders incubate and hatch in ash pits fed by live plant fuel. Fully mature at birth, salamanders can immediately breathe fire, but long-term combustion requires the consumption of live plants. Eggs and hatched salamander are killed by being doused with live water.

Live water had been mentioned at the meeting, but I still didn't know what it meant.

It's lux lucis–*enhanced water,* Valentine said when I asked.

"*Lux lucis* enhanced how?" Pure water wouldn't hold *lux lucis.*

The water has to have something living in it.

"Like swamp mold?" Ew.

I would have said yogurt, kefir, probiotics, anything with living bacteria, but if you're a fan of slimy things, head to your nearest swamp.

I made a mental note to pick up probiotics tomorrow. And to restock my refrigerator with yogurt.

"What else can you tell me?"

I've said plenty. Now it's your turn to prove you can keep your word. I don't want to be stuffed away somewhere.

I considered pressing for more information, but I recognized the fragility of our partnership. Considering I now knew how to kill salamanders and what prajurit looked like in case I came across any in the mall—sigh—I counted tonight a success.

"If I leave you out tonight, Mr. Bond is going to be all over you."

Okay. Stuff me somewhere tonight. The pages rippled in a sigh.

Five a.m. came way too early. Mr. Bond yawned and stretched when I got up and dressed, but the traitor didn't bother to get out of bed even when I filled his food dish. I prepped for battle, stuffing my lightest purse with a small water bottle, aspirin, a granola bar, pet wood, the Bowie knife, a credit card (there might actually be good deals), my ID, a hair tie, and lip balm. I wasn't nervous about the citos—I could handle evil creatures. It was the shoppers and my mom and aunt who made me long to hide under my bedspread. Grabbing a bagel and Valentine, I marched out into the chilly, dark morning.

I drove to Illumination Studios in record time due to the fact that I was one of three fools up before dawn. I parked between the only two cars in our office complex lot: Mr. Pitt's bright-orange Fiat and a late-model boxy BMW the color of baby poop.

I jogged into the building, a sharp breeze cutting through my thin green sweater. I'd dressed for an overpopulated mall, not for the outdoors. Inside wasn't much warmer; either the lobby heater didn't kick on until a reasonable hour, or it'd been turned off. Most offices in the building would be making this a four-day weekend. I tried to shake off the budding pity party, but at five thirty in the morning, its claws were firmly embedded.

Sharon perched behind her tall desk in a halo of light, her hands-free headset and forbidding glare in place. I wondered who she expected to call this early.

"Good morning," I croaked, my voice still warming.

Sharon made no pretense of acknowledging my greeting—or to acknowledge she breathed. Her stout body remained as still as a wax replica, all except her unfriendly brown eyes, which tracked me as I scurried past her desk. The woman gave me the creeps.

I navigated the darkened office using the bright light spilling from Mr. Pitt's office. In the hushed shadows, the office felt foreign. I yawned. Maybe this was a dream, one where Warden Brad Pitt had a chiseled jawline and soft dimples. He'd be young and single and—

"Good morning, Madison." Mr. Pitt's owlish eyes lifted to the clock mounted above the door, one meaty hand swiping across a forehead that ended well past his crown.

"Happy Thanksgiving." I didn't turn to look at the clock. I knew I was on time.

"Humph. Never have gotten used to these American holidays."

He motioned me to sit. I perched on the edge of a leather chair. Designed for casual lounging, the slanted seat sank occupants beneath Mr. Pitt's eye level. The furniture was either a subtle power play or a bargain buy. Up until two days ago, I would have sworn my short boss's ego had driven the purchase. After seeing Liam's office, the discount-furniture theory made as much sense, especially if the size of the region equated to the size of a region's budget.

I squeezed my purse beside me and set Valentine on my lap.

"I'm glad to see you're using the handbook."

"He's been helpful."

"Were you at the Quarry Ponds yesterday?" Mr. Pitt asked.

The abrupt topic shift caught me off guard. "The shopping center? No. Oh, you mean the Christmas tree stand next to it? Yeah, I was there." I relaxed against an armrest and smiled. He'd noticed my hard work.

"Did I tell you to go there?"

"Nope." I beamed. Mr. Pitt frowned. It wasn't the expression of a man planning on praising my take-charge attitude. Masking a groan, I sat up straight. It was a month too early for a Christmas miracle anyway.

"Did you think about checking in with me first?"

"I hoped you'd be pleasantly surprised." Which sounded better than, *I didn't feel like asking your permission to do my job.*

"I might have been if I hadn't already coordinated to have Rafi clean it up."

"I'm sure he didn't want to be working our region on Thanksgiving."

"You made me look out of touch with my region and my enforcer. If we're going to get through this, you need to stop doing things on your own initiative."

"That's a crappy way to be an enforcer." The words were out before I fully processed them, proving parts of me were still asleep.

A heavy flush suffused Mr. Pitt's cheeks. "Oh? And you know this thanks to your decades of experience?"

"I know it in my gut."

"Your gut. Bubble gum on a turd, Madison! You're a tutti-frutti enforcer. I am a warden. Trust me, I know what I'm doing."

I hadn't gone to the burned Christmas tree lot because I didn't trust Mr. Pitt to do his job. I'd gone because I thought I could prove he could trust me to do mine. But now, with his words hanging between us, I found it hard to meet his gaze. What dark event lurked in his past? Why had he been demoted to this tiny region? And could his past mistakes hurt me?

7

Shop 'til You Drop

IF, IN THE FUTURE, YOU get a hankering to dart off on one of your harebrained notions, you'll think about this little conversation and stick to the plan, right?" Mr. Pitt asked. "No matter what your organs say."

I gritted my teeth and nodded.

"Okay." He released a heavy breath. "Take six and I'll see you back here this evening for tomorrow's batch."

Mr. Pitt gestured to one side of his desk where the glass vials Rose had been working with on Wednesday were clustered inside stacked boxes. They looked like tall lipstick tubes or oversize perfume sample bottles. Picking one up, I blinked to Primordium and examined it. The clear tube glowed a creamy pale haze that shifted when I shook the bottle.

"What is it?"

"Positive emotion."

I glanced at Mr. Pitt in surprise. His boxy soul shimmered like sunlight reflected off a still pond. I blinked to normal vision to check his expression more closely. He'd never joked with me before, but he was well versed in sarcasm.

"I don't follow."

"Citos feed on negative emotions. Didn't your handbook tell you?"

I shook my head. Explaining the delicate balance of my relationship with Valentine wasn't going to impress Mr. Pitt.

"They're countered with positive emotion. These vials hold the tiniest particulates of aerosol *lux lucis*. Very expensive stuff, but useless without an empath to infuse it with the right energy."

That's what Rose had been doing. Her comments about using my date-happy emotions made more sense now.

I stood and removed the water bottle from my purse, followed by my knife, pet wood, and granola bar. Mr. Pitt's eyebrows lifted with each item I lined up on his desk. Selecting six bottles, I shoved them into my purse, wedging my ID and credit card between them to prevent their sides from clattering together. The knife and pet wood also served as barriers between the glass, and the granola lay on top. The zipper barely closed. Together, the spray bottles were lighter than the water bottle had been.

I offered the water bottle to Mr. Pitt, and he silently took it.

"Isabel tells me Jacob is meeting you at the mall, so he'll walk you through your first kill. It's simple enough." Mr. Pitt picked up a bottle and placed his finger over the spray trigger. "Point and spray." A soft hiss escaped the bottle.

I blinked to Primordium. A fine mist of *lux lucis* fell like sifted flour. Mr. Pitt dipped a hand to catch it, and it landed on his palm and absorbed into his soul.

"That's it." Mr. Pitt stood. "I'm not trying to quash your instincts, but now is not the time for lone-wolf actions. Stick to the plan. Take out the citos. Don't deviate."

"Yes, sir."

I deviated from the plan the moment I left the office. If Mr. Pitt got mad, he could explain to Mom that she needed to stay away from the mall so I could hunt citos.

"This is going to be so much fun! We've got it all mapped out," Mom said, marching toward Nordstrom. I locked the car and hurried to catch up. She fluttered a handful of newspaper ads in my direction, then consulted the list on top. "We've got the Nordstrom shoe sale first, but we can't linger; Sears has sales that last only until eight."

"It's at the opposite end of the mall," I protested.

"Don't forget See's Candies," Aunt Evelyn chimed in. She had the same small-boned frame as Mom, though Evelyn's unnatural enjoyment of marathons had left her without an ounce of extra body fat. Thanks to Dad's genes, I towered over both of them and didn't look like I'd snap when hugged too tightly.

"Did we decide between Pottery Barn or Chico's?"

"If we hurry, we can hit them both."

Zombie shoppers staggered to cars around us, red-rimmed eyes unfocused, arms already stiff under the burden of bags. A sharp, freezing gust sliced through the thin weave of my sweater. I huddled around Valentine. This wasn't fair. I should be in bed, then spending the rest of my day drinking and gossiping with Holly and Bridget. I shouldn't be attempting undercover enforcer work with my mom and aunt—and a thousand sales-crazed shoppers—in tow.

My pity party strung a few droopy streamers.

"Tell us more about this vet," Evelyn said, tugging my elbow.

"Oh no. We can't. I promised Madison we wouldn't talk about it today."

"Why not? Did he dump her?"

Cue the confetti. The pity party was in full swing. "No. He didn't dump me."

"Is he hideous?"

"No."

"Really old? Married?"

"No and no."

"Oh, dear, he's not a cousin, is he?"

"A cousin? Whose child would that make him?" I asked, amused despite my annoyance. Dad was an only child, and Evelyn was Mom's only sibling.

"Oh, right. Good point. When's the date?"

"Sunday." We crushed into a people-clogged funnel through the double set of doors and popped out in the men's section of the department store.

"But you have to work on Monday."

"Aunt Evelyn, I don't know what you're implying," I said.

"Don't give me that, Madison. What if this date leads somewhere? Like the bedroom?"

"Evelyn!" Mom tried to appear appalled, but the effort fell flat.

Without looking, I could tell she was eyeing my hips. I had childbearing hips, she'd told me, though I think it was something she said to put the idea into my head. My hips were no different than a thousand other women's hips—a little bit rounder than they needed to be, but I liked them that way. "Well?" Mom prompted.

"Well what?"

"They're young," Evelyn said. "They can go without sleep if need be."

"I remember when I was in college, before I met Oscar. There were some nights I didn't get *any* sleep."

"Mother!"

Mom and her sister burst into laughter.

"No more. Or I'm leaving you both here and going home."

The usually tidy store looked like it'd been overrun by gorillas during its all-night sales extravaganza. Clothes hung haphazardly on racks or cluttered the floor beneath them, and half the kids' shoe section had migrated across the aisle to the somber safety of men's suits. Overly enthusiastic marketers or deranged elves had bombarded the floor with Christmas, Christmas, CHRISTMAS: the pillars, counters, walls, floors, display racks, and ceiling dripped red and green, silver and gold, trees and jolly fat men, and enough glitter and shimmer to start a disco. At the heart of the store, a two-story Norway spruce pulled straight from Times Square towered beside the escalator, while "Little Drummer Boy" pounded through the speakers, the tempo sprightly and festive.

"First on the list? Let's see. Boots," Mom said.

"Do we have to?" Evelyn whined.

"Seventy-five percent off. You'll be thanking me the rest of the year."

Medusa vibrated and I checked her screen. Jacob was in the parking lot. I texted back to let him know where to meet me. Which meant I needed to distance myself from my mom and aunt. "I'm going to take a look around. Come find me before you leave, or call me."

"Okay. Hang on, Madison. Why are you carrying that book? Do you want me to put it in my purse for you?"

Glancing down at Valentine, I shook my head. "It's my notebook. I've got all kinds of important information in here." I gave Mom a conspiratorial wink, then slipped into the crowds before she could question me further.

I blinked to Primordium and hunted for an unoccupied three feet for privacy. Primordium erased the overdone red-and-green décor but emphasized the mass of people. Everywhere I turned, bright souls shopped, walked, and chatted. At least the crowd didn't include roaming imps and vervet.

"Sheri, the dreaded ding-a-ling droop has nothing to do with you," a woman near me counseled her friend on the phone as she flipped through a rack. "These things happen to men. Especially if they're cheating. Debra told me her friend's husband's brother was a complete water weenie until he confessed to an affair. No, no, I'm not saying Zach is cheating on you. It's just—"

The lady roamed out of earshot. I questioned her consolation skills but silently thanked her for solving my problem. Pulling out Medusa and putting her to my ear without turning her on, I opened Valentine and spoke without feeling overly self-conscious.

"Hi, Valentine. I need to know what citos look like."

Hi, Madison. Don't you love this music?

"Not particularly." On the overhead speakers, Mariah Carey crooned her longing for Santa to bring her true love. *You and me both, Ms. Carey,* I thought.

It needs more flute.

"More flute? Valentine, I need to work."

You're so busy you can't have a quick, polite chat with me?

I sighed. I was developing a new appreciation for reference books without personalities. "How are you liking the way I'm carrying you?"

Much better. He paused before writing, *Thank you.*

"You're welcome. Now about those citos?"

You'll find what you need now.

"Thanks." I crooked Medusa between my shoulder and ear and flipped through the pages. My thumb landed on the cito page and I tossed Valentine to the floor with a shriek. Medusa clattered on top of him. After a frozen moment of shock, I dropped to a crouch and snatched Valentine up, hugging him and pretending to not see the stares I'd attracted. Avoiding the first page, I slowly fanned the pages, then used the corners to hold the correct spread open. A giant spider wasn't squished between pages. It was a drawing. Of a cito.

Oh, crap. This just got icky.

I skimmed the text next to the disquieting sketch.

Citos are attracted to strong emotions, especially greed and envy. In the United States, citos swarm yearly from Thanksgiving to a little after Christmas in tandem with the capitalistic frenzy and corresponding stresses of the human population. Forming a parasitic relationship with their host, usually feeding at the shoulder, neck, or head, they consume negative emotions and amplify them back to the host. They can be as small as an inch across and as large as a baseball. Usually green or red.

I shuddered. I'd seen a tarantula once in a zoo; I didn't want to see one without the glass between us. Plus—green or red? In Primordium?

"Whatcha doing?"

I jerked and slammed Valentine closed. When I looked up, it was into the bright white face of a pure soul. Jacob.

"Uh. Dropped my phone," I said, collecting Medusa. I slipped her back in my purse, then petted Valentine, hoping I hadn't ruined what little rapport we'd developed by throwing him to the floor. I blinked to normal vision and cast about furtively for my mom. I found Evelyn's red head first, then my mother's taller dark head, both half obscured behind a rack of red-tagged boots.

"You see something fishy?" Jacob asked, scanning the store. In an army-green corduroy jacket, thick black thermal shirt, plaid scarf, and tight jeans, Jacob was overdressed for the mall's warm environment. Of course, he wouldn't be staying. He'd be gallivanting around my region, pretending it was his.

I crushed the uncharitable thought. Jacob was just doing the job his warden asked of him, not angling to take over my region.

"Just checking on Mom."

"You brought your mom?" Jacob's sandy brows lifted.

"Yeah."

"Seriously? She's not an enforcer, is she?"

"She doesn't even know they exist."

"Then why?"

"She wanted to go shopping. I couldn't talk her out of it. I'm pretty sure it won't be too hard to distract her and my aunt—"

"Your aunt's here, too?" Jacob's grin became a snicker. I planted my hands on my hips.

"It's really not funny."

"Actually, it kind of is. But you're in luck. It's possible to do this while escorting your *mom* and aunt around the mall."

At his inflection, I reassessed Jacob's age downward. He was young enough to still believe it "uncool" to be seen in public with a parent. I rolled my eyes.

"What do we do?"

"You've got the spray bottles, right?"

I pulled out a vial and handed it to him. "I don't have to touch them?" I wanted to be very clear on this point. Real spiders were creepy; supernatural spiders were in a realm all to themselves.

"No touching; just point and spray. It's not the difficulty of the task. It's the volume. There's one."

I blinked and followed the line of his finger to a tall woman with a light gray soul at the shoes sales counter. The salesclerk rang up box after box of shoes, oblivious to the two-inch-high brilliant green spider sitting on the customer's shoulder. I gawked at the tiny spider.

"Why isn't it black?" Everything evil in Primordium was black.

"They're parasites, nuisances, but not evil. They feed on the uglier emotions and strengthen them. When people's moods turn dark, they're more prone to do bad things. That's why it's our problem. Or your problem, this year."

That didn't explain why the cito's body was in Technicolor, but in the grand scheme of my job, its color wasn't important.

"Watch and learn, grasshopper." Jacob sauntered toward the woman. As he approached, the cito scuttled across her shoulder and onto her bare neck. I gasped and clutched Valentine tighter. *They'd better not jump.*

When Jacob passed behind the woman, he raised his hand to adjust his collar and discreetly sprayed the cito. The woman brushed at her neck, feeling the rush of air but not seeing the fine spray of glittery *lux lucis*. On her neck, the cito shrank in size until it winked out of existence.

Jacob trotted back to me. "What'd you think of that?"

"Very smooth. She didn't even know you were there."

"That's the idea. You don't want to attract attention. "

"No kidding." With my mom in tow, discretion suited me just fine. Plus, Mr. Pitt was big on the idea of me blending in as a normal human.

"Your turn. There's one coming off the escalators."

The woman in question was hardly old enough to drive. Her threadbare layered tops screamed high school, as did the skimpy jean skirt paired with midcalf Uggs. She scanned the store as if looking for her paparazzi, a cell phone pressed to her ear, gum smacking. A flat, four-inch-wide red spider sat atop her ponytail, its legs extended to hold on like a demented cap. I shivered and ran my hand through my hair. Jacob snorted.

"Are you sure you don't want this one?"

"She's all yours."

Jacob held out the spray bottle. I moved Valentine to my left hand, grabbed the cito spray, and marched after the girl.

"My best Coach bag was, like, so ruined. I should make him buy me another one. I know; totally, right?"

When I stepped within arm's reach, the cito scuttled around her head to stare at me. I froze. The girl sashayed onward, scanning the men's department for fans. The cito kept its many eyes locked on me. I glanced helplessly back at Jacob. He was on the phone but watching me, and he mimed a quick spray.

The teen tugged open a door. It was now or never. I raced up behind her and doused the cito before it could jump on me. White glitter enveloped the girl's head, and the red cito popped out of existence. The girl raised her hand to her head and shot a dirty look over her shoulder at me.

I spun to the right and waved my raised hand like I'd seen someone across the store. "There you are," I called to no one.

"O. M. G. You should see what people are wearing here." The girl pushed through the exit doors.

I relaxed my arm.

"Not bad," Jacob said. "A little overkill on the amount and a tad obvious, but good save at the end."

"Thanks."

"I think you've got things covered here. I need to take off. Isabel says there's a problem on Industrial."

My stomach flipped. "You can't leave!" There were at least a hundred people visible from where I stood, another thousand in the mall. I couldn't check them all.

"Remember, the citos going to multiply throughout the day, so stay on top of them. I normally swing through the mall for an hour or two a day during the Christmas season to wade through them, but with you here full-time, it should be a breeze."

Once or twice a day? Why hadn't I gotten that option? Why had Mr. Pitt agreed to sequester me here *all* day?

"What happens if I don't catch them all?" This was a huge mall, and I was just one woman.

Jacob shrugged and edged toward the doors. "Sometimes they dissipate on their own; sometimes citos make their hosts do bad things, and our life gets a little harder."

His nonchalance sat sour in my stomach. The underlying message was clear: Taking out citos wasn't important. It was busywork.

"Don't worry," he said, misinterpreting my furrowed brow. "You took on a demon; this will be no big deal."

Jacob slipped outside and trotted into the parking lot. I watched him go with envy so raw it made breathing difficult. Today was going to suck.

8

Don't Believe
Everything You Think

"WHO WAS THAT?"

I yelped and spun around. Valentine bounced off a mannequin's hand. Mom and Evelyn stood behind me, a bag on each of their arms.

"You're jumpy. Was that the vet?" Evelyn asked.

"Please tell me it wasn't. He's too young."

I blinked to normal vision while steadying the mannequin. "He was no one. A coworker." I palmed the spray bottle and gave Valentine a pat.

"Well, then, no more dillydallying. We're behind schedule." Mom checked her list. "We've got twenty minutes to get to Sears for the deal on the tool set your dad wants."

We surged into the mass of shoppers traversing the center of the mall. Single file, we wove past families, loiterers, and women with strollers and toddlers. Mom and Evelyn managed to keep a conversation going, but I caught only snippets over the din of hundreds of voices and the competing Christmas music of the mall and stores we passed.

I hugged Valentine with my right arm to protect him and shifted the spray to my left as I passed a couple moving in the opposite direction. The woman's hands were free, but behind her tromped a man laden with bags. A crimson cito slightly larger than his eyes twitched back and forth across his forehead. I sprayed a cloud into the air and slowed to watch the man pass through it. The cito disintegrated, and the man's dark scowl softened to a look of tolerant indifference.

I considered a laundry list of negative emotions, the topmost being anger, hate, and greed. If people left the mall with those emotions rioting beyond their usual control, it would do more than make things difficult for enforcers, as Jacob had said. Actions based on those harsh emotions would result in *atrum*, either on the person's own soul or spread throughout the environment. Jacob hadn't been worried, though, so the problems with citos must be the quantity not potency. If one person left the mall with a cito attached to her, a warden might be hard-pressed to find her blip on their radar. If a hundred hosts returned home, there'd be an uptick in evil for sure.

Was an overpopulation of citos responsible for our regions' current problems?

I almost pulled out Medusa to call Mr. Pitt and tell him my theory before realizing its major flaw. If the increased evil in our area could be blamed on citos, Mr. Pitt and everyone else at the meeting would have known. I was the only enforcer who'd never seen a cito before.

Scurrying to catch up, I fell back in line behind Evelyn before she or Mom noticed.

After a mall full of women and couples, we found the single men and hiding husbands in the crowded tools and outdoor equipment department of Sears. Mom and Evelyn disappeared into the small tools section, but I was sidetracked by the sight of the pale red—dare I say *pink*—citos hopping excitedly on shoulders of twenty-year-old men and grandpas alike as they covetously examined tools of destruction and mayhem. Sidling behind them, I gave the area a general spray, watching with satisfaction as the citos disappeared. One by one, the men looked up and blinked at their surroundings, as if seeing the store for the first time. More than one checked his watch or phone and roamed away.

"We've got it," Mom said, proudly carrying a hard plastic box filled with one hundred tiny tools. Neither of us could have said what those tools could be used for, but looking at all the tiny implements, I knew Dad would love it.

Evelyn checked the time as we pushed our way back out into the mall. "We've got to hurry. The bra sale ends in forty minutes at Vicky's." She set a brisk pace through the crowds, and Mom and I trotted in her wake.

"Why don't you slip your notebook into a bag?" Mom asked.

"This is easier when I need it."

"I haven't seen you use it once."

"That's because I'm so sneaky." The woman next to me made an expansive gesture as I passed, knocking Valentine out of my hand. I swooped to rescue him from being trampled and dropped a spray bottle. It clattered across the floor and rolled up against the front of a children's clothing store. I fumbled to pick it up, dropping my purse in the process. Evelyn and Mom stopped to wait for me.

"Look at those adorable outfits!" Evelyn exclaimed, pointing at some booties with giraffe heads and a matching giraffe-adorned cap.

"Are you sure Megan doesn't want another child?" Mom asked.

"They're determined to stop with two."

A pregnant silence fell between them, and the weight of their contemplative stares settled on the top of my head. I stood with a huff.

"I'm working on it!" I said.

"Working on what, dear?" Mom asked with false innocence, slipping back into the perpetually moving throng.

"I think that's part of what we promised not to talk about today," Evelyn said, nudging Mom in the side with her elbow. "Mr. Love and all that."

"It's *Dr.* Love," I grumbled.

Mom and Evelyn shared a look. Evelyn giggled. "There's hope yet."

I shook my head but couldn't contain my smile.

We swept past a bustling bookstore on the way to Victoria's Secret and I had a flash of genius. "I'll catch up with you guys in a minute," I said.

"I've seen the sad state of your bras. You better not take too long," Mom said over her shoulder as they trotted off.

Pretending I was invisible to the half-dozen people in hearing range of Mom's announcement, I ducked into the bookstore. Whether it should have been public knowledge or not, Mom was right. It wouldn't hurt to buy a few sexy bras, maybe something lacy with matching underwear.

I wove through the shoulder-high racks of the bookstore in search of a salesclerk, stopping to send a shot of cito spray over the heads of two teens crouched in front of a pile of manga books. A green cito hunkered down on the closest girl's neck like a malformed parrot, darting in anxious bobs back and forth from her ear to her shoulder. The other teen, a boy in skintight pants and a long baggy shirt, had a daddy longlegs–size burgundy cito slinking around his ear. Both citos disappeared under the spray. I rubbed my shoulders and spritzed myself, just in case.

"May I help you?" An overweight clerk with a formidable neck beard materialized at my elbow, frowning disapprovingly at the spray bottle. I self-consciously tucked my hand behind my back and examined his soul. Despite his scowl and beard bib, the man's soul was fairly clean. No citos crawled along his shoulders or head.

I explained what I needed and left the store minutes later, the owner of a specialized nylon strap. Padded loop on one end, rubber loop on the other, the fully adjustable book strap was designed to hold an armload of books; I needed it to hold just one. Sliding Valentine through the rubber-lined loop, I tightened the strap to secure him; then I slung the larger loop across my chest and tightened it until Valentine rested against my hip. I examined myself in the glass of the storefront. To the casual observer, it looked like I carried two purses. It also looked like Valentine could still "see" easily, and I'd freed both hands for spraying.

Pleased with myself, I hustled to Victoria's Secret.

I found Mom and Evelyn elbows deep in the underwear sale bins. After saying hi, I nudged my way through the self-conscious men and sale-hungry women until I reached the back of the store, where matching underwear and bra sets adorned the walls next to a larger-than-life poster of a nude woman. She sat with her legs crossed and propped in front of her to keep the picture G-rated. I wasn't sure how a nude woman sold underwear. Maybe it was one of Vicky's secrets.

I couldn't shop in Primordium, since I wasn't able to see the colors of the fabrics, so I assessed the crowds, found no citos, and blinked to normal vision. Tasteful hints of red and green decorated the sales floor. Ironic, since everything else nudged toward gaudy. I got a kick out of the mannequin models in G-string underwear and push-up bras sporting fluffy red Santa caps.

Scooting away from the leopard-print rack and past a rainbow of pastel bras—my usual choice—I searched for bras with more pizazz. Lost in my fantasies, I was dithering between a bra with black lace flowers and one with white lace butterflies when a sharp elbow knocked me sideways.

"Let go! I saw it first."

"What are you, two?"

Two women faced off over a single bra, both clutching the hanger. The woman facing me was old enough to be my mother but tanned, Botoxed, and made up to look closer to my age to the undiscerning eye. The other woman had her back to me. She was shorter, plump, and younger, with a yellow butterfly tattoo on her shoulder and surprisingly pointy elbows. A leopard-print lace bra with a glittery "Sexy" front clasp jiggled between them.

"You want to see childish? Are these yours?" Butterfly Tattoo grabbed a handful of lacy fabric from the table next to Botox and tossed it over her shoulder. A polka-dot thong smacked me in the face. "*That* was childish!"

Botox's face turned scarlet. Her eyes roved up and down the plump woman, disgust undisguised. "At least a thong looks attractive on me."

"Like a raisin in a G-string."

"Jealous? I've never been mistaken for a sumo wrestler in my underwear."

"Oh, that's it!" Butterfly Tattoo threw her bags to the floor and yanked a strap of the bra off the hanger. "You're embarrassing yourself over a bra no one wants to see you in."

"This is only a thirty-six, honey. You're going to need a *much* larger size," Botox said. She snatched up a strapless bra, swung it by one end like a lasso, and smacked a padded cup into Butterfly Tattoo's shoulder. A hook caught on the woman's shirt, and the bra hung down her back like an emaciated, malformed cape. Botox used the distraction to grab the leopard-print strap on her side. The plastic hanger clattered to the floor. The bra stretched between the women.

"Put a little weight into it. You've got plenty to spare," Botox said sweetly. She gripped her strap with both hands and yanked. Pins fell from her perfect French twist, and tufts of bleached-blond strands flopped above her ears like fuzzy horns.

"I am *not* fat, you plastic bimbo! I saw this first. Let go!"

Butterfly Tattoo backed up a step. The elastic of the bra creaked.

I jumped to the side before a flailing elbow hit my breast. The movement snapped me out of my shock, and I blinked.

Both women possessed normal, gray-splotched souls. Both women also had avocado-green tarantula-size citos tap dancing on their foreheads.

Ducking to avoid another face full of thongs, I scrambled through my purse for the spray. The spectacle held everyone in the vicinity riveted, and no one glanced in my direction. I gave Butterfly Tattoo's cito a spritz.

It disappeared. She released the bra, and it snapped into Botox's face. "Ow! You fat cow!"

Butterfly Tattoo twisted to unhook the bra-cape, avoiding eye contact with the audience. I sidled past her to Botox, gave the woman a spray, and made my escape. Even after Botox's cito dwindled to nothing, she lost none of her righteousness. With a triumphant flip of her mussed hair, she flounced to the nearest sales counter.

"You can't be thinking of these." All the customers who had been watching the bra fight turned in unison toward the first person to speak into the quiet: my mom. I blinked. I stood in front of a wall of boring beige bras. "He'll fall asleep when you take off your clothes. Here. Try this." Mom thrust an all-lace black bra and matching thong into my hands.

I fought the urge to crawl under a nearby table and herded Mom toward a different part of the store, grateful when the noise level returned to normal. "It's not like I'm eighty, Mom. I'm pretty sexy without the added props."

"Tell that to my grandkids."

"You don't have—" I fell into the trap before I saw it.

"Exactly."

I bought the black lacy underwear.

Several hours later, I avoided an excursion into the claustrophobic Hallmark store by suggesting I take bags to the car.

"What a great idea," Mom said, unloading her handfuls into my arms. Evelyn squeezed in a few more and tucked the rest of her stuff into the bags already hanging from my fingers.

"Hurry back, dear," Evelyn said.

Groaning under the weight of their purchases, I struggled through the thickening crowds toward Nordstrom, passing dozens of cito hosts. With my arms full, I couldn't do anything about them.

Not counting this overburdened moment, though, I'd done a good job keeping up with the citos *and* Mom and Evelyn. Between killing citos, I'd even found a belt and some discounted Egyptian cottons sheets for me, plus a few gifts for Mom and Dad when Mom wasn't looking. Not too shabby for my first cito-hunting excursion.

After spending one embarrassingly long minute hugging a mannequin until a fellow shopper unhooked my snagged bags, I stumbled out of Nordstrom into fresh November air.

Horns blared. Cars stacked three deep in front of the doors as people dropped off and picked up shoppers. Behind them, impatient drivers ranted within the confines of their cars. Tiny red citos perched on the shoulders and foreheads of many drivers, but I couldn't do anything about those, either.

Arms on fire under the strain of gifts, I waddled through traffic and up the row toward my car. A sedan crept behind me, the driver stalking me for my parking spot. I tried to wave them past, but they missed my feeble gesture beneath the mounds of bags. When I reached my Honda, I dropped everything to the ground with a relieved sigh and stretched. My arms floated, unburdened.

"I'm not leaving," I mouthed to the driver waiting impatiently behind me. The car didn't move. I pointed at my Civic and shook my head. With a squeal of tires, the car darted around me. I popped open the trunk and threw all the bags in. When I turned around, another car idled in the aisle. I did the head shake and point sign language again, and they gunned past me.

I walked back to the mall stalked by a hopeful minivan and was actually relieved to mesh back into the crowds on the sidewalk.

Savoring a moment of freedom, I strolled back to Mom the long way, spraying citos on people I passed. I didn't go out of my way to get any; there were plenty of people with citos in my path. When I reached the food court, my feet carried me straight through the bustling dining hall to the outdoor courtyard beyond.

"Joy to the World" bombarded me from hidden speakers and kids' shrieks from the ice rink echoed against the walls of the two-story buildings. Exuberant decorators had gone overboard in the courtyard, though the black-and-white world of Primordium spared me most of the visual bombardment. A huge Douglas fir, bedecked in style and dying at the center of the courtyard, drained the last of the pleasure I'd derived from escaping the crowded mall corridors.

I beelined for an empty bench and collapsed onto the metal seat. Valentine jabbed my butt, and I leapt to my feet. I'd gotten so used to the feel of the strap across my chest I'd forgotten I was wearing him.

I ducked out of the strap and freed Valentine. A quick examination proved he was fine. No bent edges. No butt marks. *What do butt marks look like on a book?*

I flopped back against the cold metal and flipped Valentine open to the first page. It was blank.

"Are you okay?"

I don't appreciate being slammed into tile.

Of course. Did I really think he'd forget me throwing him to the floor when I first saw the picture of a cito? "Sorry about that. I didn't realize citos were going to be spiders."

A spider is hardly an excuse to abuse a book.

"You're right. I'll be more careful. How's the strap?"

Fine. Then, after a pause, *Thank you.*

I shut Val and slid him back into his strap. The balls of my feet pulsed in rhythm with my heart. Despite the chill seeping through my jeans, I realized if I didn't get moving soon, I wasn't going to want to get back up.

I trudged toward the mall doors, but a blissfully empty side alley between a restaurant and Brooks Brothers beckoned invitingly. When I stepped between the tall buildings, the energy in the air shifted. The blaring music faded with the sounds of screaming children. Ahead, the wind scuttled leaves across the concrete, and beyond the alley's opening, a towering wall of fenced-in plastic wrapped a parking garage under construction. My pace sped to a jog as an extrinsic urgency invaded my limbs. I scanned the visible chain-link panels, searching for an opening. *Maybe to the left.*

Half running, I rounded the corner and slammed into Jacob.

"Whoa! Sorry." I bounced back a step and brushed my hair out of my eyes. Jacob didn't have more than ten pounds on me, and our collision sent him stumbling into a wall. I recovered my balance, but my thoughts remained off-kilter. Glancing around, I looked for the source of the urgency that had gripped me seconds before, finding nothing.

"Madison?"

"In the flesh. Are you okay?"

"Fine." Jacob rubbed his hip, which had met the sharp corner of Valentine. "What were you doing?"

"Ah, I saw you. Everything okay? I thought you were done with the mall?"

"Me too. Then Isabel sent me back to investigate a problem."

"Anything I can help with?" Maybe the urgency hadn't been a figment of my boredom. I gave the construction site and parking lot beyond another quick scan in Primordium. Inanimate charcoal-colored surfaces, untainted with even a drop of *atrum*, surrounded us, and my shoulders slumped before Jacob shook his head.

Walking to the back of the restaurant, where ivy crept up a metal lattice, Jacob rested his hand among the thick vines. *Lux lucis* slid into him, brightening his soul.

"How goes the mall?"

"Endless thrills." I leaned against the wall next to him, letting the last of my embarrassment heat leak into the chilled bricks. I blinked to normal sight and squinted against the overcast glare.

"That sounds about right." Jacob shot me a look full of pity. If he attempted to pat my shoulder to console me, he'd lose a hand. "Look, it's really great you're taking one for the team this year. It's crazy. Salamanders. No prajurit. I've never seen it this bad for this long."

"In all your years as an enforcer?"

He straightened, shoulders stiff. I'd hit a nerve.

"Sorry. I didn't mean anything. How long have you been an enforcer?"

"Two years."

"So about one year and eleven months longer than me. Seems like you've learned a lot in that time." I might have laid it on a little thick, but I hadn't meant to hurt his pride.

"Yeah. I'm a sponge." His posture eased, and he glanced toward the parking lot. "Between you and me, I'm glad Liam's coordinating everything. He's the best warden in a hundred miles. Not that Isabel isn't great. She's just a little scattered. Liam should have this figured out soon."

I made a noncommittal noise and pushed away from the wall. This arrangement might be everything Jacob could have asked for, but I wasn't finding many reasons to praise Liam.

Jacob's phone chirped, and he checked it. "I gotta go. Isabel's got me jumping today. Oh, I found a salamander this morning in Granite Bay near Auburn Folsom. Don't worry. The fire's out and the salamander is dead. Anyway, see you around." Jacob tossed me a wave and jogged back toward the parking lot.

"'Don't worry. I'm having lots of fun while you're stuck in hell,'" I mocked in falsetto once I knew he couldn't hear me. I pulled out Medusa to check in with Mr. Pitt, then slid her back into my purse. I already knew what he'd say. "No lone-wolf actions. Stick to the plan. Waste your time on citos." I gave Mr. Pitt a squeaky voice. It helped take the edge off my frustration.

I turned toward the mall, but a flap of plastic in the wind pivoted me back around. The sky darkened and a light sprinkle filtered down between the high buildings. A few drops hit my hands, soft and cool, and the heady aroma of wet dirt and ozone swirled through the corridor. I took a deep breath and listened to the soft rustle of raindrops twitching the leaves of nearby bushes.

I had this tiny segment of the mall to myself now that Jacob had disappeared. Trailing my fingers along the cold chain-link fence surrounding the parking garage construction site, I collected drops from the twisted metal on the tip of my pointer finger. Water ran down my finger to pool in my palm. I crouched in front of a gap in the fence and tilted my hand—

Plastic snapped in the wind, a sound like a gunshot, and I jolted. The water splashed onto my toes. I jerked to my feet and shook my foot before the water soaked through the porous top of my sneaker to my sock. Wet strands of hair clung to my face. I peeled them free and shook out my hair, surprised to find the top layer soaked. Rain still fell in a soft sprinkle.

How long had I been crouched beside this fence?

I glanced around. Cars crept along the road wrapping around the parking lot, but none turned into this dead end. No servers had come outside for a smoke break. I was as alone as I felt.

I crouched and squeezed through the fence, pulling my purse and Valentine through with me. When I stood, I stilled, staring down at my feet in wonder. Hadn't I been thinking I needed to get back inside? I patted my wet hair with hands bright red from the cold. Rain soaked through my thin sweater, and the thinner long-sleeve under it lay damp against my skin. Water beaded on Val's cover, and I hugged him tight to my hip.

Shivering, I turned back to the fence, then completed a slow three-sixty and wove between puddles on tiptoes across the muddy construction ground. Something called to me. My collision with Jacob had jarred it, making me doubt myself, but the internal pressure was more than a desire to escape mall crowds and blaring festive music.

After one final check to make sure I was unobserved, I slipped through a rip in the plastic encasing the five-story skeleton. My dormant good judgment made a sluggish attempt at caution, reminding me construction sites could be dangerous. The workers wore hard hats and heavy boots for a reason.

Madison Fox's crispy body was found still attached to an exposed electrical wire. She was identified only by her blackened teeth, my morbid imagination supplied. *"Trespassing is a crime," police officials said. "Justice was served."*

Temporary lights on the beams of the first floor supplemented the natural light muted by plastic and the overcast sky. Gray concrete posts and girders created a uniform grid for each floor above me and sectioned off the pewter sky, but no wiring hung ready to electrocute me. I eased a few steps from the thick plastic wall, in case its grubby opacity didn't conceal me.

Beyond the plastic, the outline of a porta-potty, small equipment, and a mobile trailer crowded within the fence's confines. I waited for a foreman to rush through a slit in the plastic and kick me out. After a dozen breaths, I turned back to the garage.

Despite the wide-open top, the majority of the gravel-strewn ground inside was dry. A dark shadow near the center of the structure called to me. It looked like a hole, but that made no sense. A crater was the last thing a parking garage needed.

Stones skittered and crunched beneath my feet, the sounds echoing in the vast space. Tiptoeing, I edged closer to the hole.

Easily three car lengths across and nearly deep enough to hide my Civic, the uneven depression looked like it'd been dug by a giant dog. I walked around the lip of the hole, rubbing my forearms, where the hairs on my arm attempted to stand. Glancing around for filler dirt, I blinked to Primordium.

The pit seethed with raw *atrum* and *lux lucis*, the two energies rolling like a nest of giant centipedes. Flares of *lux lucis* bubbled to the surface, popping soundlessly, while lightning-like *atrum* squiggled sideways across the pit, there one moment, gone the next.

I stumbled forward, tripping over nothing but my sudden vertigo. The pit loomed, massive spikes of energy filling my sight. Gravel bit into my palms. I clawed the dirt, holding on as the world tilted toward the crater.

This was impossible. *Lux lucis* and *atrum* didn't move. Outside a body, both energies lay dormant. They couldn't flare or twist or spike or twirl. They definitely couldn't coexist. Yet an inky black bubble swelled in the center of the churning inconceivable mass, fountaining back into a lake of *lux lucis*.

I scuttled backward, hugging a concrete beam to regain my feet. Valentine jabbed into my thigh, and the pinch broke through my trance.

Gulping in air, I kept my gaze locked on my shoes. The internal pressure I'd heedlessly obeyed intensified, tugging me toward the pit.

I turned and ran.

9

Trouble Has Me on Speed Dial

HOLDING VALENTINE AND MY PURSE close to my chest, I sprinted across the dirt floor of the garage. Mr. Pitt's ban on lone-wolf actions be damned, he needed to know about this—whatever this was. I stumbled to a halt at the plastic and clawed through my purse. Yanking out Medusa, I pounded the screen until the Primordium camera app opened; then I snapped a series of shots over my shoulder without turning. Still holding the phone in my hand, I burst through the plastic and hopped frantically across the muddy, puddle-strewn outer grounds. I had enough presence of mind to look around for witnesses, but had there been any, it wouldn't have mattered. I couldn't stay in the garage. Squeezing back through the fence, I sprinted to the courtyard.

Rain pelted in earnest, and I slowed to merge with the tide of shoppers scurrying to the doors, then skittered past a crowded cluster of kiosks. I didn't stop until I reached a gigantic pillar supporting the second-floor carousel near the center of the mall. I pressed my back to the smooth surface so I wouldn't be trampled and closed my eyes, willing my heart rate to slow.

"Jingle Bells" bounced through the speakers, all but drowned out by the babble of voices. Roasted coffee and expensive perfume hung in the air. Water dripped from the ends of my hair to my sweater, and I shivered, the heated air emphasizing the chill of my skin.

No sinister urge pulled me back to the garage. I opened my eyes and checked my soul. Seeing its creamy white lines deflated the tension in my stomach. I slid Valentine from his strap and shook beads of water from his well-oiled cover. After wiping my wet hands against wet jeans, I opened him.

"What was that?" I asked, too rattled to care if passersby saw me talking to myself.

Were you trying to get me KILLED? The words covered the entire page.

"Don't be dramatic." Only one of us could have hysterics at a time, and I had it covered.

More sunlight. More adventure. Valentine's writing bumped jagged across the page, larger than normal. *My life, all there to read, and I . . . bored.*

"What are you talking about? You're not making sense."

Where were the silk bookmarks? The perfume? I haven't felt an ocean breeze in a century. I've never seen a sunrise over Machapuchare, never heard a three-wattled bellbird . . . The text grew increasingly smaller until I couldn't make out the squiggled words near the bottom of the page.

I gave Valentine a shake. "Snap out of it. I need info."

Letters sloshed to the side of the page, piled up, and slid down to the bottom in a heap before disappearing. The next text was printed in neat block writing that would have done an architect proud. *Object unknown.*

"Valentine, don't be like that. Don't you have something in your pages for me?" I thumbed through his bulk, seeing only white.

My experience is not worthy of comment.

My fingers spasmed. If his jacket were a neck, he'd have been gasping for air. By the laws of Primordium, *lux lucis* and *atrum* canceled each other out. That's how I killed evil creatures: I smothered them with *lux lucis* until it overpowered their *atrum* and extinguished them. Evil creatures performed the process in reverse; they used *atrum* to annihilate *lux lucis*. The two dichotomous elements could not coexist, let alone writhe together in a pocket of soil.

"A giant crater of *lux lucis* and *atrum*, and all you've got is snark?"

Caution. Do not approach objects you know nothing about.

"It's not like I had a choice. It pulled me to it."

Caution. Don't be suckered by feelings not your own.

"So you're saying you know nothing. Mr. Pitt bought you for this very reason, and you're playing dumb. Come on, give me something."

The words disappeared and lines traced up the page, a picture sketched by an invisible pencil. Valentine took his time drawing a hand, the thumb and three fingers curled toward the palm, the middle finger extended—

"Hey!"

I slammed the handbook shut as Valentine started to shade the middle finger.

"You're as charming as you are helpful." I shoved the handbook back into his strap, feeling vengeful enough to regret my purse was too small to stuff him inside.

I scrolled through the pictures I'd taken. All but one was useless, pointed more at the sky than the anomaly. I e-mailed the good shot to Mr. Pitt, then called him.

"Mr. Pitt, I've found something."

"Unless it's citos, I don't care."

"Check your e-mail. This is bigger than citos."

"Really." His tone was dry as sandpaper. "What, pray tell?"

"We don't exactly know."

"We? Is Jacob there?"

"No. 'We' is me and Valentine."

"Who?" Mr. Pitt bit off the word.

"Valentine. The enforcer handbook."

"You named a handbook?"

I glared at my unhelpful backup. "He named himself." There was a long silence on the other end. "Are you looking at the picture I sent?"

"Yes."

"The *lux lucis* and *atrum* were doing some sort of stellar implosion thing."

"Mmm-hmm."

"Well? What is it?"

"Did Jacob show it to you?"

"No. I saw him near the garage—that's where this thing is. Maybe he doesn't—"

"The garage? The unfinished one *outside* the mall?"

Uh-oh. "Yep, but—"

"Why were you out there?"

"It sort of compelled me." Silence. I pulled the phone from my ear to see if we still had a connection.

"Compelled."

I squirmed. "Yeah."

"And you went along with it." Not a question.

Perhaps you don't know what compelled *means.* I managed to keep the thought to myself, but I could feel Valentine's "I told you so" through his spine.

"Snickerdoodle dandy!" Mr. Pitt bellowed. "I told you to stick to the plan. For this, they could take you— No inspector on the planet would believe me if— Cookie crumble!"

"So you know what it is?" I asked, interrupting his rant.

"I'm not gumdrop green; of course I know! But the situation is delicate, and your ignorance is our paltry defense. To maintain it, you need to *stay away from the garage.* Is that clear? Your job—your *only* job—is to kill citos."

"But—" He couldn't really be prioritizing citos over a crazy ball of impossible energy lurking a few feet outside, could he? "What about the danger? That was a lot of *atrum.* If Jacob doesn't know, I should—"

"Keep out of it."

"But he didn't mention it. He might not—"

"Jacob doesn't report to you," Mr. Pitt said, his voice flat. "Shockingly, if you do exactly as you've been told, you'll be fine, and we'll make it through this season. Work the mall. Don't go back to the garage. And above all, *stick to citos*!"

The connection went dead.

Mr. Pitt's offhand reassurance of my safety had done little to soothe my frazzled nerves; his refusal to share vital information sparked an unpleasant suspicion about his competence. I scrolled through my contacts and hovered a finger over Jacob's number. Just a quick call and I could get some answers.

Yet, my finger refused to hit CALL. If I consulted Jacob, it would get back to my boss. Worse, it would show everyone I didn't trust Mr. Pitt. As much as my boss irritated me, I wasn't ready to hand Liam and his conspirators another reason to fire Mr. Pitt.

I shoved Medusa back into my purse. "Run along and spray invisible spiders," I mocked. "Don't worry your inexperienced enforcer brain about the big bad ugly in the garage." Yeah, right. I was getting Mom and Aunt Evelyn out of here ASAP.

"What took you so long?" Mom asked when I caught up with them at JCPenney.

"Did you go swimming?" Evelyn teased.

"It's really coming down outside," I said, ignoring Mom's question. "I'm beat. You guys ready to go?"

I scanned the clothes racks while Mom consulted her list. No evil creatures leapt out of hiding to attack. I almost wished some would. My nerves stretched on a wire strung between me and the impossible writhing energy, and the connection grated, even if it was in my head. Doing something, even killing a few imps, would be a great distraction. I couldn't even address the citos on the nearby shoppers; my last bottle of spray had run out before I'd reached Mom and Evelyn.

Fortunately, Mom decided the two items not crossed off on her list weren't important, and after one frustrating detour to Crate & Barrel to order an out-of-stock gravy boat, we left. I didn't breathe easy until we'd cleared the mall traffic and were on the highway back to my parents' house.

"I can't wait to get home and tally how much I saved," Evelyn said.

"Me too," Mom said.

I drooped behind the steering wheel. I couldn't wait to get home. Period.

After sorting bags among their respective owners at Mom's house, I said good-bye to Mom and Aunt Evelyn, gave Dad a quick hug when he came out to help carry packages inside, and then drove straight back to the office.

Sharon manned the receptionist helm with her usual statue-like skill. She got a limp hello from me. It seemed to satisfy her as much as a cheerful greeting, which is to say, she looked as pleased as deflated pudding.

The soft sounds of the office felt like velvet on my assaulted eardrums. I waved at Rose through the glass conference room wall, and despite my quiet steps and her back to me, she waved back. Will clicked softly at his keyboard, but he glanced up long enough to give me a friendly smile. He was pleasant-looking in a way that managed to not cross the line to handsome or sexy, and if I'd looked at him in Primordium, his soul would have glowed with the inhuman warmth of a sunbeam. He was an Illuminea, a creature of *lux lucis*, but he looked human to everyone who couldn't see souls. Since he was in the office, the hotel must be doing well. Any other time, I would have stopped to ask him, but I was on a mission.

I rapped on Mr. Pitt's door, and he lifted his eyes from his computer. Polite inquisitiveness turned to his familiar scowl.

"What are you doing back so soon?"

"I'm all out." I pulled empty vials out of my purse and lined them up on his desk, then collapsed into the leather chair. "What is the thing in the garage?"

"It's none of our concern. That's not our region."

His use of *our* not *your* took some of the sting from his words. "The wardens all decided I should work the mall." *And you agreed,* I added silently. "It's not like I was trespassing on some secret project. I was told to be there."

Mr. Pitt smiled. It was a tiny twitch of his lips, but I pounced. "Wait, that's not what it is, is it? A secret project?"

"It's not a secret project, but it's none of your business. What'd the book say?"

"Nothing useful."

"Good. The less you know—about *this*—the better, for both of us. How were the citos?"

I held Mr. Pitt's hazel gaze. I really, really wanted to press for more. Keeping me ignorant wouldn't help me or him, not in any way I could see. Was he trying to sabotage me? Or was this a backward form of protection?

I drummed my fingers against my knee, cursing Niko for refusing to give me his opinion. Could I trust Mr. Pitt or not?

"Not bad," I finally said.

Mr. Pitt grunted.

"You know, it occurs to me we're going about the citos backward." I'd given this a lot of thought, especially during that last useless half hour at Crate & Barrel. "I'm taking citos out one at a time, when we could be exterminating them en masse."

Mr. Pitt flattened his wide lips but motioned for me to continue.

"We could be piping cito spray in through the vents. The circulating air would kill them for us." *And free me to do something more enjoyable that requires my talents.* "Or at least put vents at the exits, like those fly fans at drive-through windows." I mimed a downward rush of air.

"Gosh, boss, are you hearing this?" Rose asked, storming into the room. "Little Miss Dinky Enforcer has a *perfect* solution. Good thing we've got her around to educate us. How did we survive the last *umpteen* Christmas seasons without her?" Her ponytail whipped through the air when she spun to jab a finger in my face. "And who, O Wise Non-Empath, is going to make all that spray? You?"

Eyes wide, I pushed my chair back, away from Rose's hot glare.

"Oh, no, wait. *I'm* the only empath in the building. *I'm* the only one working my emotions to nubs so you can traipse around a mall all day." Rose planted her hands on her hips. "Since you've got all the brilliant solutions, how about this: How are we going to keep that cito spray fresh? Do you even know the shelf life of spray?"

I clamped my mouth shut and shook my head.

"Of course you don't. Forty-eight hours for most empaths. Mine lasts almost seventy-two. That's why I'm making spray for seven different regions."

"You are the best," Mr. Pitt said.

I leaned around Rose to double-check my boss hadn't been swapped for a stranger. I'd never heard conciliatory in his tone before. I also noticed all the bottles that had been stacked beside his desk earlier were missing.

"Pshaw," Rose said. She flounced to the chair next to me and sat near the edge, then reclined her body to rest her head on the low back, eyes closed. "You did *not* go through all six of those bottles in the last few hours."

"Um. I did. But technically it was nine or so hours. That's a little under a bottle an hour."

Rose cracked an eye at me. I'd never seen her this on edge, not even when in the vicinity of a demon.

"I swear I wasn't wasting it." I raised my hands in innocence. Guilt twisted my stomach. I *had* wasted a lot in the beginning. "I'll do better tomorrow. You can call me Ms. Conservative."

Rose glared. I did my best to project earnestness. Finally she closed her eyes. I glanced at Mr. Pitt, who watched Rose with a wariness similar to mine. Easing back in my chair, I strove for a neutral topic.

"How's the region looking today?"

Mr. Pitt's expression clouded, proving I brought good cheer wherever I went.

"The Century Theater had a small plague of vervet. Judging from the amount of *atrum*, they should have been there over a day, but yesterday the area was spotless."

"Do I need to—"

"Summer took care of it," Mr. Pitt said. "Along with a newly formed demon at the Automall."

I slumped in my chair. In one day, Summer had done as much as I'd accomplished in my entire enforcer career.

"Newly formed demons are cakewalk compared to that monster you took out," Rose said without opening her eyes.

My gratitude swelled disproportionately to her meager defense, mostly buoyed by the fact that I hoped this meant she had forgiven my ignorant suggestion.

"There was a fire near the lake, a definite salamander attack." Mr. Pitt rose from his desk and stalked to the map on the wall. "And three minor disturbances along the western border. None of this makes sense. There's no pattern." His fist smacked the wall.

"Anything I can—"

"No! You're handling the mall. Stay focused."

I took that as my cue to leave. Rose came with me. She doled out nine vials from the new batch on the conference table and a stern warning to be conservative. Stepping back from the table, she surveyed the work left in front of her.

"How was the date?"

"Didn't happen."

"Damn."

"Were you going to mooch my happiness?" I tried to look affronted, but my smile ruined it.

"You've got your tricks . . ."

"We rescheduled," I offered. I summoned Alex's handsome face but couldn't work up enthusiasm. With two more mall-filled days stretching before me, Sunday evening felt like a lifetime away.

Rose turned back to her work. "I hate this time of year."

"Let's form a club."

"Ignore the impossible maelstrom of energy in the garage," I grumbled the next day, spritzing a lime-green cito the size and shape of a black widow. "Don't you dare go near it. You might get to do something exciting." Another cito, this one maroon, disappeared in a puff of spray. "Stick with boring citos."

After four hours working through Saturday's dense horde of shoppers, I hardly noticed the people beneath the citos. I'd already gone through a little more than three vials—right on track with yesterday's use despite being consciously conservative. Rose wasn't going to be happy, but I was sure she didn't want me to let citos escape just so she didn't have to do more work. Pretty sure, at least.

I slid a hand to the base of my spine for the hundredth time. Hidden under my sweater, the knife lay horizontal against my hips in its belt sheath. Any minute, I expected the blade to clatter to the floor, despite the buckle strap holding it in the sheath. The rest of the time, I waited for someone to call mall security on me or, at the very least, to scream and point.

Despite my paranoia, I couldn't bring myself to put the knife back in my purse. I wanted the knife where I could get to it quickly.

My stomach churned. *You better know what you're doing, Mr. Pitt.*

Being forbidden from going back to the garage didn't stop me from obsessing over it. Mr. Pitt thought my ignorance could be a defense— against what, he wouldn't say—but I couldn't flip a switch on my curiosity. Plus, I could either work on the puzzle in the parking garage or contemplate all the evil being fought in my region by other enforcers. Of the two, the enigma proved more entertaining. Maybe it was a geyser of Primordium matter, a kind of source—all this *lux lucis* and *atrum* had to come from somewhere, right? Or it could be the remnants of something: When large evil creatures were killed, their remains released *atrum*, which collected and stained an area unless cleansed, much like the *atrum* left at the charred Christmas tree stand. If something had died or been killed beneath the garage, all the energy could have collected in the hole.

It would have taken the death of something enormous to leave such a massive amount of *atrum*, though, and it seemed unlikely it wouldn't have come up in the meeting. Plus, my theory didn't explain the *lux lucis*. Unless the construction site was an old slaughtering ground of evil creatures *and* enforcers—a theory too scary and gross to contemplate and fortunately one that didn't make sense. Leftover *atrum* or *lux lucis* was inert. The energy in the pit acted alive.

My top theory—and the only one that made sense—was that the raw energy was responsible for the uptick of evil. The mall squatted at the center of all the affected areas, or close enough. Given its impossible nature of interwoven *lux lucis* and *atrum*, the seething crater probably had untold abilities, including antagonizing salamanders into starting dozens of fires and attracting demons, newly formed or not.

I thought back through my conversation with Mr. Pitt after I'd fled the garage. He'd initially seemed surprised, but by the energy in the garage or the fact that I'd gone out-of-bounds to discover it, I couldn't tell. Since then, he'd seemed more concerned about regional boundaries than by the massive amounts of active *atrum*. When I'd petitioned for more information this morning, Mr. Pitt had shut me down, saying Isabel would handle her region as she saw fit. Considering a warden's job was to monitor all Primordium energy within his or her region, there was no way Isabel wasn't aware of the crater of swirling energy. If she knew about it, she would know when it had appeared and whether it was connected with the multiregional increase of evil. All of which put a major dent in my best theory.

None of my musings got me any closer to answering my core question: What was the thing in the garage?

Round and round my thoughts looped, as repetitive as my sweeps through the mall.

I was circling an indoor play area, liberally spraying the rampant cito infestation overtaking parents while entertaining the idea of the pit being a grounded Primordium storm, when I spotted Isabel. She wore a long skirt, English riding boots, and a button-up blouse, emphasizing her schoolteacher vibe, but it was her bright soul that caught my eye. It's hard to miss true white in a sea of gray and even harder to overlook the distorted soul of a warden.

"I've been trying to catch up with you for ten minutes," she said after we exchanged greetings. "You simply don't stop moving."

"Neither do the people with citos."

"Isn't that the truth? I figured you might need a pick-me-up." She handed me a tall cup. Through the clear plastic lid, the inside glowed faintly. I blinked to normal vision. A brilliant purple smoothie filled the Jamba Juice cup. Isabel held up her other hand, showing me she already had a juice for herself.

"Thank you. Was there something you need me to do?" I tried to sound polite, but my words came out cool. The last time I'd seen the warden, she'd insulted my skills as an enforcer.

"Jacob was far too busy today to check in with you, and I wanted to see how you're doing. You've so little experience, I didn't want you to be overwhelmed."

Overwhelmed? By a task Jacob had told me usually took him an hour or two a day? "It's been mundane," I said.

"I should have expected as much. You've proved surprisingly resourceful. Are you sure you didn't do some freelance work before you took your job? You know, on your own before learning about the CIA?"

"Not a drop."

"No, probably not. If you had, I suppose you would have aimed for a larger region than Brad could offer."

Isabel hadn't come right out and insulted me, but these backhanded compliments and insinuating comments felt like a personal attack. I decided to try a little offense. "I'm finding my region to be the perfect size, and Mr. Pitt has been wonderful. After all, with his guidance, my lack of experience didn't prevent me from taking on a demon."

Isabel pursed her lips. "Yes, we're all so thankful you survived. Brad really bungled that one. He knew the danger and should have pulled you out and let Niko handle it. I don't know why Brad's continuing to put you at risk, either. He should have you training under another enforcer."

Ah. Here was the real reason Isabel had hunted me down in the mall, smoothie in hand. If she could convince me to train under Jacob, the chain of command would put her in control of my—and Mr. Pitt's—region. She'd initiate the coup Niko said Mr. Pitt feared.

On cue, Isabel said, "I offered for Jacob to be your tutor. He's a quick learner, and he has really flourished since transferring to my region. He could teach you a lot, fast. Brad can't keep you in the dark if you make a formal request to work with Jacob." She gave me a motherly smile, then sipped her smoothie.

My fake smile melted from my face.

"Oh, speaking of Jacob, he said he ran into you outside yesterday."

"Yep. I was getting some fresh air." I'd been considering trying to interject a hint of my knowledge of the energy in the garage, but her attitude had stalled me. Now her forced "casual" interjection of my encounter with Jacob yesterday set off an internal alarm.

"He said you about ran him over."

"I needed an escape from all this." I forced a chuckle and gestured to the screaming children in the play area and the greater crowds flowing around us. "I got a little carried away when I spotted him."

Isabel made a noncommittal sound, then took another sip of her smoothie. "Brad's making poor decisions lately—letting you handle the demon was only one of many. If you feel unsafe in any way or need to talk about any concerns, call me."

We exchanged numbers; then Isabel said good-bye. I watched her back until the crowds swallowed her. Remembering Niko's assurance that none of the wardens were my enemy, I replayed the conversation, trying to edit out my inclination to see insults where maybe there hadn't been any. Viewed from a different angle, Isabel had been nice. She'd brought me a smoothie, actually left her office to check on me, and was campaigning to get me more training and to keep me safe. If I took out the possible political maneuvering, Isabel's actions were far friendlier than my own warden's. Maybe she was right: Maybe Mr. Pitt was making bad decisions, including keeping me in the dark about the energy in the garage. Maybe I'd been too quick to jump to the wrong conclusion about the other wardens, Isabel included.

I stared at Isabel's number still highlighted on Medusa's screen. The political jockeying among the wardens *did* exist, and pretending otherwise was foolhardy. Even if I saw insults where Isabel only expressed concerns, I couldn't go behind Mr. Pitt's back. The only reason I wanted to call Isabel was to discuss the wild energy in the garage—the very thing Mr. Pitt instructed me to ignore. Essentially, if I placed the call, I'd be telling all the wardens I trusted Isabel, not Mr. Pitt. It might be the smart thing to do; shifting my loyalties might help me retain my position if Isabel took over my region.

I shook my head. I didn't trust Isabel, but that wasn't the problem. The problem was I wasn't sure I trusted Mr. Pitt.

Stuffing Medusa back in my purse, I sipped my smoothie and returned to spraying citos, mixed feelings churning in my gut.

I limped out of the mall nearly ten hours after I'd arrived. Night had long-since fallen, and the slanting rain was illuminated in conical streams beneath the light posts. An exodus of vehicles splashed past, and I hugged the bumpers of the parked cars I passed to avoid the spray from the tires.

Chafing my upper arms, I winced when I grazed my bicep bruise. Old women and their bejeweled purses were going to be avoided tomorrow, no matter how large their citos. I'd also be avoiding the toy store. My right pinkie toe had been broken or possibly completely severed (I was too afraid to look) by a two-year-old boy in tiny cowboy boots who had spontaneously thrown a fit on top of my foot. I'd used up an entire bottle of spray in the toy store, then fled.

I didn't even want to think about the bits of rice stuck in my hair. Raw male territoriality usually reserved for lions battling over prides had roared to life between two middle-aged fathers over a four-seat dining table in the food court. By the time I reached the screaming pair and their flaming-red citos, they'd been slinging Chinese food at each other.

The whole day, images of the active crater in the garage hummed in the back of my thoughts until I couldn't tell if it called to me or if my curiosity pulled me to it.

At least twice an hour, I talked myself out of going back to the garage for another peek. I'd placated myself with the promise of marching straight to the office and demanding answers at the end of my shift.

Now, trudging to my car through the rain, I decided to save my righteous march for tomorrow. All I wanted now was a good book, my feet up in my recliner, and Mr. Bond on my lap.

I was three empty spaces from my car when I realized I'd made a mistake. The car I'd been angling for already had someone at the driver's door. I stopped and looked around. There wasn't another Civic in the poorly lit overflow lot. Sluggish thoughts engaged and I checked the license plate, then looked at the person next to the car again.

A long wire glinted in the lights of a passing vehicle. Someone was breaking into my car!

Adrenaline broke through my exhaustion. I sprinted across the remaining space. At the slap of my shoes in the puddles, the burglar spun around. We recognized each other in the same moment.

Sam froze, hand on the wire half buried between my window and the rubber seal around it. I barreled into him.

"What do you think you're doing?" I yelled. The last time I'd seen Sam, we'd been on the other side of Roseville in my region, and he'd sworn I'd scared him straight after catching him burglarizing my car. The scrawny liar! At fifteen, maybe sixteen, Sam weighed less than me, but he was all muscle. What he lacked was my anger's strength. I pressed him to my wet car, holding him at arm's length. "What did I tell you last time I saw you? That if I caught you doing anything like this again, I'd shoot you!"

His green eyes widened to perfect round circles. He raised his hands as if I were holding him at gunpoint. "I swear, I didn't know this was your car."

"That's your excuse?"

He nodded energetically, loosing tufts of orange-red hair from beneath his gray beanie.

"God, you're stupid and you've got the worst luck." I held in a sigh and considered my options. During our prior confrontation, Sam had been unwittingly hosting baby imps. I checked him now in Primordium, and sure enough, they were back, feeding from his wrists and throat.

I glanced around; we were alone—no other imps, no other people. Where was mall security when I needed them?

I reached for Sam's neck, passed my hand through the imp, and wrapped my fingers around his throat.

"Whoa," he whispered. I wanted him quaking in his ratty Vans, but at best, he looked uneasy. I tightened my grip and pumped *lux lucis* through the imp, disintegrating it, then continued to feed more *lux lucis* into Sam to wipe out the flecks of *atrum* and gray spots on his throat. I left my fingers where they were for the moment and leaned in to emphasize my point.

"You're in big, big trouble, Sam. Why are you targeting me?"

"How was I supposed to know this was your car? I just, you know, heard Civics are easy to jimmy." He rolled his eyes down to look at my breasts. "Where are your boobs?"

"I left them at home." I ground my teeth together. The last time he'd seen me, thanks to my peripheral involvement in a video game convention, I'd been in a costume I'd more happily burn than wear again.

I squeezed Sam's neck to remind him now was not the time for conversation. Counterintuitively, he relaxed against my car. I wanted to shake him, but I resisted.

"Do you want to hold hands again?" he asked hopefully.

I sighed. Yes, I needed to hold his hands to kill the imps feeding off the residual negative energy of his criminal actions. The brainless fluffs of *atrum* would feast on a pure soul, but they tended to gravitate toward those who'd already tainted themselves. The exact algorithm of how an imp selected a victim was a mystery to me. I might ask Valentine about it later. Right now, it didn't matter. Without the imps, Sam should have less desire to steal.

Of course, removing them last time hadn't changed his habits. Maybe two times was the charm. The teen years were formative for souls. If I convinced Sam to make better choices and started him off with a cleaner soul, I might be able to change the entire trajectory of his life.

Or I was deluding myself.

I took my hand from his throat and leaned back, lifting my other hand from his chest. He straightened with a cocky swagger. I shoved him back against my car. He grinned and held up his hands. I slapped his left wrist first, then his right, pumping *lux lucis* into him until the imps there exploded and the dark gray bands around his wrists and fingers disappeared. Then I took a step back, crossed my arms, and blinked to normal sight.

"I think you're scary and hot, even without the big tits," Sam said.

"Gee, thanks. That means a lot to me." I reached into my purse for Medusa. "I seem to have left my gun at home, so we'll have to settle for calling the police."

"No! You can't." Sam stepped toward me, hands pleading. "My dad will kill me. I won't do it again. I swear!"

"That's what you said last time. So how do you explain this?" I reached for the wire hanger protruding from the gap between the Civic's window and door and yanked it free. My lock clicked open.

"See, Civics are easy."

"You're not helping yourself. What were you planning on stealing?" If he said my stereo, I'd hit 911. I'd just replaced the last one he'd stolen.

Sam shrugged. "Nothing, really. Just practicing."

"Practicing?"

"You know, so I can be quicker when there . . . ah . . . Well, I don't know."

"So mine was a trial car?" Was I offended? Yeah, a little.

"You *did* park it way out here where it's all private-like, and you didn't even park under a light." He sidled toward the bumper.

"Are you saying I deserved to have my car broken into?"

"You really should be more careful."

"You really should be in juvie."

"No need. You've made me see the error of my ways."

Medusa rang, the sounds of "Sweet Home Alabama" completely out of place in my rain-soaked showdown with the teenage thief. Sam used the distraction to back up several steps. He was going to escape, scot-free, and my only option was to pretend it was my idea.

"I'm giving you one more chance, Sam," I shouted over the upbeat song. "Think of your fondest body part. Got it? The next time I see you, that'll be the first place I shoot."

He gave me a cheeky smile. "You want to see me again?"

"Hang on. I think I left my gun in my glove box." I opened my car door and leaned across the driver's seat. Through the back window, I watched Sam sprint into the darkness.

I was chuckling when I answered the phone.

"Hello, Madison," Mom said. "Am I interrupting?"

"Nope. I just saw something funny." I swiveled into the seat and closed my car door. The knife hilt bit into my back, and I wriggled to a more comfortable position. Switching Medusa to speaker phone, I placed the cell phone on the center console and tossed the wire hanger to the passenger floorboard. If I was honest, I doubted my chat had done anything but cement my weirdness in Sam's mind.

"It's not Friday anymore," Mom said.

I groaned. The truce had ended. For the next ten minutes of my drive home, I fielded and dodged questions about Alex. Dad joined the conversation on the other line, which made my evasions easier. Dad didn't want to hear the details Mom did and was more easily distracted.

"Any more fires near you?" I asked in a lull in the interrogation.

"Two today, even with the rain. Isn't it terrible?" Mom asked.

My lungs constricted. "How close?"

"Other side of town," Dad said. "They were put out almost before they started. It's the damn dogs that need more press. A pack swarmed the grocery store lot today. One of them bit a man. He was carted away in an ambulance, and the rest of us had to wait inside Raley's until the catchers could nab all the beasts."

"You didn't get bitten, did you?" My heart pattered in my throat. That didn't sound like the behavior of normal dogs; that sounded like hounds.

"Of course not. I see a dog snarling and drooling and I know to go the other way."

I relaxed my stranglehold on the steering wheel and turned into my apartment complex. I should have gone to the office to pick up tomorrow's cito spray, but I couldn't face getting out of my car anywhere but at home.

"Stop scaring her, Oscar."

"You guys should consider a vacation." I'd be a lot happier if they were out of town until the evil died down.

"If this storm dumps snow, we'll be riding the rails next week," Dad said.

"I'm sure she doesn't want to hear about trains right now, dear. Oh, is that Earl and Margaret in the walkway?"

"Shoot. I've got to get Earl that motor," Dad said. "Bye, Son." He hung up his line before I could respond.

"Uh, bye."

"Gotta go. It's screwball night. Bye!" Mom said.

"I don't want to know what that means," I told my dead phone.

Anxiety about my parents' safety made for restless sleep, and I woke with a gloomy outlook despite it finally being date day. Again. Mr. Pitt refused to discuss the garage, and his gruff "Good job staying focused yesterday" grated despite the words being the most glowing praise I'd received from him in days. My region and my parents' region were under attack while I twiddled my thumbs at the mall, I wasn't allowed near the most interesting bit of Primordium I'd ever seen, and how it related to the uptick in evil or how to counter it were the best-kept secrets in the CIA community. Even thoughts of Alex and our date couldn't cut through my pessimism.

Showing up at the mall to find the parking lot scattered with more vervet than seagulls at a dump was the best thing to happen to me in days.

10

LAUGH, AND THE WORLD LAUGHS WITH YOU; PLAN, AND THE WORLD LAUGHS AT YOU

I SLID OUT OF MY CAR, Valentine at my hip, purse stuffed with bottles, and a smile on my face. A pair of mothers pushing strollers took one look at my expression and crossed to the other side of the aisle. I quashed the desire to tip my head back and laugh maniacally. It was perverse; the sight of all those evil creatures should have upset me. Instead, they provided a much-needed sense of purpose.

I flexed my hands and checked my soul: With my stomach full of *lux lucis*–filled yogurt and the few connected hours of sleep I'd managed, I looked bright and strong.

The vervet nearest shuffled closer, attracted by my shiny soul, but those farther away scuttled across acres of parked cars, sampling from the people unloading and heading for the mall. Oddly, there were no imps to be seen. One usually meant the other. Maybe they were inside.

Humming, I locked the Civic and mentally marked my location: four spots from a light in the most patrolled section of the mall. *Take that, Sam.*

I didn't have to hunt down any vervet; they came to me.

Three jumped me from the back of a Jaguar. Two clung to my legs. The third buried its face in my bosom. I burst them all to sparkles of *atrum* dust without slowing. I was a total badass.

I swung into the mall through JCPenney's home section. A half hour after opening, and already mounds of terrycloth cascaded down display tables, pillows littered the aisles, and someone had stuck a mannequin headfirst down a display bed's duvet.

The mess I'd expected. The imps, too. Contemplating wiping out a herd or two, with frequent trips back out for the vervet, added a spring to my steps. Destroying *atrum* was a productive and welcome relief from the monotony.

It was the citos that stopped me in my tracks.

Everyone had a cito on them. Not wee little garden-size spiders or even creepy tarantula citos. Football-size citos.

I rubbed a palm against my stomach, dread curdling my breakfast yogurt.

A group of teens jostled me on their way into the store. I stumbled forward on flat feet, cringing away from the shortest girl and the bulbous fuzzy red cito wriggling finger-length legs at me. Ducking behind a plastic display tower filled with teapots, I scanned the store.

Two women across the aisle pawed through a bin of shower curtains, shoving and pushing each other out of the way. On top of each of their heads were saucer-size green citos. As they struggled, the citos doubled in size. From their flailing hairy pedipalps to their shiny eyes—four apiece and as large as cat eyes—every detail of the grotesque Primordium arachnids made my skin crawl.

Something soft brushed my neck. I slapped my skin, spinning in an uncontrolled heebie-jeebies dance before realizing the culprit was my own hair, not a spider. Just in case, I spritzed my head and upper body.

Reminding myself I'd yet to have a cito jump me, I palmed a spray bottle and darted past the women. Dousing them without detection proved easy; they wouldn't have noticed if I'd taken their purses at the same time. The citos shrank ever so slowly, like air mattresses deflating. Even when the citos disappeared, the women's actions remained frantic.

"I demand a refund right now!" a male voice boomed.

I turned to see a giant man towering over a rotund salesclerk. He had a garnet ostrich-egg-size cito bulging from his neck like an obscene Adam's apple; she had a tall and skinny splotchy red cito perched on her forehead, braced forward on all eight legs to stare the man's cito straight in its many eyes.

The man pounded the counter. The woman yelled back at him. I pushed to the front of the line and spritzed the pair, dousing the people in line as I went by, killing a cito per person. I didn't even have to be discreet about it—no one paid me the least bit of attention.

A stroller bounced off my shins.

"Hey, watch where you're going!" the mom yelled. "My kid's in there."

Yikes! A maroon cito the size of her child's head bounced around her shoulder, agitated.

I ducked around her and gave her shoulder a quick spray when she stalked by. A few minutes later, I abandoned JCPenney and escaped to the mall, praying only the one store was affected.

My prayers went unanswered. Everywhere I looked, the citos were out of proportion and the people out of control. Crap. Crap, crap, *crap. Please don't let this be my fault.*

I hid in a shadowy nook on the mall side of the store and opened Valentine with shaky fingers, refusing to let go of the spray bottle to pull out Medusa. People whisked by me, citos of all sizes urging them in frenzied haste. No one glanced at me, and if they did and they thought I was talking to myself—or worse, talking to a book—I was still the sanest person at the mall today.

"Hi, Valentine." Nothing. Just a blank page. I clutched him in a white-knuckled grip. "I know I was mean to you, but I could really use some company right now."

You called me stupid.

"I know. I'm sorry. The thing in the garage scared me." I was scared now, too. I imagined rioting mobs had citos smaller than those scuttling around most people's heads.

It wasn't much fun for me either.

"Sorry, partner." I struggled to not push Valentine. I needed his help, and yelling got me nowhere. Maybe I should give him to Mr. Pitt so my boss could learn that lesson, too.

You think of me as a partner?

It sounded better than *fella* or *book buddy.* "Yeah. Sure."

Technically, my experience far outstrips yours. I should be senior partner. Or chief.

"Let's start with coworker," I said through gritted teeth. "Just two, ah, individuals who share an *equal* status and respect each other."

It's an interesting concept.

"Darn near revolutionary."

I've never had a partner before.

I opened my mouth to ask how it usually worked between him and enforcers, then decided I had more pressing concerns. "Have you seen the citos today? You said they couldn't get much larger than, what, a baseball."

They can't. This is most abnormal.

"Is it my fault?"

I don't see how.

I sagged against the wall and let my crossed fingers relax. "What about that crazy thing in the garage? Are the citos reacting to it?"

Maybe.

"It's the cause of all the evil in our region, isn't it?"

Our region? The text swirled across the page in whimsical cursive, then disappeared. His next words were in his normal font. *No. Maybe. I don't know.*

"Are you going to tell me what it is?" If the out-of-control citos were related to the thing in the garage, it was imperative for me to get my hands on more information, no matter what Mr. Pitt said.

No.

"You're not going to tell me? Why not?"

If you insist on knowing, I didn't get a good look before I passed out.

I reread the line. I had a fainting handbook? Familiar with the fragility of Valentine's ego, I opted to tactfully change the subject.

"What's your advice?"

For the citos? Take them out quickly, before they can grow bigger.

"Why didn't I think of that?"

Maybe you should give your shoulders a quick spray, Ms. Snippy.

There was nothing on my shoulders, but I gave myself a full-body spray anyway, just to be sure. I thumbed through Valentine until I came to the entry on citos. Nothing had changed.

I turned back to the first page. "Got anything else for me?"

Proceed with caution.

"No kidding." I shut Valentine and restrung him from the strap. After dousing a glowering cross-armed couple, I pulled out Medusa and dialed Mr. Pitt.

"It's a madhouse down here," I told him when he answered. I sent him pictures and explained the mood of the crowd. The decorations might have been the same as yesterday, and the Christmas music might have been as cheerful, but the atmosphere of the mall had turned hostile.

"There were vervet all over the parking lot. I can see two nests of imps from where I'm standing. I think it all has to do with that pit."

"Which you've kept your distance from, right?"

"Yes, but—"

"I'll look into what's happening with the citos. Keep up your work, and whatever you do, don't go near the garage."

He hung up with his usual lack of a farewell.

I tipped my head back and swallowed a scream of frustration. I wanted to believe Mr. Pitt was a good, competent warden, but he was making it incredibly difficult—and possibly making my job more dangerous than it needed to be.

I should call Isabel. I should check in with Jacob. Maybe one of them knew what was happening at the mall. For sure they knew what lurked in the unfinished parking garage.

My phone didn't have a long list of contacts. A few friends, a few relatives, a few enforcers, a few wardens. Niko.

My finger paused above his number.

Yesterday, I'd convinced myself Niko's actions and words had indicated he supported Mr. Pitt, despite trying to appear neutral for my benefit. Now I wondered if his goal had been to plant the idea that Mr. Pitt was a bad warden in my head. If I revolted against Mr. Pitt while Liam held all my boss's power, it would be a complete coup. Essentially I'd be working directly for Liam, and it was a short step from there to Liam becoming my boss and Mr. Pitt's region being transferred to Liam, enforcer already in place. In that scenario, there was a strong likelihood I'd keep my job, location and all.

I liked the sound of that far more than Niko's worst-case scenario in which I'd be looking for a job four hundred to three thousand miles away. It all hinged on who I believed—or what I thought was at the heart of Niko's message.

Holding on to my faith in Mr. Pitt by willpower alone, I stepped out into mall traffic.

In an hour, I didn't make it more than fifty feet beyond JCPenney.

There, at the center of the mall, Santa had set up shop, ringed by a maze of frazzled parents and screaming, crying children waiting to commemorate the holiday with an overpriced photo with a fat man in a red suit. Invisible in the digital records would be a montage of green and red spiders worn like grotesque Christmas accessories by toddlers and children alike. It was almost unfortunate they wouldn't show up in photos; the only thing the citos had going for them was their festive colors.

I circled the lines, burning through two spray bottles dousing just the people in reach. The photographer got two passes. If only I could get up to Santa and the ruby cito pulsing like a thundercloud atop his wig— when that man finally lost his patience, it wasn't going to be pretty.

Eventually, I abandoned Santa's fans. I could spend the whole day in the same location and never cleanse the area of the overgrown citos. Meanwhile, the rest of the mall had become a playground of emotional extremes. Vervet swung from sign to sign, trotted along the second-floor railing, and bounced from human to human, taking bites of souls along the way. Given the size of the mall and my past experience with vervet, their meager numbers didn't alarm me. With this amount of people all succumbing to their baser emotions, it was no less than I expected. The problem was accessing the vervet. The crush of people disguised my bright white enforcer soul, or maybe with the buffet before them, the vervet didn't need the thrill of taunting me. Either way, they ignored me, slipping through the crowds with a dexterity denied to those of us with solid mass.

Three times I pulled Medusa from my back pocket, scrolled through my contacts, and selected Isabel's number. Every time, I justified the call. This was her territory. She'd want to know about the evil creatures. If I happened to bring up the mass of good and evil energy in the garage and she happened to tell me what it was, that wouldn't be backstabbing Mr. Pitt, would it?

Three times I put Medusa back in my pocket. Every time, my reasoning was the same. Isabel was a warden; this was her region. She already knew about the evil here. My call would be nothing more than a betrayal.

Or the smartest move I could make.

I did my best to ignore that little doubting voice.

From my vantage at the middle of the mall, everything blurred into rivers of citos. I wasn't surprised to see a smattering of street cops in uniform mixed in with the crowds. In the small area I'd patrolled, I'd witnessed three arrests for shoplifting and one for assault. I kept my distance during those tussles. I could have helped by removing citos and vervet clinging to the culprits, but I didn't want to chance getting arrested in the process.

I slumped against a pillar. For all the impact I was having, I might as well go home early and get ready for my date. There was no way I was cleaning this up in time. My knees weakened and my back slid down the pillar until I drooped against it. I wanted to be a good enforcer. I wanted to impress Mr. Pitt and Niko. I wanted to keep my region—and maybe my boss. I wanted to prove to myself I could be good at this one thing—that this special career I'd practically been born to do wasn't just another in a long line of failed jobs.

But most of all, right now I wanted to be a normal woman getting ready for a date with a man she'd lusted after for years.

My knees quivered, telling me I either needed to finish my collapse or stand up straight. I rolled my shoulders and took a steadying breath. Spritzing my head and shoulders, I dug past my longing to find the nearest exit. I wasn't going to impress anyone by giving up.

I imagined a ticker on Mr. Pitt's computer registering each cito I wiped out. The numbers flickered so fast they jumped by double digits as I swept past a cluster of shoppers around a cell phone kiosk. Mr. Pitt couldn't help but be impressed—and see the cito population was out of control.

If only it were that easy.

I pulled out a fresh bottle of cito spray, then ducked into the long hallway to the public restrooms. Clusters of moms with strollers and dads with children clinging to their legs clogged the stretch to the restrooms. I gave the group a pass, breathing easy when I'd finally created the first cito-free zone in the mall. Planting myself near the hallway opening, I reached for Medusa and called Rose.

"This better be good news," Rose said.

"I'm alive." It was the best I could come up with.

"For now."

"Is Mr. Pitt pissed at me?" Hearing my words, my frustration snapped. If anyone should be pissed, it was me. I was calling Isabel as soon as I hung up. This was her region; she should be updated.

"Not at you, girl. He's positively chipper about you."

"What?" I pulled the phone away from my ear and stared at it. "Are we talking about the same warden?"

"Short, balding, looks like he's going to have a heart attack every time you walk in his office?"

"That's the one." Mr. Pitt was *happy* with me? Had that ever happened before? "Does he look less heart attacky when he's happy?" Maybe I'd been missing the signs.

"You should hear him yelling at Isabel and Liam. Here. Listen."

Muffled, I heard, "Lemon balls and sour grapes! Now is not—"

"See?" Rose asked. "If anyone else in the building was here on a Sunday, I'm sure they would have called the cops on us. Now I need deets. What did you find on Friday?"

"I honestly have no idea, and Mr. Pitt won't tell me." I shelved my astonishment to describe the crater and its seething *lux lucis* and *atrum*. Rose had never heard of anything like it. I forwarded her my picture.

"Does it look like he's sending me to do something about it?" I asked.

"Girl, you've got a death wish."

"Actually, I'm desperate. If the garage thing is responsible for today's madness and I could neutralize it, maybe the citos would go back to normal, because right now, they're out of control."

Rose groaned. "That's what Brad said. I'm making more spray as fast as possible, but I'm pretty tapped out."

"Oh."

"Oh, what?"

"I was calling to tell you I need more soon."

"Soon! You just got there."

"I swear, I'm being as conservative as I can. I—"

"I know, I know. I saw the pictures you sent. Hopefully what Jacob has will be enough to tide you over until I make more."

"Jacob?"

"Damn it. I told Brad to call you before he called Liam, but he must have been too worked up after how long it took to convince Isabel to send Jacob as your backup."

"I'm getting help?"

"Hang in there."

Discombobulated, I slid Medusa into my back pocket. Mr. Pitt was happy with me. Because I'd avoided the garage and followed his orders? Because I wasn't mucking up our region? The former made the most sense but hardly seemed worthy of making Mr. Pitt cheery.

More important, I wouldn't have to tackle the whole mall on my own. With two people, the odds of making my date tonight doubled. Pulling my hair into a ponytail, I waded into the fray, following a bouncing pack of imps.

By the time I received Jacob's text to meet him by the ice rink, my usually buttery soul looked closer to pale parchment and could use a recharge in the tree-filled courtyard. Perfect timing. Avoiding the madness of the food court, I ducked out a side door and into the bracing November air.

Though bursting with people and children, the plant-filled courtyard appeared only marginally affected by the madness inside the mall. Thanking the *lux lucis* gods for a reprieve, I trailed from one tree to the next, careful to stay on the far side of the courtyard, away from the alley to the garage. No compulsion other than normal curiosity pulled me toward the construction site, but I wasn't taking a chance.

I spotted Jacob when he was still far across the parking lot. Our gleaming white enforcer souls really did stand out like targets in a world full of sullied norms. No wonder evil creatures found it hard to avoid us, even when they knew the danger we presented to them.

I waited at the edge of the courtyard, my bare hand resting on a tree's soothing bark. Thin enough to wrap my hand around, the sapling held the same quiet, peaceful energy of a tree three times its age. Timeless serenity was part of every tree's makeup.

Jacob stalked through a fresh wave of shoppers. Judging by his scowl, he wasn't pleased to be taken away from his region. That made two of us.

"Hi, Madison." He greeted me with a handshake, but his polite smile didn't hide the irritation tightening the corners of his eyes. "I got a call from Isabel. Brad doesn't believe you can handle a few citos. I have time for a quick sweep; then I've got a half dozen more pressing problems to get back to."

"Did you see my pictures from this morning?" I fell into step beside Jacob, biting the inside of my cheek to avoid telling him to stuff his self-important attitude. I needed his help.

"No need."

"The citos have gotten large."

"The citos get large every year."

"Not like this. I think it might have something to do with the energy in the garage."

Jacob stopped. People grumbled and veered around us. "What do you know about that?"

"Nothing. What—"

"When did you see it?"

"A few days ago. It's kind of hard to miss. What is it?"

"Nothing."

"It's not *nothing*."

"It's under control, and it has nothing to do with citos."

"Seriously? That's all you're going to tell me? Maybe we should go check, in case you're wrong."

His smile dripped condescension. "I know you think you're a hotshot for taking out a demon in your first week, but trust me, I know what I'm doing. Leave the garage alone. It's got nothing to do with citos, and it's got nothing to do with you. Let's get this over with so I can get back to important problems."

He knew about the bizarre, impossible cluster of energy in the garage. That must have been the problem he'd been investigating on Friday. It had looked far from under control when I'd seen it. It had looked dangerous, like the kind of mystery anomaly a fellow enforcer should be informed of, since we were all supposed to be on the same team.

I contemplated the parking lot, weighing the satisfaction of leaving this self-important prick to handle the massive citos by himself against the karma of not assisting all the helpless people hosting those citos. The innocent citizens of Roseville won by a slim margin. Glaring at Jacob's back, I marched after him toward the mall.

"I don't see why you got Brad all worked up over this," Jacob said. He'd stopped to survey the parents cluttered around the ice rink and the normal-size citos crawling on their heads. I stepped to the side to let people behind me pass, swiping a wayward imp with my foot. It puffed into a cloud of *atrum*.

"Come on. I can help you catch up, but then I've got to go." Jacob headed for a woman with an apple-size cito on her shoulder, pulling a spray bottle from his jacket pocket.

"She's not worth it."

Jacob spun and stalked back to me, pointedly spritzing a couple with a golf-ball-size cito apiece. "I think we've found the problem. If you don't take out *every* cito you encounter, they will grow. No wonder this is out of hand."

I glanced around the calm courtyard and laughed. Jacob crossed his arms.

"Follow me."

With a huff, Jacob trailed after me, lagging to take out a handful of baby citos. I conserved my spray, not letting my backup see me roll my eyes at his blatant attempt to school me. I held the door to the mall open for him, and when we stepped across the threshold, oppressive malice settled around us. Jacob slowed, his hand holding the spray bottle suspended before him, forgotten. Parents yelled at children, customers berated the hallway retail kiosk staff, and teenagers and elderly alike shoved their way through the crowd—and atop every person's head crawled sewer-rat-size citos. In the distance, the line of children and parents around Santa's chair looked as if I'd never sprayed them.

I pulled Jacob to the side of the doorway so we wouldn't be trampled and drew his attention to the far wing of the mall. Two stores away, officers led a mother and daughter out of GameStop in cuffs. All four people hosted hen-size citos in shades of pink, green, and red. The crowds swallowed them, and their four citos were obscured by a dozen others sprawled atop people's heads like brain-sucking parasitic props from a bad science-fiction movie. The citos nearest us turned upon their hosts' heads, tracking us with beady eyes.

I swung Jacob around by his shoulders to face the other direction. As far as I could see, people carried ever-larger citos.

"Impossible."

"Where does this rank in your priorities?" I asked with false sweetness. It was almost worth the cito insanity to savor the expression on Jacob's face.

"I've never seen citos this large. They're everywhere!"

"Now do you believe I'm not the new girl crying wolf?"

Jacob's mouth snapped closed. "Yeah. I thought you were being lazy."

That didn't fall anywhere on the apology spectrum, but I let it go. "Still say it's not the garage thing?"

"Apples and oranges."

I clasped my hands together so I wouldn't shake him for more information. Was it possible the wunderkind's reticence stemmed from ignorance? Or was it more likely he was a self-inflated jerk? "So what's the plan? Do we split up or stay together?"

"Together. You take one side of the walkway; I'll take the other. Let's see what we can accomplish."

A fresh surge of hope spurred me through the rest of my spray bottle. With two of us working, I could actually see a moderate decrease in citos in our wake. Imps fell between us, having no escape except by latching onto a host. I had to let a fair share get away, attached to knees and ankles of shoppers, but I consoled myself with the dozens I exterminated.

When I got the chance, I watched Jacob to see if I could learn any special tricks, but he was no better at spraying and slaying than I was. Score one for the newbie. Even if we were only performing menial tasks at an overwhelming rate, the only thing the wunderkind had that I lacked was a fierce scowl, as if he were personally affronted by the size of the citos. I didn't have the energy for that.

Forty-five minutes later, I slid another empty bottle into my purse and gestured Jacob close to a fake potted plant so we could talk.

"I've only got two bottles of spray left. What about you?"

"I only brought one." He had the grace to look embarrassed. Mr. Big Shot hadn't planned on being much help at all.

"Why don't I give you what I have left and go pick up more from Rose?" I could have let Jacob go, but I wanted a break from the mall, and I wasn't above using his guilt against him.

"Okay. But don't take long. I can hold the numbers down for a while by myself, but not forever."

I bit my lip to keep from smiling. Jacob sounded like he pictured himself as the final guard of a castle, braced to hold the gate barehanded against an army. He didn't stand a chance, but I wasn't going to burst his bubble.

"I'll be back as fast as possible." I handed over the last of my spray bottles. "Good luck."

I detoured to an eatery not connected to the food court for a to-go sandwich, wishing I'd kept a spray bottle. After three days of hunting citos, I'd never seen one jump from a host, but I didn't want to be caught helpless if they changed tactics.

With a turkey and vegetable sandwich in one hand and a soda and a bag of chips in the other, I exited the mall. I kept an eye out for evil creatures, but I didn't give chase to any vervet bounding between parked cars. In the grand scheme of things, racing around the parking lot to kill a few bits of evil fell far below the importance of getting more spray.

When I got into my car, I unwrapped my sandwich carefully so I could eat while I drove. Finally, I let myself think about the elephant in my head: I wasn't going to be done early tonight. I had to let Alex know I was going to be late for our date.

"This sucks!"

11

Powered by Delusion

I THOUGHT ABOUT CALLING ALEX, BUT having already done that once, a second call would look like a flaky pattern. Backing out of my spot, I headed for his office. Hopefully Jacob could handle the masses as well as he thought he could. Plus, leaving Jacob alone with oversize citos in his own region's mall, if only for an hour, tickled my vindictive funny bone.

I scarfed both halves of the sandwich during the drive and then parked where I couldn't be seen from the office windows so I could check my teeth in the rearview mirror before getting out of the car.

I fluttered my hands around my outfit, tugging at the V-neck sweater to settle it evenly across my breasts, wishing for more cleavage, running my hands down my jeans, wishing for clothing that looked more professional and less college student. I left my hair in a ponytail. If I took it down now, it'd be flat on top with a strange bump around my crown before frizzing into fluffy waves reminiscent of bad hippy hair. At least a ponytail tamed it. Mostly.

Patting flyaway strands around the crown of my head, I walked across the parking lot. I hadn't worn makeup today. I didn't, usually, but now I wished I'd at least dabbed on a little mascara. I caught my reflection in the door's window as I reached for the handle. I looked like I felt: tired and nervous.

I just want to move the date back an hour or so. If Alex didn't understand, then I didn't want to date him.

But I *so* wanted to date him.

"How can I help you?" the receptionist asked. She was an older, round woman with an easy smile. Like everyone who worked at Love and Caring Veterinary Clinic, she wore vet scrubs.

"I'm here to see, um, Dr. Love." After convincing myself to think of him as *Alex* and not *Dr. Love*, it sounded like I'd blundered. Surely that was the reason a blush heated my cheeks and not because I was nervous and embarrassed.

"Is he expecting you?"

"Not exactly. I'm Madison Fox. We've, ah, got a later appointment." I didn't want to tell this motherly woman we had a date; it seemed inappropriate in Alex's workplace.

She bustled off, stopping to pat the head of a German shepherd lying on a bed behind her desk, one of his feet bandaged. He thumped his tail on the floor and watched her walk away with sad eyes. I scooted around the counter and squatted next to him. When I held my hand out for the dog to sniff, he licked my fingers and his tail started thumping again.

"Did you hurt your paw, you poor thing?" I blinked to look at the German shepherd in Primordium. His soul shone a pristine, snowy white. I scratched behind his ears, and he tried to get his back foot up to join in. "None of that, cutie. I've got this."

The dog relaxed to his side, and I continued to scratch my hands through his fur. Despite Christmas Muzak piping softly through overhead speakers, the clinic's peaceful energy bled tension from my body. Weariness surged forward. The last three days had drained me in ways three days hunting imps and vervet wouldn't have. Being on my feet all day, dodging people, trying to blend in, hunting down creatures that were not necessarily more evil than their hosts took its toll. Even without citos, being crushed in the mall crowds for three days would have taken its toll on my spirit. Crowds were part of the reason I moved away from Berkeley; concentrations of people and pavement sucked away my will to live. I couldn't wait for this cito gig to be over.

The German shepherd sighed and closed his eyes when I massaged down his spine.

"I think you've made a friend."

I jumped and steadied myself against the wall. Dr. Love—Alex— leaned against the counter. I stared at him in Primordium a long, slow moment before I got my brain working. "Hi."

"Hi."

Alex's soul flowed in beautiful smooth lines of white hardly blemished with dabs of gray. For a normal human, he was utterly delicious. I wetted my lips and forced myself to blink to normal vision.

Not that he was any less beautiful in color. Tall, with broad-shoulders, a golden tan, and kind blue eyes, Alex was the whole package. He smiled at me, tiny crow's-feet forming at the corners of his eyes. I smiled back.

The receptionist bustled back to her seat with a discreet cough, walking between us and breaking our eye contact. Flustered, I jerked to my feet, realizing I must have looked like a lovesick fool kneeling on the floor, staring adoringly up at Alex. I pushed my hair back from my face, only to realize it was already in a ponytail, and turned the gesture into a quick tug on my hair.

"It's nice of you to drop by," Alex said. It must have occurred to him to wonder why I was there, because his expression turned guarded. "Is everything okay with Mr. Bond?"

"Mr. Bond? No, I mean, yes. Everything's fine with him. I just wanted to see—ah, talk to you."

"Oh. Okay. Come with me."

The receptionist's curiosity tickled my neck as I followed Alex to the back. He opened the door to a small exam room. I went through first, stepping a tad closer to him than necessary, breathing in as I did. Faint traces of cologne or aftershave bent my body toward him, but I forced myself to keep walking. Maybe later tonight I would get a chance for more than a sniff. The thought set off internal flutters.

Alex closed the door behind him. I tried to look casual and leaned against the exam table. He remained by the door.

"I'm sorry to drop in on you like this at your work," I said.

"I don't mind. Are you sure everything's okay? You look kind of tired." He presented the way out without expression. Déjà vu.

"Work's been crazy these last few days."

"You don't get the weekend off?"

"Not with the holidays." Alex thought I worked in sales at a bumper sticker company, so there was only so much I could say. But I didn't want to talk about my job. Alex looked more reserved by the second, and I wanted his smile back. "The only thing that's kept me going has been our date." Saying it out loud made me blush. Alex's arms dropped to his sides and he smiled a little, making my discomfort worth it.

"I've been looking forward to it, too."

My heart somersaulted. Maybe I could get off early somehow. Maybe I could race through the mall from end to end, a spray bottle in both hands, spraying everyone I saw. If I made ten passes, I might kill all the citos. If I could get more than two steps without running into someone. If I could convince Jacob to stay late on my behalf, or another enforcer could take my place—

There were too many ifs, all completely unrealistic.

"I really don't want to say this, but I think I need to move our date back a couple hours tonight," I blurted out. "Everything's so busy, and I know we're not going to be done by seven, but if I rush, I should be able to get out of there by eight, and then it won't take me long to get ready, so you could meet me at eight thirty. No. Eight forty-five. We would still have time for dinner before the restaurant closed, especially if we ate at the bar, which stays open a half hour later than the restaurant."

"Whoa, slow down." Alex stepped away from the door and captured my hands, which had mimed my plan. His long fingers wrapped around mine, and I froze, entranced by the heat of his touch. "That doesn't sound like much fun."

"Oh." My heart pounded hard against my chest. *It's okay. I can do this. Just walk out. I had my chance and I blew it.* But Alex's body language wasn't saying he was upset, so I clung to a shred of hope.

"I don't want a rushed date with you."

"Okay." Check: One shred of hope incinerated. I took a deep breath and waited for him to release my hands.

"I don't want to have to rush anything. You're clearly tired already. Are you here on your lunch break?" I nodded, my hope reborn like a phoenix. The corners of my mouth curved up tremulously. Alex rubbed his thumbs in slow circles on my palms. I was glad for the support of the table I leaned against. "Let's pick a different day."

"But—"

"It's okay. Really. I don't want you falling asleep in your meal. It'd do horrible things for my self-confidence."

I giggled—literally giggled—and he chuckled with me. "I wouldn't want to damage your ego," I said.

"Good. When works for you? Is tomorrow too soon?"

I grinned but shook my head.

"I know, I know. How about Friday?"

Something had to give between me and the strange surge of activity at the mall. If nothing else, Mr. Pitt would have to give me a day off.

"Friday should work." I would have crossed my fingers, but they were still delightfully wrapped up in his warm hands.

Alex winked at me. "Third time's the charm."

I think it surprised him to realize he still held my hands because he started and let them go, backing away a step. My smile grew wider.

"Oh, hey. Do you have a minute before you go?" he asked.

What a silly question. "Sure."

"Come with me."

Alex opened the door at the back of the room and gestured for me to follow him through the cluttered workstation running behind the exam rooms. Medical supplies, scales, monitors, paperwork, and animal toys lined the counters. We rounded a corner to a much larger, open room with operating tables and gadgetry I purposely didn't look at too closely. I'd nearly passed out when Mr. Bond had to get a shot—I didn't want to witness anything faint-inducing.

Two other people, a woman around my age and a man slightly older, stood at the opposite end of the room examining an X-ray. They glanced our way but didn't seem especially curious.

Alex walked to the far side of the room, where large cages lined the entire wall. Dogs and cats of all sizes and states of intoxication lay inside. Alex beelined for an empty top cage. He opened the large mesh door carefully and reached inside, coming out with a bundle of fluff; the kitten was so tiny I hadn't seen her amid the rumpled blankets. I recognized its tabby coat right away.

"This is one I found, right?" I asked, whispering since the kitten was asleep. One of the biggest highlights last week had been saving a trio of kittens, including this diminutive fluff ball.

"Yes. The healthier ones adopted out almost immediately, but she's still waiting." Cupped in his large hand, the tiny kitten looked hardly a few days old. Being both the runt of the litter and malnourished had stunted her growth. Watching the gentle way Alex held the kitten, any last driblet of emotional detachment for our date evaporated. I was a sucker for men who loved animals.

Alex handed me the kitten. I cradled her close to my body. She blinked sapphire eyes at me, and a deep, rumbling purr revved inside her, almost too large for her size. I scratched her chin, and she closed her eyes in contentment. Through her staticy downy fur, I could feel her slender ribs, and her tiny head was hard and heavy compared to her thin body.

I had rescued Mr. Bond from a Dumpster when he was barely larger than this kitten. It had been love at first sight—for both of us, I liked to think. A similar stirring swirled through my chest now. Maybe it was a trick of Alex's proximity, but I didn't think so.

What would Mr. Bond think if I brought home another cat? Would he hate her? Hate me?

"I wanted you to see she's doing well," Alex said. "You probably have to get back to work, though."

"Work. Right. I wish I could stay here all day." Cuddling kittens and staring at Alex's soul. Or his pecs, or his smile, or his butt.

"That'd be distracting."

I glanced up to find Alex watching me with open warmth. My body temperature spiked. I looked away, embarrassed but pleased. Reluctantly, I slid the kitten back onto her blanket and Alex shut the cage.

The man who'd been examining the X-ray walked across the room, stopping a few feet away, clearly waiting on Alex.

"I think I can find my way out from here," I said. "See you on Friday."

"I'm glad you stopped by, Madison. See you soon."

We shared a final smile that I knew would keep me energized for hours, and I walked out feeling as if a trampoline were beneath every footstep. Maybe Rose would hate me a little less if I brought this energy to her.

When I slid my key into my apartment door eight endless hours later, all traces of flirtation euphoria had leeched from me. Stepping inside, I tossed my keys into the blue bowl beside the door and bent to take off my shoes. Mr. Bond raced from the bedroom and threw himself against my legs. I ran my fingers through his silky coat, suffering through several head-butts. By the time I got my shoes off, he was happy to lead me to his empty food dish.

I warded the apartment, showered, and brushed my teeth, then fell into bed. On a normal night, I would have stayed up later, but extra sleep was the only thing that'd get me through tomorrow. Jacob and I had traveled the mall in a nonstop loop, and even then, we hadn't gained the upper hand. We'd gone through three days' supply of cito spray, and I'd come home only because the mall had closed.

Citos danced behind my eyelids, red and green, big and small, polka dotted, striped, and calico. I opened my eyes and stared at my ceiling.

Today had been a futile endeavor. Running around, spraying individual citos was akin to placing twigs in the gap of a splitting dam: It simply wasn't going to hold. Jacob and I could run around all day tomorrow, but if the citos were the same size and out in the same number, we wouldn't make a dent. Citos might not be evil, but loosing emotionally unstable hosts into our regions would be dangerous. People filled with that much anger, greed, and jealousy couldn't help but make idiotic, *atrum*-tainting decisions.

Jacob was wrong about the parking garage. I knew it in my bones. The wild bundle of *lux lucis* and *atrum* had to be linked to the out-of-control citos.

I swung my legs out of bed and stood. My body was tired, but my mind wasn't. I paced my small bedroom, then decided to get dressed rather than shiver.

The mall bordered on my region. The mystery pit could easily spill its wicked energy over to my territory, creating a mess worse than the demon. If everyone in the city became linked to a cito, their emotions amplified out of control, chaos would ensue.

I didn't want a mess. Mr. Pitt didn't want a mess.

I had my shoes on and jacket in hand when I realized what I was doing.

"No. I can't. Mr. Pitt would kill me." I tossed my jacket to the chair, but I couldn't quite bring myself to take off my shoes and clothes and go back to bed. I needed a better look at the crater. A *careful*, quiet reconnaissance. If I could prove the energetic crater was linked to the bloated citos, bringing Mr. Pitt the information might give him leverage against the other wardens. He might even thank me.

My argument was feeble, but two days without answers had worn down my good intention to do exactly as Mr. Pitt said. Besides, it wasn't a lone-wolf action if it was on my own time and all I did was observe.

Shrugging into my coat, I grabbed a black beanie, my purse, and my car keys and said good-bye to Mr. Bond. He flopped dejectedly on a book I'd left on the floor.

"I'll be back soon. I promise." I shut the door, trying to shut the guilt inside, too. My next day off, I'd spend the whole day playing with Mr. Bond to make up for giving him so little attention lately.

None of the scant Sunday-night traffic turned with me into the deserted mall parking lot, but I kept an eye out for mall security. Fortunately, the mall was vast, and I made it from the entrance to a parking spot in the shadows of the half-built parking garage without spotting a white Securitas truck.

The skeletal garage loomed in the shadows above the lamps, plastic rustling. The structure sounded restless, like a caged animal ready to break free or like a huge beast breathing erratically.

You're not helping yourself.

I almost climbed back into my car. Being brave had been a lot easier in the warmth of my apartment. I scanned for people or creatures in normal sight and Primordium. A cold gust blew my hair in my face, and a tapping behind me had me whirling and reaching for the Bowie knife on my belt. I let out a huge breath when I realized the sound had been nothing more than the skitter of dry leaves across the pavement. I was alone.

I slithered through the gap in the fence surrounding the construction site and hopped across the puddle-strewn mud, wincing at the echo of each squishing step. After one last glance at my car, I shoved through a slit in the plastic affixed to the towering frame of the garage.

The lights on the beams illuminated the dirt floor. I checked my shadows. None fell on the plastic to give away my position, and the grimy plastic was too thick to see through from the outside. I chaffed my hands together, and the dry rustle bounced around the interior like the soundtrack to a horror movie stalker scene. I stopped immediately. Wind moaned through the plastic, and I eased away from the agitated walls. Fumbling through my purse until my hand clamped down on the petrified wand, I yanked it free and extended it, then pushed *lux lucis* to its tip. I clumsily unsnapped the Bowie knife next. Weapon in each hand, I crept across the construction site.

Neon plastic ties hung from the rafters and fluttered in the ebb and flow of air, dancing at the corner of my vision and casting flickering shadows on the ground. I tried to keep everything in sight, jerking left and right as I walked across the floor like a spazzing FBI agent. I would have laughed at myself if my heart hadn't been clogging my throat.

I made myself look at the pit. It gaped like an open mouth, making me think of Venus flytraps and sea anemones that ate foolish enforcers. I blinked to Primordium and crept closer, standing well clear of the rim.

Lux lucis swelled from the center of the pit and burst, white particles falling back to the crater like water droplets. *Atrum* undulated around the rim of the pit, swirling faster and faster until the crest of the wave caught up with the tail of it, and it spiked to the sky, flattened, and oozed down toward the center of the hole. Arches of *lux lucis* spiraled in and out of the *atrum*, some twice as high as my head, some so small they didn't clear my knees. None of the *lux lucis* or *atrum* canceled each other out.

"This is *so* not normal." I looked for a connection to the mall, perhaps tendrils of *atrum* stretching toward the shops, but all the energy remained contained in the pit.

The pit started to boil. All the *lux lucis* and *atrum* combined and frothed along the edge, bursting in huge bubbles in the center, simmering denser and denser until I couldn't see the ground beneath it.

A long arm of candy cane–spiraled *lux lucis* and *atrum* surged from the center, pushing the bubbling pool over the edge of the pit and toward my toes. I backpedaled frantically. The energy receded, but the candy cane arm remained like a horn pointing from the center of the hole. Then it dropped. Soundlessly, weightlessly, absorbed into the boiling mass too quickly to follow.

I barely saw the cresting wave of *lux lucis* that arched out of the crater and swallowed me whole before the world went black.

12

NEVER DO A BAD JOB WELL

A COCOON OF COMFORT WRAPPED ME, warm and soft. I reached—not with my hand or any body part because my body wasn't responding, but somehow I petted something and sank into dense, soft fur. A fake bearskin rug? A real bearskin rug? *A real bear?*

Fear constricted my chest and stuck to the insides of my lungs, utterly foreign and overwhelming. I fought, punching and kicking with phantom limbs. I flailed until I couldn't remember what had frightened me. Relaxing again, I rolled in the warmth. Soft fur caressed my face. Mr. Bond?

I remembered my cat, and with that memory came a rush of all the memories of Mr. Bond. Mr. Bond as a kitten pouncing on my toes; Mr. Bond batting a plastic bottle cap around the kitchen; Mr. Bond curled up on my lap, asleep and uncaring that I had to pee.

But this thing was too big. Mr. Bond fit in my lap. If anything, I fit in this thing's lap.

I trembled. Big things with fur were usually scary. I couldn't see what this was. I couldn't see anything. My heart pounded. I strained my hearing. A whip cracked; a car's engine revved.

I remembered the pit. I remembered the surge of energy cresting over me. I remembered the hard, cold ground of the garage as my limp body slammed into it.

I found my hands. I lost the warmth and fur.

Plastic snapped. Fluorescent light pierced my eyes, eliciting instant tears. Beams and wires crisscrossed above me.

I jackknifed up and spun on all fours to face the pit, blinking to Primordium. The crater frothed, but softly now. *Atrum* undulated like a placid lake, not like water in a centrifuge. *Lux lucis* floated across it, expanding and shrinking like an ever-changing Rorschach test. I scrambled to my feet. My head thumped in pain. My vision tunneled and I crouched while blood rushed back to my brain.

Mud coated my pants. I brushed at my jeans, stopping when I noticed my palms. They must have taken the brunt of my fall. Pebbles pressed into the skin, held in place by dry mud. I picked the rocks off, thankful to find no abrasions underneath. I didn't relish the pain in my future when my numb hands thawed.

Gingerly, I probed my head. My ear hurt, as did a spot behind my temple, where more dirt and gravel caught in my hair and beanie, but overall my head seemed okay. Even my soul looked good. In fact, it looked better than good; I looked like I'd slept pressed against a four-hundred-year-old oak tree and had absorbed the entire thing. If there were such an event as an enforcer pageant, my soul would have given Niko's a run for its money. I glistened.

The whip crack of plastic snapped me out of my soul-gazing trance. I checked the crater. Still calm.

Much more carefully this time, I straightened and assessed my limbs. They creaked and popped and shivered, but they worked.

How long have I been out? Given my bone-cold body, at least an hour. The better question was, how much trouble was I in?

I stumbled a few steps, arms outstretched for balance, to collect my wand and knife from where they'd fallen. I'd been lucky to not skewer myself on either. With stiff fingers, I sheathed the knife, then collapsed the wand and slid it back into my purse; both weapons had proved useless against the pit. I kept an eye on the tranquil energy the entire time, and I didn't turn my back on it until I'd backed halfway across the garage. By then, my legs had recovered enough not to wobble with each step, and I chanced a jog.

If everything worked in my favor, I wouldn't be in any trouble because no one would know about this foolhardy venture.

With my fingers crossed, I peeked through the plastic. Seeing all was clear, I trotted to the fence and slipped through to the other side.

Only then did I slow and look at the sky. Blackness stretched above the light poles.

"Thank you, thank you, thank you," I chanted softly as I hobbled toward my Civic. I grabbed the blanket from my trunk and tugged it over my driver's seat before I crawled behind the wheel. The ignition turned over, and warm air blasted from the vents. I had a feeling the air wasn't really warm; I was too cold to know better.

The dash clock lit up.

"Seven thirty? You've got to be kidding me!" I checked the sky and my clock again. "There's no way it's already morning."

I gunned it for the main road. As I drew clear of the confines of the mall, I spotted the eastern horizon. Clouds had fooled me. It was morning.

I drove home like a madwoman with the heater on full blast. My hands stung on the steering wheel, the warmth waking bruises. The heat burned my cheeks, but by the time I got home, the blocks of ice that were my toes had thawed enough for me to run up the stairs two at a time. For once, I didn't even pause to say hi to Mr. Bond when I burst through the doors. I raced for the shower, shedding clothes as I went. Twenty minutes later, I was dressed again and headed back out the door for work, detouring long enough to fill Mr. Bond's empty food bowl and grab a banana.

I paused on the threshold and opened Valentine.

"What happened to me?"

I wouldn't know. Then, scrawled in what I could only call a sarcastic font: *Partner.*

"I went back to the pit last night."

Good for you. If you'd taken me, we could have skipped this whole conversation.

And wouldn't that have been nice. I took a deep breath and let it out softly. "I'm sorry I forgot to take you with me. I was in a rush. But the last time I took you near the pit, you accused me of trying to kill you. You remember telling me you passed out?"

I'm a book. I don't have a memory. I have archives, and they are infinite.

"Good. Because last night the *lux lucis* was wild and swallowed me and *I* passed out. What do you make of that?"

Are you attempting to elicit empathy by having a shared experience?

"What? No. I want to know what happened."

I can't tell you anything from your recollection. Viewing an event through your perspective skews the original reality. If I had been there . . .

"Is that a long-winded way of saying you still don't have a clue?" He didn't respond. I ground my teeth. "Check out my soul. I'm like a super-enforcer. Any thoughts on that?"

Must be nice for you.

"Why don't I give you some time to access your 'archives.' I'm sure you'll come up with something." I shut Valentine and slid him gently into his strap, then stomped my feet to vent my frustration. If I put extra bounce in my hips down the stairs, jarring the book more than normal, I would never admit to it.

I found another good reason for a hissy fit when I reached my car: Sam crouched in the open driver's door of the Impala parked beside my Civic. Seeing me, he emptied his hands in the pockets of his zip-up sweatshirt and shut the car door.

"Hi!" He smiled at me like we were reunited high school friends.

"What were you doing?" I demanded, even though I knew.

"I got bored waiting for you, so I did a little sightseeing."

"Sightseeing?" No, wait. There was a larger issue. "You were *waiting* for me? Are you stalking me?" I eyed him up and down. He didn't look threatening, not even in his wannabe gangster apparel of baggy dark jeans, gray sweatshirt, and black beanie pulled down so low it partially covered his eyes. Nothing short of a full head wrap would disguise his neon-orange hair, though, and curly tufts poked out over his ears.

He held up dirty palms as if to pacify me, his fingers bright pink from the cold. "I'm not *stalking* you. Geez. That's creepy. I just wanted to see you again."

"So you figured out where I live and followed me? That's the definition of stalking!"

"When you put it like that, it sounds bad. But it's not like I followed you up to your apartment. I don't even know which one is yours. I saw your car and was, like, 'I'll wait for her here.'"

"I drive a Civic, the most popular car in America. You happened to miraculously know this one was mine?" I crossed my arms over my chest and glared at him.

"It has your license plate on it."

He'd memorized my plate. I didn't know what to say.

"I want to join your group."

"What?"

"Your superhero group. I want to become a member."

I glanced around reflexively. We were the only two people in the parking lot. I stepped up to the bumper of the Impala, stopping within arm's reach of Sam.

"I have no clue what you're talking about."

"The costume. The guns. You admitted that you've got a region and you fight crime. You're a superhero! I know it."

I opened my mouth but nothing came out. I flashed back to finding Sam breaking into my car—the *first* time. I'd been working the convention dressed as a video game character, yes, with guns. Flush in the first week of my job, I'd said things I shouldn't have, hoping to straighten Sam out. Clearly it had backfired.

"I'm not a superhero," I hissed, denying the one thing I could. It did have a good ring to it, though. Madison Fox, Illuminant Enforcer, Superhero Extraordinaire.

"I'm not delusional," Sam said, his eyes huge and earnest. "I don't think I've got powers. But I could help you out. You know, like a sidekick. Or an errand boy. Or your whipping boy. Whatever. And maybe you could teach me things. I won't tell anyone. Your secret's safe with me."

Whipping boy? "Sam! There is no secret! I'm an office worker. I make bumper stickers." I stopped short of telling him where the headquarters were or the fake name of my company. The last thing I needed was for Sam to show up at work.

"Right." He winked with enough exaggeration to move his whole body.

I rolled my eyes. "Shouldn't you be in school?"

He rolled his eyes right back at me. "I'm in independent study. I work on my own time. Don't you see how perfect this is? I could be your lackey."

It would be nice to hand over the cito spray and devote my day to something more exciting. Of course, if Sam had the enforcer gene, he wouldn't be burgling cars. I'd been silent too long, though, and Sam took it as encouragement.

"It could be like an internship." He swiped off his beanie and struck a pose fit for a puppy. Curls sprang around his head in a fiery halo.

I fought to contain a smile he'd see as more encouragement. "Unless you want to intern at juvie, you'd better put back what you took from that car."

"Aww, but they were practically begging to have this stuff taken."

"Leaving something in your locked car is not an open invitation to have it stolen. Just like not parking under a light is not an invitation to have your car broken into."

"Bet you haven't parked in a dark spot since."

"Put the stuff back."

Sam looked at the Impala. "But it's locked."

"You got into it the first time. Get into it again."

"The first time I had motivation. I can't do it without motivation. If you promise to teach me some superhero stuff, that'd do the trick."

"You should be motivated because it's the right thing to do."

"Nope. That's not working for me."

Enforcer material he was not. "That's it. I'm calling the cops." I fished in my purse for Medusa.

"Hang on. I'm feeling motivated." Sam pulled a piece of flat metal from his hip. It looked like a ruler but longer.

"You've upgraded."

"Yeah. I had to. You stole my hanger."

"I didn't steal anything!"

"If that makes you feel better." He pulled his beanie back on. "Keep a lookout for people, okay?"

"I'm not participating in this."

"If someone comes along now, you're an accessory to me breaking into this car."

"What!"

"I don't have to put the stuff back." Sam turned to me, his face the picture of innocence.

"Yes, you do. Now hurry." I glanced around for people, my heart racing. At any moment someone could walk by, see Sam jimmying the lock, and call the cops. No cop would believe I was making sure Sam returned stolen items.

Sam popped the lock and poured the loose change into the center console. He started to shut the door.

"All of it," I ordered, bouncing from foot to foot.

Sighing, he pulled an MP3 player, a parking pass, two lighters, and a pair of sunglasses out of his pockets. He dumped them all on the passenger seat.

"Is that where you found them?"

"Nope." He locked and shut the Impala's door.

"Get away from the car."

Grinning, Sam held up his hands in surrender. I moved so he could walk past me. He stopped just beyond the car's bumper and held out his hands.

"I know the drill," he said.

It took me a moment to realize what he was doing. With a sigh, I blinked. Gray spots speckled his soul, and as I expected, several chinchilla-like imps fed off his wrists. I circled his wrists with my fingers and fed the imps *lux lucis* until they exploded, then fed Sam a little more to cleanse his soul. I wasn't sure why I bothered. Clearly my attempts to wipe away his clepto tendencies by cleaning his soul were not working. But doing nothing felt like giving up on the kid.

I glanced around. A few imps sucked on my ankles. I clamped down on a yelp and let go of Sam's wrists so I could concentrate. The imps attached to me exploded in sparkles of *atrum*.

"See. You wouldn't do the handholding thing if you weren't a superhero," Sam said.

I had to admit, it was an odd ritual for a normal person. "I'm trying to send you good intentions and curb your evil ways."

"Uh-huh. I'd hold your hand anytime, superpowers or not."

"I'm not a superhero." I sounded like a recording.

"If you say so. I'll be around."

He jogged off through the apartment complex with a jaunty wave. I watched him go, wondering how things had gotten so far out of hand and how I was ever going to convince Sam I was an ordinary person, especially when I wasn't.

I glanced down at my soul. Cleansing Sam had done nothing to dim my unnatural glow.

"I don't need your help yet, Will," Rose said when I poked my head into the conference room. A familiar collection of spray bottles covered the table in front of her. I waited for Rose to end her call, then realized she wasn't on the phone. I glanced behind me. Will was across the office, walking out of the break room.

"Um," I said.

Rose spun and gaped. "That's *you*. Damn, did you have a date with Jesus?"

"What?"

"You feel like—" She held her hands out to me as if warming them against a fire. "You feel . . . amazing."

"Thank you."

"Don't give me 'thank you.' What the hell happened with your love doctor?"

"Nothing."

Rose propped her hands on her hips and tapped a tennis-shoe-clad toe.

"No date last night. Just a bit of foolishness. I'll tell you about it later." If Rose could feel the difference in my soul, I needed to be twice as fast as planned if I hoped to escape the office without Mr. Pitt noticing my soul's unnatural glow.

Rose arched her eyebrows at me. Squaring my shoulders, I marched to Mr. Pitt's office.

"I've resented your implication all along, Liam. My territory's experienced no more evil than— Sure, I've had two demons, but you can hardly count the one Summer encountered—"

I paused, then ducked into my cubicle before Mr. Pitt saw me. Rose leaned out of the conference doorway and mouthed, *"Wimp."* I made shooing motions at her. I wasn't afraid of Mr. Pitt; I wanted to eavesdrop.

"If my enforcer wasn't doing the work of—" Pause. "She may be untried, but she's not *untrained*. Niko—" Pause, then at full volume, "Says who! Let's look at the records, Liam. How was Summer or Rafi their *first* week on the job?"

Was he defending me? Two times in as many days? This had to be my Christmas miracle come early.

"Excuse me. I have real work to do." Either a sledgehammer broke through concrete in my warden's office, or Mr. Pitt had slammed the phone into the cradle. "Madison! Get your glowing Tootsie Pop in here and explain yourself."

Stomach plummeting, I straightened, patted Valentine for good luck, and presented myself for sacrifice.

"You're not hurt?" Mr. Pitt asked when I finished recounting my short tale.

I'd expected an explosion of candy-laden profanity. His quiet question caught me flat-footed. "Nope. Nothing a warm shower didn't fix."

Mr. Pitt watched me, head tilted. His complexion remained a pale pink. The vein at his temple didn't dilate. I wrung my hands. Yelling I was used to. This somber version of my boss was worrisome.

"Good. I'm glad you told me." He clapped his hands and I jumped. "You've got Jacob and Claire helping out today. Isabel ordered more spray from out of state, so we don't have to kill Rose over this." He raised his voice for the last sentence.

"Thanks, boss," Rose said from outside the doorway.

"But we'll need twice as much for Madison today."

"Gotcha. I'll get back to work."

"That's it?" I asked. I was pushing my luck, but as long as I was having an out-of-body experience, I might as well enjoy the euphoria.

"Are you asking if I'm mad?"

I nodded.

Again, Mr. Pitt favored me with a head-cocked stare. I couldn't read his expression, other than that he wasn't angry.

"Do me a favor and don't tell anyone else about your adventure last night. If you feel another compulsion to get close to the pit today, call me. And trust your instincts."

My eyebrows tried to merge with my hairline. "So what am I up against?" I asked.

"Your specialty."

"And that would be?"

"Trouble." Mr. Pitt's froggy smile offered no comfort.

"Anything specific?"

"Let me put it this way: If the energy in the garage isn't resolved by the end of today, I'm pulling you back to our region."

I almost hugged him. My return to normal work was all but guaranteed. Still, his lack of an answer kept my celebrations subdued as I walked to my car. Mr. Pitt knew more than he was telling me; that much was obvious from my escape without a single raised word. If I didn't know better, I'd say he was concerned for me. There was a scary thought.

I settled a flat of spray bottles on my passenger seat, then walked around to the driver's side. I also couldn't reconcile my lingering feelings of goodwill—and my visibly brighter soul—with the dangerous energy that had knocked me unconscious. A giant hole in a parking garage crackling with Primordium energy didn't exactly go with my vision of warmth, fur, and comfort. Mr. Pitt hadn't commented one way or the other. Maybe the pleasant dream had been my mind's way of shielding me from my painful collapse and chilled body.

I fielded a call from my mom as I pulled into the mall. Naturally, she wanted details about my date, which hadn't happened.

"You can't keep leading a man on like this, you know," she said. "Sooner or later, he's going to get tired of it. I don't want you to lose your chance with him."

I gritted my teeth, telling myself she meant well. "I'm not doing this on purpose."

Mom sighed. "I know. I just want you to find someone you're happy with. You need more than Mr. Bond in your life."

It was my turn to sigh. Loudly. The traffic clogging the lane skirting the perimeter of the mall trickled away into the aisles as I coasted around the back of the mall. "I promise I won't stand him up again."

"And when is the new date?"

"Good-bye, Mom."

She laughed and rang off.

I spotted Jacob where Mr. Pitt said he'd be, near the entrance to Macy's. I parked next to his Acura as a giant black SUV pulled into the space in front of me. Claire slid out and flounced through the cars to Jacob. I stuffed my purse full of spray bottles, fitting only half what I'd brought before joining the group.

"I can't stay past noon. I have to get back to *my* region," Claire announced as I walked up.

"Don't you have school?" I asked.

"I'm a senior," Claire said, as if that answered my question. She graced me with a soft, openmouthed sneer before dismissing me. I thought my question was valid, considering she looked like she'd come from school, with her knee-high white socks, short plaid skirt, and button-up white blouse. Of course, I bet school policy did not allow the shirt to be unbuttoned down to her bra or her skirt to be pulled up quite so short.

I spared a wish for the more pleasant company of Summer or even Rafi.

"Hey, Madison. Long time, no see," Jacob said. "Whoa! What'd you do to your soul?" His eyes roved up and down my body with frank admiration and a touch of something darker. I blushed.

"A good night's sleep does a girl wonders," I said dismissively.

Claire made a short gagging sound and drummed her nails on the top of my car.

"At least this explains things," Jacob said. Before I could ask what he meant, he changed the subject. "Isabel's got more spray coming express, but it won't get here for a few hours. Did you bring extra?"

I popped open the passenger door. Jacob filled his jacket pockets and Claire dropped three spray bottles into a tiny leather backpack. If this were a normal cito day, those three bottles might have lasted her until noon. Today, she'd be out in less than an hour. She wouldn't believe me if I told her, though.

"Here's how we'll do this," Jacob said. "Claire, you'll focus near the center of the mall. Madison, you'll take the Macy's half, and I'll take the Nordstrom half."

This left me closer to the garage, so I didn't complain. Mr. Pitt had all but instructed me to keep an eye on it.

"Do we even need Madison?" Claire asked, as if I weren't standing close enough to slap her. "If she hadn't screwed up, *I* wouldn't be here *wasting* my time."

"I didn't screw up."

"It's different this year," Jacob said. "It's not Madison's fault, either."

"Whatever." Claire spun on her heel in a huff, flashing us white bikini underwear. I averted my eyes.

We caught up with her inside the doors to Macy's, where she'd stopped in shock. Jacob hooked an arm around Claire's frozen body and pulled her to a rack of fur-lined coats and out of the line of traffic. She moved with him, unresisting, wide eyes bouncing from all the gargantuan citos to their frantic, volatile hosts.

"This is bonkers," she said.

I'd known what to expect, and I still needed a steadying breath.

Today was going to be a long day.

I stumbled out of The Body Shop, nose buried in my elbow, several hours later. A ten-year-old girl had turned the store into a war zone, goaded by a green cito the size of Mr. Bond. While her distraught father bellowed at the salesclerk for not stocking the perfume his daughter wanted, the tiny terror had climbed the display rack of glass bottle perfume samples, her resemblance to Godzilla uncanny as she shattered the heavy glass stoppers, one after the other, against the floor. I had used half a spray bottle on the lot, gone back to the girl for a second pass that finally shrank her cito out of existence, then fled the store.

My hair swung in front of my face, coated in a dozen competing perfumes. I coughed. For once, the crowds parted for me, driven away by the stench exuding from my clothing. I blundered into an open space in front of Sears and collapsed against the wall. Lifting my hair in a fist, I shook it, hoping to air it out, flapping the front of my sweater with the opposite hand. My eyes watered. I swallowed bitter-scented alcohol and resisted the temptation to scrub my tongue with my fingers.

"Hello, Madison."

I glanced up. Isabel stood a few feet away, a heavy leather bag on one shoulder, her glowing bulbous white soul unmistakable. She wore slacks today and a button-up sweater made from patches of coarse fabric, both charcoal gray in Primordium. I straightened, trying to find my sense of humor when she took a discreet step back.

"I come bearing gifts." She opened the top of her bag to reveal a collection of full spray bottles.

"Perfect timing. I'm almost out." I gave my half-full bottle a shake.

"I can see why. You're holding up much better than the other enforcers."

"Must be all my practice," I said, shrugging off the uncomfortable compliment. I didn't need a reputation for being the go-to enforcer for citos.

"Here, hand over your empties, and that one. I can finish it off on my way out."

I tried to hide my surprise. Not only had she hand-delivered fresh supplies, but she was also offering to do a little enforcer work while she was here? I pictured Mr. Pitt making a delivery run. The image of him cursing his way through the crowds was oddly funny.

I restocked my purse while Isabel held her breath.

"Brad told me you saw the little energy fluctuation in the parking garage."

"Um, yeah, I did." How dare Mr. Pitt tell me to keep my ill-thought-out adventure to myself and then blab about it to another warden. Was he trying to make me look bad, so they wouldn't hire me if he was fired?

"I don't know what Brad told you. You'd think there were enough problems in his own region to keep him busy, but he seems determined to make more of this than there is, and he's claiming you're in danger. I'll tell you the same thing I've been telling him the last few days: Don't worry; I've got my eye on it, and Jacob has it under control," Isabel said.

The last few days. She was talking about the first day I found the pit, not last night. Mr. Pitt thought I was in danger? Was that the source of his irate calls to Isabel and Liam? Maybe he'd promised to pull me from the mall tomorrow if things didn't change because he feared for my safety. I didn't know if I should be pleased. An enforcer's job was naturally dangerous. I'd have been happier if he'd given me some information—any information—to help me counter all that wild *atrum*. And I wasn't going to miss my opportunity to question Isabel, not when she'd brought it up.

"About that," I started. My words were drowned out by a loud screech. I spun to see a man jerk a shopping cart to the middle of the aisle inside Sears. He jammed a curtain rod into the cart so it slanted from the back right corner to the left front, with the sharp metal tip extending past the front of the cart by several feet. With a cherry-red cito tap-dancing on his shoulder like a deformed parrot, the man positioned himself behind the cart. I followed his line of sight. Down the aisle, another man revved the handle of a cart, the blunt end of a wooden shovel handle sticking out the front of his cart. The ruby cito braced on his shoulder was as large as a second head.

"CHARGE!" shouted the man nearest us.

The men sprinted toward each other. Shoppers leapt from their path.

Dear God, they were jousting. I bounced on my toes. I wanted answers, badly, but I couldn't let this medieval madness go unchecked, especially not in front of Isabel. Not only could people get seriously hurt, but I'd also look like a terrible enforcer if I stood around chatting while it happened. "Thanks for the spray. I'll be right back."

The carts collided, impromptu lances bouncing uselessly in the baskets. On the men's shoulders, their citos swiveled to keep the other in sight when the men jerked their carts apart and paced back to the end of the aisle. I darted through a ring of spectators and prepped a spray bottle.

The second pass toppled a display of Shake Weights and yoga mats. I crouched amid the lawn mowers, dusting the air between the men from a safe distance. On the third pass, their carts locked, and I rushed past with a mom and her four kids, spraying liberally. The citos dwindled to nothing, and the men separated their carts and sheepishly parted ways.

With Sears freed of wayward knights, I rushed back out into the mall, but Isabel was gone, along with answers to my questions.

The crowds grew rowdier after lunch, with more people shoving and cussing through the crush and a few fistfights breaking out. Claire stayed on, which didn't improve her attitude, but her blinding-white soul would have been easy enough to avoid if I had the spare time to care. I kept a fraction of my brain tuned toward the garage and slipped outside at lunch to move my car closer to it and surreptitiously check it out. From outside the fence, the compulsion to approach the live energy was a muted buzz, easily ignored. In the courtyard, it might not have existed. Contrary to the crazed cito activity in the mall, the pit appeared to have calmed. Disappointed, I trudged back inside, telling myself it was a good thing.

I skimmed the edges of a crowd clustered inside the doors, killing a dozen citos. People parted to allow a middle-aged man with a black-smeared soul to be marched out between two Roseville police officers.

Ragged black lines like stretched varicose veins webbed across a bright pink cito pulsing atop the suspect's head. My skin crawled. Inside, two more officers stood with a young mother, who clutched a bawling little boy to her chest.

"Tried to snatch him when my back was turned but—"

I walked past, directed onward by a free officer managing the crowd. Crap, I'd let a child abductor leave with a rampaging cito. Not that I could have sprayed it without alarming the officers, but I still had to resist the urge to race after them.

A dark shape in my periphery spun me toward the long bathroom hallway on my left. A huge black ghost made of broiling black soot floated next to the drinking fountain. It grew from a point in the floor and expanded outward like a cone, and along its bulk, a dozen faces twisted and moved, tracking people in the hallway. As I gaped, a new face pushed to the surface and focused shiny ebony eyes on me.

13

Speak Softly
and Carry a Big Gun

I SCREAMED.

The sound echoed down the tiled walls, spinning a dozen people in my direction. I fumbled to the wall for support, backing up in the process.

"Spider," I said, seizing on the first excuse that came to mind to soothe the wary onlookers. The irony was lost on the dozen cito-infested hosts. Nearly as one, they turned away from me.

A preteen boy strode through the many-faced ghost, shivering and rubbing his arms when it engulfed him. He escaped out the other side, unscathed. "Wuss," he said when he passed me.

"It happened right there," said a woman sitting on one of the benches farther down the hallway.

"Can you believe people?" her companion asked. "Who knows what perverted plans he had for that boy."

As tempted as I was to sidle back into the main thoroughfare, then run from all those sickening, moving faces, I kept the monstrosity in my sight and slowly pulled Val from his strap. I held him up, closed, to my mouth, and whispered against his binding.

"I'm sorry I forgot you last night. I really am. I'm sorry for yelling at you. The garage has me on edge. The citos, too. I shouldn't have taken it out on you, Val."

Saying a silent prayer that his fragile ego had been properly stroked, I opened the handbook to the first page.

Did you just give me a nickname?

"Do you like it?"

I've never had a nickname before. I guess it would be all right.

For Val, that admission was on par with a little child clapping his hands in delight. When I glanced back up at the thing, my smile faded.

"I need some help, Val. What is that?" I held him up in case he somehow missed the giant boogeyman in the hallway.

Check page 95.

Page numbers? He must have liked his nickname more than I realized. I thumbed ahead. Even though most of the pages were still blank, they all had numbers on the bottom like a proper book.

"Page numbers are great," I said. Between screaming at nothing and now conversing with a book, I was doing a great job projecting the vibe of a crazy lady. Fortunately, most people were too self-absorbed to notice, and the few who looked at me sideways hurried on their way. Hopefully not to return with mall security.

I reached page ninety-five and stopped caring about my potential arrest.

WRAITH. A Primordium manifestation of an incredibly intense emotion generated by an evil action, anchored to the location of the action. Once formed, they blanket anyone they touch with the emotion of their origin. Wraiths gain strength by re-creating the original action in subsequent people. Their area of influence extends no farther than they can stretch. Do not get caught inside one. Exterminate at the source.

I glanced at the accompanying picture, which looked remarkably similar to the wraith in front of me: cone shaped with five visible faces. A tiny notation at the bottom of the picture said, *A wraith forms a face for each person currently in its line of sight.*

I studied the wraith as a woman and a gaggle of children left the restroom and headed my way. Each one shivered as they passed through the sinister cone. I shivered, too, when four new faces rotated around the wraith to follow the family's progress, disappearing when they rounded the corner.

Lifting Val once more so I could read and keep the wraith in sight, I flipped back to the main page.

"Is this because of the attempted kidnapping?" I remembered to keep my voice down this time and used Val to shield others from seeing my lips move.

Yes.

My skin crawled under the rock-steady gaze of the wraith's face trained on me. Another bubbled to the surface next to it.

"Take a picture, it'll last longer," Claire said at my elbow.

I jumped and jerked Val away from her, shielding him with my body. I didn't want to share Val. It also seemed prudent to separate the two people with the most volatile personalities.

"Have you encountered one of these before?" I hated the rush of relief that followed my initial surprise. Of all the people to admit a weakness in front of, why did it have to be Claire?

"You haven't? Oh, that's right. You're stunted with a loser warden."

An insult for me *and* my warden; at least Claire was consistent.

"How do we get rid of it?" It was the question I'd planned on asking Val when Claire interrupted.

"See that spot?" Claire asked, pointing to the pulsing black circle of *atrum* hardly larger than a quarter beneath the wraith. "That's the anchor."

I hadn't noticed the spot before she pointed it out, having been too distracted by the faces. Now that I studied the tiny dot, I realized the wraith's upper body didn't quite meet the anchor. A gap of empty air existed between the two pieces.

"It's floating."

"Duh. That's, like, a projection." She pointed to the wraith. Then she pointed to the anchor. "That's the source. Or what we can see of it. Anchors tunnel down, like roots."

I peeked at Claire to see if she was pulling one over on the new girl. For once, she looked earnest.

"Spiral *lux lucis* into that spot until it disappears."

"Spiral?"

"You know." She pointed her finger at the ground and spun it in a circle. "Spiral."

"I know what 'spiral' means. I don't know how to do it."

"Don't you know *anything*?"

"I can loop—"

Her sigh cut me off. "Watch." She shoved her palm into my face. I flinched and she gave me a saccharine smile. *Lux lucis* collected in her hand, then flicked over her thumb and reappeared swirling around her pinkie, splashed across her palm, and disappeared to the back of her hand again. The second time around, it spiraled up to her fingertips. They flared bright as the energy backed up with nowhere to go.

"Is that going to be too much for you?"

I glowered.

Claire drummed her foot while I gave spiraling a try. It was similar to looping energy, but harder, because rather than uniformly moving the energy around my entire hand, I had to move the energy in spinning increments up my hand, from my palm to my fingertips. Claire's quick demonstration had been blatant showing off, proving she not only had more knowledge but also better control and possibly more strength, despite being eight years my junior. I kept flubbing the process and ending up looping all the *lux lucis* in a single sweep around my palm.

Claire huffed. "Just let me."

She flounced toward the wraith, but I grabbed her arm to stop her. She glared at my hand holding her.

"I need to learn how to do this," I said. I'd rather be getting a lesson from anyone else, but given the fact that I'd been sequestered to cito duty while evil overran my region because of my lack of experience, I couldn't let personal bias stand between me and any bit of useful knowledge. Gritting my teeth, I added, "Please."

"Hurry up."

"Right." I didn't need Claire to tell me it was dangerous to postpone destroying the wraith; in the scant time we'd been in the hallway, the wraith had grown a few inches in height with each victim who walked through it. If it could induce the original emotion in others, as Val had said, it was only a matter of time before it influenced another person to attempt a kidnapping.

Foot tapping, Claire watched an approaching man. When he drew close to the wraith, she suddenly stepped into his path, forcing him to go around her and down the safe side of the hallway. Then she stomped back to my side, dividing her attention between me and the hall. Her fidgeting ate into my concentration.

"Focus!" she demanded. "You totally lack control. Build energy in your palm, *then* move it up your fingers."

She deigned to demonstrate again, slower this time, and I saw what she meant. It took two more attempts, but using my left palm as a pretend anchor, I eventually spiraled *lux lucis* through my right palm and up my fingers. The spinning energy released into my left hand with a feeling like wind against my soul.

"Whoa." I shook my left palm. I would have said it tickled, but my soul didn't have the right receptors.

"Finally. Now do that right into the anchor."

I eased closer to the wraith. The face observing me swiveled to keep me dead in its sights. Cold black eyes watched the *lux lucis* gather in my hand, then slowly spiral toward the tip. When I was certain I had the energy moving correctly, I crouched and duck-walked forward. The face moved with me, sinking down to eye level, distorting around the thinner circumference near the base. My antics earned me more stares from people in the hallway. Unable to see the monstrosity, they saw only a woman waddling across the wide tile hall, one hand raised in a frozen wave. Since I could see the wraith, I didn't care what they thought.

With the energy spiraling through my hand, I touched my fingers to the floor, right on top of the anchor. *Lux lucis* whirled from my fingers into the tile. The wraith arced above me, then engulfed me in darkness. A whimper half escaped my throat as goose bumps raced down my arms and legs. Claire snickered. Just as quickly, the wraith flopped the other direction, dwindling in size.

I shoved more energy into the anchor. *Lux lucis* tunneled into the floor, disappearing into the tile. The wraith shrank in proportion, as if my *lux lucis* were a drain, sucking the horror into the floor. It wasn't until the wraith winked out that *lux lucis* built up on the tile and spread in a pool at my feet.

"Overkill much?" Claire rolled her eyes at me and tromped off.

I stood and wiped shaky fingers down my pants, then pulled out Val.

Nice move, partner.

"Thanks. That was scary."

I know. Your palms are sweaty.

"Sorry." I wiped them on my pants again, then asked, "Anything to add?"

It was nice to do something other than hunt citos.

The comment surprised me almost as much as the praise. It was the first time Val had showed an interest in what we were doing. "Getting tired of the mall?"

I think we should go back to the bookstore.

"Any reason in particular?" I pulled a spray bottle out of my purse and prepared to step back into the main traffic.

To free the books, of course.

I couldn't tell if he was joking.

The day didn't get much better. The three of us worked nonstop, never clearing the citos but at least thinning the masses, and if I counted anything a success, it was that no more wraiths formed on my watch. As far as victories went, it was lackluster.

In a last-ditch effort to thin the cito population, Jacob, Claire, and I divided the three most traffic-heavy exits between us when the mall closed, and I chose the doors closest to the garage. When I stepped outside with the last of the shoppers, the world tilted toward the garage. On faltering steps, I wove through the stragglers, a jittery energy dancing down my spine. Then the plastic-wrapped construction site came into view and all thoughts of my tired feet and the overgrown citos escaping on shoppers fell away. Blindly, I ran to the garage.

I didn't remember squeezing through the fence or checking for witnesses to my trespassing. I was running through the dark alleyway; then I was inside the plastic around the garage's framework, staring at the magnetic, hypnotic energy.

Lux lucis billowed from the sunken ground, *atrum* riding the inner wall of the enormous bubble like a second skin. Higher and higher it swelled, like an inflating hot-air balloon, arching past the steel beams of the first floor, then the second. The bubble grew wider as it gained in height, until the rim reached the fifth floor and expanded like a roof above me.

"Shit, shit, shit," I chanted, staring in horror at the mass of deadly power. The energy moved silently, only the sounds of my whispered words and the shush-shush of plastic sliding against itself filling the still space of the garage. Crouching, I squinted toward the crater. The wraith came to mind, specifically its anchor. Maybe this energy had an anchor, too, buried in the bottom of the crater. If so, too much *lux lucis* and *atrum* swelled between me and the enormous divot to pinpoint a source.

Something tapped my head. I spun around, but nothing was there. Another tap, this time on my shoulder. I spun again. Nothing. I stood still after the next tap. It was soft, like a raindrop against the skin while swimming, absorbed as quickly as I felt it.

Another submerged drop hit my back, only this time it stung. I tipped my head back.

A thunderstorm of *lux lucis* and *atrum* bubbled and swelled to fill the edges of the plastic enclosure, releasing droplets of raw Primordium energy. Fat *lux lucis* drops splattered soundlessly across the ground. They soaked into the dirt, leaving no trace behind. When the drops landed on my skin, they absorbed into me, too.

It was *atrum* drops that made my heart pound in my chest. Quarter-size drops of pure evil energy fell with random consistency, soaking into the ground as quickly as the *lux lucis* did. Just as easily, dollops of *atrum* soaked into my skin where they hit, stinging as the inky drops contaminated my soul.

"Holy shit."

I lurched into action, sprinting for the plastic opening. Another *atrum* drop speared my scalp. Sliding through the half-dried mud by the fence, I glanced up. The clouds of raw energy stretched beyond the parking garage, heavy tendrils questing.

My sweater snagged on the fence and I jerked it free. Another dozen steps, then I chanced a glance over my shoulder. The storm deflated, swirling dark and light energy sucking back into the confines of the garage.

I collapsed against a wall of bare white ivy vines, pulling *lux lucis* from them to exterminate the contamination of *atrum* on my soul. When I glanced up, a brilliant white man marched out from between the buildings, headed for the fence.

"Jacob," I said.

He jumped. I think he tried to spin around, but with his hands full, he ended up swaying in place. A heavy bag slipped from his right hand and clunked against the cement.

"Christ, Madison! What are you doing? Were you inside?"

"Whatever's in there just turned into a Primordium storm. I don't think it's under control, like you and Isabel say."

"Oh. And you think you could control it?"

I flinched at the hostility in his tone. "You're kidding, right? I don't know what that thing is, but it scares me, and it can't be good for your region. I'm just here to help."

"I'm supposed to believe Brad didn't tell you *exactly* what's inside?"

"He won't tell me crap." I didn't add that Mr. Pitt had denied me knowledge for my supposed safety. Staring into Jacob's accusatory glare, it occurred to me that Mr. Pitt hadn't specified what—or who— my continued lack of knowledge kept me safe from. Hadn't he said my ignorance was my only defense? With complete honesty, I added, "Mr. Pitt told me to focus on the citos. I think he's afraid if I muck this up, he'll be out of a job."

Jacob stared at me, weighing my words. Trying not to fidget and simultaneously ignore the massive energy's pull, I waited for him to offer an explanation for his bizarre reaction. Finally, he blinked and stooped to grab the handles of the bag he'd dropped.

"It's a pooka."

"What's a pooka?" I crossed my fingers behind my back, hoping I was making the right call. If Mr. Pitt had seen the enormous swell of energy a few minutes ago, I was certain he would have lifted his ban on information.

"A pooka's a dangerous, powerful creature. Unaligned, it's deadly."

"I thought you said you had this thing under control."

"I did."

"And now you don't? It's hard to tell the difference." Anger nipped my words, but darn it, he and Isabel had been all assurances for three days, and now he told me it was deadly. What had they been waiting for? The end of the weekend?

"Before, it was dormant. Now it's rising." Jacob set everything on the ground and unzipped a duffel bag. "I can't play mentor right now, Madison. Stay. Go. I don't care. Just keep out of the way."

Charming. I stalked to his side, arms crossed. Jacob lifted bolt cutters from the bag and snapped through the chain holding the fence closed. He swung the gate wide, then collected his gear.

"Why do you have a spear gun?" I'd never seen one before, but the harpoon shape was unmistakable.

"Pookas always rise in their largest form."

"So you're going to kill it?"

He sighed and finally turned to look me in the eye. I danced back to save my shins from scraping against the barbed tip of the spear. "If I have to. It's too dangerous to leave loose."

Jacob marched across the dirt and through the sheet of plastic into the garage. I checked the sky. The wild energy had deflated, but I'd seen its power. The storm cloud had contained more than enough *atrum* to snuff out my soul three times over. Yet despite the danger, it took concentrated willpower to resist the pooka's call.

My pulse dancing in my throat, I jogged back into the den of insanity.

"Who has a spear gun lying around?" I asked, trying to sound composed. My gaze locked on the pit.

It appeared calm, as if minutes earlier it had never so much as dreamed of swallowing the entire structure. From where I forced my feet to stop near the plastic, I could barely see *atrum* lapping gently around the edges of the crater and *lux lucis* sprouting in small knee-high fountains.

Jacob examined the energy, boldly standing at the rim of the crater. I almost called out a warning to him, fearing he was in the pooka's thrall, but he appeared more annoyed than entranced. Against the swirling backdrop, his soul glowed solid and pure, sizzling with harnessed energy. The young enforcer rubbed his hands down his pants, then chaffed his palms together.

His small concession to nerves pleased a pettiness in me; even the big bad wunderkind enforcer was scared.

Smarter parts of me were alarmed by the tiny crack in Jacob's confidence.

Fumbling into my purse, I pulled out my pet wood and stuffed it into my jeans' rear pocket. I tucked my sweater into my pants and cupped the hilt of the belt knife at the small of my back. I pulled it loose, then sheathed it again.

Dropping my purse atop a duffel bag, I gave in to the compulsion and crossed the garage. I stopped well short of the lip of the pit.

"I think I know how a moth feels," I said. "All that energy, it calls to me, even though I know it's deadly, too." I pulled my gaze from the hypnotic black-and-white energy to meet Jacob's assessing gaze. "You know what I mean?"

Jacob snorted and stalked past me to his supplies. I turned reluctantly away from the pit and followed him.

"You don't feel it?" I asked.

"I'm a little too experienced to get all tingly about some ball of energy."

Tingly was a far cry from my urge to rush to the pit and throw myself into the energy, but Jacob's superior attitude quashed my desire to explain. Striving for a neutral tone but succeeding only in making myself sound monotone, I asked, "What's your plan?"

"Capture the pooka, then leash it to me."

"You're *not* going to kill it?" My light-headed relief swelled out of context with his statement, lifting a weight I didn't remember shouldering. It would take the *lux lucis* of half a forest of redwoods to quell the *atrum* in the pooka, but maybe if we worked together, we could make a dent.

"Not if I can tether it. Killing it is a last resort."

My gut knotted around a lump of lead. The pooka's boatload of *atrum* made me want to put another hundred feet between us, but it also possessed an equal amount of blazing-bright *lux lucis*. Any creature with that much good energy couldn't be evil. My encounter with it last night had proved as much. Yes, it had knocked me unconscious, but I'd woken with a stronger soul than I'd fallen asleep with. It could just as easily have layered me with *atrum*.

My logic tightened the knot in my stomach. "How do we capture it?"

"The same way you catch anything. With a net." Jacob strode back to crouch beside his pile of supplies. I followed, blinking to normal vision to get a better view of his arsenal. In addition to the harpoon, he had a slender sword, a shotgun, and another gun with a barrel half as long as the shotgun but three times as wide.

"You said pookas rise in their largest form. What did you mean—"

My feet chilled. I looked down. Mud coated my white and orange tennis shoes and splashed up the hem of my pants. It wasn't a pretty sight, but it wasn't responsible for the cold that washed along my shins and feet.

"Holy mother of a poltergeist!" Jacob leapt to his feet.

I blinked to Primordium and screamed.

Fluffy black imps swarmed into the construction site, oozing under the plastic in every direction. Clumps darted through my legs, smearing my soul with flecks of stinging *atrum*, but none paused to snack. In a mindless mass, they rushed to the pit. Movement at eye level spun me around; vervet scaled the concrete pillars with razor claws and swung along beams above us on the second and third floors, converging over the pool of energy. Whatever a pooka was, it had as much pull over these evil creatures as it did over me.

My left hand clutched the pet wood; my right gripped the belt knife. I didn't remember grabbing either. I forgot how to breathe. Already the garage thronged with more evil creatures than I'd killed in the last week, and more kept coming. *Atrum* smeared across my ankles, creeping upward. I swung to face the plastic, spearing the extended wand through the next clump of imps headed my way. Beside me, Jacob held the shining fencing sword but didn't move.

"A little help," I said.

"What are they doing?"

I dispatched a cluster of imps and followed Jacob's perplexed stare. Above us, the vervet crowded the gray beams, scratching and clawing each other. It was typical vervet behavior, and the only thing holding my panic at bay. So long as they remained occupied and out of range, we could concentrate on the imps first.

A kamikaze vervet leapt from the rafters into the pit.

Lux lucis sucked the vervet under like a giant vacuum, leaving no trace of its black body. Three more jumped to their deaths. I relaxed my white-knuckle grip on the pet wood. Maybe this battle wouldn't be so bad; we could let the pooka do the work.

A snarl of vervet fell into the pit midfight. My cheer caught in my throat: Most vervet died, but those that landed in *atrum* rather than *lux lucis* leapt free at twice their previous size.

The leading edge of imps reached the lip of the crater, and in a brainless lemur rush, they tipped into the swirl of energy. *Lux lucis* frothed and bubbled, consuming dozens of imps in indiscriminate swallows. *Atrum* hopscotched across the surface, kissing a few imps along the way. Those imps ballooned in size, bounced another step, and disappeared into *lux lucis.*

Energy within the pit swelled, *atrum* arching and ballooning toward the rafters. Vervet bounded through it, exiting as large as baboons. They turned on their brethren, using tiger claws to rend smaller vervet to pieces. The rafters fast became a cannibalistic feeding frenzy.

On the ground, *lux lucis* flared with maddening irregularity, killing a handful of imps, then allowing another group to slip through *atrum* and swell to the size of wolfhounds. What was cute at the size of a gerbil or bunny became a nightmare of fuzz and forearm-long teeth when tripled and quadrupled in size.

Their rapid growth didn't faze the imps. They bounced around the pit like moths around a bug zapper. As quickly as the imps grew, most died, their larger bodies vulnerable to the slightest touch of frothing *lux lucis.* But for every twenty that disintegrated, five enormous imps didn't.

My ankle twinged. I tore my gaze away from the insane spectacle to look behind me. The flood of imps and vervet hadn't slacked. If anything, it was increasing.

"Help, please." I'd barely whispered the words, but they carried in the eerily quiet garage. Despite hundreds of clawed feet all around me, not one of their steps made a noise discernible to human ears, not even enforcer ears. Neither did the increasingly agitated energy of the pit.

Jacob shifted his feet, and the scuff of his shoes on dirt made the hair on the back of my neck stand on end. Deliberately, I kicked my foot against the ground, reaffirming my own solidness in a world overwhelmed with pure Primordium energy. Unlocked from paralysis, I fought against succumbing to a panicked dash to my car.

A Clydesdale-size imp bounded toward the plastic to my left, dinner plate–size ears vibrating with each bounce. *Have they always had ears?* I'd never looked that closely before. The imp almost reached the plastic before I realized it was going to bounce right out of sight, mindlessly unleashed upon the world. A normal-size imp could, over time, deposit a fair amount of *atrum* on a person's soul as it fed. What would an imp the size of a small tractor do?

I sprinted across the seething ground, leaping clumps of imps whenever possible. Behind me, I heard Jacob curse, then scuffle into action. How much *atrum* comprised this imp? More than had coated the charred remains of the Christmas tree stand. More than my entire body's balance of *lux lucis*?

Tightening my grip on the pet wood, I darted around a concrete pillar just as the Clydesdale turned. Glistening black eyes latched on to me. A boneless jaw dropped open, stretching from the base of the imp's eyes to its feet. Sword-length teeth spiraled into the infinite blackness of its throat.

I shrieked and dove to the side, rolling through piles of normal-size imps. Gravel bit into my back and arms, but I sprang to my feet before the Clydesdale turned, thanking the *lux lucis* gods for not increasing the imp's intelligence with its size. I jabbed my pet wood into its flank and pumped a wallop of *lux lucis* through it.

The imp jumped forward, unaffected.

"This is *so* not good."

Where a normal imp's hop would have covered a little over a foot of ground, this beast bounced as high as the first beams and easily the length of my Civic. My eyes felt like saucers as panic skittered through my veins. I searched for Jacob, finding him on the opposite side of the pit, his sword swinging through two gorilla-size vervet. *Lux lucis* flared in the pit, blocking my vision before I could tell if Jacob's efforts were more successful than mine.

The Clydesdale imp jumped in an exaggerated circle, clumsily orienting on me. I lurched for its flank, using its cumbersome size against it. My second copious dose of *lux lucis* disappeared within the imp's inky, airy body without effect before it bounded out of range again. After my third attack, I thought I saw a minute decrease in the imp's size, but I couldn't be sure it wasn't wishful thinking. This was hopeless.

"Madison! Behind you!" I whirled and leapt aside as an imp the size of a sheep pounced. Its feet slid through my shoulder on the way by, sending a jolt through my soul like an electric charge. One knee buckled. I gasped and staggered to my feet. A heavy smear of *atrum* clung to my shoulder, but I didn't have time to cleanse myself. More agile than its larger companion, the sheep imp pivoted and attacked, a double layer of razor teeth leading its charge.

I swung my pet wood through its body as I scuttled out of reach, pulsing *lux lucis* through the wand. When the imp landed, it had decreased to the size of a goat. It sprung several steps before realizing I wasn't in front of it. I used the reprieve to sprint away from the Clydesdale imp, which had finally maneuvered its mouth toward me again.

My eyes glazed across the sea of *atrum* mayhem. I hadn't been mistaken earlier: The tide of evil creatures had increased. Wall-to-wall vervet and imps, most of them abnormally large, littered the garage. It was too much. Too much to take in. Too much to fight. I didn't have enough *lux lucis* in my body to disintegrate the two imps who'd fixated on me, let alone half the evil creatures rushing in. Maybe if I had a forest to recharge in, but all I had at my back now was an angry-looking pooka pit, and even its *lux lucis* had proved dangerous to me.

I had a vision of the pooka overwhelming me again. If I blacked out, I'd be covered by imps. They would suck the *lux lucis* from my body while I was unconscious, and I'd awaken . . . changed.

"Madison!" Jacob dashed to my side. "We've got to drive them to the pooka. There's no way we can take them out by ourselves, but maybe it can."

We dodged in separate directions as a lion-size imp leapt for us. Jacob swung his sword up through its body, and it fell to the ground at half its size.

"How?"

"These ones are after you. Run toward the pit, and they should follow."

I stared at him incredulously. "What happens if the imps get a boost of *atrum*? Or I do?"

"Make sure that doesn't happen."

"Your plan sucks." Unfortunately, I couldn't think of anything better. "What are you going to do?" I shouted, dodging the clumsy Clydesdale imp.

"Try to round up some others. Use your knife. It'll pack more of a punch." Jacob darted across the garage, sword swirling.

Ooo-kay. I looked at my short knife, then at the three feet of pet wood. Hadn't I been excited to make some up-close kills yesterday? For some reason, I couldn't muster the same enthusiasm now.

"Here, little impy," I called, jogging a few steps toward the pit.

As if they shared one brain, three monstrous imps cocked their bulbous heads, then leapt as one in my direction. A fresh spurt of adrenaline tingled through my toes, and I zigzagged through the bouncing, oversize imps, attracting a few bloated vervet in the process.

Though the sheer number of normal-size creatures could take me down if they coordinated their efforts, to say nothing of the stronger imps and vervet, the pit scared me more. The closer I got to it, the more active the energies became, though I hoped my mind was playing tricks on me. *Atrum* swelled like a sheet blown from below, flapping high into the air before deflating again and again, its movements unpredictable. *Lux lucis* snaked across the floor of the garage in long tendrils like live electric wires, disintegrating swaths of imps and leaving clear charcoal patches of gravel that just as quickly refilled with imps again. Heart pounding, I gave those strands a wide berth.

A vervet chasing me pounced on the back of the Clydesdale, ripping a chunk from its back and swallowing. The imp deflated and the grotesque monkey inflated in direct proportion to its bite. The vervet's spiky head swiveled. Shiny black teeth grinned at me.

I bounced off a girder beam and careened out of the trajectory of a leaping vervet. Nearby, a rush of imps flowed over the lip of the crater and into the *atrum*, swelling like dry sponges at the first touch of water. Most continued their hop, landing in *lux lucis* beyond the *atrum* and disintegrating. A few bounced out, whole and hungry-looking.

I was the closest snack.

A swell of *atrum* billowed into the sky, dwarfing me.

"Oh God, oh God, oh God." I stopped a few feet from the largest swells of activity, peripherally aware of the pooka's incessant pull. This was close enough. If I timed it right, I could force my stalkers to leap directly into the pit. From there, luck would determine whether they landed in *lux lucis* or *atrum*.

Dropping into a tennis stance, I readied myself to run in whichever direction would save my life.

Lux lucis twined between my feet. My breath caught. The bar of light slithered through the endless tide of imps, killing with impunity. Before I could leap aside, another branch of *lux lucis* speared the air by my right hip, then my left. A fourth bar arced over me toward the girders, dividing like lightning strands. I trembled. I stood against the underside of a *lux lucis* octopus, with all its legs fanned out around my body, reaching, stretching, preparing to engulf me and suck me under.

Yet not a single strand touched me. The arms lengthened, encountering the oversize evil creatures by chance. The tip of a strand of *lux lucis* brushed a bear cub–size imp, and it disappeared. Another tendril took out two imps and a vervet. Another touch disintegrated the Clydesdale imp and the vervet feeding off it.

I held my ground, afraid to move a muscle, barely breathing. A base sense of self-preservation screamed for me to run or at least turn to face the source of all this energy, but my better instincts preserved me. Power flowed through the white energy outlining my body, vibrating against my skin and soul. My bones hummed. It was like standing a hairbreadth from a high-voltage wire, only there were a fistful of wires around me, and each could electrocute my soul.

Then, one by one, the tendrils receded, writhing back to the pit like snakes. I took a hesitant step, then another. When I was sure I was clear, I sprinted several feet before spinning to face the pit. It had calmed to a quiet storm, like the center of a plasma ball, just waiting for someone to stick their hand in it and cause it to spark.

In the moment of reprieve, I leaned my hands on my knees and listened to the harsh sound of my breathing in the still air.

"Not exactly what I had in mind, Spark Plug," Jacob said. He trotted across the gravel to stand in clear ground with me. *Lux lucis* flowed down his body, cleaning the smear of *atrum* from his ankles.

I looked at my hand. My soul gleamed like solid ivory, and almost too bright to take in.

"You'll learn to move faster with practice," he said.

I straightened, a sour taste in my mouth. If light in Primordium traveled the same as in normal sight, Jacob would have been engulfed in the glow of my soul. Instead, I stood next to him, looking stronger than Niko and he as weak as I had after my first encounter with a hound. Yet he had the nerve to lecture me.

"I thought you couldn't mentor me. Should I get out of the way and let you handle this?"

"That's not what I meant."

"Then don't talk to me like I'm brainless." I stalked away from Jacob. My insides vibrated like a struck gong, and not completely from fear. I sheathed my knife. Jacob was wrong; it was too short to be useful against these oversize insubstantial creatures, even if it could pack a stronger *lux lucis* punch than pet wood.

A small, bright creature zipped in front of my vision. Fear and *lux lucis* wrapped so tight around my muscles that I levitated backward in a move that would have done Mr. Bond proud.

The blur crystallized, hovering at eye level as steadily as I might hold out my hand.

I stared into the large eyes of my very first prajurit.

She was no taller than the length of my hand, and absolutely flawless from the tiny braids holding her long hair away from her triangular face down to minuscule toes peeking out of the cloth wrapping her arches and ankles. She might have stepped straight from Val's sketch, with a tight top and loose pants sewn with amazing details. In each hand, she held a slender sword glistening with *lux lucis*.

I'd encountered evil creatures whose bodies didn't have normal-world counterparts, but prajurit were the first good creatures I'd met who didn't look one hundred percent human. It was like being confronted with a griffin or a mermaid—a creature of solid magic hovered before me, and I did my best to wrap my unsophisticated mind around it.

"Uh, hi?" Madison Fox, woman of eloquence.

A handful of prajurit dropped beside the first. I jerked. Most were male, and all held toothpick-length swords.

The first prajurit darted forward and brushed a kiss across my forehead, zipping back out of reach before I fully registered the sensation. She giggled, tipped over backward, and did a series of loops toward the floor before zipping away.

One by one, the other prajurit kissed my forehead, then twirled into the garage. I stood, transfixed. Their wings had moved my hair. They had physical form. I'd been told as much, but it still made the reality of the tiny flying humanoids no less shocking.

"It's your soul," Jacob said. "They like the taste."

I blinked, coming out of my daze. Across the garage, tiny white beelike bodies dove through the vervet, swords slashing. In nimble aerial feats, they evaded claws and stingers, and everywhere they passed, sparkles of dissipated *atrum* sprinkled to the ground.

"Jacob!" The cry came from outside; then the plastic parted, and

Claire raced into the garage, her steps high and exaggerated. Beneath her feet, a fresh wave of imps and vervet surged into the unfinished building. Three vervet leapt onto her back from behind, sinking their teeth into her soul.

Jacob and I moved as one, but she disintegrated the vervet before we reached her.

"What's happening? I was almost to my Escalade when the imps came out of nowhere—everywhere. I tried to stop them, but they didn't . . . they . . ." Claire's gaze snagged on the pit, and her words dried up.

Bubbles of *atrum*-soaked *lux lucis* lifted from the crater and floated in a slow rotation around the main energy like planets suspended in space.

"It's a pooka," I said.

Claire's wide eyes blinked at me. "What the hell happened to you?"

I threw a thumb over my shoulder at the pit.

"Whatever." She turned to Jacob. "I called Gavin. Did you call Grace? Isabel?"

I let Jacob finish answering her questions and surveyed the garage. I needed to do something with the energy pulsing inside me or I would explode. The number of enlarged vervet and imps was growing, and the incoming tide hadn't slackened.

Rushing into the fray, I squashed a compulsion to sing. Nerves made me giddy, and darting around singing "Eye of the Tiger" wasn't going to win me any points with my fellow enforcers. Plus, who was in charge of my inner sound track? It obviously wasn't me.

For a while, nothing registered but the end of my pet wood, the dark bodies dying against it, and the accompanying scuffle sounds of Claire and Jacob battling nearby. I fought without much skill, dodging and sprinting as much as I hacked and slashed. For the most part, it worked, but I grew clumsy. Physical exhaustion emphasized by *lux lucis* depletion weighted my limbs. I'd been on my feet, battling evil in one form or another, for sixteen hours. I suspected the only reason I remained upright was the two generous boosts from the pooka—one this morning while I lay unconscious and the other more recent but rapidly expended against inflated imps. Even terror and adrenaline could keep me going only so much longer.

I turned from disintegrating a knee-high imp and came up against a wall of *atrum*. Backpedaling, I cast about for my bearings, afraid the pooka's ever-present compulsion had pulled me closer to the pit than I realized.

The wall moved with me. Flaky fish scales glistened in the ebony surface. I lifted my head, my body moving too slowly. A thick cluster of black spikes protruded from the vervet's chest, and scaly snake skin twisted up its pillar neck. From above the first girders, glossy obsidian eyes the size of my head gleamed over a wide, sharp smile. My heart thundered against my eardrums. Two massive three-clawed paws punched the ground on either side of me, cutting off my escape.

The vervet opened its mouth. Rows and rows of jet-black teeth receded into its throat. I backed up, but not fast enough. Fast as a snake strike, all those teeth snapped around me, and my scream echoed through the structure.

14

WHAT DOESN'T KILL YOU MAKES YOU STRONGER

BLACKNESS, PURE AND UNRELIEVED, COATED my eyes, blinding me to anything beyond the coalesced *atrum* of the vervet's throat. I expected a smell, but there wasn't even a change in air pressure. The vervet was still little more than evil air, despite its size.

Shafts of *atrum* teeth skewered me from waist to ankles. Ice-cold and pain-free, those sharp blades couldn't hold me physically, but they pierced my soul clean through. The vervet swallowed, and a wave of nausea coursed from my head down to my waist as *lux lucis* poured from my soul in reaction, sliding through the jagged cuts. My feet numbed.

I shoved at nothing with my arms and stumbled backward. My heel caught on a rock, and I landed hard on my tailbone. The vervet's teeth jerked up my body, slicing tatters through my soul but leaving my head engulfed in *atrum*.

Another swallow, and the vervet guzzled *lux lucis* from every wound in my soul. I screamed again, hand convulsing on useless pet wood.

The world spun, and I collapsed on my side. Saliva pooled in my mouth. The *lux lucis* comprising my soul faltered and slowed like molasses, oozing into the vervet in a painful sludge. I pushed up on wobbly arms, crashing back to the ground when they gave out. The impact jarred my sight.

Yellow overhead lights blinded me. *Normal sight,* my sluggish brain supplied. The vervet still existed, invisible now; I was still skewered on its teeth and could still feel it sucking my soul down like a thick milkshake through a straw. Black fuzzy clouds narrowed my peripheral vision. My head insisted the world was dumping me off its surface, but my eyes confirmed I was lying on my back.

"Hang on!" A man raced to my side, a wooden staff raised like a javelin.

I blinked to Primordium when the pressure eased in my chest. *Atrum* sparkles rained down around me, turning gray as they fell. I tried to sit up, tried to thank the stranger, but he had disappeared. I scanned my soul, staring long and hard before I realized the feeble stutter of light was me.

My arms gave out again. The rocky ground cradled me, reminding me of the giant furry creature that had held me this morning. I rolled my head to look at the pit. Bubbles of *atrum* moved within a column of *lux lucis* like an enormous lava lamp. The bubbles shifted and flowed, up into the rafters and down into the pit.

"Hey, pooka. Do you like me?" My words slurred around a tongue too thick for my mouth.

Someone grabbed my head and shoulders, jerking me up and breaking my hypnotized stare.

"Here. Take a sip." It was the stranger holding my shoulders. Upside down, he was a study of rounded shapes: round arched eyebrows, large round eyes, round downward-curved lips circled with facial hair. Even his round scalp was haloed by a puff of hair.

"Holy crap."

I rolled my eyes to my feet. Jacob stood there with Claire, both looking dim. Beyond them, *atrum* smeared the ground, but nothing moved. I rolled my eyes upward. The rafters were similarly empty.

"It's just us," I mumbled.

"You need to drink this," the stranger said.

"He's a doctor, Madison," Jacob said. "A medical enforcer."

It took too long to drag my gaze back and forth between the men. I closed my eyes. Everything was going to be better after a nap.

A firm slap snapped my eyes open. Hard metal pushed at my lower lip.

"Stay with me, Madison. I need you to swallow this."

Sweet, cold liquid spilled into my mouth, and I swallowed when it hit the back of my throat.

Fire burned down my esophagus, licking outward to my lungs, stomach, and limbs. My jaw locked in pain as a hundred ragged wounds in my soul mended; every inch being healed was a precise agony. When the flames reached my toes and fingertips, the heat backwashed, this time a gentle warming rush. I collapsed, realizing only then I'd been bowed off the ground, supported by only my heels and the man holding my shoulders.

For several deep breaths, I relaxed against the hard ground, listening to the ringing in my ears abate. When I opened my eyes, it was to normal sight.

"Sorry about that," the medical enforcer said. The man possessed kind brown eyes, with a deep furrow of worry between them.

"It had her swallowed," Jacob said, his tone disbelieving.

"What's it like in a vervet belly?" the ME asked.

"Dark," I croaked. "What did you give me?"

"Liquid *lux lucis* concentrate. A little goes a long way. Which is a good thing, because it's expensive."

The fire of the *lux lucis* concentrate burned off before I had time to appreciate its warmth. The ME raised the flask again.

"Here, this time I'm just going to put a dab on your lips."

He dribbled a little liquid on my lips and I licked it up, shuddering as the warmth rekindled in my middle.

"There. You're looking a little better now." The ME took a tiny sip from the flask, then handed it to Jacob.

I remembered that I didn't know the man who cradled my head in his lap and that I wasn't fond of lying on dirt. Plus, the pooka's wild energy still fluctuated a few feet to my right. Time to move. Casting off the languor of my third *lux lucis* boost of the day, I rolled to my feet.

"Whoa! Take it easy," the ME said.

The world spun as blood rushed to my head, and I collapsed back to all fours until everything stabilized. I blinked back to Primordium and surveyed the garage again. Aside from the prajurit swirling around the pooka's energy, the construction site was free of Primordium creatures. Unless we counted. *Am I a creature of Primordium?*

"Where'd they all go?"

"They just stopped coming," Claire said, coming back through the plastic. "It looks like a zoo out there, but it's all good creatures."

Pushing back on my heels, I held out a palm to the ME.

"Thanks for saving my life. I'm Madison," I said.

"Gavin Holt," he said. "And it was my pleasure." His handshake was firm, his hand solid and calloused. He couldn't have been more than a decade older than me, and he looked fit enough—in body and soul—to keep up with Niko.

Bridget was going to swoon.

Along with my soul, the liquid *lux lucis* had recharged my tired muscles. A five-hour nap wouldn't have been more restorative. "I've really got to get me some of that stuff."

"You'd need a prescription, and even then"—Gavin took the capped flask from Claire and raised it for us to see—"this was thirty grand."

"Thirty grand! But that's hardly three ounces!"

"I told you it was expensive."

Still, I could see the value. Not only had it saved my life, but I was also more than ready to keep fighting. "Why would I need a prescription?"

"It's highly addictive and tends to be abused. Enforcers start thinking they can take on more than they can. They stop listening to their bodies and push themselves beyond their limits. Trust me, you'll understand tomorrow." Gavin slipped the flask back into his medical bag and picked his staff up off the ground.

I admired my glowing hands, which brightened before my eyes. I looked fresh. Turning to the pit's swirling energy, I watched twin spires of black and white stripes twirl to the ceiling and fall back to the pool without a splash or sound. Prajurit darted around the *lux lucis*, but none tried to touch it. If they'd expended any personal *lux lucis* fighting the vervet, I couldn't tell. Their tiny bodies glowed with power, and I wondered if they'd recharged via proximity to the pooka.

The pooka might be the most powerful creature I'd almost met, but it was fickle. It had saved me once from the monstrosities it had created, but then it allowed the King Kong–size vervet to nearly kill me. As irrational as it was, that felt like a betrayal.

"When will it rise?" Claire asked.

"Soon," Jacob said.

I reached for Val against my hip. Scratches and dust marred his leather cover, and pieces of gravel bit into the pages. I brushed him clean, then let him fall to my hip without opening him. Before checking in with the handbook, I needed to call my warden. Mr. Pitt had told me to keep an eye on the crater's activity today and notify him of any changes. This more than qualified.

I grabbed Medusa from my purse and dialed Mr. Pitt while walking toward the plastic. I wasn't sure what to expect from him. This morning, he'd been shockingly calm, but it was too much to hope he'd remain so after I told him about the pooka rising. Just in case, I wanted a little distance between me and the other enforcers for privacy.

"Madison." Mr. Pitt packed exasperation and relief into his greeting. "I've been calling for ten minutes."

"Sorry. I've been busy." *Busy* sounded better than *almost dying*. "There's a—"

"Pooka. I know. Isabel finally confirmed today. Not that she had a choice. It's November thirtieth."

"What does the date have to do with anything?"

"I'll tell you later. Who's with you?"

"Jacob, Claire, and Gavin. It'd be nice if Niko were here." This really felt like an optivus aegis kind of job. I was positive Niko could beat the combined combat experience of everyone in the garage, Jacob's wunderkind status notwithstanding.

"He's got his hands full with a rash of salamanders."

As if on cue, the wail of a siren swelled and faded as a fire truck raced down the nearby boulevard. In my ear, a delayed siren echoed beneath Mr. Pitt's voice.

"Stay inside." The connection went dead. Across the garage, Claire's phone rang.

I shoved Medusa into my back pocket and pushed aside the plastic.

A heavy, repetitive honk echoed through the tall buildings. Along the rooftops, a flock of geese shuffled for space, honking and snaking necks at each other. I gaped at their white bodies. They weren't the only birds. Seagulls, crows, doves, pigeons, and smaller finches and sparrows lined the rooftops and fluttered among the buildings, all jabbering at top volume. Some alighted on the ivy vines, more on the trees in the parking lot. The dark sky of Primordium appeared star-studded with the number of birds circling, coming from all directions.

Atrum smeared the parking lot, hugging corners and skirting plants, the aftermath of a thousand evil footsteps worn into the dead concrete. Rodents and rabbits scurried in frightened bursts from one hiding spot to the next, often chased by house cats and hawks, their bodies bright against the black backdrop.

"It's a wildlife madhouse," Gavin said, coming up beside me.

I closed my mouth before a bird pooped in it. What the hell was a pooka, other than a magnet for life of any kind? I absently reached for Val, but most of my attention was on the three white enforcer souls who stood near a cluster of cars in the otherwise empty parking lot. My shoulders sagged. We had backup.

Footsteps pounded behind me, and I spun. Still talking on the phone, Claire unsheathed a knife as she jogged. Where had she been hiding that?

"How many hounds?" she asked the person on the phone. "Okay. I'll be right there."

"What's going on?" Jacob demanded.

"Rafi says hounds are coming."

"Rafi's here?" Jacob pushed through the plastic to stand next to me.

"Rafi, Grace, and Summer. The pooka attracted hounds." Claire looked up at the riot of birds. "If I get pooped on, I'm going to be pissed."

"Poop is the least of our worries," Jacob said. I tended to agree.

"Says you." Claire rubbed her arms and darted through the muddy grounds to the parking lot. I followed, noticing after a few steps that Jacob and Gavin had remained behind.

Mr. Pitt's distorted soul leveraged out of his Fiat and hustled to meet us. Isabel's Toyota Corolla screeched to a stop near the fence and she ran past me toward Jacob. It looked like we were having a full-blown CIA party.

Mr. Pitt barreled up to me, moving surprisingly fast on his stocky legs. "Turn around and get back to the pooka, Madison."

"I'm going to help with the hounds."

"No, you're not. They've got it covered." He grabbed my arm, his thick fingers gripping with almost bruising strength. "The pooka is your priority."

Frowning, I jogged with Mr. Pitt back to the garage. He kept his hand clamped on my arm, as if he thought he'd have to drag me. Gavin pulled the fence closed behind us. A hair-raising howl silenced the racket of birds. In the eerie quiet, I heard the scrabble of claws first, then the pounding of paws. I twisted in Mr. Pitt's grip. A pack of hounds rounded the far building, their black bodies glistening like wet blood. Sliding into each other, they took the corner tight, then fanned out, glowing black eyes locked on the enforcers.

Atrum soaked the hounds from their coats to their hearts, corrupting once normal dogs into killing monsters. It was possible to rehabilitate most hounds and restore their natural *lux lucis*, but the process took time. Meanwhile, they would make every attempt to rip your throat out.

"They know what they're doing," Mr. Pitt said. As I watched, one of the enforcers—Summer?—tossed a bright white net over a charging hound. The enormous beast fell to the ground with a heart-wrenching cry, but it didn't attempt to escape. "Jacob's going to need your help."

Two hounds, both as large as German shepherds, sprang for Claire. She swerved out of their paths, shoving one in the side so it fell. Snarls lifted the hairs of my arms.

Reluctantly, I let Mr. Pitt turn me around. He was right. The enforcers were competent and experienced fighters. By dashing out to join them, I wouldn't be adding much, but maybe I could help Jacob with the pooka. Taking a deep breath, I parted the plastic, my eyes going immediately to the pit.

A chill frizzled down my spine. I thought I'd used up the last of my adrenaline, but my body had saved some for the main event. Or to escape it. Sprinting to my car sounded better than ever.

Dandelion puffs of *atrum* and *lux lucis* swirled high in the air, catching intangible currents and drifting in every direction, only to disappear like popped soap bubbles when they floated more than twenty feet from the pit. As I approached, the air thickened with power, messing with my perception of space. My feet connected with the ground seconds before I expected, lifting for the next step before my brain acknowledged I'd touched ground. Mr. Pitt shook himself, releasing my arm.

We stopped near the others, who stood so they could keep the pit in sight. Isabel rubbed her arms, and Gavin fluttered his fingers through the air in front of him—I wasn't the only one feeling the oppressive pressure coming from the pooka. It didn't negate the compulsion to get closer, though. I opened my mouth to comment on the peculiarity of being pulled and pushed by the same force when a flurry of prajurit dove from the rafters and swirled around Isabel. They talked fast and high-pitched, incomprehensible in their rush; then they shot to the sky and disappeared beyond the garage.

"That's unfortunate. I had questions for them," Isabel said. She turned back to Jacob. "I got here as quickly as I could. It's too bad this pooka didn't bond with you. I was hoping we wouldn't have to kill it."

"Yeah. I'm not looking forward to this," Jacob said.

I frowned. Despite everything, I hadn't written the pooka off yet.

"Drink this." Gavin sidestepped Jacob and held a yogurt out to me. The medical enforcer tried to pop his ears, but I didn't think he was successful; it wasn't that kind of pressure. "*Lux lucis* concentrate can get you only so far. You need something with substance."

I took the yogurt because he was right. My soul gleamed, but it felt saturated rather than strong. I had power at my fingertips, but my reserves were shallow.

"Are you sure I don't need more concentrate?" I tried to peer into Gavin's doctor's bag. *Lux lucis*–imbued food would help normalize my internal *lux lucis* after a large drain, but the pooka's pressure against my insides made eating sound miserable.

"You've already had too much."

"I've hardly had any!"

"You've had two doses within twelve hours. That's enough."

"I think the situation calls for it."

"That's how it starts."

"That's how *what* starts? Are you saying I'm addicted?" I glared at him, then resumed trying to visually suss out the flask.

"I'm saying you're headed that way. Hey, Jacob." Jacob turned and Gavin tossed him a yogurt. Jacob uncapped it and drank it in one movement, tossing the plastic canister aside to kneel beside his arsenal.

"Drink your yogurt and be happy," Mr. Pitt said.

Another complaint wormed on the tip of my tongue, but I drowned it with boysenberry-flavored yogurt. Arguing would only feed Mr. Stingy's ridiculous theory. The yogurt hit the bottom of my stomach, reminding me dinner had been hours earlier. When it sloshed in a fresh pulse of pressure, I decided against asking Gavin for another.

Mr. Pitt watched me with calm, buggy eyes. "Isabel and I can't interfere—or won't—unless this gets out of hand."

"You can interfere?" From what I knew of Mr. Pitt's skills, none translated to being useful in the field. If I needed to know where the nearest patch of evil was—aside from the colossal pool right in front of us—he could tell me, but otherwise, his skills seemed far more suited to the office. I started to say as much to Mr. Pitt, but he interrupted me.

"Jigglin' Jell-O! Focus, Madison. Unless someone's dying, Isabel and I are here only in an advisory and supervisory capacity."

Isabel shot us an indecipherable look, then turned to hold a whispered conversation with Jacob. My stomach churning with fresh anxiety, I eyed the long shotgun lying beside the wide-barreled mystery gun, then the swirling energy of the pit. Did the pooka fall under Mr. Pitt's "unless someone's dying" qualification?

"You've proved you have the instincts of an enforcer, if not the expertise," Mr. Pitt continued, his voice softer so it didn't carry beyond the two of us.

"Um. Thanks?"

"So don't do anything stupid." He took a deep breath, as if girding himself, then added, "And trust yourself."

My eyebrows shot up. That sounded like contradictory advice, at least from Mr. Pitt's perspective, and I opened my mouth to call him on it, but he winked, then turned to talk with Isabel. What the hell was I supposed to make of that? My volatile, cranky boss, I understood. This half-supportive boss was a mystery.

A flurry of movement over the pit jerked my attention from my internal musings. The puffs of *lux lucis* whisked away from the *atrum* and coalesced, forming four enormous twirling spires of *lux lucis* anchored at the cardinal directions. Simultaneously, the *atrum* bits collected into black tendrils that stretched and wove between the pillars in complex designs reminiscent of Celtic knots. Power spilled tighter around my body, squeezing. Soundlessly, the *lux lucis* pillars crashed outward to the ground, pulling the lacework of *atrum* with them and stretching the whole deadly design around the crater like a fine Persian rug. I jumped but didn't retreat despite the closest band of *atrum* landing less than ten feet from me. The others held their ground, too.

Fingers fumbling in the power-thick air, Jacob looped the spear gun's strap diagonally across his chest, the way I wore Val. He left it hanging and stretched toward the widemouthed gun, legs braced extra wide to compensate for the pressure's interference with balance. I glanced to Mr. Pitt, looking for more concrete advice. He dropped his hand to his side to hide it from everyone else's view, then shooed me toward Jacob. Frowning, I walked with exaggerated care through air that felt only slightly less dense than water.

"What's that?" I asked, pointing to the peculiar gun Jacob now held. I knew as much about guns as I did about pookas.

"It fires a net."

I fidgeted, struck by an almost overwhelming desire to tackle Jacob. I still didn't believe the pooka was evil, not purely, and I hadn't had a chance to get any answers.

I stepped forward. "Do you need—"

"Stay back. Give me room," Jacob said, not looking away from the pit.

On the floor, the *atrum* and *lux lucis* sucked back into the dirt crater, taking with it the thick pressure. I stumbled, off balance with the lack of resistance, and savored a deep, easy breath. From the corner of my eye, I saw Gavin steady himself against a nearby beam, but Jacob didn't appear to notice. He stalked the retreating energy, and I trailed behind him, ready to jump in. With as much power as the pooka wielded, it could cause untold damage in all our regions. Something had to be done to restrain it, but my heart constricted at the thought of killing it. Unless we absolutely had to, we didn't kill hounds, because they could be rehabilitated, despite the total *atrum* of their souls. The pooka was at least half good. It deserved the same chance as a hound to be saved.

If it gave us a chance to save it.

Jacob reached the rim on the crater and stopped. I eased closer. Like a plug had been pulled, the last of the *lux lucis* and *atrum* circled the hollow ground and disappeared into the soil. The crater looked innocuous, just an enormous charcoal divot in the middle of a construction site. But all that energy hadn't just disappeared; it still existed somewhere beneath the dirt's surface.

I opened my mouth to ask Jacob what we should do, but I clamped my mouth shut when the loose dirt in the pit quivered, and pebbles shivered down the sides.

The pooka was rising.

At first, the movement was barely noticeable. A tremor went through the crater's base; clumps of silt slid in a barely audible, gentle waterfall. Then it became a horror movie, where the vampire was clawing its way from its grave, rising hungry and ready to eat something.

Only the pooka was much, much worse.

Spikes stabbed through the ground first, pointed straight to the sky, and they kept coming, two white blades longer than I was tall. They curved in a gigantic arc, separated at their tips by a few feet, then swelling outward before wrapping back to either side of the creature's face. Its massive head came next, a shaggy riot of contained *atrum* and *lux lucis* with a thick, snaking trunk.

Beyond the thick neck, the body ballooned larger and larger as it thrust into the air; then enormous feet broke free of the soil, flinging dirt in twin sprays. I shielded my face from the falling dirt, keeping my eyes locked on the point of origin. The base of the crater shook, but not as much as was warranted, as if the pooka wasn't a fully formed creature buried beneath the surface, but one taking shape inches below the ground, displacing only the top layer of soil.

That's it, Dice. Worry about the laws of physics.

With the rumble of a contained earthquake, colossal shoulders burst free, pulled upward by legs thicker than I could wrap my arms around. Even only partially emerged, the pooka was the largest creature I'd ever seen, its body a swirl of combined *lux lucis* and *atrum*. It dug into the crater with saucer feet, lowering its head as it strained to heave its lower half free from the dirt.

A fresh shower of loamy soil hit my head and shoulders from a wayward kick of its foot, and I backed up only far enough to keep dirt out of my eyes. The air filled with the rich odor of churned earth and a deeper, musky scent of fur and animal—the familiar-foreign smells an intoxicating mix. When I realized I'd stepped forward again, drawn by the pooka's magnetism, I forced myself back and darted a glance around the garage.

Jacob circled the pooka until he faced it head-on. He raised the wide-mouthed gun, sighted down it, and fired. An enormous bright white net flared wide, then slapped the pooka in the face and fell across its shoulders, the long ends draping the ground where its body was still emerging.

Lux lucis sparked like electricity against the *atrum* swirls. The net may have resembled a jumbo-size hound net, but its size didn't appear to enhance its strength. Enraged, the pooka bugled, throwing its head back and tangling its trunk in the holes of the net. With a massive surge and a thunderous, rattling pop, it cleared the surface of the earth; in another lunge, it scrambled free of the pit on all four feet.

My jaw dropped. At its crown, it had to be at least twice my height, probably taller. A kaleidoscope of *atrum* and *lux lucis* swirled in the thick, woolly hair covering the pooka's body from the top of its head down its sloping back and all the way to its saucer-like feet. Yet unlike the vervet or prajurit, this wasn't a foreign creature. Those weren't blades protruding from its face but enormous tusks. The pooka was a woolly mammoth!

Seeing skeletons in a museum didn't do mammoths justice. Add the girth of two elephants and fur, and the effect was dwarfing, awe inspiring, and terrifying. And beautiful.

The wildly sparking *lux lucis* net that had looked so enormous when the pooka was still half submerged didn't stretch past its shoulders; even if Jacob could have reshot the net, it wouldn't have covered the gigantic creature, not by half.

The pooka threw its trunk to the sky, rearing and releasing another earsplitting trumpet. When its front feet crashed to the ground, I braced my legs against the earth's tremor. Beside me, the concrete beam quivered. The mammoth shook, sending hair and dust in every direction, and I buried my eyes in the crook of my elbow. When I lowered my arm, the net lay in a useless heap beside the pooka.

Going to one knee, Jacob spun the spear gun into his hands and aimed it at the mammoth's chest.

I reached my hand out, ineffective. "No. I don't think—"

The mammoth lowered its tusks and charged Jacob. The metal harpoon whistled down the shaft of the gun, the sound crystal clear between pounding footfalls. My ponytail whipped against my cheek as I tracked the spear's flight, the sharp tip furrowing through thick hair along the mammoth's side as if through air, before burrowing into the pooka's enormous rump.

The mammoth barreled into Jacob. The enforcer lurched to the side, but one long tusk caught him in the leg. Like a cat with a mouse, the pooka plucked Jacob off the ground and tossed him over my head. He slammed against a concrete beam fifteen feet behind me and bounced to the ground beside his duffel bag.

I was running for Jacob before I remembered moving, but I craned to see the mammoth when it cried out and fell. The impact of its body hitting the ground threw me to my knees. I scrambled to my feet, torn between getting to Jacob and doing something—anything!—enforcerish to defend us from the mammoth.

A heavy click echoed through the structure. Jacob slumped against a beam, but he'd pulled a long rifle from the duffel bag to his lap, and he had it pointed straight at the mammoth's forehead.

I had woken this morning beside the pit, soothed by a fluffy creature that could only have been this mammoth. The pooka had saved me from the equine-size imps. It had been calling me to it for the last three days, trying to reach out to me. It hadn't done anything to harm me—or Jacob, until he'd tried to capture it, then shot it. The pooka wasn't the problem.

Fury burned through my confusion, and on a burst of superhuman speed, I sprinted for Jacob and kicked the barrel of the rifle.

A shot blasted before the gun flew from Jacob's hands to bounce across the hardened dirt. It must have made a loud clatter, but I couldn't hear it. I spun to look at the pooka, expecting to see a gruesome wound and dying mammoth.

The mammoth trumpeted and thrashed where it had fallen earlier, but no blood marred its head or chest that I could see.

"Are you crazy?" Jacob yelled.

I stared, dumbstruck, at the blood soaking Jacob's leg, turning slowly from bright *lux lucis* to charcoal gray. I'd never seen a wound in Primordium before, and it jarred me.

"Are you okay?" I shouted over the ringing in my ears.

"You broke my fucking finger!" He started to push himself to his feet; then his mouth flattened and he dropped the few inches back to the ground. "Get me a fucking weapon. We need to take it out now, while it's down."

The pooka braced its front legs, half standing, before crying out in pain and collapsing back on its side. I winced and took a step toward it.

From this angle, I couldn't see the three-foot-long harpoon piercing its flank, but I knew its movement must be making the wound worse.

Gavin darted to crouch beside Jacob, his medical bag clutched under one arm. "Here. Press this over your leg." Gavin held out a large gauze pad, and Jacob pressed the pad in place with his left hand. He cradled his right hand to his chest, and his pointer finger was already swelling. I hoped I hadn't really broken it, but I didn't feel any guilt. If anything, I felt guilty for not feeling bad. My thoughts weren't making sense.

Gavin picked up the rifle and aimed it at the pooka.

"No!" I jumped in front of the barrel.

"Get out of the way, Madison."

I stepped closer to the tip of the gun, my heart a frantic bird trying to take flight in my chest. Gavin glared at me. The pooka was wild and in pain, and even if it were in perfect health, it would still be the most dangerous creature in the room, yet I felt safe with it at my back.

"You can't shoot it."

"It just took down one enforcer. Do you want to be next?"

"Move, Madison," Jacob growled.

"No."

"Why not?" Gavin demanded. "Do you need more proof it's dangerous? We need to take it out now." He'd straightened from his crouch but lowered the gun so it pointed at the ground. I had a feeling he could raise the gun and pull off a shot before I could stop him, if he wanted to, but I tensed, ready to try if necessary.

"It's not evil," I said.

"Neither are citos, but we kill them," Gavin said. "We wouldn't tolerate a cito this large running around."

"It's not a cito."

"It's worse," Jacob hissed, and leaned back. The gauze was already soaked through with blood. Gavin looked at him, and I saw the ME waver: The doctor in him wanted to tend to Jacob, but the enforcer in him wanted to eliminate the threat first. "You don't know what you're doing, Madison. Look at all the *atrum*. It's evil."

"Kill it," Isabel said. She glowered at the pooka, fists clenched. "Kill it now."

"You heard the warden," Jacob said. "One shot between the eyes should do it."

"Everything will be better once the pooka stabilizes," Mr. Pitt said, ignoring me.

"I evoke a council," Isabel said.

Gavin's head shot up, startled. I glanced back and forth between the wardens, sure I'd missed something. "I witness," Gavin said, turning back to Jacob.

"We'll need a third, but we'll do it in my region," Mr. Pitt said. Isabel started to protest, but he talked over her. "My enforcer, my region."

Isabel crossed her arms, expression seething. Her head jerked in a sharp nod. "I want the pooka removed now."

Mr. Pitt's smile came and went almost too fast to see. "Done. We'll move it to my region immediately."

"We can't move it. It's injured. It can't walk." Not to mention people were bound to notice a mammoth walking the streets of Roseville.

Everyone ignored me.

"Council will convene in the parking lot of my office in a half hour." Mr. Pitt stalked over to one edge of the garage. Isabel squatted beside Jacob, turning her back on me and the pooka.

I remained standing, hands still raised to fend off the gun no longer pointed at the pooka. What just happened? More important, what did they mean the pooka had imprinted on me? For that matter, did anyone want to explain how the pooka had solidified out of *lux lucis* and *atrum*? Anyone? Anyone at all?

There was one person with all the answers. I waited a moment to make sure no one was going to tell me what to do; then I walked a few feet closer to the pooka.

"Shh, I know it hurts. I'm going to help you," I said. "I just need to figure a few things out."

Large eyes of spinning vortices of white and black tracked my movements. I looked away before the pooka hypnotized me.

Loosening the strap around Val, I pulled him out and dusted off his spine.

"How are you doing, Val?" I asked. I really wanted to jump straight to my questions, but I didn't want to risk alienating Val. Plus, he'd been with me through the whole crazy evening. He was liable to feel fragile, especially in the presence of the pooka. I prayed he hadn't fainted again.

I'm not bored.

Soft sarcasm. We were in business. "You're okay?"

I could use a polish and a good cleaning, but who doesn't like a little dirt in their binding every once in a while?

I took that as a yes. "Sorry about the vervet swallowing us."

It was informative.

I waited for complaints, but Val let the words fade back to a blank page. I wanted to thank him for not making my crazy night harder, but I couldn't think of a way to do so without offending him. "Do you need any *lux lucis*?" I wasn't sure it worked that way, but I'd happily give the book some energy if it could use it.

I feel as good as the day I was pressed. You?

I glanced toward Jacob. Gavin had cut away the enforcer's bloody pants and wrapped his leg. Isabel stood beside them, on the phone. I swung around to look at the pooka. It twisted to reach for its flank, the long trunk falling well short of the spear. The sight of Jacob's wound made my legs feel funny. The pooka's pain made my heart ache.

"Confused," I finally said. "Can you tell me anything about pookas?"

Yes. They're deleterious to enforcers and hazardous to handbooks. They should be avoided.

"Let's say that's not possible."

If you'd brought me with you last night, I could have warned you away before it imprinted on you. But the ink's dried on that deal.

I veered away from the potential argument. "Can you start with how it's possible that it's solid? It was pure Primordium energy just twenty minutes ago."

Whoa. Okay. Let me flip back to the basics of the basics. You do realize I'm lux lucis, *right?*

"Sure." The pages glowed white. The book had a brain. The higher levels of *lux lucis* magic were clearly at work in Val.

Illuminea are solid, too. They came from lux lucis.

"I thought that was figurative. Like little girls being made from sugar and spice and everything nice."

Val's first page remained blank, but the bottom edges of the paper curled up, fluttering. *That's funny.*

"You're laughing at me?"

No, no. With you, I'm sure. Here, I've accessed the pooka entry for you.

I turned to the page number he indicated, miffed. The book could laugh. I'd contemplate that later.

POOKA. Pookas incubate underground for approximately 20 years in regions of massive population growth. Between 1966 and 1984, pookas were moderately common in the United States. In the last 30 years, they've become rare here but remain common in Nigeria, Pakistan, and India.

A pooka is born with a perfect balance of atrum *and* lux lucis. *When its birth nears, it imprints upon a being of its choosing. Once imprinted, a pooka is tethered to that being, and its development in life will depend upon the imprintee and the pooka's experiences.*

Pookas are always born in November. In some cultures, they are revered for their ability to bestow prophecies upon others regarding the next year's events. Other cultures kill them outright.*

No picture accompanied the entry, but that was moot now. I read the small footnote at the bottom of the page.

**This pooka's birth in the last minute of the last day of the month is auspicious.*

I flipped back to the front. "Auspicious how?"

It's said the later a pooka rises, the more powerful it is.

"Is that myth or fact?"

Most don't rise larger than a grizzly.

Great. I could stack two bears atop each other and still not make a single mammoth. "'Tethered' means . . . ?"

Roped. Chained. Fastened. Locked.

"Never mind. What am I supposed to do with a mammoth? People are going to notice it following me around."

It will stabilize.

The pooka's moans wedged tension between my spinal joints. As long as it had a harpoon in it, nothing was going to be stable about the pain-filled animal. I'd figure out the specifics of being imprinted upon later. This poor creature had been incubating for twenty years, only to be attacked and wounded less than a minute after its birth.

"Thanks for the info, Val. I promise I'll get you cleaned up soon."

Thank you. A third word appeared faint, then came into focus, like ink soaking into the page from the other side. *Maddy. May I call you Maddy?*

I hid my wince; I'd hated that nickname since childhood. "My best friend calls me 'Dice.' Would that be okay?"

Dice? I like it . . . Dice.

I grinned, the movement tight against cold cheeks, and gave the book a pat before sliding him back into his strap. "We need to help the pooka," I said loudly.

Gavin and Jacob looked up. Isabel stalked away, talking into her phone.

"I've got my hands full. Jacob needs more attention than I can give him here," Gavin said. I looked at Jacob. Pain glazed his eyes, not unlike the mammoth's.

Gavin dug into his doctor's bag and pulled out a jar. He tossed it to me, and I surprised myself by catching it.

"What's this?"

"It's an antiseptic powder. Normally I'd say use a small pinch, but in this case, dump whatever's left in there in the wound after you remove the spear. It will help it coagulate. I've got to get Jacob to a hospital."

The jar fit easily in my grip, which meant it was ant size to the mammoth. I stared at the pooka. How was I supposed to get close enough to the wound to pull out the spear and pour this on it?

"Madison."

I turned back to the ME. Gavin had pulled Jacob up on his good leg. Jacob leaned heavily against Gavin, but he kept a wary eye on the pooka behind me.

"Be careful and try not to get hurt. If you do, Brad knows where to find me."

Together the enforcers hobbled across the garage and disappeared through the plastic. A stab of abandonment, illogical and unwanted, hollowed my gut. I could really use the support of another enforcer right about now.

As if conjured by magic, Niko strode through the plastic, soul shining with strength. My relief was so profound that for once I was grateful I didn't know the man better; if I had, I might have rushed into his arms and made a fool of myself.

"What's going on?" he asked.

"The pooka imprinted on Madison. It's wounded, and we're moving it to our region," Mr. Pitt said. My warden didn't seem surprised by Niko's appearance—he must have called him.

"Okay."

Okay? Okay! Just like that, he accepted Mr. Pitt's incredulously simplistic recap?

"Be ready to move in twenty minutes, Madison." Mr. Pitt strode out of the garage.

"What now?" Niko asked.

I pivoted to the injured mammoth. *Lux lucis* and *atrum* lapped on the floor around its massive body.

"Now we take that horrible thing out of its butt and tend its wounds." Somehow.

"How do we get close enough to do that without getting hurt?"

"Very carefully."

"You first."

I lifted an eyebrow at the optivus aegis.

"It's your pooka."

"Have you ever seen one before?"

"Not in my region."

"Do you think it's evil?"

"Right now? Yes. Exactly half evil. Stop stalling."

The mammoth lay flat on its side, its long curving tusks crooking its head at an awkward angle. I tugged my sweater straight and tightened my ponytail. The pooka's thickly lashed left eye tracked my movement across the garage as I came toward it. When I got close, it struggled to rise.

Not *it*. *He*. It was hard to miss mammoth testicles.

"It's okay. I'm here to help." I stopped walking. Up close, I got an unobstructed view of the massive ivory tusks, one coated dark gray with Jacob's dried blood. The tusks were thick at the base and long enough to skewer ten or eleven enforcers and still have room left over.

Think about something else. I shook my head to rid myself of the picture of me as a shish kebab.

The mammoth lunged for me, surging to three of its feet and taking a few awkward steps. I bounced back out of range, heart racing. Even wounded, the pooka moved fast. *Atrum* and *lux lucis* sprinkled from his neck and tusks, and he trumpeted at me, glaring. He remained half standing, his left rear leg limp, his front knees bent.

"Can he understand me?"

Niko shrugged.

I pulled Val free and jerked him open. "Val?"

Pookas absorb the languages they're exposed to while incubating. Also, please note my supple leather binding would not hold up well against a tusk. Books don't make good shields.

I thrust Val back into his strap and cleared my throat. "I'm not going to hurt you. I want to help. I can take the harpoon out and patch you up. Would you like that?"

I felt like a dolt talking to the enormous creature as if he were a child. The mammoth shifted when I eased forward, angling his head to keep me directly in impaling line of sight.

"I shouldn't have let Jacob shoot you." The pooka arched his trunk over his head and screamed at me, a deep bellow meant to strike fear into the hearts of saber-toothed tigers. My knees quaked. Little voices in the back of my mind clamored for me to run. *This thing can crush you with one foot.*

I eyed the mammoth's saucer feet and tree-trunk legs. I'd make a messy pancake.

"I promise to never let anyone shoot you again." I felt Isabel's and Niko's eyes on my back, felt the grit in my shoes, under my shirt, in my hair, felt my exhaustion and the bruises forming on my knees and arms, and most of all, felt the weight of the pooka judging me.

"We're linked together, you and me. I didn't understand before. I still don't, actually. But if you're mine—"

The pooka tossed his head, agitated.

"And if I'm yours—"

He blinked vortex eyes at me.

"Then we need to trust each other."

I eased forward two steps. The mammoth remained tense. Two more put me within striking range. My heart migrated to my throat.

"I want to take you somewhere safe. But first I need to tend to your wound."

The mammoth snorted and moved his head restlessly from side to side. I froze for half a heartbeat, then forced myself to keep moving. The tip of one long tusk brushed the air above my head. If he attacked, I'd never escape in time. I forced the thought aside.

Faster than I could follow, the mammoth snaked out his trunk and wrapped the end around my arm, yanking me toward his mouth. I screamed. Behind me, Niko shouted my name. The mammoth pulled me under his tusks, then lowered them around me like a cage. He brought his head close to mine, until I stared into one large spiraling intelligent eye from less than two feet away.

I held perfectly still, not even daring to breathe. The trunk flexed on my arm, circling me from wrist to elbow in a tight, warm vise. Coarse hairs along the trunk scraped against my wrist. In my peripheral vision, *lux lucis* and *atrum* spiraled down each tusk and back up, the energies never pausing, but the trunk remained pure *lux lucis*.

I stared into the whirlpool eye and took a slow breath. The pooka's earthy scent swirled through my fear, sweeping it aside, and I relaxed in his grip. An absurd vision of vaulting onto the pooka's back and riding out into Roseville lifted the last of my fear.

Untamed energy billowed within the confines of the pooka's prehistoric body, the monochromatic clouds defined by the fluffy lines of the colossal pooka. I brushed my free hand across its leathery forehead where a large patch of *lux lucis* lay. "I don't know why you look like an extinct creature, but I think you're lovely."

"Madison? Talk to me."

The worry in Niko's voice pulled me around. He shoved a cartridge into the enormous rifle Mr. Pitt had emptied and snapped it closed.

"I'm a good shot. Just duck."

"No! It's okay. I think we just bonded."

"Is it hurting you?"

"No."

The mammoth released my arm. I patted his trunk, then turned back toward Niko. The pooka lifted his head so I could walk under the tusks.

"Thank you," I said to the pooka, but Niko nodded as if I spoke to him. "Okay. Let's do this." The mammoth flopped back on his side, raising a cloud of dust. He lifted his head to watch me walk to his flank. I tried not to think about what I was doing. Too much thinking would bring back fear.

The harpoon pierced the middle of the mammoth's left flank, too high up for me to reach even with the pooka lying down. I rubbed my palms down my pants.

"I need to climb on you."

"Do you think that's wise?" Niko asked.

"I think it's the only way." I eyed the injured flank, which was larger than my bed, and the thick hair in which the harpoon was buried. The pooka craned his neck to get a better look at me. I swore I could read the pain in his eye, and I stopped procrastinating.

"Stand back. I don't know what he's going to do when I yank this out." Niko didn't move, and he didn't set the gun down. I frowned, but I didn't have time to argue. Isabel watched from near the plastic, arms crossed and face pinched.

"Okay, my beautiful pooka. Try to hold still."

I closed my throat around a bubble of hysterical laughter. I was about to climb atop an extinct animal composed purely and equally of *lux lucis* and *atrum*. My job had lost any trappings of normalcy.

I adjusted Val to rest against my back. My pockets were too tight for the jar, so I tucked my sweater into the front of my jeans, then pulled the neck of it away from my body and dropped the jar inside. It rolled past my negligible cleavage to rest, hard and cold, against my stomach.

"Don't let the *atrum* touch me, please." I patted the mammoth's hair. My hand sank into thick wool, releasing a fresh earthy aroma. *Okay. This is it.*

I sank my fingers into the hair at my shoulder height and placed a foot on the mammoth's thigh, then checked to see if he looked upset. The pooka laid his massive head back on the ground. Trying to be gentle while using clumps of hair as grips and digging my feet into his leg and belly, I leveraged myself up the pooka's body.

"I'm sorry," I said when I yanked his hair. "Sorry," I said when I planted my tennis shoe in his gut. "Sorry," I said when I perched on top of its hip, my knees and feet digging into his muscle and flesh. The pooka remained quiet, and he kept a patch of *lux lucis* beneath me at all times. The rest of his body fluctuated with mixed energies.

I'd never been more aware of how tiny and fragile my life was.

Thick fur covered the harpoon's tip, and blood matted the wound and oozed down his leg. It wasn't human blood, or even mammoth blood. The pooka bled a liquid energy, an oil-like *atrum* and *lux lucis* mixture.

I reached for the harpoon, then paused. Once I yanked the barbed tip free, I didn't think the mammoth was going to hold still for me to apply the antiseptic. I dug into my shirt, pulling the jar free. It fell onto the mammoth's fur, sinking until it disappeared. I snatched it up and unscrewed the cap. Inside was a fine powder, dull gray in Primordium with glints of white sparkles that could only be tiny shards of *lux lucis*. I eyed the *atrum* and *lux lucis* fluid seeping from the wound and hoped the pooka didn't need *atrum* to heal.

"This might sting a little."

The pooka rolled his trunk toward his forehead but otherwise didn't respond.

I grabbed the harpoon with my free hand as close to the base as I could without touching the mammoth's blood. Aside from making my grip sticky, I wasn't sure what *atrum*-tainted blood would do to me, and I didn't want to find out while crouched atop a prehistoric beast. I yanked the harpoon.

It came halfway out. The mammoth bugled and shifted, trying to rise. I held on to the harpoon and tried to grip the rounded flank with my thighs.

"Hang in there," I said, more to myself than the mammoth.

I gave the harpoon another, rougher tug, and it sprang free with a dreadful sucking sound. The mammoth's pain-filled trumpet deafened me. Tossing the harpoon to the ground, I smoothed aside tufts of thick wool and dumped the contents of the jar onto the fleshy, torn opening. The mammoth bugled and lurched to his feet.

I squawked as my perch shifted from horizontal to vertical. I half slid, half fell down the mammoth's side, trying to roll out of the ten-foot drop like I'd seen stunt people in movies do.

I would have made a terrible stunt person. My ankle buckled under me, and I fell to the side. Sheer adrenaline and fear of being flattened beneath the mammoth's massive round feet prompted the roll I'd been aiming for. Just for good measure, I rolled again before standing and darting across the garage to Niko.

He caught me as I barreled into him.

"Steady," he said, righting me.

I turned to face the mammoth. He was standing. He limped a few steps forward, then to the side, but he managed to put weight on the leg. If he hadn't been right there in front of me, his tufts of wool still tangled around my fingers, I would have found it impossible to imagine a creature could be so large.

I realized Niko still supported me and I took a hasty, embarrassed step away from him. My right ankle buckled, spearing pain through my foot and up my leg. I cried out and clutched Niko's arm to steady myself.

"I thought you might have hurt that." He knelt before me and probed my ankle.

"Ow!"

"Yep. You've sprained it."

The perfect cap on a perfect day. Pain throbbed up my leg, collecting exhaustion along the way. I slumped.

"Sit."

I sat, chilly gravel poking into my jeans. Rubbing my arms to create warmth, I watched Niko. He glanced around, then strode to Isabel. For him, she smiled. I doubted she'd ever smile at me again, let alone bring me Jamba Juice. I'd poached a pooka on her land, whatever that meant. My bigger crime was hurting Jacob, I thought; first letting him get skewered, then crippling his hand.

Niko returned with Isabel's scarf. He pulled off my shoe and peeled my dirty sock down until it covered only my toes; then he probed my ankle.

"Enough with the torture!"

"We need to know if it's broken."

I flexed my toes and carefully circled my foot to prove I could still move everything. It hurt, but I tried to appear unaffected. "See. Not broken. Now stop poking."

"Fine." He deftly began wrapping my ankle with the scarf. I thought about the fairy tales all girls are raised on, where the handsome prince fits the poverty-stricken woman with the crystal slipper, proving a woman's foot size could determine true love. Here I was with the handsome prince of enforcers kneeling over my foot, but the rest was a typical Madison-and-men catastrophe. I was filthy. My foot was sweaty, grimy, and probably stank, but I couldn't tell over the general mammoth aroma permeating my clothing. My ankle was already swollen enough to make me wince at the thought of sliding it back into my cushy tennis shoe. As far as fairy tales went, this one wouldn't pass muster.

Over Niko's shoulder, I watched as the mammoth stopped testing his back leg and turned to examine his surroundings. After snuffling up a pillar to the beam above—and almost getting his tusks caught on the beam—the massive pooka pivoted to face me. He lifted his trunk and his mouth gaped open. I could have sworn he smiled.

Screw fairy tales. My life was way more interesting.

"Did you know the enforcer the other pooka you met imprinted on?" I asked.

"It imprinted on a demon."

I gaped at the top of Niko's shaved head. "What?"

"They're born half good, half evil. They have a choice who they imprint on. It's not always an enforcer."

"What happened to the pooka?"

"I helped kill it."

Niko tied off the ends of the scarf while I processed his words. The scarf wrapped my foot and ankle, leaving only my toes and heel exposed and making my sock redundant.

"It looks like the prajurit leggings," I said, more to force myself to think of something other than Niko having to kill a pooka.

"You saw one?"

"Four. No five. They helped with the vervet earlier."

"Where did they go?"

I shrugged. "It was hectic. They left before the pooka rose."

Niko handed me my shoe and I wiggled it back into place. It fit snug, and it hurt to tighten the laces, but my chilled toes appreciated the coverage.

Niko helped me stand, and I tested how well the ankle was going to hold me. It didn't hurt as much as I expected, thanks to Niko's first aid skills.

"Truck's here," Mr. Pitt called from across the garage. "Let's get going." He disappeared behind the plastic. Isabel marched after him.

"You don't by chance have a mammoth collar and leash in your trunk?"

Niko shook his head. "I left them at home this morning."

"Damn." How in the world was I supposed to take a five-ton creature for a walk?

I blinked to normal vision on the off chance the pooka would look like something completely different in normal sight—if the demon had taught me anything, it was that Primordium and normal sight didn't always translate shape in the same manner.

Harsh bright overhead lights cast a dozen bulbous mammoth shadows across the garage. I squinted, shielding my eyes to take in the pooka's complete form. He looked exactly the same in normal sight, only entirely onyx black from trunk tip to short, swishy tail. I doubted generations of archaeologists had mistaken the color of an entire species, which meant the pooka wasn't completely in line with natural rules. Considering it had just birthed itself from pure *lux lucis* and *atrum* generated or accumulated by the human population growth in the area, I shouldn't have been surprised.

"What's the rush?" Niko asked.

"Isabel. She wants him removed from her region. She says I poached him. Does that make sense to you?"

Niko nodded. "I'll explain. Later. Where's your coat?"

"In my car." As if my body needed the reminder I was underdressed for midnight in November—no, December now—a shiver chattered my teeth.

"Lead the way." Niko gestured to the pooka rather than the exit.

I took a deep breath. From what I knew of species who imprinted, they tended to follow the creature they imprinted on. I hobbled up to the mammoth, stopping short of his tusks, which left me nearly eight feet from his face. In normal sight, his eyes were liquid gold, beautiful, and much easier to look at than the swirling vortices in Primordium. "You ready to move this party to my region?" The pooka blinked thick lashes, and while my mammoth-expression-reading skills were rusty, I thought he might be confused.

"This way." I turned and hobbled toward the exit. When I looked back, the mammoth hadn't moved. "Come on." I motioned with my hand like I would at another person. He curled his trunk at me.

"Maybe if you touch it," Niko suggested from where he'd remained across the garage.

I blinked back to Primordium, wary of the pooka's dual nature. I didn't want to blindly rest against *atrum*. Wincing, I hobbled back to the pooka and reached a hand out to him. Mirroring my tentative gesture, the pooka lifted his trunk to my fingers. He snuffled my hand and arm with the tip of his *lux lucis* trunk and I gently petted the coarse skin.

Thinking of the *Black Stallion* movies I'd been enamored with as a child, I decided to test Alec Ramsay's way of "leading" the black stallion by walking beside his neck. I turned to face the same direction as the mammoth. The mammoth gently wrapped his trunk around my forearm. Taking a deep breath and trying to project what I wanted, I took my first hobbling step. Then another.

The pooka let me walk three steps before he moved, shuffling along beside me as calm as could be. I grinned at him.

"We make great gimp twins."

The mammoth's tusks pushed through the plastic before I got close, but I tried to hold what I could aside so it wouldn't hit his face. The plastic ripped as it spread around the mammoth's massive body, and I thanked my luck the pooka wasn't spooked by the sound.

The world outside had righted itself. The hounds were gone, as were the enforcers and their vehicles. The flocks of birds had scattered along with the smaller creatures in the shrubbery. A faint glow of *lux lucis* coated the roof edges like a dusting of snow. On the ground, swaths of *atrum* remained from the stampede of imps and vervet, though a few charcoal strips showed the enforcers had done some cleanup work after netting the hounds. There was a lot more work to do, but fortunately no one expected it of me: Keeping my feet clean of *atrum* while walking across the blackened ground taxed my current energy level.

I glanced behind us. Where the pooka stepped, faint impressions of mottled black and white footprints remained. However, once the pooka lifted a foot, the energies canceled each other out, acting the way I'd learned *lux lucis* and *atrum* were supposed to behave. I breathed a sigh of relief. At least I wouldn't have to run around after the pooka, cleaning up every footprint.

Niko walked around us, moving faster than my shuffle despite being weighed down with Jacob's artillery. The pooka followed him with his whirling irises. I saw a gorgeous man with an impressive and enviable soul. I wondered what the pooka saw. He'd imprinted on me, a woman with a soul of pure *lux lucis*, but the pooka was equal parts *atrum*. Did he find Niko repulsive? Did he have the usual evil creature's desire to devour enforcers?

I checked the trunk wrapped around my arm. Still solid *lux lucis*.

Niko dumped his armfuls beside his BMW, then strode to my car, my purse in his hands. In my pooka preoccupation, I'd forgotten it. I patted my hip, checking for Val; the book lay securely against my side.

We navigated the opening in the fence that someone had pulled wide. Our destination was obvious. Backed up to the edge of the construction site idled a wide-load flatbed trailer attached to a semi. The driver waited in the cab, and Mr. Pitt stood near the back of the flatbed. He eyed the pooka hungrily, and when we got closer, my boss gave the pooka a shallow bow. The pooka inclined his head in return.

I hissed in pain when I stepped onto the ramp with my sprained ankle and the slant engaged swollen ligaments. I staggered toward the pooka and latched on to his offered tusk. When I grasped it, he lifted me into the air, and I dangled two feet above the ground for a few shuffled steps before the pooka set me down on the flatbed.

"Thank you," I said when I remembered how to breathe. I hobbled forward, knees absorbing the wobble of the trailer when the pooka climbed aboard. I situated us near the middle of the flatbed. It was plenty long, but not wide enough for my comfort. I would have appreciated some walls or railings. This kind of truck usually hauled oversize tractors and construction equipment. In other words, items that didn't possess legs attached to a brain that could spontaneously decide to disembark while the truck was in motion.

"Madison." Niko stood beside the trailer, holding my coat in his hands. "Here."

I crouched and took the coat from his hands, straightening too fast and making myself dizzy. The mammoth was big enough to step on me when I was standing. Crouched, it might not see me before squishing me.

I shrugged into the coat, shivering despite the added warmth. The mammoth poked the thick fabric with the tip of his trunk, snuffled, then took hold of my wrist again.

The ramp retracted automatically, and Mr. Pitt gave a signal to the driver. The truck lurched into gear and eased away from the construction site. Exhaust billowed from the tall pipe behind the cab, blowing over us. I eyed the pooka, waiting for signs of panic. In turn, he watched me, as if waiting for the same signs in me. Not knowing what to do, I petted his trunk with my free hand.

"This won't take long."

I glanced back toward the garage as we crawled across the smooth blacktop of the parking lot. Niko crouched near his car, and *lux lucis* shot from his hands, racing across the *atrum*-tainted ground, eating away the blackness in an enormous arc. He stood, lifting a phone to his ear as he walked to the driver's door of his BMW. Mr. Pitt was already in his tiny Fiat, and he zipped down the row beside us before pulling out in front of the truck. Isabel followed him in her Corolla. I looked for Illuminea or security guards or even imps lurking in the bushes, but other than our small entourage, the grounds were empty.

Cold air trickled through the warmth of my coat and numbed my legs. I shivered and shifted closer to the mammoth. All fear, even of being trampled, blew away with the wind. The peace I remembered feeling when waking up in the construction site returned. I snuggled against the pooka's woolly leg, and he shifted his energy so I lay against pure *lux lucis*. I braced myself as the truck took the first gentle corner, and the mammoth shifted to regain his balance. The flatbed rocked, then steadied when the mammoth stilled.

Nothing in my life prior to this moment prepared me for standing on the back of a wide-load flatbed, one arm held by a prehistoric creature, my body pressed against his warm front, traveling down Roseville's nearly deserted streets at forty miles per hour, yet it felt as natural as breathing.

I wondered what the few people who passed us thought. Cars slowed and drivers stared. Did they think the pooka was a prop for a float or an exhibit for a museum? How did they reconcile how impossibly alive the mammoth appeared? For once, the magic of my secret world was visible to everyone, but did they really see it, or did they discount it, inured to the fantastical by movies and their limited grasp of reality?

Would they remain so conveniently dismissive when I walked around with a mammoth every day?

The wind scooped up my worries and carried them away. On the rim of the horizon, a faint glow announced the approaching dawn. I yawned, careful to avoid a mouthful of bugs and fur. I went on alert as we neared ground zero. If anything was going to call lingering evil to the surface, it was my pooka.

The truck barreled past the hotel without incident.

We drove straight to Illumination Studios. The driver parked on the curb rather than attempting to navigate the tree-studded lot. Niko pulled into the parking lot behind us, joining a cluster of cars and white-souled people.

"Welcome to my region," I said.

The pooka looked around. Tucked against his chest, I didn't have to duck to avoid his swooping tusks.

The driver leapt from the cab. Gray patches clouded the man's soul, but I thought he might have been CIA anyway; he didn't glance at the mammoth or me, didn't say a word, and didn't look the least bit curious. He hit a button that lowered the ramp before jogging back to the warmth of the cab.

The flatbed didn't have room for the mammoth to turn around, and the drop-off was too steep for his injured leg. That left us with backing up, which proved much slower for the enormous beast than going forward. I stood between his tusks while the mammoth navigated one careful footstep at a time. He maintained his grip on my arm the whole way, and I fancied myself his safety blanket, which amused me.

When he reached the pavement, I gripped his tusk. He obligingly lifted me over the ramp to flat ground. Together, we turned toward the congregation.

Kathleen, Liam, Isabel, and a wiry woman with a geometric soul that marked her as a warden stood to one side. Mr. Pitt stood near them but clearly not with them. Clumped between the factions were Summer, Rafi, and Liam's warden-in-training Sheila. Niko pulled into the lot and strode to stand near the enforcers, unaligned with either Mr. Pitt or the other wardens.

Sheila tried to maintain a stoic expression, but her eyes kept widening each time she looked at the pooka. Everyone else stared with serious eyes and heavy frowns.

Dread settled in my midsection. This wasn't a welcoming committee.

16

MAGIC HAPPENS

N O ONE SPOKE AS THE pooka and I traversed the otherwise empty lot. I'd all but forgotten the promised council. It hadn't been important while I'd been bonding with and unskewering the pooka, and I honestly hadn't expected it to include me.

The worries I'd dismissed during the surreal drive settled into my body with each step. Isabel's face was set in grim lines echoed by the wardens flanking her. I swallowed, my throat dry, and gave the pooka a reassuring pat. Whatever this was, I would make sure no further harm came to him.

"I recognize the evoked council," Liam said once the pooka and I came to a limping stop.

"I answer." Mr. Pitt stepped forward. I gasped when his soul *pivoted* as if attached to an axis anchored in his belt. The strange white shape stretched and spread around him like a bizarre, angular tutu.

"I evoked," Isabel said, stepping forward. Her soul fell flat around her waist, the long smooth line of one side aligning with Mr. Pitt's.

"I preside." Behind my warden, Liam's soul sprawled across two parking spaces, aligning with portions of Mr. Pitt's and Isabel's soul.

"I preside," said Kathleen. By the time her soul fell, I recognized the pieces: Their souls held the shape of their regions, and they fit together like puzzle pieces. Mr. Pitt's was by far the smallest, right there for everyone to see.

"I preside," said the warden I didn't know, stepping in front of Mr. Pitt, making her the warden to the area north of Roseville.

"Evoked, answered, and locked," Liam said. A cycle of *lux lucis* shifted through the wardens before their souls snapped back into place. Mr. Pitt checked faces warily and the warden I didn't know shuddered openly. Only Kathleen of Folsom seemed unaffected by the energy transfer. Liam stepped back, a deep furrow between his brows. The rest resumed a semicircle around me, but gossamer strands of *lux lucis* stretched between the wardens. Summer, Rafi, and Sheila discreetly shifted to avoid coming in contact with the immaterial filaments. Niko stood well clear.

"Margaret," the wiry warden introduced herself to me. She glanced over my shoulder at the pooka. "I'll shake your hand later, if you don't mind."

I closed my gaping mouth and nodded.

"Here is the source of all our problems." Isabel pointed at me.

I bristled. I may have been untrained and new, but that didn't make me a source of evil. Then I realized no one was looking at me. They were all looking at my pooka. I opened my mouth to protest, but the words didn't materialize. The pooka *had* raised holy hell in the garage just a few hours earlier.

"Tonight's problems, yes, but not those of the last weeks," Niko said calmly.

Everyone turned to face the optivus aegis.

"Of course it is," Isabel said.

"No, Niko's right," Kathleen said. "Even one this big can't be blamed for our problems. By its nature, a pooka's half *lux lucis*, half *atrum*. If it were exerting power over all the localized evil, it would have exerted the same pull over all the creatures on our side, too."

I released a pent-up breath. The pooka had knocked me unconscious, saved me from horse-size imps, and left me to die in the stomach of a vervet. I wasn't deluded into believing he was a good creature, but I didn't want him to be responsible for the plague of evil in the area.

I checked to see how the pooka took the news. His eyelids drooped. I hobbled a few steps forward. If he fell asleep, I didn't want to be crushed.

"It may not have been responsible for the evil we've faced, but look at it." Liam gestured at the pooka. I didn't care for the calculating look in his eyes. "It's huge. It's twice the size of the last California pooka.

And it's in the hands of an untrained enforcer. This is a catastrophe waiting to happen."

"I claim territorial right to the poached pooka and enforcer," Isabel said. Liam jerked to stare at Isabel, clearly shocked. Isabel tilted her chin higher. "It's my right."

Territorial right? I needed a translator for this conversation. I glanced toward Summer, but the friendly enforcer watched me and the pooka with equal wariness. There'd be no whispered answers to my questions in this meeting.

"Madison didn't poach anything," Mr. Pitt said. "She had no knowledge of pookas before tonight—a fact I repeatedly spoke out against the last few days, considering the dangerous proximity in which she worked with it."

I frowned. Mr. Pitt had been the first person to deny me knowledge of the pooka. He could have told me all about it before reporting my discovery to Liam and Isabel on Black Friday. Or was I missing some unspoken warden code?

"Furthermore," Mr. Pitt continued, "she was exactly where you all decided she should be."

"None of us knew there was a pooka rising," Liam said. He shifted to put space between himself and Isabel.

"*None* of us?" Mr. Pitt asked, arching a brow at Isabel.

She huffed. "I don't report to you, Brad, or anyone else. Of course I knew there was a pooka incubating in my territory. I've known about it for years. Jacob's been monitoring it since he took on the region. It should have imprinted on him."

"You admit to inviting an enforcer into your territory, into the pooka's *hatching grounds*. You can't claim it was poached when you gave consent," Mr. Pitt said.

"You put her up to it," Isabel said, pointing at me. "You refuse to get her any training, and we all know it's because you're so damn scared for your job that you won't give another warden authority over her. And this green, naive enforcer happens to stumble upon the pooka *and* bond with it? We're all supposed to think it's a coincidence and not your manipulation?"

"Wasting Madison at the mall was your idea, yours and Liam's," Mr. Pitt said. "But if you want to talk about power manipulations, we could start with your and Liam's attempt to maneuver me out of my job through this butterscotch snickerdoodle 'allocation of enforcer resources' that deprived me of *my* enforcer."

The pooka shifted restlessly, eyes fully open after Mr. Pitt's increasingly booming argument. I patted his trunk, pleased to have my boss's impressive lung power used in my defense, yet unable to verbally reassure the pooka without ruining Mr. Pitt's moment.

"Brad's right," Margaret said, gaze shifting from the arguing wardens to the pooka and back. "It wasn't his decision to place Madison in the mall. Isabel, you didn't have to report the pooka, but if you had, we could have prevented this."

"There was nothing to prevent. *She* should never have been in the parking garage."

I met Isabel's furious glare and opened my mouth to defend my actions, but Kathleen beat me.

"You just said you know how untrained Madison is. You should never have allowed her to be put anywhere near a creature as powerful as a pooka, even one not yet risen. She didn't even know not to approach it."

"I agree," Liam said. "You don't have a right to back a poaching claim." Kathleen, Margaret, and Mr. Pitt nodded, a signal that apparently ended the discussion. Isabel shoved her hands into her pockets and glared at Liam. Not all was peachy between the wardens; it almost made me smile, until Liam continued. "The extremes of the current situation dictated Madison be stationed at the mall. But linking an untrained enforcer to a powerful pooka may prove more dangerous than any evil we've faced. Leaving that enforcer under the guidance of a weak warden would be gross negligence on all our parts."

"What are you proposing?" Kathleen asked.

I clutched the pooka's trunk. *Crap on toast*. Liam was going to use this to push Mr. Pitt out of his region. I waited for Mr. Pitt to protest, but my warden merely watched Liam, arms crossed, familiar vein bulging in his forehead.

"Brad's tiny region is too small to contain the effects of a pooka this size. Even if it were penned in the very center, we would all still suffer a ripple effect of its influence on our regions. The pooka needs to be moved to the largest available region."

"Yours, of course," Mr. Pitt said.

"Yes. I will place Madison in the center of my region. With my three enforcers around her and the pooka, we can contain its influence and protect Madison at the same time. She is weak, vulnerable. The pooka will use that against her. If we're not careful, and if we don't act quickly, the pooka will overrun her."

Overrun me? The only person here trying to use any weakness or vulnerability against me was Liam, yet no one protested. Sheila looked away when I met her gaze, but not before I saw her undisguised hate. For me? For the pooka? Isabel ran hungry eyes over the pooka, but she was nodding to Liam's words. Kathleen looked contemplative and Margaret impatient. Did they all think I'd be overrun, too? Or was this simply a convenient excuse to force Mr. Pitt out?

"What a shocking proposal," Mr. Pitt said, his voice heavy with sarcasm. "Almost as if you planned the whole thing."

"Saddling myself with an incompetent enforcer and the most dangerous creature we've encountered in the last decade? Yes, that was my plan all along," Liam said, matching Mr. Pitt's tone. "*I'm* not clinging to my job, throwing my clueless enforcer into situations far outstripping her abilities in the desperate hope it'll keep me employed another month or two. Of course, you've always been careless with your enforcers."

Mr. Pitt's fists tightened and he stepped toward Liam. "I'm *never* careless with anyone's life."

"Right. Unless you need to look important. Having a pooka in your region would sure look good to the Triumvirate."

"Which never occurred to you when you decided to steal Madison," Mr. Pitt said.

Liam threw up his hands. "Listen to yourself, Brad. *I* don't need to look good to the Triumvirate. I've got three enforcers and three wardens training and working under me. My region is four times the size of yours. I can absorb a pooka into my region, and you'd never know. You can't even keep ahead of the *vervet* in your region. For once in your life, think of the safety of your enforcer, Brad. Madison will stay in my region—"

"No."

I think they'd forgotten about me, because the wardens all looked surprised at my protest. I released the pooka's trunk, and he let me go, shifting restlessly, with the *lux lucis* and *atrum* beneath his woolly coat swirling in agitated whirls. I understood the feeling. My hands shook and my heart beat too fast.

"I'm not moving, and neither is the pooka."

"Fresh off an imprint, you're not thinking clearly, Madison," Liam said. "Let us decide—"

"No." I didn't have to raise my voice to cut him off; my tone did it for me. If the imprint had any impact on my thinking, it was that it had cleared away my confusion. It was obvious that of all the people at this meeting, only Mr. Pitt had my best interest at heart. Liam was wrong: Mr. Pitt had never endangered me. Every single time I'd gotten in trouble, my impulsiveness was to blame. If anything, Mr. Pitt coddled me too much. Whatever secret lurked in Mr. Pitt's past, that's where it remained. He was a dedicated warden who'd taken a chance on me. I wouldn't repay him by jumping to work under a more powerful warden.

"We've played along, followed your advice," I said. "I gave up my region and worked in Isabel's, just as you wanted. And look where that got us." I started to pat the pooka's trunk, but *atrum* coated the mammoth's face, so I turned the move into a gesture. "If your enforcers are good enough to contain the pooka's influence if I was inside your territory, I'm sure they're more than capable of dealing with the same influence on the fringe of their regions."

The pooka curled his trunk to his forehead and bugled. I wanted to clamp my hands over my ears, but it would ruin my stare-down with Liam. The pooka swung his tusks back and forth over my head, feet stomping restlessly. The council shifted but only Sheila backed up a step before catching herself.

I crossed my arms, knowing how imposing the pooka looked behind me. I didn't understand how, but the pooka gave me power, and Liam wasn't going to take it from me.

"If you're all done yelling, let's get back on track," Margaret drawled. "An enforcer imprinting a pooka is not grounds for transfer without the enforcer's consent, and it never has been. If you have a problem with the arrangement, take it up with an inspector."

"As always, it's good to have your sound mind in attendance," Mr. Pitt said. Then he turned a bland expression to Liam. "Shall we continue?"

Liam's sharp smile chilled me. "I'm sure my next meeting with the Director of Inquisitions will be informative."

"I know the rules and so does the head of the inspectors. I've done nothing wrong, and neither has my enforcer," Mr. Pitt said with a shrug, all earlier anger hidden behind a new calm. I tried to absorb some of his confidence. Burrowing my chilled hands into my coat pockets, I surveyed the others. Sheila looked as if she'd happily decapitate Mr. Pitt and me. Isabel looked frustrated; she hadn't expected her accusations of me poaching the pooka to be so quickly dismissed. Summer appeared wary, Rafi unreadable. I couldn't get a read on Kathleen and Margaret, either.

I'd hoped to see a friendly smile or encouraging gesture from Niko, but he studied me with as much wariness as Summer, if not more. I'd convinced myself he was on Mr. Pitt's side, but my doubts resurfaced. I shrugged them aside. Niko had told me to make up my own mind, and I had.

When Liam addressed me, I snapped back to attention.

"Madison Fox, of sound mind and pure soul, do you accept the full responsibility of the pooka, including resolving all disturbances caused by it? Are you committed to molding the pooka into a creature of *lux lucis* and overseeing its growth and progress until such time the imprint is no longer valid?"

I stilled, eyes wide. Liam's words carried the formal weight of ceremony, and I realized the rest of this council had been political preamble. This was the purpose, to formally bind me to the pooka in the eyes of my peers and the CIA.

Did he say I was responsible for turning the pooka into a creature of pure *lux lucis*? I twisted to take in the massive frame of the pooka. I couldn't just shove *lux lucis* into the pooka and call it a day. A month of feeding the pooka *lux lucis* wouldn't cleanse his soul.

What if I said no? What would they do to me? To the pooka? I wouldn't let them harm him; my conscience wouldn't allow it. At least I was pretty sure that was my own impulse. I couldn't distinguish my normal emotions from those influenced by the pooka. I hadn't forgotten the overwhelming rage that had made me ambivalent to Jacob's injuries, including those I inflicted on him. But even if I weren't emotionally attached to the pooka, I couldn't let a creature this powerful roam through my region without doing my best to exterminate his *atrum*.

I swallowed my questions. No answer would change my mind. I'd figure out the details of this arrangement later.

With false confidence, I said, "I accept the responsibility of my pooka."

Liam pivoted on a heel to Mr. Pitt. "Brad Pitt, of sound mind and pure soul, do you accept full responsibility for Madison Fox and agree to report any maleficent influence the pooka exerts over her?"

"*If* the pooka controls her, yes."

Liam's lips tightened. "Do you agree to engage in all known precautionary procedures and agree to the appropriate oversight?"

"As warranted and as necessary, yes. Madison will be safe with me."

Liam wasn't the only warden displeased with Mr. Pitt's qualifiers, but no one objected.

"Then we need to discuss the relocation of Madison."

"What?" I thought we'd settled this.

Liam turned to me. "You cannot live in my region with a pooka. You must move. If you're centralized in Brad's region, we'll all suffer your foolishness less."

"But I live on the border," I protested. Technically, my apartment sat on the upper fringe of Summer's region, but so close to the border it hadn't mattered. Until now.

"Which means the pooka will be in my territory as much as yours."

"Only while I sleep." I still had no clue how I was supposed to control, let alone hide, a mammoth *anywhere*, but I decided to stick to the point at hand. I loved my apartment. I wasn't letting it go without a fight. Especially not on Liam's say-so.

"The pooka's tether will stretch, and I doubt your control will improve. He'll be roaming through Summer's region, causing her trouble she didn't sign up for."

I glanced at Summer, expecting her to protest on my behalf. She didn't meet my gaze. I gritted my teeth. Obviously our tentative friendship didn't hold weight against her boss.

"Technically, our region should now include the pooka's hatching grounds," Mr. Pitt said, drawing everyone's attention.

"You can't be serious," Isabel said.

"The pooka will feel an affinity to its birth location," Mr. Pitt continued. "It will return there whether it is within our region or not. We are within our legal rights to claim a league around the birth grounds."

No one moved. A league was at least three miles long, right? If Mr. Pitt was right, by imprinting the pooka, I could take almost a fourth of Jacob's region—the good fourth, the one with all the people and activity. I was pretty sure a league would stretch into Margaret's region and possibly to the upper corner of Liam's, too. It also overlapped with some of our region, but in one swoop, we could expand our region by nearly a third its current size.

"You can't manage what you have now," Liam said.

Mr. Pitt shrugged. "So you say."

Isabel looked like she wanted to hit something, or someone. Liam folded his arms and glared at Mr. Pitt.

"Now look here," Margaret said. "You can't just—"

"I can," Mr. Pitt interrupted.

Margaret closed her mouth into a thin line. Kathleen shook her head, disapproving but not saying anything.

This was going to turn into a lynching. If any of these wardens had been on Mr. Pitt's side, they were rethinking their loyalties. Plus, something more heinous occurred to me: If we took control of the hatching grounds, I'd be responsible for the mall, too. A series of future holiday seasons unfurled before me, each filled with endless rounds of citos and shopping madness.

Praying Mr. Pitt would understand, I spoke up. "Or you can give us my apartment." We had leverage, and I pushed. Mr. Pitt wasn't the only ruthless person in this region. "Of course, to prevent future problems for Summer, Rafi, and you, Liam, we should take over a little extra room to give the pooka space. Say from—"

"Twin Oaks," Mr. Pitt said. "Twin Oaks to Sunrise to Old Auburn to East Roseville Parkway to Barton. The freeway to the west, the lake to the east, as before."

The area Mr. Pitt defined spread our region over a mile deeper along our entire southern border. It was a smaller swath of land than the league around the mall's parking garage, but it meant we overtook only one warden's region—the one warden who already hated Mr. Pitt. It seemed like a good compromise to me.

Liam's jaw bunched and relaxed.

"I approve of that compromise," Margaret said, her tone dry.

"Of course you do," Liam spat.

"I approve as well," Kathleen said. Liam ground his teeth. Our proposal would increase the acreage of the border we shared with Kathleen. If anyone was going to protest, it would have been her.

"I approve," Isabel said.

They backed Liam into a corner for Mr. Pitt and me, and for a moment, the wardens were united with Mr. Pitt against Liam. It felt pretty good.

Liam spit out his words. "I approve."

"You can't," Sheila said, only to be shushed by her boss. The woman's pixie face tightened with embarrassment, but she didn't bother to disguise her hate when she glared at Mr. Pitt.

My boss stepped forward and Liam matched him. The two men clasped forearms. Even in Primordium, I could tell Liam's fingers bit into Mr. Pitt. *Lux lucis* flared from Liam to Mr. Pitt, and then they parted. From a few feet apart, their souls rotated to flare around their middles. I rubbed my stomach. The move looked nauseating and uncomfortable, but Mr. Pitt's expression remained neutral. The edges of their puzzle-piece souls connected and *lux lucis* flared along the connecting border. Mr. Pitt's soul brightened and popped, reshaping its southern line to follow the new roads delineating my region from Summer's. Liam's soul contracted, and he flinched.

"Witnessed," Kathleen said, and everyone in the circle echoed her.

I got to keep my apartment and my job, and my region was larger. Three wins for team Pitt-Fox. Liam should have had steam escaping his ears. I was surprised I couldn't hear Isabel's teeth squeak with how hard she clenched them. Kathleen frowned at the pooka, and I wondered if she regretted the council's decisions. For my part, I hoped we'd done the right thing.

"Council closed," Liam snarled. Isabel jerked like he'd jabbed her. The slender *lux lucis* strands connecting the wardens snapped apart.

No one spoke as they departed. Summer gave me a cold glance before driving away. My heart constricted. I'd been so focused on Liam, I'd forgotten my new territory had carved into Summer's region, too. My play for a larger region had ruined our budding friendship.

A caravan of cars departed, leaving the parking lot empty of all but Niko, Mr. Pitt, myself, and a mammoth-shaped pooka.

The pooka wrapped his trunk around my arm, holding only *lux lucis* against me. He'd calmed with me and now looked sleepy again.

Finding a bed sounded spectacular, but first I had to figure out what I was supposed to do with a mammoth.

"We should be close," Niko said. He glanced at his watch. "Its control has become more defined, and I think it's tiring."

Mr. Pitt studied the pooka and nodded.

"If Isabel could have waited, this would have gone smoother," Niko said.

Mr. Pitt nodded again.

"You probably wouldn't have gotten any of Liam's region, though."

Mr. Pitt's nod was accompanied by a self-satisfied smile.

"You're not upset?" I asked.

"It wasn't a bad compromise." My boss shrugged. He was playing it cool, but he kept having to rein in his grin. Beside him, Niko snorted and shook his head.

"So how am I—"

The pooka released my arm and shuffled backward, tusks swaying above me. I ducked and stepped out of range.

"What are you doing?" My question ended with a squeak.

The pooka's energy contracted, all his wild *lux lucis* and *atrum* condensing. It pulled away from the mammoth's skin, dwindling beneath the surface only to reappear in stutters. The mammoth's long tusks retracted. I blinked and rubbed my eyes. It wasn't my imagination: The pooka was shrinking.

In halting increments, the mammoth reduced to the size of an elephant, then a hippo. His shoulders narrowed, his leg shortened. The woolly fur disappeared. In moments, he was eye to eye with me, then shorter. His torso thinned and his trunk retracted into a muzzle. *Atrum* and *lux lucis* pushed within him like pudding, thick and slow.

My knees wobbled and I dipped, then gave up and landed on my butt on the cold pavement. Fumes of old oil puddles caught at the back of my throat. My injured ankle protested, and I flopped it out straight, not looking away from the pooka.

A creature who could change shape and size—that was magic, plain and simple.

I pushed loose strands of hair out of my face with shaking hands and tried out a little reasoning. I'd killed a demon. I'd seen wardens with souls shaped like their regions, not like their bodies. I carried around a sentient book. I'd met prajurit. After all that, what's a little shape-shifting?

Impossible, of course, but with a pooka around, I had a feeling I needed to strike that word from my vocabulary.

Where moments before had stood the only living mammoth now shivered a Great Dane. He gave himself a vigorous shake, then wagged his tail, turning to watch the movement. The wound on his hip had healed during his transformation, but with his liquid, mixed soul, there was no mistaking he was still the pooka.

"I take it no one told you it could change shapes?"

I tore my gaze from the dog and looked up into Niko's laughing eyes.

"That failed to be mentioned." *Thanks, Val.* I blinked to normal sight. A cone of light from a lot lamp haloed the pooka, setting his glossy black coat shimmering. Golden eyes blinked at me; then the dog trotted to me. From where I sat, he still towered over me. He sniffed my shoes, crotch, and hands, then licked my face from chin to part.

"Ew! No, bad pooka." I used my jacket's sleeve to wipe the slime off. The pooka sat on my lap with a doggy smile and a cloud of horrid breath. One hundred plus pounds ground my thighs into the gritty pavement. "Seriously, this isn't working for me. I need to get up."

The pooka furrowed his brow in a pitiful expression, then stood. I reached for the top of his head and patted him—after checking his coat in Primordium. The pooka's tongue lolled out, and his eyes half closed. When I glanced down at my legs, I swallowed a few choice cuss words: *Atrum* coated my thighs from my knees to my hips where the pooka had sat. Summoning *lux lucis*, I cleaned my soul, my control sluggish. The pooka watched me with curious eyes when I finished. I shook my finger in his face. "No *atrum* on me. Ever." His tail drooped and his whole body slumped. I gave him another pat and softened my tone. "*Lux lucis* only from now on, please."

Niko stepped in front of me and gave me a hand up, steadying me as I readjusted to my hurt ankle. I used the opportunity to get control of my expression. It was easy to drop my guard around the pooka, but I couldn't forget how dangerous he really was.

"His tether is short right now," Mr. Pitt said. He hadn't moved and didn't look inclined to get any closer to me or the pooka. "For now, he won't leave your side, day or night."

"But my apartment is tiny." Up until a minute ago, I'd assumed the pooka would remain outside. "What about his *atrum*?"

"Niko will set you up, but you'll have to learn to exert your will and not allow him to leak *atrum* on your things or you."

"Like metaphysical potty training?" I pictured rubbing the pooka's nose in a puddle of *atrum* and shook my head at the absurdity.

"Something like that. This isn't going to be easy. This is a strong pooka, and you're new. The sooner you gain control of it, the better. For now, get some sleep. I'll see you this afternoon." Mr. Pitt took a few steps toward the offices before turning back. "And, Madison. You did really well tonight."

He strode into the lobby without looking back. The pooka sat and leaned a shoulder of pure *lux lucis* against my hip. His eyes drifted closed on a big yawn. My jaw unhinged, and my yawn squeezed out a few tears. I staggered when the pooka relaxed against me.

"Let's get you both home before you fall over," Niko said, a laugh in his voice.

It took a vigorous rubbing of the pooka's shoulder to rouse him. "Come on, sleepy head. Let's go home."

He plodded beside me to Niko's car. Niko jogged ahead and laid a blanket across his backseat. I got the pooka settled on it and tucked his tail tight to his body before shutting the door. The Great Dane stretched across the BMW's entire backseat. How was this pony-size dog going to fit in my apartment?

More important, would Mr. Bond ever forgive me?

Niko held the passenger door open for me. I must have looked pretty awful if he thought I couldn't handle the door myself. Unhooking Val from my shoulder, I slid into the car. My shoulder, chest, and hip felt naked without the familiar weight.

I lifted Val to my lips. "Would it have killed you to mention pookas can turn into dogs?" I gave the book a pat that almost qualified as a spank, then set him on my lap. The knife sheath and handle digging into my back would have made the seat uncomfortable if I weren't so tired. I clicked my seat belt into place as Niko settled behind the wheel.

Cool air trickled from the vents against my face, and Niko turned it off. We took the back exit out of the lot, heading into the glow of the sunrise.

"Everyone's rushed you through this, but I want you to understand the dangers of the pooka," Niko said.

I covered a yawn with both hands and tried to look attentive.

"They're rare, not well understood, and dangerous because they're magical creatures."

"Aren't we all?" At Niko's sharp look, I realized the comment had sounded flippant. "I mean, everyone in the CIA. We can do things other people can't."

He turned back to the road. "What we do is not magic, no more than people with twenty-twenty vision have magic. We're using a sense or function we were born with. Magical creatures, like the pooka, have a different set of rules."

"Like changing shapes."

"Like that. Pookas are one of the strongest unaligned magical creatures, which makes them dangerous on their own. They're also attractive to those who sense them, and especially to those who would use them. Tonight gave you a condensed glimpse of what your life is going to be like while looking after the pooka."

"I'm going to be fending off human-size imps and vervet every day?" I turned to face Niko fully, hoping he was joking.

"Not necessarily. But just by living, by being, the pooka will continue to draw trouble. Other creatures can't resist it."

"Good and bad," I clarified.

"We're not worried about the good creatures. It's going to attract a lot of evil, and you're going to have to deal with it all. Which is why it might be better off dead."

I controlled my impulse to slap him. Niko wasn't attacking the pooka, he was just explaining things to me. Not caring for his logic didn't give me the right to assault him.

"Just because the pooka is going to be trouble doesn't mean he should be killed," I said. "If that was how we did things, Mr. Pitt would have killed me my second day on the job."

Niko smiled, but it barely took the edge off my anger.

"Stand down, Madison. I don't want to kill your pooka."

"Then why'd you say that?" I let go of my death grip on my seat belt and leaned back in my seat, taking several deep breaths.

"After the baby boom, there were several trials regarding pooka poaching," Niko said, not answering my question. "More than one enforcer was transferred and confined as a result."

"Like Liam wanted to do."

"The only warden with a potential right to claim you and the pooka as their own was Isabel. If Isabel could have convinced the other wardens you were Brad's pawn, she would have claimed you as her enforcer, and you would have been transferred by the CIA. Your extreme naïveté worked in your favor for once."

"I tried to find out what the massive energy was, but—" But Mr. Pitt hadn't let me. He'd been insistent that I remain ignorant. What had his exact wording been? *The situation is delicate, and your ignorance is our paltry defense.* He'd known since Black Friday that I might imprint the pooka, and he'd intentionally kept me in the dark!

I worked my jaw, hunting for the appropriate emotional response. Anger didn't surface. Neither did surprise—I'd known Mr. Pitt had been hiding *something* from me these last few days. I tried on indignation, but that didn't work, either. Mr. Pitt had recognized the pooka for what it was, and just as quickly, he'd seen the possible implications. If he'd told me too much information, it might have looked like I'd known about the pooka all along, and Isabel surely would have won her poaching claim.

"I wouldn't have gotten a say about the transfer?" I asked.

"No."

"That's a stupid rule." Especially since I didn't want to work under Isabel, and I definitely didn't want to be *forced* to work anywhere. "I didn't ask to be imprinted. I didn't try, and I wouldn't even know how you would go about forcing—enticing?—a pooka to imprint on you."

"I know. Every warden at that meeting could tell, too."

"What's the big deal who he imprinted on? I mean, I wouldn't give up the pooka now if I had a choice"—words I realized were true only as I spoke them—"but he's going to make my life harder. Who would volunteer for that?"

"Those who want to advance faster. Linked to a pooka, you're going to be tested twice as much as any other enforcer in the region. You'll either get stronger faster or you'll fail."

"Great. As long as I get a nap first."

"Pay attention, Madison. The stronger a warden's enforcers, the stronger the warden, so having an enforcer linked to a pooka is a boon to a warden. If the decision to put you at the mall had been Brad's—or if he'd been suspected of talking you into trying to imprint the pooka—

he'd already be removed from his position. The CIA doesn't stand for gross power grabs, especially through the intentional endangerment of enforcers."

"I get it. This is serious. And dangerous." I covered another yawn behind my hands.

"You need to be vigilant. The pooka can shape you as much as you change it. More than one enforcer got too close to their pooka and lost perspective."

What a cheerful thought. How was I supposed to always be on my guard, especially while I lived with the pooka? It sounded exhausting on a normal day, overwhelming now.

The car rocked to a stop and I glanced up, surprised to see we were in front of Safeway. I checked the backseat. The pooka breathed in soft snores, his eyes closed tight. It was hard not be jealous.

"How long will the pooka and I be linked?"

"I don't know."

"Ballpark it for me."

Niko hesitated. "Months to years. Depends on how fast the pooka learns."

I closed my eyes and held my breath until the urge to panic subsided.

"It'll be dependent on you for now," Niko said. I kept my eyes closed, listening to the deep timber of his voice more than the words. "We'll shut it in your bathroom and set up protection over the doorway tonight. Once you have better control, this won't be as important."

I nodded to show I heard.

"I'm going to get some food. It hasn't eaten since birth. I'm sure it's hungry."

I nodded again, making no effort to undo my belt. If I went into the store with Niko, the pooka would come, too, and we'd all be kicked out.

How was I going to function tethered to a pooka?

Niko opened the door, and cold air swirled in. The car rocked, and when the door didn't shut behind him, I opened my eyes. Niko leaned back into the car.

"You negotiated your region's expansion like a pro. Congratulations."

"Thanks. But honestly, a larger region wasn't my goal."

"It's been Brad's goal every day since he got here."

Niko shut his door before I could respond. It was just as well.

Explaining that my motivation had been rooted in my desire not to alienate every single local warden would have taken too much energy. Especially since I'd also been motivated by a far more selfish reason: I didn't want to move. I loved my apartment, and the thought of hauling my belongings down those stairs was too much to contemplate after today. Dodging responsibility for the mall was the whipped cream on top.

I listened to the muted sounds of people and cars through the windows, closing my eyes against the growing light of day. My hair felt gritty and wild, which summed up how I felt, too. Dirt caked my clothing. My hands stung from bruises and cuts. If I weren't limp with exhaustion, I might have dashed from the car to see if I could escape the pooka and all the unasked-for responsibility the creature entailed. How was I supposed to control a creature with free will?

Maybe we could come to an understanding. If I'd learned anything from Val, it was that respect and friendliness worked far better than being demanding and controlling.

I undid my seat belt and twisted to look at the ebony pooka in normal sight. "Hey, are you awake?" He lifted his massive Great Dane head and opened eerily intelligent yellow eyes. *Here goes nothing.* "Do you have a name?"

The black head bobbed in a distinctive nod.

"Are you going to tell me?"

He barked two connected syllables.

"I don't speak dog. I'll call you Trouble. Is that okay?"

A pink and black spotted tongue lolled out of his mouth, and a string of drool missed the blanket and dripped onto Niko's leather seat. Perfect.

Niko opened the trunk, and I jumped. Through the back window, I watched him load a huge bag of dog food. Huh. I hadn't considered exactly what a pooka would eat. I guess dog food was appropriate.

My apartment complex sprawled behind the Safeway center. It wasn't worth putting my seat belt back on for the minute-long drive, but I did so anyway out of habit. Three speed bumps later, Niko pulled down the alleyway of covered parking. I indicated my vacant spot, wondering how I was going to get back to my car tomorrow with a Great Dane. Niko started to park, then stopped when Sam leapt up from where he'd perched on my concrete tire stop.

I dropped my head in my hands. "Uuuggh."

17

I'll Sleep When I'm Dead

DO YOU KNOW THIS BOY?" Niko asked.

I looked up. Sam backed up to the lawn in front of the parking spot and waved enthusiastically, a broad smile on his freckled face. Niko finished pulling into my spot and turned off the car.

"That's Sam. Local truant. I'm trying to teach him the error of his ways."

Niko arched an eyebrow at me, but Sam opened my door before I could explain.

"Madison, how's it going?"

"It's been a long night," I said. The pooka tried to climb between the seats to get out with me and I motioned him back. "Excuse me, Sam." The neighbor's Impala hugged the line, leaving little space between our cars. I squeezed past Sam. His icy fingers grazed mine, and I took a second look at the boy. How long had he been sitting here in the cold, waiting for me?

Trouble teeter-tottered out the back door, walked to the bumper, and spun back around to push his nose past me and into Sam's crotch.

"Whoa! Dude. Wait for the second date."

"Back up, Trouble." I urged the pooka backward. He ducked his head and watched his feet, and when he cleared the cars, he looked at me with obvious pride. "Yes, yes. Good job backing up."

Niko stood near the trunk, stern optivus aegis expression in place.

"Yo, my man, it's Sam." Sam held out his hand to Niko. Niko gave the boy's hand a firm shake but didn't offer his name. "You guys been out partying?"

"Sure, Sam. What are you doing here?"

"Waiting for my training to begin."

"Training?" Niko asked. Though he looked at me, Sam answered before I could open my mouth.

"Madison's going to train me to do stuff like her."

"Stuff like her? Like what?" Niko asked.

"Yeah, Sam, like what?" I asked him, hoping Niko would play along until I could explain.

"Like help you with your superpowers."

"Which would be?"

Sam shrugged. "Something in costume."

"We met last week over some petty crime," I said for Niko's benefit. "Lately Sam's been shifting more toward grand theft."

"Hey, now! I'm helping teach people to be safer."

"Tell that to him," I said, jerking my head toward Niko. The optivus aegis shifted and somehow grew six inches, transforming from interested to imposing. It was a neat trick and one I needed to master.

"Aw, man, you're not a cop, are you? You kind of look like one, but Madison said she wasn't a cop." Sam took a few steps back. He made it seem casual, but it was clear he was gearing up to bolt. Trouble sniffed his fingertips and barked.

"Nope. Not a cop. Curious why you don't look like you've been committing all those crimes, though."

"Because I've been helping people. I'm not a criminal," Sam said, relaxing to pat Trouble's head.

Niko wasn't looking at Sam. He was staring hard at me, as if waiting for me to answer. It took me a moment, though in all fairness, I had been up almost twenty-four hours.

"I've done a little work with the boy," I said.

"How much 'work'?"

"I don't know. Two times. No, three."

"You haven't done anything with me yet," Sam protested. "But I'm not giving up. I'm ready for my superhero training. I'll do whatever it takes, even if it means camping out here."

"I'm not a superhero," I said. I closed my eyes, then snapped them open when the world swayed. Niko caught my arm and steadied me. I blinked blearily at him.

"Madison, are you, like, okay?"

Niko ignored Sam. All traces of humor were gone when he tipped my head up to force me to meet his gaze. "We're going to have a serious talk as soon as you get some sleep." He turned to Sam. "You are coming with me."

"What? What'd I do?"

"You said you wanted to learn how to be a superhero. I can show you."

"All *right*!"

"What?" I gaped at Niko, unconsciously mimicking Sam. "What did I do?"

"Later. Sam, I have to carry some things up to Madison's. I want you to wait for me here. If you move a step, the deal's off."

"Right-o."

"Didn't anyone ever teach you about stranger danger?" I groused.

"Any dude who's okay with you is okay with me," Sam said. A shaft of sunlight sparked off his curls. The boy danced in place, exaggerating the fact that he never lifted his feet from the ground. "Plus, look at him. He's the shit, right?"

"The total shit," I agreed.

Niko carried a canvas bag and the dog food up the stairs in front of me. Trouble gave Sam's fingers one last lick, then paced at my hip to my apartment, head swinging from side to side to take it all in. The first set of stairs gave him trouble. Coordinating his hind legs with the front took his concentration, but by the second set of stairs, he plodded next to my limping steps without my assistance.

Niko pulled my purse from inside the canvas bag. It was a testament to my fatigue that I hadn't considered how we'd get into my house without my keys. Niko let me in, then stopped on the welcome mat. I explained to Trouble I would be right back for him. The pooka whined when I shut the door in his face; Niko took it with more grace.

Mr. Bond crouched in the hallway, body hair puffed in a ridge on his back. Even inflated, my obese cat looked tiny after hanging out with a mammoth.

"It's okay, panther," I said. "It's just me."

The dark Siamese crept up to my fingers and sniffed, then investigated my dirty sleeves before letting me pet him. I buried my cold fingers in his sleek fur, babying my ankle when I crouched awkwardly to rub my forehead against his. Mr. Bond jerked back, then sniffed my face, my grimy wisps of hair, and my shirt's collar before he deigned to a forehead rub. Outside, Trouble whimpered. Niko was silent, and I wondered what my neighbors thought of me leaving such a gorgeous man on my doorstep. Other than I was a complete idiot.

Mr. Bond caught sight or scent of Val and darted around my knee to reach the book.

"Okay. Let's get you some food." I stood, shifting Val behind me and breaking Mr. Bond's laser focus on him. When I picked up the bowl instead of filling it, Mr. Bond meowed. Grabbing the ceramic food canister, I headed for my bedroom, accompanied by Mr. Bond and his increasingly insistent yowls. I set the bowl and canister next to my desk and scooped fresh food atop the few remaining kibble. Mr. Bond twined through my legs, then buried his face in his food. I slipped out of the bedroom and shut the door behind me.

"Come on in," I said, swinging the door open. Niko picked up his supplies and stepped into my apartment. Trouble roused himself from his sprawl across my welcome mat and plodded into my front room. My apartment shrank to half its normal size, and I didn't know if the blame lay with Niko or the Great Dane.

"What's going to happen to Sam?" I asked.

"We'll talk about it later. Grab bowls for food and water, and we'll get the pooka set up." Niko swung the bathroom door open. "It's going to be a tight fit, but I think it'll work."

I mentally measured the bathroom against the length of the Great Dane and silently agreed. Trouble listed against the kitchen wall while watching me pull two enormous bowls down from my seldom-used baking shelf. The pooka looked like he could nod off any moment.

Niko waited in the hall while I set the bowls next to the tub and filled one with water, the other with food. Trouble perked up at the smell and moseyed to the food bowl. Kibble disappeared in enormous bites, and I added more food to the bowl, then squeezed between the Great Dane and the toilet to get back to the hallway.

Maybe this wouldn't be so bad. The pooka would come and go with me, and he could sleep in the bathroom at night. It wasn't ideal, but we could make it work.

"This is a lichtwand," Niko said, holding up a rod that looked like a fluorescent tube light without a cord. "You will have to recharge it daily."

I blinked to Primordium and surreptitiously checked my soul. It was easy to forget Trouble had the patchwork soul of a pooka when I looked at him in normal sight, and I'd forgotten to be careful about where I touched him. I was clean, and I made a big deal out of thanking the pooka before closing the bathroom door. Positive reinforcement couldn't hurt.

Niko set the lichtwand against the base of the door and flipped an on-off switch. A sheet of *lux lucis* lifted from the lichtwand to coat the entire doorway in light. I reached into it, expecting resistance, but *lux lucis* wrapped around my hand with a soft feathery sensation. The energy connected above my hand, like water flowing around a rock. *Lux lucis* spread an inch to either side of the lichtwand, which was exactly the width of the threshold, and extended a few inches up the frame above the door.

I'd seen Niko use one of these before, but I hadn't had time to ask about it. Nor had I ever expected to need one in my own home.

"A ward won't hold in the amount of *atrum* the pooka might release. This has a better chance."

"How much do these cost?" I braced myself for sticker shock.

"Even a standard-size one like this isn't cheap. For now, keep mine. Hopefully this won't be a long-term solution."

Once the pooka has control, then what? I wanted to ask, but I wasn't sure I was ready to hear the answer. The pooka on a short tether was complicated enough. Picturing the pooka free to roam unsupervised made my stomach contract.

I trailed Niko to my front room and leaned against a wall while he warded my sliding glass door. His movements were fast and efficient, leaving a sparkling barrier between me and any creatures the pooka might attract while I slept. Fear moved sluggishly up my spine at the thought. I redirected my attention to the pull of Niko's jacket across his shoulders and the steady glow of his soul, and I didn't allow a tendril of anxiety to take root.

Niko walked past me down the hall and I followed. Even numb with exhaustion, I wasn't going to miss the sight of Niko in my bedroom. I slipped through the door and breathed a sigh of relief: I hadn't left any underwear lying out.

Mr. Bond supervised Niko's warding from between the optivus aegis's feet, mewing the whole time. Niko gave him a pet when he finished and Mr. Bond used a paw to pull Niko's hand back for a second inspection, then rubbed his face against Niko's warm palm. I wondered if I could get away with the same maneuver.

"You're moving pretty well on that ankle already," Niko said, interrupting my wayward thoughts. "Don't forget to take some anti-inflammatories."

My ankle twinged as if in agreement.

Niko warded my front door, told me to call him if I needed him, then let himself out. I locked up after him and put my back to the door. The temptation to slide to the floor and sleep right there almost overpowered me, but I pushed back into motion.

After taking Val out of his strap and wiping most of the grime off his cover, I stored him in my filing cabinet. Then I devoured a banana and two ibuprofen and stripped, putting my filthy clothes into the washing machine. I had to give Trouble a push to get into the bathroom. The Great Dane sprawled from the doorway to the tub, making a bed of my bathmats. I stepped between his feet and over his head into the shower. He woke when I turned off the shower and watched me with sleepy eyes while I dried off.

"I'll be just across the hall and I'll come get you when I wake up," I said. His eyes tracked me to the door; then he flopped back onto his side. I closed the bathroom door and activated the lichtwand. Mr. Bond darted to the wall of light and batted his paws across the surface, sniffing along the top, with his face submerged in *lux lucis*. When he finished his investigation, he tore around the apartment to his scratching post.

I towel-dried my hair and crawled under the covers. Sleep dragged me under before Mr. Bond settled on my feet.

I woke to a shaft of pain cleaving my skull. Clutching my scalp, I cracked an eye. Sunlight fractured the pain into jagged shards. I moaned and burrowed under the covers.

The front door clattered shut, and I bolted upright. Pain turned my breath to a strangled gasp. Footsteps moved through my front room, then back to the kitchen. Muted thumps registered as cupboards opening and closing.

Only three people had keys to my house: Bridget and my parents. I glanced at the clock. At two in the afternoon, Bridget was still at work. My parents had no reason to stop by, and if they had, they wouldn't barge in. They'd call. Furthermore, Mr. Bond was fond of all of them and would have darted out of the bedroom to greet them.

Instead, my overweight cat perched on the end of my bed, body stiff with tension. When I moved, he crouched, primed to hide under the bed skirt. Sadly, he was too large to fit under the bed. So was I.

I clawed the covers to my chin and tried to think over the pounding in my brain. A stranger had broken into my house. I'd seen enough news stories to know that when burglars discovered people at home, it never ended well. My only real weapon, the knife I'd purchased for my job, wasn't going to help me. It lay atop the washing machine, where I'd left it after stripping last night—which was exactly where I'd left my cell, too. With my home phone in the front room cradle, my chances of calling 911 dwindled to nil.

I swallowed a whimper. As much as I yearned to pull the covers over my head and pretend they'd keep me safe, I had to get up.

Sucking in shallow, quiet breaths, I slid the covers back and eased to the floor. Cold air pebbled my naked skin from my breasts to my toes. I found nightgowns strangulating and pajamas constricting, but I'd never wished harder for the protective illusion of clothing. I wasted precious seconds pulling on dirty sweatpants and a T-shirt from the hamper.

Metal screeched, and I collapsed to my hands and knees next to my bed before I recognized the sound of the accordion door leading to the cramped laundry closet. I grabbed a tuft of hair and squeezed my scalp. My head was telling me I'd polished off a bottle of tequila last night, but I hadn't had a drop of liquor.

The possibility of a connection between the stranger rooting through my apartment and the pain made me blink to Primordium. I expected to find a swarm of vervet gnawing on my scalp. Maybe a demon drilling into my head.

The room glowed with peaceful energy. Across the hall, the lichtwand radiated *lux lucis* against the closed bathroom door. Behind me, Niko's strong ward haloed the window, and my forest of plants shone strong and untainted, as did Mr. Bond and my own soul.

My brain bounced adrenaline-fast through possible explanations for the intruder and my headache. *Lux lucis* concentrate. Gavin said I would feel the effects today. What an understatement!

Of course, if I could have woken without my heart beating like a hummingbird's, maybe it wouldn't have been so bad.

The sounds from the front of the apartment quieted. That couldn't be a good sign. So far, the intruder hadn't made a move toward the bedroom, but my luck wouldn't hold. I had two options, escape or hide. My eyes darted around the room. My closet was too shallow and packed to disguise me. My desk was too small to crawl under. My wicker laundry basket creaked when I tossed in a sock; there was no way to hide beneath my smelly clothes without alerting the burglar. Which left escape.

My legs trembled, but I forced myself to a crouch. If I went down the hall, not only would the squeaky floor give me away, but I would also have nowhere to hide. I could chance it, grab the phone, and run for the front door. If I was fast enough, the police would arrive before the intruder caught me.

I didn't have a lot of faith in that plan.

The only other option was the window. My apartment's tiny porch stretched from the sliding glass door in the front room to the bedroom's window. If I could sneak outside, I could hide in the corner, out of sight, until the stranger investigated the bedroom. Then I could dart through the sliding glass door and out the front before he could catch me. Like the first plan, this meant abandoning both Mr. Bond and Trouble until I could return with the cops. I didn't like it, but I'd like it less if I were dead. So would they, I thought.

If there had been a third option, I would have taken it. Moving on quaking tiptoes, I eased the sliding window up. The metal screen frame creaked when I popped it free. I froze, but the footsteps I expected didn't manifest. Chilly December air spilled over the windowsill, slithering across my bare feet. Mr. Bond slunk across the bed, puddled to the floor on silent paws, and crouched next to me. Before I slid through the window, I grabbed a heavy brass bookend.

The window ledge sat a foot and a half off the floor, making my escape easy. I hugged the short wall, crouching with hands, knees, and feet on the ice-cold balcony concrete. Mr. Bond hopped out after me, his tail lifting to a happy wag. He explored the porch almost daily, but never through the bedroom window. To him this had turned into a new adventure. At least outside he was less likely to be noticed by the intruder.

A shiver made my teeth chatter. Why had I chosen the third floor? From the second floor, I could have survived the fall. From this height, I'd break my legs on landing, or my spine. Either way, I wouldn't be escaping.

What if I was making a big deal of nothing? What if the person in my apartment was someone I knew? It could be Niko, come by to check on me. It wasn't hard to picture him picking my lock or making a spare key. Or Sam. He knew how to pick locks, and he was obsessed with becoming a superhero. Niko supposedly had taken him away this morning, but the boy was tenacious.

Rough concrete bit into the tender flesh of my bruised palms as I inched forward. My heart knocking against my ribs, I peeked through the sliding glass door.

A man stood in the center of my living room wearing a floral pleated skirt and a WWF T-shirt printed with the image of the Earth and the words "Hotter Than I Should Be." He stuffed a handful of salt and pepper potato chips into his mouth and examined the picture collage above my TV. His feet were bare and muddy.

His soul swirled with liquid *atrum* and *lux lucis*.

18

QUESTION EVERYTHING

UMBFOUNDED, I STARED AT THE human-shaped pooka.

A human-shaped pooka. The lichtwand still coated the doorway of the bathroom.

Oh precious lux lucis *gods, please let there not be two of them!*

The man turned. When he spotted me, he waved vigorously, exactly as Sam had when we'd pulled up last night. Potato chip crumbs scattered across the carpet. He strode to the sliding glass door and pulled it open.

I pushed to my feet and raised the brass statue. The man-pooka paused, then burst out laughing. "I scared you!" he exclaimed between breaths. He mimed round circles around his eyes. "Your eyes!"

Lowering the statue, I blinked to normal sight. The pooka was exactly my height, slender, with thick black hair and the same golden eyes of the Great Dane. On the dog, the color had looked natural. On a human, it was shocking.

"Trouble?" My voice shook.

"Who else?"

The brass statue fell from numb fingers. My knees wobbled, and I braced a hand on the sliding glass door. Trouble twisted under my scrutiny. The red and black skirt flared; the bright pink shirt pulled tight across his shoulders.

"Are those my clothes?" Because *that* was important.

"Yep."

Mr. Bond hissed from behind a potted dwarf lemon tree. Trouble regarded my cat and Mr. Bond deflated, then trotted to him, tail raised, and threw his body against the pooka. I backed up a step. Had Trouble just mind-jacked my cat?

I blinked back to Primordium and realized the answer was simpler if no less frightening. Trouble had rearranged his soul so a fine layer of *lux lucis* camouflaged all his *atrum*. To the untrained eye—and to my cat—his soul looked as clean as an enforcer's. The pooka had gained a lot of control in the few hours I'd slept. What else had he learned?

A hard shiver jarred my body, setting off a cascade of pain through my brain.

"Inside," I said. Trouble backed up and Mr. Bond followed. I swiped the bottom of my dirty feet clean on the threshold, then stepped onto the warm cushion of my carpet. Keeping a wary eye on the pooka, I slid the door closed behind me. Whatever endorphins I'd experienced when we imprinted were gone. For the first time, I doubted the wisdom of remaining linked to the creature. It was too late to back out, but damn; what had I gotten myself into? The pooka was far more powerful and magical than I'd comprehended.

I took a deep breath to settle my nerves—and gagged.

"Dear God, what is that smell?"

Trouble looked at the ceiling.

"Can't you smell that?"

Trouble shrugged slender shoulders. I stalked across the front room into the kitchen, ignoring the muddy footprints strewn from the laminate foyer across the carpeted apartment. A tart, deathly odor coiled in the back of my throat. Grabbing my shirt, I pulled it over my nose. I jerked open the fridge. Nothing. I peeked in the trash bin. It smelled like old pizza and moldy cardboard—almost refreshing. Then I remembered the screech of the laundry closet. Normally I kept the door cracked wide enough for Mr. Bond, since his litter box was inside. Now the slatted accordion door was shut tight.

Holding my hand over my cloth-covered nose, I eased the door open.

Mounded in the center of Mr. Bond's litter box, completely exposed, was the largest dog poop I'd ever seen. I spun to face the pooka.

Trouble blinked wide eyes and pointed at Mr. Bond.

The cat peeked around the kitchen corner, eyes squinted against the stench. I opened my mouth, thought better of it, and settled on a scowl for the pooka. Grabbing the litter box, I stuffed my feet into shoes, wincing at the twinge in my injured ankle.

"Shut the door after me and don't touch anything," I said.

Pain pinched my ankle with each step as I raced down the stairs, arms straining and eyes watering, but the mild pain didn't slow me. I shoved the entire litter box into the Dumpster, darted back up the walkway, and took a deep breath. Noxious fumes hung in the air, or in my nose, but I no longer felt like dry heaving.

Back upstairs, I threw open the sliding glass door despite the chilly winter air. Pulling a wrapping paper bin from beneath my bed, I dumped the contents into a pile, then set up the plastic bottom in the laundry room and filled it with fresh litter. Mr. Bond sniffed around the new box and the washer, the only one of us immune to the stench.

The pooka stared at me with wide gold eyes and flinched when I stomped to the kitchen sink. Standing in the middle of my front room, shoulders hunched in my pink shirt, bare toes curled into the carpet, and a half-empty potato chip bag dangling from one hand, the pooka looked lost and afraid. I deflated. The last jittery tremors of fear abated. The pooka was a powerful mystery, but he wasn't all bad. It was my responsibility to make sure he became less evil every day, and I couldn't do that with him scared of me.

I dried my hands and beckoned the pooka closer. He took a few steps, and the cotton skirt swishing around his hairy legs made me fight back a smile.

"You frightened me, and I didn't find it funny. Sorry for getting upset."

"Should I change to a dog?"

"No. I like getting to talk to you. I just wish—" My brain stuttered over a memory. I flushed. "You watched me shower this morning!"

"No, I didn't."

"Don't argue semantics. You saw me naked." I'd stepped *right* over the pooka. He hadn't just seen me naked; he'd seen parts of me last viewed by my gynecologist.

"You've seen me naked," he said, visibly confused.

I decided against explaining my embarrassed indignation. "Why didn't you pick this form last night? It would have made everything a lot simpler."

"I didn't have these." The pooka plucked at the hem of the skirt, shuffled his hips, then gave a leg a shake. I flashed on the image of his mammoth testicles, then forced the picture from my mind. Everything had been proportional when he'd changed to the Great Dane. I was *not* going to picture what was hidden under the floral print.

"Okay. You have a point." If he had turned into a naked man in the Illumination Studios parking lot, it might have complicated things. "Why become human now?"

"This place is stifling. Too much *lux lucis*. I wanted to go out."

I'd been avoiding thinking about the pooka roaming around while I slept. I dreaded what he might have done, though everything had looked normal when I'd dashed down to the Dumpster. "You could go outside as a Great Dane. You'd probably have blended in better." Barefoot, in women's clothes—yeah, a dog off a leash would have been better.

"I couldn't work the handles."

I closed my mouth, defeated by logic. The pooka twisted in place, still unsure of me. I sighed. "Do you know about germs?"

I explained the importance of hand washing and supervised while he played with the soap and water for twice as long as necessary. Then I explained the purpose of a toilet. Flushing fascinated the pooka, so I also explained California's drought and the importance of water conservation. He followed along, proving he was far more intelligent than a day-old creature had a right to be.

"I can't keep calling you Trouble. What's your real name?"

"Jamie." The pooka planted his hands on his hips as he said his name, clearly proud. He looked like a cross-dressing superhero. He deflated when I didn't immediately respond, but *Jamie*? I'd been expecting a much more exotic name, maybe one with some *x*'s and *z*'s in it. After all, he was an entirely different species.

"That's a nice name. I like Jamie," I finally said, and his chest visibly inflated again at my moderate praise. He was cute, like a teenage boy before testosterone kicked in, both in looks and confidence, and I suppressed the desire to tousle his thick hair. I couldn't treat him like a child—he was too sharp for that, and too dangerous—but the last of my trepidation disappeared. This wasn't imprint pheromones or post-terror euphoria. It was simply the pooka's natural charm working on me.

Niko's warning about getting too close to the pooka and letting him influence me rang in my ears. Jamie didn't look or act dangerous, which was the real hazard. It would be easy to forget he might not have my best interest at heart.

I made us both peanut butter and jelly roll-ups on tortillas because the bread was moldy, and I gulped down two glasses of water and ibuprofen. Jamie thought the cobbled-together meal was divine, proving he'd imprinted on the right enforcer. Mr. Bond alternated between hissing at Jamie and wanting to curl up in his lap, depending on Jamie's soul. I'd suspected Mr. Bond possessed sensitivity to *lux lucis* from the way he'd responded to Niko and Val, but this proved it. When Jamie's soul fluctuated to show more *atrum*, Mr. Bond acted as if he were the enemy; when Jamie shone with *lux lucis*, Mr. Bond wanted to be best buds. I didn't know what it said about Mr. Bond that he was so easily swayed and didn't make the connection that, no matter what his outward metaphysical appearance, Jamie wasn't changing. Maybe my cat wasn't equipped to rationalize a creature as powerful and rare as a pooka.

I ate my roll-up slowly, savoring the novelty of not being at the mall. With Jacob recovering from Jamie's attack and me on pooka watch, I wondered who'd been stuck with the citos. The emotion-enhancing spiders would still be active even without Jamie's presence, though they'd be back to manageable sizes and numbers . . . hopefully. Maybe Claire had been given the task. Watching Jamie lick jelly from his fingers and forearm, I grinned. Whoever was responsible for taking care of the Galleria citos, it wasn't me.

After I cleaned up and moved Mr. Bond's food bowl back to its usual location, filling it under his supervision, I couldn't put off the rest of the day any longer. As much as I wanted to climb back under the covers, I was awake, Jamie was awake, and untold evil brewed in my region. I didn't think Liam would be willing to continue sending Summer or Rafi to cover my region, either. Taking some of his region and refusing to become his enforcer hadn't won me any favors with the man. Good thing that hadn't been my goal.

I showed Jamie a game on my cell phone, then used my landline to dial Mr. Pitt.

"The pooka has a human form," I said without preamble.

"Yep."

"Yep?" That was the best Mr. Pitt could muster for my shocking news? Let him wake up with a stranger in his home and see if he responded with equal aplomb.

"The last two hundred years of pookas have had human form. I hoped it would be the same."

"Anyone think that might be worth mentioning to me?" My headache pulsed, and I lowered my voice. "Anything else I should know?"

"Come to the office. Your car is in your spot. The key is under your welcome mat. Is the pooka still in human form? I want to meet it."

"Him. You want to meet him. Jamie. Yes, he's in human form."

"Good." Mr. Pitt hung up.

I stalked to my filing cabinet and pulled out Val. "What's your excuse?"

Good afternoon.

"You gave me a history lesson. You told me about pookas on other continents. But you didn't mention Jamie would have different forms?"

I did, too.

"No, you didn't."

Look who woke up on the wrong side of the page. I told you the pooka would stabilize.

"And I was supposed to know that meant change shapes?"

A pause, then, *I guess I could have been clearer.*

"Any other surprises?"

Why don't you ask him?

"Val, between you, me, and a one-day-old pooka, who do you think has the most expertise?"

You're showing new wisdom every day. Words continued to flow across the page before I could respond with the appropriate sarcasm. *I've updated the entry.*

"Thank you." I flipped ahead to the pooka entry. The first paragraph remained the same, but the second had new information.

Once imprinted, a pooka is tethered to that being, and its development in life will depend upon the imprintee and the pooka's experiences. The relationship formed between the two is symbiotic, each influencing the other. When a pooka imprints on an enforcer, it is up to the enforcer to mold the pooka into a being of lux lucis, without, of course, succumbing to the allure of the pooka's dual nature.

Pookas have three to five forms but always rise in their largest form. Most pookas can assume the form of the creature they imprint upon.

"Would it have hurt you to include this information last night?" I flipped back to the first page.

Val's words formed in uptight typeface. *It was an exciting evening. I was a little distracted.*

I sighed and forgave the book. "Been a while since you've been swallowed by a vervet?"

Something like that.

"What's that?"

I jumped, sending a sharp pain through my ankle. Jamie stood in the bedroom doorway, and I hadn't heard him approach. His soul shifted beneath his skin like feathery clouds against a black sky. Behind him, the lichtwand glistened, a pure white backdrop.

"It's Valentine. Val, meet Jamie; Jamie, Val." I lifted the book and Jamie scooted closer. When he reached a hand toward the book, *NO TOUCHING* flashed in enormous letters across the page. Jamie jerked back. "He's pure *lux lucis*. I don't know how he'd respond to you," I said.

Jamie nodded. "Hi, Val."

Hi, Jamie.

This was my world. A talking book, a cross-dressing pooka, and me, all cozy in my bedroom.

"You can read?" I asked.

"You can't?" Jamie looked startled.

I dropped it. Stepping around him, I turned off the lichtwand and blinked to normal sight. "We need to find you more suitable clothes."

"I like these." Jamie lifted both sides of the skirt, and I averted my gaze before being flashed.

"We're headed to work, and I don't want you to be cold."

Thankfully Jamie didn't have a football player's body. I pulled out my baggiest jeans and a men's black thermal shirt I usually wore around the house. I selected socks for him, too, but drew the line at giving him my underwear. We'd deal with that problem later.

Jamie examined each item I handed him, then yanked the WWF T-shirt off and slipped into the thermal shirt. I closed my bedroom door and revealed the full-length mirror attached to the back. Jamie admired himself, rolling his shoulders and running his long, slender fingers down his abdomen to smooth the shirt. I was struck anew by his exotic eyes when he smiled at me.

Jamie unzipped the skirt and bent to tug it down, giving me an eyeful of paper-white buns.

"Whoa, there!" I spun around, cheeks flaming.

"What? Are you okay?"

"I'm fine. It's just people . . . humans . . . we don't show each other our"—I hunted for the word and settled on—"privates. Unless its, ah, an intimate thing. Not that you're going to be doing anything intimate with anyone anytime soon. I mean, not that it's a bad thing. You're just far too young, and—" *Stop talking, Dice.*

"What's a private?"

"It's your—" *Crap.* "Your reproductive parts."

"But those are the most interesting parts."

He was so earnestly confused, I couldn't hold in my laughter. He circled around in front of me—thankfully with pants on and mostly zipped—and checked my face.

"Are you teasing me?"

I shook my head. "Humans like to save our privates for those most special to us."

He grinned. "That's why you showed me yours last night."

"Um, that's—"

"You're special to me. I should show you my—"

I grabbed his hand before he could unzip his pants. I didn't need a mirror to confirm I was scarlet from my eyeballs to my clavicle. "That's, well, thank you, but I've already seen yours."

"Oh, that's right." Jamie turned back to the mirror and buttoned his pants. I pressed cool fingers to my cheeks and tried to dismiss the last two minutes as easily as the pooka had.

"I think I should change back to that." Jamie pointed to the skirt with one hand, using the other to tug at the crotch of the pants. "This pinches."

"No. Keep it. You look very handsome." It was the truth and also easier than arguing, or worse, continuing our conversation about his man parts.

Jamie cocked his head and reexamined himself. Maybe the lighting earlier hadn't been right, but his soft oval face had more definition than I'd noticed before. Looking at us side by side in the mirror, I tried to see the pooka the way the rest of the world would, and found myself oddly proud of his attractive appearance, as if he were my own child. His skin was fair enough to be a newborn's, which technically it was, and his hair made my chestnut waves look sun-kissed. His hair had style, too. Close at the sides and longer on top, Jamie's hairdo was both trendy and disarming, which was a lot for a hairstyle to accomplish. With those golden eyes, he was exotic enough to model. The pooka knew how to choose forms to impress, that was for sure.

I shooed Jamie from the room and changed into jeans, a green and tan striped shirt, and an ivory cloth jacket with a zipper that bisected my body from my right hip to my left shoulder. I hoped I wouldn't regret wearing such a light, easily ruined jacket, but it was either me or Jamie in this jacket, and it was too feminine for the pooka. He got my black coat. I settled Val in his strap after I gave his cover a quick buffing, strapped on the knife belt, and grabbed my purse.

We left Mr. Bond on the threshold, both of us giving him a pat good-bye. As far as I knew, only I carried guilt down the stairs. I'd barely been home seven hours, and most of those I'd been unconscious. My poor cat needed more company than that. The tiny fluff ball tabby at Alex's clinic came to mind. At least Mr. Bond would have a playmate. Maybe he needed a cat sitter, too. He'd been fond of Niko. I could offer to let Niko room with me while he was in town.

I needed more sleep if I was entertaining ideas of playing house with the optivus aegis. In lieu of more sleep, caffeine would have to do. Since I wasn't a coffee fan—possibly the last holdout on the planet—I stopped by Jamba Juice for a Chocolate Moo'd Smoothie, then added a Matcha Green Tea Blast, just in case. Jamie ordered a smoothie from every menu. I stifled a sigh and gave the cashier my overworked credit card. I hadn't taken into account the financial impact Jamie would excise on my bank account. Maybe I could convince Mr. Pitt that imprinting a pooka was raise worthy. If nothing else, new territory should warrant a pay increase.

I sucked down the chocolate shake while Jamie played with the radio and heater dials on the drive to the office. Jamie as a dog I could fit into my life; I'd never planned on a roommate. I couldn't make him sleep in the bathroom every night. Did I get him a twin bed or a doggie bed? What about his goals and plans? What did a pooka do all day? Eventually, he would tire of following me everywhere. Or was it the other way around? Was I now supposed to follow him around like a perpetual moral teacher, instructing his every decision?

Great. The caffeine had woken me up, but it'd also demolished the buffer of surrealism left over from last night. The reality of imprinting a pooka jounced around my head, rekindling my headache. I set the shake down.

When we got to the office, I checked Jamie in Primordium. His soul swirled black and white, looking no more one energy than the other. I also checked the seat after he got out, having found a fine film of *atrum* on my bathmats this morning. The seat was clean.

I greeted Sharon as if we were old friends. It'd become a one-sided joke, and if it irritated the stoic woman, I couldn't tell. For once, her cold gaze merely glanced off me. She locked on Jamie, unblinking eyes as expressionless as her drab face. The pooka halted. His tray of half-finished smoothies dipped, and he didn't notice when I lifted it from his hands. He fixated on Sharon with a reciprocal, eerie intensity.

Blinking to Primordium, I checked souls. Sharon's managed to look heavy and gritty despite being the same pure *lux lucis* as mine. Jamie's made me set the drinks on Sharon's desk and take a deep breath. Tennis ball–size bubbles of *atrum* lifted from his skin, dissipating as soon as they formed, and *lux lucis* swirled beneath, soft and frothy. I shook out my hands and prepared to tackle Jamie, but as quickly as it had changed, his energy settled, the *atrum* washing back into the *lux lucis* in tendrils so thin he looked pinstriped. He bowed his head to Sharon, grabbed the tray of smoothies, and turned to me with his wide smile, all without saying a word.

I glanced back and forth between them, decided better of asking questions or making introductions, and continued as if we hadn't paused. Jamie fell into step beside me, slurping a thick raspberry smoothie through a straw. My spine stiffened under the weight of Sharon's stare.

Rose peeked out of the conference room door. I jumped and only half contained my yelp of surprise. Jamie giggled. Rose finished stepping through the doorway and closed the glass door behind her. A grid work of cito spray bottles covered the conference table, all but three rows glowing with the Rose's special blend of cito pesticide.

"I thought I felt you," she said, then looked at Jamie. "You, I couldn't mistake."

These two, I introduced. Jamie didn't offer his hand, perhaps not knowing the custom, and it was just as well. I doubted the empath wanted to touch the pooka. She kept her soul as clean as an enforcer's, though today weariness tinged its natural glow. When I blinked to normal sight, I saw that fatigue rested in the dark circles under her eyes. She stood barefoot in stockings, a tropical-print sundress, and matching turquoise jacket, which brightened her appearance. I hoped her more typical attractive apparel was in celebration of the citos decreasing to normal levels now that Jamie had left his hatching grounds, but since I didn't want to even whisper the word *cito* out of fear of jinxing myself back into mall duty, I didn't ask.

She narrowed her eyes at Jamie. "I expect you to treat Madison nicely. She's a *lux lucis* girl. Let's keep her that way."

Jamie cocked his head and studied me. He obviously was looking at my soul. What did the world look like through pooka eyes? "But that's so limited."

Ooo-kay. That was an answer of a sort: He didn't see things the same way I did.

"It's an intentional choice," I said, urging Jamie toward Mr. Pitt's office. I was slacking on my first day in charge of the pooka. We needed to talk about morality and its importance. If only I didn't feel like I'd be wasting my breath. How do you convince someone that half their nature is wrong?

You don't, at least not when you're supposed to be chatting with your boss.

"Madison! How's it goin'?"

I spun to face the cubicles, dread worming through my intestines. "Sam?"

The teen popped up beside Will's desk.

"In the flesh, superwoman. They said you were out today, which was a total bummer. Will my man's been teaching me all kinds of exciting bumper sticker stuff. This job is wicked cool."

Niko's big plan was to give Sam a job in my office? Was this for Sam's benefit or my punishment?

"Yeah, wicked cool," I echoed. It must be the Illuminea rubbing off on him, because I had a hard time believing a teenager used to breaking into cars would find anything *cool* or *exciting* about bumper stickers.

Sam sized up Jamie. "Hey, man," he said with less enthusiasm.

"Sam, this is Jamie." I made the introductions on autopilot, barely hearing myself over the voice in my head nattering about what a bad idea it was to introduce the pooka to Sam.

"So, do you, like, work with Madison?" Sam crossed his arms, a challenge in his gaze.

I flicked a glance between the two guys. Jamie could have been Sam's age. Did Sam think I'd apprenticed Jamie instead of him? He certainly looked jealous.

"Jamie's a close friend," I said, earning a beatific smile from the pooka.

Will stood up beside Sam and clapped a hand to his shoulder. A trickle of *lux lucis* moved from the Illuminea to Sam. I stared, shocked. What the hell was going on here?

"Do you work here?" Jamie asked. His gaze slid to Will, then dismissed him.

"Yep." Sam puffed out his chest.

"Wicked cool. You want a smoothie?" Jamie offered up the tray.

While Sam dithered over the choices, I slipped around to the other side of the cubicles to whisper to Will. "Why is Sam here?"

"I'm weaning him." Will watched Sam and Jamie with narrowed eyes.

"From what?" Breaking into cars? I'd tried that, too, but an Illuminea stood a better chance of having a long-term influence.

"From the *lux lucis* you've been feeding him."

My stomach dropped. "Is it bad?"

"He should be fine in a week or two."

I slumped against the cubicle. Weaning implied an addiction. My well-meaning attempts to straighten up Sam's choices by cleansing his soul had done more damage than good. Will's voice and expression contained no censure for my ignorant actions, making my guilt thicken.

"Madison was swaggy, like, bam, bam, BAM!" Sam did some impressive karate moves against the cubicle wall. "I thought I was merked, but she's, like, one of my mains now."

Jamie ate up Sam's gibberish, eyes alight. Smothering a groan, I hurried back to Jamie's side. The last thing I needed was a slang-spewing pooka.

"We've got to go, Jamie. Mr. Pitt is waiting."

"Aww," Sam said, and Jamie echoed him. I urged the pooka down the hallway, tossing a wave to Will. He smiled, but his expression turned downright frosty when he looked at Jamie. Shivering, I hurried the pooka along. I'd never seen the Illuminea look anything but pleasant. Will's cold expression was as shocking as seeing hatred on the face of a beloved uncle. Jamie let me dictate his speed, but his head swiveled to keep the Illuminea in sight, all easygoing cheer from his conversation with Sam gone. In the flat fluorescent lights, Jamie's youthful face looked broad. My coat creaked on his shoulders, stretched at the seams.

"Relax." *Before you rip my coat or, you know, start a battle with my coworker.* The Illuminea didn't fight evil. They concentrated their efforts on influencing people toward good choices and enhancing *lux lucis* where it already existed. I hoped their policy extended to pookas.

"What was that?" Jamie asked.

"Sam? A teenager." As foreign as a person from another planet.

"No. The other one."

"Will's an Illuminea."

"He's a half person."

"Pretty sure he's whole."

"He's unbalanced."

Like me? I wanted to ask, but we'd reached Mr. Pitt's office. I released my tension on a long breath. I hadn't been prepared for the office to feel like a gauntlet with Jamie at my side. Behind us, Sharon glared from her receptionist chair, and Sam waved over the wall of Will's cubicle. I gave them both weak smiles and knocked on Mr. Pitt's door frame.

Distracted as I was, I didn't notice Mr. Pitt's off-tune humming until he stopped.

"Come in, come in."

He greeted us smiling. With teeth. Not his familiar thin-lipped "I'm smiling because otherwise I'd be banging my head on my desk" smile. This was genuine happiness, something I'd never before seen on my boss.

"Jamie, this is my warden, Brad Pitt."

"We met last night."

"Indeed." Mr. Pitt waved us to the leather chairs across from his desk, then perched a hip on the corner of his desk. "You've made a good choice in Madison," he said to the pooka as if I weren't sitting right there. "Let me know if there's anything you need."

"Thank you."

"Um, why *did* you choose me?" I couldn't believe I hadn't asked Jamie earlier.

"I like you."

I waited for him to elaborate. He sucked up the last of a pink smoothie, then moved to a purple one.

"You didn't know me," I prompted.

"I could feel your soul."

"And I didn't feel like a half person?"

Mr. Pitt raised his eyebrows but didn't interrupt.

"You have potential."

Coming from the pooka, that was no compliment. He thought I had potential to balance the *lux lucis* of my soul with an equal amount of *atrum*. Seeing the scowl on Mr. Pitt's face, I realized I should have waited to have this conversation in private.

Don't ask questions you don't want answered.

Jamie glanced up, noticing my silence. I smoothed my features and reassured him. "I'm glad you picked me. Do you mind throwing this away for me?" I handed him my empty cup and gave him directions to the break room. He went, clearly more eager to explore than to do my bidding since I had to remind him to take my cup.

"What are we supposed to do all day?" I asked the moment he moved out of earshot. It was a genuine concern and a diversionary tactic all rolled into one. I didn't need Mr. Pitt fixating on Jamie's belief he could turn me—halfway—to the dark side.

"Your job. Take Jamie with you. Show it how to do good." Mr. Pitt resumed his seat behind his desk.

"Him." I wasn't going to convince Jamie he wanted to be more like me and all the people on my side if they continued to refer to him as an *it*.

Mr. Pitt gave me a concessionary shrug. "Him."

"And if he doesn't want to stay with me?"

"He will, for now. I checked a few records, called a few old enforcers who imprinted. In the early days, they always stay close."

"When he grows up?"

"We'll deal with that later."

I would have pressed for specifics, but Jamie returned, so I asked, "How's the region look?"

"Good." Mr. Pitt leaned back in his chair and smiled, eyes half lidded with satisfaction. On the wall, the laminate map of our region had been replaced with one showing our expanded territory. Several points were marked with red circles. "We weren't sure how long you'd be out, so Summer and Rafi are continuing to work our region, directed by Liam." His familiar scowl returned. "Since you're here, I'll let Liam know Summer can focus on Jacob's region."

"How is he?"

"In the hospital still."

"I hope there's no permanent damage."

Mr. Pitt eyed Jamie. "He'll recover. Madison?"

The pooka scowled, fingers tight on the armrests. I blinked to Primordium. Jamie's soul boiled with *atrum*, leaking onto the leather chair.

"Hey, there. No one's saying Jacob was right to attack you," I said. Jamie turned glowing whirlpool eyes to me. "I think he's suffering an appropriate retribution, don't you?" Jacob would likely be stuck in a cast for weeks, while Jamie hadn't exhibited a wound since he shifted to Great Dane form. I felt like a heel for not asking the pooka about his injury earlier, but expressing concern now would seem contrived and emphasize my thoughtlessness.

"He deserved more."

"His actions weren't malicious. He didn't know better and didn't understand."

"He hurt me. What else matters?"

"His intent matters. He thought you were going to harm us all. He thought he was saving us."

"So you think it's okay he shot me?"

I shook my head. "He got what he deserved." I'd missed a prime opportunity to explain forgiveness and being the better person, and I hoped I didn't regret it. I didn't condone an-eye-for-an-eye mentality, but I couldn't make myself lie to Jamie, either. As much as I'd prefer otherwise, I wasn't sorry Jamie had impaled Jacob. I didn't want to see him do it again, though.

"Help me clean this up, would you? Mr. Pitt likes a tidy office."

I rolled *lux lucis* off my fingertips and across the arm of his chair, countering a swath of *atrum* as if removing the stain of evil from our headquarters was the most natural activity in the world.

Jamie looked down, surprised. Without needing a second demonstration, he repeated my maneuver, setting the chair awash with *lux lucis*. He beamed at me, and I at him. I hoped he couldn't see the trepidation in my eyes. The pooka was a fast learner and immeasurably powerful. It wouldn't take him long to figure out that what he could do with *lux lucis*, he could do with *atrum*.

Mr. Pitt cleared his throat. "Going forward, a good rule of thumb is to not hurt enforcers."

Jamie cocked his head and contemplated Mr. Pitt. The warden turned to me.

"We're spread too thin and we're not sure about citos around Jamie, so you're off cito duty."

Hallelujah. It was good to have confirmation. "Out of curiosity . . ."

"Sheila and Dominic have taken over."

"Liam's apprentice wardens?"

Mr. Pitt nodded.

"You mean they could have been doing it all along!" I shot from my chair. "Why did Liam insist *I* needed to work the mall? It was all part of his plan to kick you out, wasn't it? He wanted to make you look weak, so he stuck me in the mall when I could have been doing actual helpful work." I'd been a pawn. I'd known it all along, but to have confirmation made me want to hit something. Or someone. "The man's diabolical."

Mr. Pitt gave me one of his rare, true smiles. "It worked out in our favor."

I threw myself back into my seat, arms crossed. "Well, yeah, but . . ." Had Mr. Pitt known about the pooka? Had he gone along with Liam's plans in the hopes of having me imprint Jamie? Wardens could feel the movement of *lux lucis* and *atrum* in their regions. It was part of the job description. But how far beyond his region could Mr. Pitt feel? The mall garage where Jamie had incubated was less than a mile from our region's border. Had that been close enough for Mr. Pitt to feel the massive energy of a pooka coming to the surface? It didn't seem like a stretch.

If so, Mr. Pitt had taken a huge gamble. If I hadn't imprinted the pooka, it wouldn't have taken much more than a nudge after the holidays for Liam to push my warden out and assume his territory. Or if the other wardens had suspected Mr. Pitt had gone along with their plans just to get me closer to the pooka, he would have lost his region even faster. But with the pooka, we'd gained a swath of Liam's territory and a great deal more power. Mr. Pitt was either devious or lucky.

My boss steepled his fingers and watched me with a smaller smile. I'd put my money on devious. Which meant he'd used me. I waited to be offended. I was irritated I'd had to work the mall and swallow the insult of others assuming I wasn't enforcer enough for my region, but Mr. Pitt had taken worse insults *and* had reported to Liam the whole time. Maybe we were even.

It still didn't explain the uptick of evil.

"If all the evil lately isn't Jamie's doing . . ."

"It's not," Mr. Pitt said, giving me the assurance I needed.

"Then we still don't know what the culprit is?"

"That's for us to figure out."

I liked that Mr. Pitt included me. Unfortunately, the events of the last few days had proved to me what Mr. Pitt's repeated declarations hadn't: I knew next to nothing about the world of Primordium. I wasn't sure I could be of any help to my boss. The best I could do was hope I stumbled onto the problem using my usual bumbling, trouble-magnet method. It wasn't a comforting thought.

19

ONLY YOU
CAN PREVENT WILDFIRES

M R. PITT SENT ME TO explore our new territory, warning me to stick close to my phone. "I'll try to go easy on you, but the more you handle, the less ammo Liam has against us."

I tried to get myself psyched. I was reinstated in my territory, far away from citos and crazed shoppers, and doing the work I'd been born to do. I was literally going to make the world a better place. I might not know what the root of the problem was, but I could handle cleaning up individual evils. And along the way, I'd teach Jamie how to love *lux lucis*. Somehow.

My phone rang before I'd latched my seat belt.

"Salamander at Maidu Park," Mr. Pitt said. "Do you have a yogurt and water?"

"Not yet." It appeared my boss was familiar with Val's do-it-yourself salamander-extermination cocktail.

"Get on it."

I tossed Medusa back in my purse and threw the car in reverse. Jamie lurched against his seat belt, laughing when I plastered him back into the seat as I peeled out of the parking lot.

Sunrise Natural Foods, a local all-natural food store, was the closest grocer. I flew through the aisles, dumping yogurt into my handbasket, circling back for probiotics in capsules, just in case. Jamie added two snack-size bags of organic chips and chocolate Annie's Bunny Grahams while I scooped up two gallons of water. We dashed out of the store, not waiting for the cashier to hand over the receipt.

Jamie poured an entire bag of chips into his mouth before we were clear of the parking lot. The second bag disappeared on the short drive down Rocky Ridge Drive. A thin stream of light gray smoke on the eastern horizon pinpointed the newest fire. I cut left down McLaren Drive, checking my rearview mirror for fire engines or police. Sirens wailed, faint but approaching. There was a chance I'd beat the firefighters to the scene, and I couldn't decide if that was a good thing. If I could get to the salamander before there were witnesses, it'd probably be easier, but the thought of racing into a blazing, unchecked fire made my palms sweat.

I barreled past the park's main lot, barely slowing for stop signs. Sprawling over one hundred fifty acres, Maidu Park could devour three normal city parks whole and have room for dessert. The sports side, with four baseball diamonds, a similar expansion of soccer fields, a skate park, batting cages, and two children's playgrounds, covered only half the park. The other half was open space, with a paved bike trail winding through native terrain that included a stream surrounded by enormous oaks and rolling valleys blanketed with dead brown grass. The smoke rose from the middle of that tinderbox landscape. My heart rate kicked up.

I swerved to park at the curb several blocks from the plume. As tempted as I was to drive closer, a siren's screech beyond the bend in the road convinced me to stop. I may never have fought a salamander before, but if firefighters saw me dashing toward the flames, I'd be tackled. I needed to utilize stealth.

Jamie leapt from the car, tore off his jacket and shirt, and ducked down, morphing into a sleek Great Dane. I closed my mouth. No matter how many times I witnessed his transformations, it was never going to seem natural.

He shook, and the jeans clinging to his hips dropped to the ground. With a happy wag, he trotted out of his shoes. By the time I recovered and got out of the car, Jamie had circled to my side to frolic around me. I shooed him out of the empty street, checking the house windows to see if anyone had witnessed Jamie's transformation.

Maybe the pooka in dog form would work in my favor, mainly because Jamie couldn't say the wrong thing at the wrong time.

I shoved his borrowed clothes into the car, then popped the trunk and wiped my palms on my pants. My salamander-extinguishing ingredients waited.

Loosing Val from his strap, I asked, "You ready to hunt a salamander?"

I could watch from the car.

"Where's the fun in that?"

Crispy edges only work for old treasure maps. On me, it would look trashy.

"I promise, you won't get burned. I got the supplies like you said. Any idea how much I should mix in a gallon? How much does it take to kill a salamander?"

How should I know? Tell you what, you go ahead, and I'll stay here and do some research.

"Research? Val, I need an answer now."

More is better than less.

Good enough for me. I shoved Val back into his strap and opened the top of both gallons of water. After dumping out some water to make room, I poured two yogurts and ten capsules of probiotics into each jug, capped them, and shook them. It formed a pink-tinged sludge, but when I checked the jugs in Primordium, they glowed faintly of *lux lucis*. We were in business.

With Jamie at my side and a gallon straining each arm, I raced across the street and down a packed dirt trail into a valley of dry weeds. Nature swallowed us. In a dozen strides, the houses and road disappeared, blocked from sight by a steep hill and a dense canopy of barren oak limbs. Pain jolted through my injured ankle when I slid on scree and caught my balance, and every step after pinched. I slowed, but the distant shouts of firefighters soon spurred my steps. A fire truck roared by out of sight, joining the cacophony of sirens closer to the blaze. My winding path next to the park's stream wasn't as direct, but I stuck to the trail and didn't blink to Primordium. Even on the uneven dirt, I was afraid I'd catch a toe and finish off my ankle.

I didn't have the strength to run with my arms bent, so I bounced between straight arms, smacking my thighs repeatedly with the jugs, my shoulders aching from the ungainly weight of the gallons. My lungs burned from the smoke thickening the air, and my brain jarred against my skull with each step, hammering through the ibuprofen relief. Jamie loped in expanding circles around me, pausing to investigate the scents on downed logs, a muddy hole, a fork in the trail before galloping back to my side, tongue flapping. I stifled irritation as the jug smacked a new bruise in my thigh. It wouldn't have helped if Jamie were miserable, too, but did he have to look so happy?

I rounded a curve in the hillside and spotted flames. Wheezing, I collapsed against a tree trunk and dropped the gallons.

"Stick"—pant—"close."

Jamie glanced up the hill toward the bulk of the park, ears perked.

"Jamie." I drew his name out in warning. His head jerked toward me. Golden eyes met mine. He barked, then galloped up the hillside and disappeared. "Jamie!"

Damn it! I didn't have time—or lung power—to chase after him. Flames licked up an oak a dozen yards away and advanced along the dry grass. The fire burned through the shallow gorge, clogging it with smoke and obscuring my view beyond. Somewhere in the inferno was a salamander that needed to be killed. I stared at the ridge, willing Jamie to return.

He didn't.

I opened my mouth to call for him again but thought better of it. I was attempting to be stealthy. Leaving the water bottles against the tree, I scrambled three steps up the slope, only to slide back to the base on a protesting ankle. I glanced around for a different route up, then back at the fire. The flames weren't waiting on me or my wayward pooka.

In the early days, they always stay close. "Any other gems of wisdom, Mr. Pitt?" Sarcasm didn't mask my fear. Had Jamie been afraid of the fire, or had something caught his attention? The thought gave me a chill. I pictured a congress of salamanders at the top of the hill and Jamie frolicking among them, feeding them *atrum*. He had a knack for growing creatures out of proportion, enhancing all their negative qualities. I glanced down at the jugs; I didn't need to see a salamander to know two gallons against an overgrown one would be laughable.

If I lost control of Jamie on the first day, I didn't stand a chance of turning him into a good creature. If he went dark on my watch, my region—and my life—would be destroyed.

No. I wouldn't jump to the worst-case scenario.

This was *only* the first day. I would get better. A lot of enforcers had worked with and turned pookas in the past. If they could do it—

They were real enforcers with lots of experience. What makes you think you can?

Maybe he'd just wanted to explore. On his own. While I was occupied.

Enough. I shook out my hands and turned to face the fire. The pooka had proved he could cause trouble as easily as he breathed. Left unattended, there was no telling what sort of mess he'd make. But a salamander's destructive potential was evident: It had already started a fire. If this blaze got out of hand, it'd destroy homes.

I hobbled back to the water bottles. *Stay safe, you stupid pooka. Please.*

I collected the gallons and crept closer to the flames. Blackened smoke settled in the twisting gully, turning afternoon sunlight to murky shadows. Farther up the trail, several powerful arcs of water bathed the fire from both sides of the gully banks, and I caught glimpses of firefighters through the smoke. I stayed well back from the main blaze. I wasn't here to battle the whole fire. My quarry was much smaller.

I blinked to Primordium and stopped in my tracks. The thick smoke had vanished. More shockingly, so had the blaze. I could still smell smoke and feel it heavy in my lungs, could still hear the fire crackle and pop, could still feel warm swirls of hot air mixed in with the cool moisture of the stream, but the flames themselves were invisible. Like a swarm of locusts moving over the tall trees, a gray tide ate up shining *lux lucis*, leaving behind dead charcoal trunks and limbs. Flecks of bright white lifted into the air before evaporating. I couldn't see the flames— they were another form of normal-sight light that didn't translate to Primordium—but I could see their destructive aftermath.

My palms grew slick on the gallon handles. Facing down a creature who could breathe fire was scary enough without being blind to the perilous flames.

I switched back to normal sight, and the flames reappeared, brilliant red and yellow among the black smoke. It would have been a relief, but in normal sight, I wouldn't see a salamander approaching. Heart hammering, I backtracked to a side trail and jogged to higher ground, then crouched behind a tree to think. I couldn't run into the flames, brandishing a few gallons of water and probiotics, and expect to evade the firefighters, find and extinguish the salamander lurking within, and escape unharmed. I needed a plan.

Using Primordium for an unobstructed view of the gully, I searched for my prey. Most noticeable at first were the firefighters. Without the interference of smoke, their glowing souls highlighted them against the dying landscape. None were close, but they were working my way. I needed to move quickly. I turned my attention to the center of the fire.

Atrum flickered in the center of the scorched landscape. The plastic gallons sagged to the ground, and I stood to get a better look. It wasn't a trick of the distance making the dark energy appear to move: It flapped and flared like real flames burning at the heart of the larger, currently invisible fire. Outside of Jamie's soul and pre-hatching energy, I'd never seen *atrum* move of its own volition. Worse, the unnatural ebony flames would make a perfect blind for a black fire-loving salamander.

I traced the line of *atrum* along the base of the gully. Pockets of black flames dotted the dead grass ahead of the main fire. The firefighters might assume these smaller fires sparked from floating embers, but as I watched, a fresh burst of *atrum* flared several feet ahead of the previous patch. The evil energy caught on charcoal-dead plants and *lux lucis-*filled ones alike. I blinked back and forth between visions, swaying from self-induced dizziness. Where the *atrum* flames started, small white-hot flames smoldered and caught, spreading quickly in all directions despite water-soaked grounds and a concentrated effort from the firefighters. The aberrant flames were quelled only after all burnable vegetation had been consumed.

I finally grasped the magnitude of evil the rampant salamanders represented. Most evil creatures attacked individuals directly, infecting people and sometimes animals on a case-by-case basis. Salamanders used fire to spread evil through the physical world on a wholesale basis, leaving nothing behind but *atrum*-soaked scorched earth. Salamanders destroyed *lux lucis* at its roots, robbing the world of the passive, perpetual enhancement plants supplied.

Those anomalous *atrum* fires were my target, the salamander. It moved away from the main action, which worked to my benefit. I wouldn't have to attract any attention. All I had to do was plant myself in front of the salamander, douse it, and slip back to my car before the firefighters noticed me. All while avoiding real and *atrum* flames. Real fire would scorch my flesh; the salamander's flames would burn through my soul.

I patted Val, taking as little comfort from his company as he probably took from being dragged along with me. I was tempted, oh so very, very tempted, to call Niko for backup. I didn't want to confront a living flamethrower. Putting myself in the path of a moving, uncontrolled fire was idiotic—especially when I couldn't see the real flames in Primordium.

Hefting the jugs, I switched back to normal sight. Unfortunately, nerves did not justify the call. Other enforcers handled more danger than a single salamander on a daily basis, and they'd been doing so in my region while I worked at the mall. Calling Niko now would be admitting I wasn't capable of doing my job and would give Liam all the ammunition he needed to fold me into his region and steamroll Mr. Pitt. Worse, it would negate my insistence on being able to handle my region—and Jamie—on my own.

Please be safe, Jamie. And good.

Why did I have to prove myself in a test of fire?

Circling back to the base of the gully, I crouched in the salamander's path. My heart pounded in my eardrums. From my precarious position, I couldn't see the main blaze, which meant I squatted out of sight of the firefighters—and any potential rescue, should I need one. Wind swirled smoke in every direction now, and each breath burned. Bouts of flames ate up my buffer of safety, revealing the advance of the salamander. I waited until the latest burst of fire ignited a mere five feet away before I locked wobbly knees. It took willpower to blink to Primordium and blind myself to the deadly flames.

Waddling through tall stalks of dead grass, a foot-long salamander advanced on stubby legs. It chewed on bites of *lux lucis*–filled ground cover still thriving in the shade of the dead plants, then opened a triangular mouth and belched an *atrum* fireball the size of a basketball. The grass in front of it caught fire, flames of *atrum* eating through the dead material as easily as the live bits at the base. Real flames followed the *atrum* ones; I could feel the heat on my face. The salamander walked through the fire.

I fumbled forward, afraid to remove my eyes from the salamander to check my footing. The lizardlike creature stopped, a front leg suspended in the air. It swiveled to look at me. Small dark eyes glowed against a dark body, jaw moving as it chewed. I tensed for a charge or, at the very least, to dodge a fireball.

In a flash, it turned and scurried toward the hillside, sprinting on tiny legs and disappearing into the gray weeds. My burst of light-headed relief that it hadn't attacked was drowned a millisecond later in sickening alarm: The salamander was escaping.

"Oh, no, you don't." I ran after it, jumping the *atrum* flames. Heat licked up my legs; then I was clear. I kicked in an extra burst of speed, ignoring pain shooting from my ankle to my knee. Ripping a cap free with my teeth, I upended a jug of *lux lucis* water onto the salamander. It shot forward, panicked, and I leapt after it, dousing it with the second gallon. The salamander didn't make it more than three feet before it shrank to half its size. I leaned closer, drowning it in glops of yogurt.

I waited, reserving half a jug's contents. My breath rasped loud above the crackle of flames. When nothing moved beneath the mound of gelatinous dairy and water, I grabbed a stick and poked the viscous mass, poised to leap aside if the salamander launched *atrum* flames. Rooting through to the soil, I found nothing but a puddle of speckled *atrum* half eaten through by the yogurt.

"We did it, Val." I straightened, grinning. *Take that, Liam.* I doubted even wonder enforcer Jacob could have done any better.

Blinking back to normal sight, I checked the distance between me and any real flames. The last patch burned a few feet away. A sharp wind flattened it, almost extinguishing it, but the *atrum* flames rekindled the blaze. Seeing as my salamander chase had gone undetected, I crouched and rolled *lux lucis* toward the flames. Pushing *lux lucis* across the bare ground wasted energy, but not having to get up close and personal with the fire made it worth it. When I'd negated all the *atrum*, I doused the patch of flames with my reserved water.

Inspired, I crept to an untouched, healthy oak tree and planted one palm on its bark and the other on the ground. The *atrum* flames would burn until they ran out of fuel no matter how much water the firefighters used, but I had something more powerful than water.

The zigzagging and dotted path of *atrum* flames clearly marked the salamander's progress through the larger blaze. I gathered a wad of *lux lucis* in my hand and rolled it into a fast spin from the tips of my fingers to my wrists and back again. When it whirled in an almost seamless blur, I released it. *Lux lucis* shot up the scorched gully, eating through the first two patches of *atrum* and starting on the third before dwindling out. My other palm sucked fresh energy from the oak, replenishing the expended *lux lucis* as quickly as it escaped. I repeated the move twice more, checking the tree between each blast to ensure I didn't overtax it. Each time, my *lux lucis* rolled farther, as if it slid frictionless across the white energy already coating the ground before slowing to counter the *atrum*.

Satisfaction suffused me with giddy energy. This was what it meant to be an enforcer. In ten minutes, I'd made more of a difference than I had in three days at the mall.

"Ma'am, are you okay?"

I whirled and sprawled on my butt when my ankle gave out. A beefy firefighter in head-to-toe gear hustled toward me, alien behind an air mask. I must have looked equally frightening, covered in dirt and soot, crouched with a hand on the ground and another on the tree, as if I were a cave woman cowering from the fire, afraid to run.

"You need to leave."

You think? "I got turned around," I said, which I realized was the truth.

A deep baying jerked my gaze toward the slope. Jamie the Great Dane stood at the top of the hill, grinning.

"That's my dog. I need to—"

"This way." The firefighter took my elbow, forcing me to leave the empty jugs behind. He marched me up a steep trail to the top of the park where Jamie waited, and I used his support to baby my throbbing ankle up the incline. I would pay for my ardent salamander chase, but it'd been worth it.

At the top of the slope, the smoke thinned to reveal three fire trucks parked across the bike trail, firefighters using hoses to douse the flames below. No bloated imps bounced among them. No Godzilla salamanders loomed on the horizon. Whatever had distracted Jamie, he hadn't fed it. My knees weakened with relief, and it took repeated astringent assurances of my well-being before the firefighter allowed me to leave without calling an ambulance. He radioed ahead to a policeman at the exit to let him know I was coming. He probably thought I was too brainless to leave the park on my own.

Jamie kept his distance, trotting to my side only after I'd left the firefighter behind. I'd also received a truncated lecture about leash laws and dog safety. I'd happily promised to never leave the house without a leash again. Physically tethering Jamie to me was the best pooka-training idea I'd heard.

I found if I didn't push it, the pain in my ankle subsided to a dull ache. It was a good thing, too; with my shortcut through the nature trail designated off-limits by the firefighter, I had to walk a good half mile to the park's exit and back to the car.

I savored my victory on the long walk. I'd survived my first salamander encounter. So what if I'd lost control of Jamie for a few minutes? He'd come back, and in the meantime, I'd saved the park. Well, I'd *helped* save the park, and I'd saved the firefighters a worse blaze.

The dried weeds and stately oaks of the native section of the park gave way to manicured soccer fields that glistened like an endless white carpet in Primordium. A gentle breeze pushed the smoke away, lifting the fumes from my clothing, and a few bends in the trail muffled the cacophony of the ongoing battle. Jamie ranged near me, examining the plethora of curiosities the world offered the keen senses of a dog. I'd deal with reprimanding him later, when he changed back to human form. For now, with my heart rate returning to normal and post-adrenaline jitters fading, I savored the unexpected tranquility.

I didn't expect to encounter anyone else in the evacuated park, but when I neared the path between the soccer fields and the baseball diamonds, a man bustled toward me, waving to get my attention.

"Hey, are you okay?" he asked. He was big. Tall, with shoulders too wide for the average doorway and a chunky middle gone soft. Despite the sixty-degree weather, he wore shorts and a T-shirt, exposing tribal tattoos on both biceps and swirly Old English text down his forearms. If not for his average gray soul and the teacup Yorkie prancing on the leash at his side, I might have hurried in the other direction.

"I'm fine. Just got a little close to the flames." My voice rasped over the words, and I swallowed a cough. Soot smeared my cream coat, and my pants looked like I'd camped in them for a week. Not my best look.

"My wife sent me to check on the fire. I had to sneak in. They've got all the roads into here blocked. We live in this neighborhood and have a right to know what's going on. If that fire gets out of hand, it could be my home in jeopardy."

Since he indicated his home stood in the opposite direction of the fire, his only worry would be getting all his windows closed to keep out smoke, but I assured him the firefighters were in control.

Jamie trotted out of the bushes, and the Yorkie went on point, barking in high-pitched yips. It threw itself against the end of the leash, straining on hind legs to get to Jamie.

"Don't worry, he's friendly. I, uh, lost his leash back there." After the lecture from the firefighter, I felt defensive.

"Now there's a real dog," the man said. "This thing's my wife's, but who's the one picking up Princess's poop? George, that's who." He thrust a thumb at his chest.

"Uh-huh." George thought he had it bad; the Great Dane had poops larger than Princess.

Jamie touched noses with the runt. Her tiny tongue darted out to lick his face and I cringed on his behalf. I've never been one for sharing saliva with other species or seeing others do it.

"Well, I've got to . . ."

Jamie's soul flared from his body, enveloping the dog in *atrum*. In a flash, Princess's soul changed from bright white to heavy pewter.

". . . go."

20

DOG IS MY COPILOT

PRINCESS SPUN ON GEORGE AND sank her teeth into the excess flap of his Birkenstock's strap.

"Princess, no!" George stomped his beefy foot. Princess hung on, growling through her mouthful. "Let go, you little shit." Princess tried to shake her prey and tipped herself over. She recovered, launching herself back at George with furious, squeaky barks. When she latched on to the toe of the shoe, he scrambled out of it. "Bad Princess!" George remembered he had an audience and said apologetically, "Damn dog's never liked me, but she's never tried to bite me."

I nodded. Princess wasn't Princess anymore. Not by half, at least. With shocking ease, Jamie had changed her. She wasn't a full-blown (if world's smallest) hound, but she was halfway there. A glimmer of her inborn good nature remained in the residual *lux lucis*, enough to turn an attack on George into a mauling of his shoe. A hound would have gone for blood.

Jamie barked, dropping his front legs to the ground, his hind end wagging. Princess looked up from the tooth-marked shoe. Yipping, she raced under Jamie's belly, then around his front toes, growling when he playfully bit the air near her.

I found my voice. "Jamie, you can't do this."

Princess's leash wrapped around Jamie's front legs, and she spun to attack the nylon. Jamie rose and casually stepped on the strap as he untangled himself. The loop jerked from George's hand. I lurched to grab the leash, but Jamie bounced sideways, blocking me as he dipped for another playful strike at Princess. She ignored him, prancing by with the leash in her mouth like a prize, tail high. When George lunged for the trailing tip, she whirled to snap at him, and he jerked back with a curse.

"Jamie, this isn't a game. She's going to hurt someone."

George shot me a confused look. Jamie ignored me.

I had to get my hands on Princess. If I did, I could cleanse her soul. A dog her size couldn't hold more *atrum* than a handful of imps, especially only half tainted. One thing was certain: I couldn't leave her and hope she'd revert back to her previous pure *lux lucis* soul. Every time she lunged for George, her soul dimmed. Already, the pewter had darkened to a grim soot.

Snarling, the ankle-tall Yorkie charged George. He windmilled backward, then jogged a few steps. When Princess didn't pause, he sprinted in a circle, grabbing for the trailing leash. Princess cut him off, biting the air where his hand had been. George yelped. I lurched to assist, stopping when a coughing fit doubled me over. Through watering eyes, I watched Princess herd the large man across the soccer field. The tiny dog all but disappeared in the grass, making George's frantic, erratic path appear the run of a madman, or perhaps a man attacked by bees. Jamie raced around the pair, barking, a doggy grin splitting his face. He thought this was funny.

I forgot about how powerful the pooka was. I forgot I had no real authority over him. I forgot he temporarily looked like a dog. In that moment, he was a misbehaving child, and my inner mom roared to life.

"Jamie!" I snapped my fingers and pointed to my side. The pooka swung his head my direction. His tail drooped, and he trotted over to me, sat on my foot, and whined. I extricated my foot, then squatted, which put me below eye level with the seated Great Dane. "Jamie, you need to fix Princess. She's going to hurt George or herself. Or me."

The energy of the pooka's soul divided, his left side becoming solid *atrum*, his right pure *lux lucis*.

Whoa. I took a stab at interpreting his soul's statement, ignoring the frantic litany of "No, Princess! Bad Princess! I'm going to skin you and turn you into a slipper, Princess!"

"I know you think one form of energy is boring, but some of us like being all *lux lucis*," I said. "Like me. By changing Princess to half *atrum*, you robbed her of her choice and her *lux lucis*." Jamie whined, and I petted his right side. "You're special. You get to be both energies. But the rest of the world doesn't cherish the same balance."

I chose my words carefully. It wasn't the right time to tell him I hoped he'd embrace one side—my side. Such a blatant approach seemed doomed for failure. It was actions that mattered and that would convince Jamie to see my side. If I told him now that I would prefer a world without *atrum*, he might think I hated half of him. It might make him hate me, or himself.

"Can you change her back?"

Jamie's whirling eyes held mine. When he loped away, I stood, fingers crossed behind my back. He easily overtook the charging Yorkie, and a bar of pure *lux lucis* extended from his soul, sliding through the teacup terror. As easily as he'd transformed her the first time, he eradicated all traces of *atrum* from Princess's soul. The Yorkie skidded to a halt and sat. George continued to run for several strides before noticing Princess no longer chased him. He'd lost his other shoe somewhere along the way.

I sagged, hands to my knees, and fought the compulsion to cough again. The pooka's strength terrified and awed me. For now, he obeyed me, but it was his choice, and I wouldn't forget it.

"Thank you." I petted his head when he trotted back to my side.

We left George creeping up on the Yorkie, who sat watching him with her head cocked, cuteness and goodwill restored. Jamie trudged at my side, tail drooping, back to the car, while I contemplated scary thoughts, like whether the pooka could change my soul as easily as he had Princess's.

When I blinked to normal sight, I was surprised to see the sky washed red and orange in the sunset and the smoky street shadowed with twilight. Between the salamander and the Yorkie, we'd spent almost two hours in the besieged park. It'd felt like half that time. I opened the passenger door and Jamie stepped his front legs onto the floorboard. With his butt in the air, he morphed back to human. I yelped and covered my eyes.

"Give a girl some warning." I trotted to the driver's side with my eyes averted while he dressed.

I slid into my seat, and Jamie, fully dressed, flopped into the car next to me, then batted large gold eyes at me in the dim light. Instead of inciting compassion, his pitiful look rekindled my irritation. Jamie had disobeyed me when he'd run off and scared me when he played pooka god with the Yorkie. He might be a magical creature with one very restricted day under his belt, but I couldn't let his actions go without remark. I settled on honesty, stripping my voice of as much emotion as possible.

"I'm mad at you."

Jamie stilled, soft smile melting.

"You ran from me."

"I wanted to explore."

"You should ask first. You could have been hurt."

"I wasn't."

"You imprinted on me so I could help you, right?"

He cocked his head, considering. "No."

"No?"

"I chose you because I like you."

I sighed. "I like you, too. That's why I don't want you to get hurt. You need to let me help you until you understand the world better." I pressed my lips together, then asked a question that'd weighed on me during the walk. "Did you change anyone's—any thing's—Primordium energy while I was taking out the salamander?"

"No."

"Thank you." I sagged into my seat and closed my eyes. They stung from the smoke. It hung in the air like a fog, burning in my lungs. "Let's get out of here. I'm hungry."

"Me too."

I turned on the car, then took a moment to check in with Val.

"You okay, Val?"

Shazam! That's how it's done!

Shazam?

You were rockin' and rollin', groovin' and oozin'.

"Oozing? Are you okay?"

Val's pages bunched and fluttered, and I dropped him into my lap.

Yowza. Anytime. You and me, Dice. We're unstoppable.

"Are we going to get food?" Jamie asked. He lifted his chin, pointedly not looking at Val. What was that about?

I'm full. Full, full, full. To the glue holding me together.

Now that he mentioned it, Val did look brighter than usual.

"You didn't have to erase the *atrum*," Jamie said, gaze focused out the window. "It would have dissipated with the new growth."

Yeah, but where's the fun in that? Ka-pow!

I closed Val and slid him back into his strap. He seemed okay even if he was acting weird. "That would have taken months, and I didn't want any of the firefighters to get hurt—or anyone or anything else—in the meantime."

"Oh."

"Are you upset I cleaned up the *atrum*?" I pulled on my seat belt.

"I thought—" Jamie's gaze darted toward Val. "No."

Was he jealous of Val? If he weren't a book, I'd say Val was drunk. Maybe he was. I'd pulled a lot of *lux lucis* out of the tree when cleaning up after the salamander. How much had he absorbed?

"Hey." I took Jamie's hand. His entire left side shimmered with *lux lucis*, and I wondered if it was his way of apologizing. "I'm really glad you came back."

Jamie peeked at me with softly whirling irises. "Really?"

"Really."

My stomach growled. I released his hand, blinked to normal sight, and pulled from the curb. When we cleared the police barricades and were beyond their sight, I pulled over to the side of the road and called Mr. Pitt. As aggravating as it was to hear that Rafi had taken care of three other problems while I'd been at the park, it did leave us a free moment for dinner. If I'd been alone, I would have gone to In-N-Out, then straight home to shower. Figuring Jamie deserved to see more of the world than the interior of my car and apartment, I turned the car toward downtown Roseville, crossing the freeway into Isabel's territory. Since wardens could sense all *atrum* and *lux lucis* in their region, I wondered if she could feel the moment we crossed her border. Could Mr. Pitt pinpoint us at all times in our region? I'd have to ask.

I pulled the tip of my ponytail to my nose and coughed. Eau de Burn Pile was not a good scent on me. I rolled down the windows and cranked up the heat. After we got food, a shower moved to top priority, for both of us. Separately.

By the time we reached Vernon Street and found parking, Jamie's cheerful disposition was restored. He bounced out of the car and darted around to my side, showing remarkable constraint. Two blocks of the main street through downtown were blocked off for the weekly food truck extravaganza. Though the crowds were smaller tonight than during the warm summer months, plenty of people lined up at every truck's order window, and most of the bench tables were at capacity.

Greasy, fragrant aromas emanating from a dozen trucks elicited dueling growls from our stomachs.

"Every truck has something different, so check your options before making a decision," I said after explaining how food trucks worked.

Jamie bounced into the crowd. I kept an eye on him but headed straight for my favorite vendor. Normally I'd get fish tacos or their gourmet burger, but the sluggish feel of *lux lucis* inside me changed my order to a taco salad. The wild fluctuations of my soul in the last two days were catching up with me, and as much as I preferred otherwise, the best way to help my body recover was to consume live foods. I added a side of sweet potato fries, because I'm only human, then a second order for Jamie. I joined him in line at a truck featuring a pizza oven. He polished off the fries before we made it to the front of the line, then ordered a pizza with everything. We carried our food to a table and, by mutual consent, didn't look up or speak until we'd cleaned our paper plates.

"You ready to try dessert?"

"What's dessert?"

"A party for your mouth." I led Jamie to the Belgian waffle vendor and demonstrated the best combination of waffle, ice cream, chocolate, whipped cream, and chocolate chips. Jamie ordered exactly as I did. When he took his first bite, his eyes widened and he opened his mouth, pointing at the unappealing mash of food.

"This is sooo good." At least, that's what I thought he said.

He forked bites into his mouth with a teenager's speed. I laughed at his blissful expressions, then twice as hard when he clutched his forehead and almost fell off the back of the bench seat.

"That's what happens when you eat cold things too fast."

"Why didn't you tell me?" He moaned and hunched forward, massaging his forehead.

"I wasn't sure you could get an ice cream headache."

He ate slower after that, but not by much. Then he went back for a second waffle with the works and managed to finish it, too, before I polished mine off.

Wishing I hadn't eaten quite so much, I decided to take the long way around the block back to the car, passing through the empty town square rather than through the dining crowd. In the summer, fountains of water speared through the concrete square for kids to run through, and the green lawn beyond hosted weekly events. Tonight, tall lamps illuminated the emptiness. Cold wind cut across the open space, and I drew my jacket tighter to my body. I brushed ineffectively at soot smudging the creamy fabric. To save money, I was going to buy only drab brown clothes from now on. Outside of cito duty, it seemed like every enforcer activity involved dirt—and me rolling in it.

One minute, Jamie walked beside me, head swinging to take in everything. The next, he slid out of his coat and yanked off his shirt, and a midnight-black Great Dane sprinted free of his jeans into the park.

"Wait—" I cut off my cry, glancing around. A little girl pointed and stared, tugging on her father's sleeve, but she was the only person who'd witnessed Jamie's transformation. I scooped up his dropped clothes and hustled after him, food sloshing in my stomach.

Jamie barked, running in circles on the concrete, pouncing and rolling on nothing. I slowed, blinking to Primordium. A stampede of imps surged from behind the post office across the street, bounding to the pooka. My lungs constricted. *Not again!* They swarmed Jamie, and the pooka barked with delight. Chinchilla-shaped bits of evil chased through the Great Dane's legs, nipped at his hips and belly, and leapt to his back, tumbling down when Jamie rolled.

My feet took root. Imps were the smallest form of evil, born of pure *atrum*. They existed to feed on anybody they encountered and were as likely to try to swallow my pet wood as they were my ankle. They had no self-preservation and no rational thinking skills, yet they played with Jamie like real, thinking creatures.

Despite *atrum* layering his entire soul, Jamie didn't feed the imps energy and, miraculously, none tried to feed on his soul, which meant all the imps remained smaller than Mr. Bond. After the initial swarm, no more imps appeared, and I relaxed my stranglehold on the bundle of clothing. Over forty imps clambered over my pooka—more than enough to tax me, but compared to the previous night's endless stampede, the seething bundle of imps looked downright manageable.

My feet still didn't move. Jamie raced back and forth across the concrete square, dodging between lampposts, a trail of imps bouncing after him. When he turned back toward them, the imps jumped him, disguising the Great Dane beneath their excited pile. Jamie broke free, tongue lolling, whirling eyes spinning with unmistakable delight.

I should have raced into the fray immediately. Clustered as they were, the imps were easy targets. But Jamie looked happy, so I stood there, hugging his borrowed clothes to my chest.

Niko's warning surfaced. *You need to be vigilant. More than one enforcer got too close to their pooka and lost perspective.*

Exhaling heavily, I set the clothes on a bench and pulled the pet wood from my back pocket. With a flick of my wrist, I extended it to full length, then filled it with *lux lucis*. Trudging into the frolicking mass, I waved the long wand. Imps trailing at the back of the pack swiveled to face me. The pooka held untold allure, but I was closer. True to their nature, a handful charged me. I swiped the pet wood through their bodies, pulsing *lux lucis* into the wand in coordination with each strike. The imps disappeared in sparkles of *atrum* before they touched me.

Jamie circled me, and a dozen imps spun from him to attack me. More *atrum* glitter fell around my feet. Slowing, Jamie approached me at a trot, head cocked and a bundle of imps astride.

"You and I need to talk about where it's appropriate to change," I said, striving to remain neutral to his woeful expression. "For starters, never in public."

He barked. Imps tumbled from him. Half tried to regain purchase while the others turned on me. This time, several managed to latch on to my soul before I disintegrated them. By the time the last of the imps abandoned Jamie, my movements were sloppy, my soul dim. The imps might have been small, and I'd gotten stronger, but I wasn't strong enough to shrug off expending the volume of *lux lucis* necessary to wipe out that many imps.

Jamie trailed me from tree to tree until I'd topped off my *lux lucis* levels, and together we turned to face the empty square. *Atrum* coated the concrete where Jamie had run repeated figure eights. If the imps had made a single pass, they wouldn't have deposited a noticeable trail, but the frequency combined with their excitement had built up a thin smear. I crouched, looped *lux lucis* through my palm, and set it rolling through the closest swath of *atrum*. Jamie bent his nose close to my hand, then licked my face before I could jump out of reach.

"Blech." I swiped slobber onto my coat sleeve. "We need to discuss tongue boundaries, too."

Jamie pranced to the next patch of *atrum*, his soul swirling with black and white energy again. His left paw turned pure white and whirled with energy. When he released it, *lux lucis* shot from his nails across the pavement. The long line stretched across the square, then spun like the hand of a clock with Jamie at the fulcrum. *Lux lucis* washed over my shoes, tickling me from my toes to my ankles. After one sweep, it winked out, leaving the square completely clean.

The lecture on the tip of my tongue withered. "You're so going to have to show me how to do that."

Jamie woofed.

We investigated the post office to see what had attracted so many imps in the first place. It backed up to the tip of Roseville's rail yard, where three sets of tracks diverged into dozens. A heavy rumble announced the approach of a freight engine. When the engineer blasted the horn, Jamie jumped, tucking his tail and running to me. I patted a safe patch of his side and pointed out the locomotive, and Jamie watched the train rumble past with a fascination that would have done Dad proud.

I kept looking for the source of the imps, finding a clue only when I turned to get Jamie's attention: A faint trail of *atrum* bumped across the rails to the cluster of shops hugging the other side of the tracks.

Since we couldn't hop the fence and follow the trail across the tracks, Jamie and I returned to the car, where Jamie changed while crouched next to the car and then dressed in the dark, and I surreptitiously provided cover from passersby. A few minutes later, and a few complaints about the uncomfortable constriction of jeans, and we were on our way.

"Why can't I change in front of other people?" Jamie asked as we curved around the Oak Street roundabout and headed under the tracks on Washington Boulevard.

"Because it'll frighten them and cause them to ask too many questions."

"What kind of questions?"

"They'll want to know what you are and how you do it."

"I'll tell them I'm a pooka."

"You can't."

"Why not?"

"Because they don't know pookas exist."

"They should."

"Most people don't know enforcers exist. Or vervet. Or prajurit. It's better that way."

"Why?"

"Because most people can't see Primordium. What they don't see, they don't think exists."

Jamie frowned. "Are you teasing me?"

"Nope."

Divided from the rest of downtown's shopping district by the tracks and bracketed by historic housing, this pocket of Roseville contained a handful of struggling mom-and-pop shops and a plethora of businesses typically not welcome elsewhere. In three short blocks, four bars, two nightclubs, and a hookah lounge mixed with tattoo parlors, a questionable hotel, and, oddly, two recording studios and an organic donut shop. In the early evening on a December weeknight, it looked like a ghost town.

Parking next to the Owl Club, I turned off the Civic's headlights and blinked to Primordium; the gray on gray of asphalt, sidewalks, and streetlights made using Primordium too dangerous while driving. Flickering yellow light from the streetlamps and the neon in the club's window disappeared, replaced by a uniform directionless light; day and night were indistinguishable in Primordium.

A dozen beady black eyes surrounded us. I squeaked. Four imps bounced onto the hood of the Civic, and beyond them, two vervet dangled from the Owl Club's protruding sign. I twisted to check behind us. Vervet hunched, vulture-like, on the two-story rooftops. A ball of imps scuffled across the road like an *atrum*-soaked tumbleweed. When they bounded atop the trunk, the car remained motionless beneath their weightless hops. Every single eye focused on Jamie.

"Can I go play?"

"Yes. Great idea. Out you go. Stay human. Wait. Promise not to feed them."

"I promise."

I shooed Jamie from the car. The pooka emerged as if through a sheet of *atrum*, shifting his soul's energy as he stepped out. The imps mobbed him.

I pulled the door shut and grabbed Medusa.

"Mr. Pitt, I might have a problem," I said when he answered.

"Not that I see. At least for the minute, our region's clear."

"I'm not in our region." I explained the imps at the food truck event and the greeting party surrounding the car. "Aside from last night's hatching, I haven't seen a concentration of imps and vervet like this since ground zero. *Before* I killed the demon."

"I'm looking at Liam's most current map, and Isabel didn't report anything where you're at."

"Can I take care of it?" I was outside my jurisdiction, in the territory of a warden who'd been none too pleased I hadn't defected to her region. I wasn't sure what the rules were.

"Yes. I'll notify Liam so he doesn't send Summer. Come by the office when you're done."

I tucked Medusa back in my purse. I would have liked a chance to talk to Summer in person. I'd decided against calling her today; my "sorry I stole part of your region" conversation was going to be awkward enough without adding on the lack of expressions and body language clues of a phone call. Setting the problem aside for later, I stepped from the car.

The vervet swiveled to watch me. I don't know how they looked away from Jamie. I couldn't. He *juggled* imps.

They climbed his body or leapt from the roof of the Civic to his hands, and he spun their fluffy bodies through the air. Some he caught, while others landed unfazed beside him and climbed back up for another go. He should have looked ridiculous. He *did* to people who couldn't see Primordium. I struggled to wrap my brain around imps who clearly enjoyed being catapulted into the air, using Jamie like some indulgent uncle at a family gathering.

A vervet sprang from the club sign and latched on to my soul through my hip. I jumped, trance broken, and shoved *lux lucis* down its throat. *Atrum* sparkles drifted to the ground. A trio of imps on the hood of the car spun to sink teeth into my soul at my forearm. They died in one quick pulse.

"Are you going to kill them all?" Jamie asked.

He'd stopped juggling, and imps crawled over him, falling from his shoulders in easy tumbles. I shuddered. The pooka's eyes whirled with a spiral of *lux lucis* and *atrum*, sadness unmistakable. I hardened my heart. "Yes."

"I don't want you to."

"I have to. If they're left alone, they'll harm people and cause people to harm others, too."

"You're killing them. That's the ultimate harm." Jamie scooped up a handful of imps and cradled their chinchilla bodies to his chest. A few took bites from his soul, but true to his word, Jamie didn't allow them to feed on his energy. "Do you only like *lux lucis* creatures?"

Up until yesterday, I would have said yes. But looking at Jamie, I knew it wasn't true. I liked him as he was, even half *atrum*. I would have *preferred* he was solidly *lux lucis*, but his dark half didn't repel me. In a way, he was a more extreme version of a normal person, partially tainted but still a lot good.

I hadn't expected to have to explain why good was good and evil was evil, especially not to someone who could *see* it. I searched for a simplified rationale.

"I like individuals who don't seek to feed off or hurt others, whatever species they are." I felt that covered my parents, with their tarnished souls, and Jamie with his half-and-half soul, while excluding everything coated in *atrum*.

My answer satisfied Jamie. For now. I was sure this wouldn't be our last conversation on the topic, but it seemed like a good start.

"Do *I* have to kill them?" He gazed at the imps the way I'd looked at the tabby kitten at Alex's clinic. My heart cracked.

"Not unless you want to."

I walked to the sidewalk, and the vervet perched above us dropped on me. I killed them all, intentionally using too much *lux lucis* so patches of my soul flared. Like moths to a bug zapper, imps peeled away from Jamie and sank teeth and claws into me. In deference to Jamie's sad face and the few pedestrians, I didn't use the pet wood, letting each creature land on me before disintegrating it. Jamie played with the remaining imps until the last one leapt from his hands to die on my soul.

I took a deep breath and shrugged off a pang of regret. Just because the imps enjoyed playing with the pooka did not elevate them above brainless evil varmints. They were small trouble but still important to exterminate before they cultivated a larger problem.

Jamie didn't say anything, and when I started down the block, he fell into step beside me. Vervet followed us, diving from the rooftops and swinging from balconies to bury their claws in my soul. Jamie watched two tear into my soul, a small frown between his eyes. The vervet were all normal size, and it was no more difficult to kill them than it was to do a sit-up: I flexed a metaphysical muscle and exerted energy in its rawest form. It was repetition that tired me. I rested against trees more and more frequently to regain my lost strength as we traveled.

The ninth leaping vervet died before it reached me. Jamie's soul flexed above my head in a glowing umbrella of *lux lucis*, and the vervet puffed out of existence.

"You didn't have to do—"

"They all want to eat you." He glowered at the rooftop. The vervet paced, agitated by the pooka's action.

I smiled. Score one for the good side.

Jamie took care of the majority of vervet after that. I moved on to cleansing the standing *atrum*.

"Why do you do that?" Jamie asked after I rolled *lux lucis* up a brick wall to the *atrum*-smeared balcony above.

"Because the *atrum* doesn't belong." I avoided saying, *And it'll hatch more imps if allowed to remain*. Likely, Jamie knew that. "The balcony is inanimate. It's not meant to hold energy. So I negate the residual evil to restore it to its natural state. Do you want to try?"

"Okay."

When he swept a patch of *lux lucis* from the front of the donut shop with looped *atrum*, washing away the positive energy and leaving a gray doorstep, I shuddered and fought to keep fear from my expression. Technically, the *lux lucis* didn't belong on the inanimate surface any more than *atrum* did, and rather than risk undermining Jamie's growing trust, I focused on my goal: making *lux lucis* fun for the pooka.

We made a game of who could cleanse the most *atrum* from each clump we found. Jamie never repeated the amazing radar-sweep move he'd wowed me with earlier, but he still won every contest. Seeing as it was the first game he'd ever played and the first time he'd won anything, he found the entire experience thrilling, racing from one black patch to the next. I did my best to keep up, then made sure he recharged. I didn't want his expended good energy to free up room in his soul for *atrum* to creep in.

I drove to the office pleasantly tired and proud. If we could keep this up, Jamie and I were going to make an unstoppable team.

"Before we get out, which form do you want to take?" At night, the parking lot in front of Illumination Studios contained only a few empty cars. Mr. Pitt's bright orange Fiat was one of them. "No one's here to see you change, so now's a good time if you want to."

"There's not enough room to change in here."

"Okay. But stick close to the car when you do."

Jamie shrugged out of his clothes. I didn't look away. He shifted fluidly, like his bones and muscles were a reshapable illusion. His metamorphosis seemed slower this time, though, or maybe it was the weak lighting. Maybe six shifts in one day took its toll.

Giving his tail a wag, Jamie tottered over to a nearby bush and lifted a leg, making me wonder if getting to freely pee on the great outdoors was the reason he'd changed. He trotted at my side as I walked to the office, close enough to brush my hip with his shoulder. *Lux lucis* coated his head and shoulders, giving way to uneven patches beyond my reach. I scratched my fingers through the short hair between his shoulder blades. Was it weird I felt okay with petting him in this form knowing he wasn't really a dog? Probably, but since he seemed to take comfort from it, I didn't think about it too hard.

Sharon locked eyes on the pooka when we entered. Jamie sniffed the corner of her desk.

"Jamie, no!" I grabbed his shoulders before he could lift a leg. "No peeing inside except in a toilet, okay?"

He lolled his tongue at me before curling it back into his mouth on a yawn. I nudged him down the hall toward the light spilling from Mr. Pitt's office. For once, I felt I deserved the censure in Sharon's glare.

Jamie preceded me into my boss's office. Mr. Pitt held a phone to his ear, but he waved me to a seat. In the quiet office, I caught a few murmurs from the person on the other end of the line, but I couldn't make out any words.

Jamie clambered into the second chair, circled on tall legs, and tried to curl into a ball on the seat. He overflowed in every direction. In squeaky increments, his feet slid along the cushion. Grunting, he shifted back to the center of the chair, only to start sliding again. His head dipped, eyes closing. When his front paws flopped off the chair, he jerked upright. The chair tilted backward. He yipped and tipped forward to compensate. I grabbed for the arm to stabilize the chair. Jamie's front feet slipped to the floor, and the chair landed on all four legs with a thud.

Jamie harrumphed, his cheeks flapping on the exhalation. I sat back in my chair, holding in my smile. He looked ridiculous with his rear end perched on the chair and his front paws on the ground. Almost immediately, his head bobbed, eyes drooping closed. His hind paws slid toward his armpits, and he tipped forward in a nosedive. The chair scooted back into the window blinds with a clang, and Jamie sprawled onto his side. I clapped a hand over my mouth to hold in laughter. Jamie shoved to his feet, not looking at me, and headed back to the chair. When I looked up, Mr. Pitt had his forehead resting in his free hand and he was shaking his head, the phone still to his ear.

I pointed to the space previously occupied by the chair. "Why don't you lie down there?" I couldn't keep the chuckle from my voice. Jamie gave me a hard look, then walked to my feet and flopped across them. "Or there."

Mr. Pitt hung up the phone without saying more than ten words. He seemed as subdued as the hushed office. It occurred to me I could "forget" to tell Mr. Pitt about Jamie sullying Princess's soul. Since the incident, he'd been a model pooka—or far better than I'd expected— and I didn't want to tattle on him. But the main reason I wanted to avoid relating the experience to Mr. Pitt was because I didn't want him to blow up at me and my lack of control.

At the moment, Jamie's soul twisted calmly, soft waves of *lux lucis* and *atrum* circulating through his upper body, his belly a clean white against my toes and shins. He looked harmless, but only his own volition stopped him from overpowering my soul as easily as he had Princess's.

I wanted to cleanse Jamie's soul, to teach him to be a pooka of pure *lux lucis* and use all his amazing power for good. Making sure I achieved my goal was far more important than getting in trouble with my boss, so I explained the incident to Mr. Pitt, keeping an eye on Jamie while I spoke. The pooka snored into the carpet. Mr. Pitt took it in stride.

"He's a pooka. It's up to you to make sure he fixes things when he blunders in the wrong direction."

No vein throbbed in Mr. Pitt's temple. He didn't even raise his voice. Not wanting to push my luck, I left out Jamie's playful interactions with the imps when I recounted cleaning up the tiny section of Isabel's region.

"I never found a source. Maybe it was in the back of a bar where I couldn't see."

"It's possible. It could be as random as what cropped up here today. Isabel will follow up on it."

"How's our region doing?"

"Fine, for the moment. Rafi took care of another small demon today as well as five of those unexplained pockets of evil. Our region is getting hit hard, more so than the areas around us."

"Any theories yet?"

"I've seen something like this before."

I leaned forward in my chair. "Really?"

"Years ago. When I worked in LA."

"Is that what got you demoted?" I regretted the question before the last syllable escaped. Mr. Pitt sat back, setting his elbows on his armrests and steepling his fingers in front of him. "I'm sorry. I shouldn't—"

"No. Tell me what you know."

I squirmed. "Just that you used to have a larger region and then you got stuck with this one."

Mr. Pitt dropped his eyes to his desk and nodded. "I had a region with five enforcers working under me in the heart of LA. That's about as high brass as you can get in this state, and I got the position shortly after finishing my training. I didn't even work the city as an enforcer."

"An enforcer?" Jamie lifted his head at my shocked outburst, then settled back down, rolling to put more of his weight against me.

"There was a time, a short time, when I held your position."

"That's possible?" I'd figured wardens were like enforcers, born with the skill set.

"It's a career choice a lot of enforcers make in their later years. More stability, fewer physical risks."

"But how?"

"What's the handbook say?"

"I've never asked."

"Go ahead."

Miffed, I pulled Val free. I wanted Mr. Pitt to explain it, but I had a feeling he was making a point. I needed to be asking Val more questions.

"Hi, Val. I'm here with our warden, Mr. Pitt. What can you tell me about wardens?"

Oooh, sitting down with the boss. Got to be on our best behavior, right?

"Darn tootin'."

"You have a most peculiar approach to everything, Madison."

I waited for Mr. Pitt to explain, but he waved a hand for me to continue my conversation with Val.

"Whatcha got for me?"

I've been listening, so the relevant passages are highlighted.

He gave me the page number near the back of the book, and I flipped to it. By *highlighted* he meant only certain text was visible.

WARDEN. A human or humanoid working for the CIA in charge of a defined section of land or sea. Wardens monitor evil within their region and coordinate and dispatch those under their command to combat any atrum *or* atrum-*based creatures.*

Like illuminant enforcers, wardens can work lux lucis. *However, more than minor* lux lucis *use is frowned upon, as using* lux lucis *decreases a warden's awareness of his region by softening the shape of his soul. The less defined his soul, the less precise his knowledge of his region. Similarly, if an enforcer does not regularly use* lux lucis, *her soul will harden into the shape of her region.*

"What's it say?"

"Wardens are dormant enforcers."

"We're a little bit more than that."

I pulled my gaze from Val's pages at Mr. Pitt's wry tone. "Of course. It's just, I thought we were different."

"We are, Madison. Very, very different. Just not when it comes to *lux lucis.*"

I closed Val and set him on my lap. I couldn't wrap my brain around a young Mr. Pitt chasing vervet or netting a hound. My mind stuttered on picturing him young and got stuck. I cleared my throat. "So you were in LA."

"My region wasn't huge, but the population was dense and it kept my enforcers busy, and they strengthened fast. My region became the most requested transfer in the state. There was talk of expanding it by almost double. It would have made me the most powerful warden in the western United States." He lapsed to silence, eyes focused on empty space between us.

I held still, barely breathing. This was the most Mr. Pitt had ever shared about his past, about himself. I didn't want to blurt out a stupid question and ruin it.

"I thought I was talented. The best. I was wrong. One of my enforcers was a rogue." His jaw bunched, and his eyes focused on me. "I can tell from your blank stare that you don't understand. A rogue is an enforcer who works both sides."

"Like, they manipulate *atrum*, too?"

"Maybe eventually, but at first Cheryl just made bad decisions, then covered them up. Like you did with our latest hire, Sam."

"I'm not working both sides!"

"I know. No one could fake your ignorance. Otherwise . . ." He sighed. "The rogue enforcer, she did bad things intentionally, cultivated evil, if you will. Then she'd go in with *lux lucis* and clean it up and be a hero."

"And you couldn't sense that?"

"I should have, but Cheryl was careful. She cleaned her soul before each meeting. She confined her evil actions to places that didn't set off my alarms and spread it around to all the enforcer regions under my domain."

A shiver slid down my spine. I'd never considered the implications of my ability to cleanse my soul of *atrum*'s taint. Conceivably, I could commit all manner of crimes, do untold evil, then walk up to a tree and wash away the evidence with *lux lucis*.

"Then she got greedy," Mr. Pitt continued. "She hunted down evil in other people's territories and carted it to hers for big scores. I should have seen what Cheryl was doing long before then. If I had, Lupe would still be alive. She was my second-strongest enforcer and thought she was strong enough . . ." Mr. Pitt chaffed his hands and refocused on me. "After that, I was lucky to get this small region."

Part of me wanted to ask how Lupe died, but a larger part didn't want that fear sitting in the back of my head.

"You think it's happening again?" A rogue enforcer in our midst? Suddenly I found myself wishing for another demon.

"Maybe. I haven't told anyone of this except Niko. It's too serious an accusation to make without solid proof."

"You suspect Jacob. Everyone says he's a fast learner." It was a logical conclusion, even if I felt traitorous voicing it. Just because he shot Jamie didn't make Jacob evil.

"He's fast, yes, but if that were the only criteria, then every warden in the area would have claimed you rogue by now."

"Then who do you suspect?" The wardens thought *I* was advancing quickly?

Mr. Pitt shook his head. "You don't need doubts in your head."

"No doubts? Now I suspect everyone." Though Jacob still topped my mental list. My next realization overwhelmed all other thoughts. "That's why you're not having me train under anyone!"

Mr. Pitt nodded. "You're the only enforcer I implicitly trust right now, other than Doris, of course. She'll be back soon enough to handle your training. Plus, Isabel wasn't wrong: Giving another warden authority over you would be career suicide."

I realized I hadn't given Mr. Pitt enough credit: He'd been rightfully worried about his job, but he'd also been protecting me this whole time, despite how bad that made him look. I pulled my thoughts back on topic with an effort.

"Why did you decide to tell me your rogue theory now?"

"Because I need your help in a very unorthodox way." He leaned forward. "I need your *lux lucis*, Madison."

"My *lux lucis*?"

"I need to see the larger picture. I'm missing something. Our region's expansion weakened me. I'm not complaining. I'll recover and adjust, but we don't have time to wait. Your *lux lucis* will give me the strength I need."

"Why not take it from a plant?"

"Yours will be far stronger. Enforcer *lux lucis* always is. If you want the scientific explanation, ask your handbook. More important, by you giving me *lux lucis*, I won't be actively using it, which means my soul's map remains precise and I'll be able to see beyond our borders."

"And you think doing so will let you see who's a rogue?" It didn't seem like such an odd request if it could pinpoint the root of our problem.

"Rogue enforcers are rare; Cheryl was only the third in the United States since the birth of this country. The other wardens might not know what they're looking for. Or I'm wrong, and it's something else, but between the combined experience of six wardens, it seems unlikely we haven't figured this out. Unless someone's not telling the truth."

"Why would anyone lie?"

"To fix the problem on their own. To be the regional hero."

Was that what Mr. Pitt was trying to do? If he could pinpoint the source of all our problems, he'd be a hero, and it might secure his position.

"What I'm asking you to do is simple: You push *lux lucis* into me the same as you would anything else. But it's dangerous. If done wrong, it could drain you—kill you."

"How much do you want to take?"

"As much as I can."

I swallowed. In other words, my boss wanted to *almost* kill me.

21

Always Give 100%...Unless You're Giving Blood

I DON'T ASK ON A WHIM, Madison, and I don't want you to say yes lightly, either. Give it some thought." He stood and exited the room, heading toward the break room. The silence of the nearly empty office settled around me.

I knew Mr. Pitt's ugly secret now: He'd unwittingly fostered a rogue and an enforcer had died under his command. Some wardens thought that reason enough for Mr. Pitt to be forced into retirement. Liam had gone so far as to accuse Mr. Pitt of being careless with his enforcers.

I hadn't thought much of Liam's accusation at the time. Mr. Pitt was not careless with my safety. And if Liam had meant to imply Cheryl going rogue had been Mr. Pitt's fault, he gave my boss too much credit. Morality choices were never made by a second party; my attempt to force good into Sam proved that. Mr. Pitt couldn't have forced an enforcer to work both sides. That had been Cheryl's choice. And if Liam had been inferring Mr. Pitt was to blame for Lupe's death, I couldn't make that accusation stick, either. Mr. Pitt erred on the side of caution to the point of irritation.

Which brought me back to the heart of Mr. Pitt's request: Was I ready to put my life in his hands? The answer came immediately and with remarkable ease. Yes. I'd trusted Mr. Pitt with my safety since the day I'd been hired. Knowing the mistakes and misfortunes of his past didn't change anything.

"What do you need me to do?" I asked when he returned with a fresh mug of coffee.

Mr. Pitt rearranged his office furniture so the two leather chairs faced each other. He sat in one, and I took the other. Jamie crowded close to my chair, alert now and focused on Mr. Pitt.

"Take my hands."

Mr. Pitt's hands were small, meaty, and faintly damp in my cold fingers.

"Push *lux lucis* into me as if I were an imp."

I blinked to Primordium. Mr. Pitt's now-familiar soul, with its bulky lines and odd angles, hugged his body. My own soul looked crisp. Letting out a breath, I pushed *lux lucis* from my fingertips into Mr. Pitt. A film of resistance pushed back, then my energy slid into him.

It didn't take long for the strong white lines of Mr. Pitt's soul to sharpen and harden until they resembled opaque glass. It reminded me of how my soul had looked after Jamie had supercharged me while destroying the imps. I wanted to look at the pooka to see his reaction, but I couldn't draw my gaze from Mr. Pitt. Pressure built inside him. I could feel it against my hands almost like a physical barrier. Then the intangible boundaries of his soul burst, and *lux lucis* spread in a corona around Mr. Pitt. The shape of his soul morphed, encroaching in an ivory tide across the map lines of the adjacent regions. Sweat dripped down Mr. Pitt's face, but he remained perfectly still.

I no longer pushed *lux lucis*; it pulled from me, draining into Mr. Pitt. The sensation mirrored being trapped inside the vervet without the pain. My foot jiggled. This was Mr. Pitt, not an oversize vervet. I was safe.

My breaths shortened. Just in case, I cut back the flow to a trickle— or tried: My *lux lucis* didn't respond. It gushed through my fingertips, swirling up from toes and sinking from my head in a dizzying rush.

We needed to stop. Soon. *Now.* I tried to speak, but the words stuck in my throat. Mr. Pitt's soul bulged and flexed, pulling the urgency from me and replacing it with lassitude. My foot stilled and I slumped in my chair, sinking into the fluid energy of *lux lucis* gliding through me. My eyelids drooped, but I held them open to watch Mr. Pitt's soul, fancying I saw shapes in its outline. A shield. A heart. A book. Was Val influencing this? I giggled.

My fingers tingled, and the sensation spread up my arms straight to my head. Darkness pulsed at the edges of my blurred vision. I floated, but my feet stuck to the floor as it receded, and my shins stretched like taffy. I ran a tongue around my mouth, and the sensation bubbled through my head.

An angel stood over me, with wings so vast they looked like a solid sheet behind him. Fleshy froggish lips moved, but the language of the heavens was incomprehensible babble beneath the roar in my ears. Maybe not an angel. Maybe a cherub. Angels had full heads of hair, or they should.

He pressed a cold dropper between my lips. Liquid fire trickled down my throat, and I crashed to earth, gasping. The cherub laid a heavy forearm across my collarbone, holding me down and pouring another thimbleful of flames into my mouth. Coughing, I pushed him away. Heat speared from my stomach to my limbs, but when the burn receded, I could feel my fingers and toes again, and everything in between.

Mr. Pitt stepped back, capping a tiny thimble of *lux lucis* concentrate. I groaned. Not that stuff again. I'd barely gotten rid of today's headache.

"How do you feel?"

"Have you ever noticed how much space exists between your cells?"

Mr. Pitt arched an eyebrow. "Here." He handed me a water bottle. I downed it, then accepted a yogurt and spoon. The dairy sat heavy on my tongue, like squishy velvet. I pushed each bite around my mouth, finishing the container far too soon. Mr. Pitt paced the office, his exaggerated soul sweeping through the walls and furniture.

"Did it work?"

He planted a foot and spun to face me, his soul haloed around him like a peacock's plumage on display. "It's far too soon to be sure. I can't rush this. I need to . . ." He tapped his chin and resumed pacing. I scooted my chair back to avoid the sweep of his soul when he turned. Sinking into my body, I assessed my *lux lucis*. My levels were low, but no longer dangerously so. Between the *lux lucis* concentrate and the yogurt, I was in pretty good shape, considering Mr. Pitt had almost drained me dry minutes earlier. I flexed my *lux lucis*, looping it around my palm, savoring being back in control.

Mr. Pitt jumped when I tossed the empty yogurt container in the trash, confirming my suspicion he'd forgotten me.

"Did I hurt you?"

I shook my head. It'd been intoxicating and frightening, but not painful. "Have you done that before?"

"Yes, but only from your position."

That surprised me. "How do *you* feel?" I blinked to normal sight. Mr. Pitt's cheeks were flush with good health, his eyes bright.

"Heavy. You should go. I need to concentrate before I lose this."

I left him pacing his office, muttering to himself. Jamie supported me with his shoulder, watching me with large puppy eyes. Sharon rose from her desk to unlock the front door for us. I tried not to gawk. I'd never seen her move. She was tiny, inches shorter than my chin, with a brisk stride on black orthopedic shoes, and after Jamie and I were through the doors, she stepped out into the hall, her weighted glare tracking us to the lobby.

"I need to recharge." Once we were outside, I angled for a walkway lined with trees. Jamie sniffed at the base of trunks, relieving himself on several while I soaked up *lux lucis*. Less than twenty-four hours ago, I'd stood in this parking lot with a mammoth, yet already Jamie didn't feel like a stranger. He felt like a part of me. I wondered if the imprint still clouded my thoughts and realized I didn't care.

"Do you want to change back or stay a dog?"

Jamie barked. Unsure how to interpret that, I opened the passenger door to give him access to his clothes. He waited. I opened the back door and he jumped in. I needed to stick to yes or no questions while he was in Great Dane form.

I slid behind the wheel. Despite leaving the windows cracked, the Civic reeked of smoke, reminding me of my own stench—and reigniting my craving for a shower. I powered the windows all the way down, and we rode home with the sound of the wind and scents of the city filling the car. I drove on autopilot, grateful for the limited traffic and short commute. After everything that had happened today, my concentration was shot.

I sent Jamie to shower first. That involved teaching him how to work the knobs, and since those required hands, it meant I spent an uncomfortable minute in the close confines of my bathroom with a naked pooka man who possessed zero modesty. Despite using the curtain as a shield between us, I still got an eyeful. Proportional was relative. Of course, if I could choose my form, and if I were a man, I'd have made similar endowment—

Nope. Not going there.

I fled the bathroom with scarlet cheeks and slammed the door behind me.

Mr. Bond chirped. He'd polished off the top layer of fresh food I'd poured when I arrived, and now he twined between my legs. I scooped him up and snuggled him. He tolerated being held long enough to sniff my sweater, hair, and face, then shoved to the floor. With his supervision and steady stream of critiques, I affixed fresh wards to the doors and window, started a load of laundry, laid out wet food for the obese and spoiled cat, then joined him on the floor because I didn't want my grubby clothes on the furniture.

I propped Val up on the seat of my recliner and opened him so we could chat hands-free.

"How're you doing? Any weird effects from that energy transfer?"

The words started at the top of the page in a huge font and dwindled down to an unreadable size. *You should not have done that. It was dangerous and hasty and foolish and half-baked and senseless and—*

"Val, you're babbling."

Pigheaded, harebrained, insane. That's what you humans are. As a species, you need to learn patience.

"So you're fine?"

I'm fine. Are you? You were . . . not there for a bit.

"I'm fine. I passed out."

You'll never do that again?

"I don't know. You mentioned needing to research earlier. How do you do that?"

Are you trying to distract me?

Maybe. "I want to help you as you've helped me."

Humph. He actually wrote out the word. *Fine. I research by reading up on subjects.*

"You can read?"

Val remained pointedly silent.

"It wasn't a dumb question. I meant, how? By osmosis?"

You give me far too much credit. I read like anyone else. The next words were almost too small to see. *I just require assistance turning the pages.*

I pictured holding Val over an encyclopedia for hours, turning the pages on command. It sounded like a mild form of torture. "What about audio books?"

I'm unfamiliar with that species.

I grinned. After explaining what an audio book was, and privately wondering why no enforcer in the last few decades had brought Val up to date, I asked, "Do you want to listen to a few tonight? See if you like them?" I crossed my fingers behind my back.

I might.

Such rousing enthusiasm. "Anything in particular? I'm not talking research books here. What about a little fun reading? We've both been working a lot lately. It might be good for you to unwind." Plus, he'd be more likely to use audio books if he enjoyed the first few.

Reading for fun?

"You know, fiction. Escapist reads. Funny things."

His answer took a few beats. *What do you like?*

"Romance. Fantasy." My interest in fantasy was new, but it was fast becoming the most relatable genre.

Okay.

Mr. Bond had settled himself across my folded legs to clean his whiskers and he didn't budge when I wiggled the laptop in place on the recliner's seat. After logging on to an online bookstore, I selected a few of my favorite authors and lifted Val to see the screen. Val read the book blurbs while I petted Mr. Bond. Splashing sounds emanated from the bathroom. It was a remarkably normal, homey scene despite the fact that of the four sentient creatures in my apartment, I was the only human.

Val selected Jim Butcher's *Storm Front*, Robin McKinley's *Sunshine*, and Robin D. Owens's *Heart Mate*. He had good taste. I loaded all three in a library so they'd play back-to-back, with *Heart Mate* first at Val's request. I set the laptop to not go to sleep, then attached my headphones and carried it and Val to the closet. Mr. Bond, dumped from my lap, followed. I placed the headphones against Val and adjusted the volume to his liking, then closed the book and laptop safely in the closet, out of Mr. Bond's reach. My cat pouted all of five seconds before darting into the open bathroom door where Jamie stood, naked, towel wrapped around his head.

"Around your hips. The towel goes around your hips," I said. I shielded my eyes and chose a baggy pair of sleep shorts for him. Then I rushed into the bathroom. The hot water relaxed the stress in my limbs, and the exhaustion from the day's events caught up with me before I emerged from the steamy room. I gathered blankets for Jamie and set a bed up for him on the recliner, with a promise that he would not leak *atrum* in his sleep. Jamie gave me an affronted look ruined by a huge yawn. I brushed my teeth—making a note to buy Jamie a toothbrush, too—and climbed into bed. Mr. Bond flopped across my stomach, and I petted him until the rumble of his purr lulled me to sleep.

Salamanders chased me through my dreams, lighting fires in my apartment. When I extinguished the flames and killed the salamander— using a pizza topped with yogurt sauce—Jacob burst through the blackened doorway. He carried a spear gun in each hand, and he shot Jamie through his human heart with one gun and through his dog heart with the other.

I woke drenched in sweat. Peeling back the covers, I stared at the light of the alarm clock: 6:42. My head throbbed. Since I wasn't going to get good sleep in the next eighteen minutes, I swung my feet over the edge of the bed, pleasantly surprised that the sharp pain in my ankle had subsided to a sore ache. My toes hit something solid and warm. I jerked back and clicked on my bedside lamp.

Jamie lay tangled in his blankets on the floor beside the bed, his hair mussed a dozen different directions. Gold eyes blinked at me.

"Everyone was in here. I was lonely," he said.

We took turns in the bathroom and squeezed together in the kitchen. Jamie decided he wanted dog food for breakfast, and I insisted he eat it as a dog, which he thought was amusing. I found it nauseating to watch him eat kibble as a human. Of course, since he remained seated at the table, his front paws on either side of his bowl, and drooling as much as he ate, it ended up ruining my appetite anyway. Mr. Bond sulked atop the back of the recliner, either because Jamie got to eat at the table or because it was the first time he'd seen the pooka's dog form.

"What'd you think of your first audio book experience?" I asked Val when I collected him.

It merits further study.

"And your first paranormal romance?"

Humans are very preoccupied with each other's bodies.

"And you're not attracted to a book with a well-turned spine?"

That's different.

I'd been teasing, not expecting Val to get the joke. Biting my lip, I dropped the subject. I did not want to venture into the-birds-and-the-bees conversation with a book.

I convinced Jamie he didn't need another shower, then helped him pick out clothes. I made another mental note to get the boy underwear after a lengthy argument about the uncomfortable ridges of the only pair of jeans I had that fit him and the necessity for him to wear them. Not just underwear: I needed to get him a whole wardrobe of his own. Which reminded me I needed to check for a pooka budget to assist newly imprinted enforcers.

Mr. Bond circled us, demanding attention throughout the morning, but when we headed for the door, he flopped on the recliner and stretched his head out on his paw. Sad eyes tracked us. Jamie wanted to bring him with us, and I was more than a little tempted. Surely I could add one more creature to my traveling menagerie. Except bringing along a cat was far different than a pooka or a sentient book. Mr. Bond would end up spending the day in the car instead of the apartment, with nothing to eat and nowhere to go to the bathroom. He'd also likely escape and get hurt. With a heavy heart, I shut the door, and his forlorn expression haunted me.

We stopped at the grocery store to restock salamander-exterminating supplies. Jamie loaded the cart with two grocery bags' worth of snacks while I filled the rest with gallons of water, a tub of the cheapest yogurt, and a small ice chest. We were transferring everything to the trunk when my phone rang. I dug Medusa out of my purse.

"Get to the office. Now," Mr. Pitt said, then hung up.

Adrenaline sparked in my stomach and frizzled to my extremities. He'd found something. I shoved the rest of the groceries into the trunk and zipped out of the lot.

Sharon greeted us with her usual cheer. Jamie ignored her, which I decided was an improvement over their first staring match. I waved jauntily to make up for him.

"In here, Madison."

I'd rounded the conference room wall, expecting to see Rose creating more cito spray—those working the mall would continue to need it through the end of the year—but Mr. Pitt had commandeered the large room. A huge map covered most of the long table, and the pull-down screen against the back wall contained a projection of the map Liam had made for the meeting a week ago. The markings on the map flickered every five seconds with the time stamp, noting spots of evil in the last two weeks, complete with yesterday's data. It was my first viewing of the map since the meeting. We weren't doing well. The frequency of evil had increased in the last week, despite everyone's best efforts and group coordination.

Mr. Pitt looked like he'd aged a dozen years since I'd left him last night. Gone was his healthy glow and bright eyes. This morning, his skin lay sallow under the fluorescent lights, dark purple underscored his eyes, and weariness sat heavy on the corners of his mouth. He wore yesterday's clothes, now wrinkled like tissue paper, the previously neat blue shirt untucked and unbuttoned to reveal a few inches of a white undershirt. Steam rose from the coffee cup in his hand, and the burnt smell of it permeated the room.

"You should not have agreed to do this."

I jumped at the deep, irritated voice. If I'd had any doubt I'd been working too hard lately, overlooking Niko proved it. He leaned against the wall beside the door, leather-clad arms crossed over his chest, long legs braced shoulder width apart. His dark eyes smoldered, and his full lips were pulled flat. Yep, even pissed off, he was hot enough to lick up.

"Hi, Niko."

He pushed off the wall and stalked toward me. I backed up a step, bumping into Jamie. The pooka twined his fingers in mine and squeezed, sticking close to loom in my periphery, shoulders taller and wider than they should have been. I darted my gaze away from Niko's to the pooka. Jamie's jaw was hard and defined.

Niko grabbed my shoulders. Heat from his fingers seared through my thin sweater. I jerked my gaze back to the optivus aegis.

"What's wrong? Are you okay?" I asked. Over Niko's shoulder, I could see Mr. Pitt drumming his fingers on the tabletop and glaring at Niko's back. What had Niko's panties in a bunch?

"Giving Brad your *lux lucis* was foolish and dangerous."

Ah. That. If I opened Val, *I told you so* would be written in huge letters across his main page. Niko studied my face from far too close, then ran his eyes down my body. He was checking my soul, but it didn't prevent me from blushing. Didn't this office have air-conditioning?

"You did the same for me once," I said, referring to my disastrous first run-in with the demon and the energy Niko had fed me to help me recover.

"I gave you enough to bring you back to consciousness. I didn't drain myself into you. I didn't—" Niko's fingers squeezed my shoulders with bruising force.

"You did what was necessary. So did I." Without looking away from the furious heat of Niko's eyes, I asked, "Mr. Pitt, did you find what we need?"

"Yes."

"Then it was the right thing to do." I leaned back, tired of being held. I'd done nothing wrong. My voice came out hard. "I followed my warden's wisdom. Just like you said I should."

Niko's jaw bunched; then he released me. I caught my balance and shook my wrist a little to remind Jamie he was squeezing the blood from my fingers. The pooka uncurled his fingers and stepped back.

"Did Brad tell you how dangerous it was?"

"Of course."

"I think we can all see Madison survived, Niko. Now, if you two are done with your hellos, we've got problems to take care of."

Problems was an understatement. Thanks to my *lux lucis*, Mr. Pitt had used his enhanced warden senses to label the paper map on the table with dozens of red dots, each signifying a hot spot of evil. His labels extended deep into Liam's region to the south, past Isabel's region to the west, and far into the foothills to the north and east. The discrepancies between Mr. Pitt's map and Liam's map were blatant. Liam's map made our region appear to be the epicenter of evil. Mr. Pitt's map put the bulk of the problems in Isabel's region and added a fair number to Liam's region.

When I commented on the discrepancies, Mr. Pitt released a disgusted snort.

"That's the problem with getting the inspectors involved," he said. "Now everyone wants their caramel crap to look lemon drop sparkly."

"Are you saying Liam and Isabel haven't been reporting some of their problems?" I asked.

Mr. Pitt spread his arms wide, sweeping the map in a vigorous "see for yourself" gesture.

"Some of this could be skewed by Jacob not being present," Niko said, ignoring Mr. Pitt's theatrics and tapping the middle of Isabel's heavily marked region. "But not all of it. Maybe Jacob isn't as good as we've been told and Isabel's covering for him."

Or maybe my original suspicion of Jacob was spot-on. If he was rogue and cultivating evil in his region, it would flourish while he was laid up. Summer and Grace would have their hands full today.

"I don't give a cinnamon stick about Isabel's region!"

I jumped at Mr. Pitt's explosion. His mask of fatigued impatience gave way to pure, vein-pulsing fury. Mr. Pitt jabbed a blunt finger at two locations on the map marked in red and circled until the pen had ripped holes through the paper. One sat within the confines of our new territory, the other on the northwestern fringe where Isabel's, Margaret's, and our border met. "Something's here and here. Something big. Sitting right under my butterscotch-blind nose. The rest of this"—he swirled his arms over the red-splattered map—"is taffy turds."

"What's so special about those?"

"Both are big evils, bigger than all the rest, and ringed in *lux lucis*."

"So they're contained?" I glanced between the men, confused.

"We don't contain evil," Niko said. "We eliminate it. Someone or something planted these problems and then disguised them."

"They did a sugary job, too." Mr. Pitt scrubbed his face. Stubble rasped against his palm. "They could have been here a day or a year. Gofer gumdrops on fruitcake! All the *lux lucis* around them blinds my normal senses. I probably could have stood right next to them and never felt them without Madison's enhancement."

"How do we know who put them there?" I asked. Was Jacob hoarding evil in our region?

"There should be clues on-site," Niko said. "I think you've found the source, or sources, of this area's problems."

"At least we weren't the only target. It looks like this one"—I pointed to the southern circle in our new territory—"might have been meant for Liam."

"Maybe," Niko said. "Or it could have been placed there in the last twenty-four hours."

"That's the cookie-crumble problem: I didn't even know they existed yesterday!" Mr. Pitt drummed heavy fingers on the tabletop. "The location of both is suspect. They're both close to the borders of multiple regions, yet still within our region. If I were setting someone up, this is exactly how I'd go about it."

"How do you want to proceed?" Niko asked.

"We don't have time to waste. Niko, you take whatever's here," Mr. Pitt said, pointing to the circle previously in Liam's region. "It's the stronger of the two. Madison, you're on the other one." Mr. Pitt fixed his bug-eyed gaze on me. "It should go without saying that whatever you're walking into is dangerous and you should use all the caution you've yet to exhibit. If it's something you've never encountered, call me. Niko will check in with you as soon as he's cleaned up his area."

My heart thumped in anticipation. Considering I'd fought less than ten types of evil, the odds were high I'd be on the phone with Mr. Pitt in a few minutes.

"He told me about his LA past," I said to Niko when we were nearly to our cars.

"Good." Niko divided his attention between me and Jamie, who trailed behind us, peering into the sleepy offices along the hall.

"Do you think it's happening again?"

"A rogue enforcer?" Niko stopped, his dark eyes unreadable. Wind lifted my hair into my eyes, and I tucked it behind an ear. "A person who is learning too fast, who seems capable of handling more than she should? That sounds familiar."

"Are you talking about me? Do you think I'm rogue?" I expected him to laugh, but his serious expression didn't change.

"I think it's dangerous to jump to conclusions. Be careful, Madison."

"Feeling cryptic, are we?" I grumbled, but I waited until I closed myself inside the Civic before I spoke.

"You're strong," Jamie said. "You could be full rogue in a few days."

I goggled at him. "Ah, thank you, but no. I like being all *lux lucis*."

Jamie sighed.

Medusa played "SexyBack" as I merged onto I-80 at Eureka. I hit speakerphone and gunned the Civic in front of a semi.

"Niko? Are you okay?"

"I'm fine. I've found a turbonis, a large one. About the size of my car. This is going to take me a while. If you encounter the same, call me. Do *not* attempt to unravel it on your own."

"Do you need help?"

"No."

"What's a—" The phone went dead. "Turbonis."

I peeled off the freeway at Rocklin Road and spun a hard right onto the frontage road. "Jamie, do you know what a turbonis is?"

"Twisted." He powered down his window, filling the cabin with freezing wind. I turned the heater on high. I should never have introduced him to Sam. Somehow he'd picked up the teen's slang in the few seconds they'd talked.

We arrived at our destination minutes later. With the accuracy of my *lux lucis*, Mr. Pitt had pinpointed the mysterious disguised evil spot down to a specific house. I checked the address and parked a few car lengths from the end of the driveway. Interstate 80 ran a few hundred yards behind me, hidden by several twists in the road. Farther ahead of me, subdivisions bisected the rise of the hill in tidy rows, but here huge native oaks surrounded a smattering of homes on large irregular lots twisting around a creek and old quarry.

The house looked innocuous. Like the rest in the neighborhood, it was a single story, with the bland architecture indicative of homes built in the '90s and a carport instead of a garage. The house sat farther back from the road than most, and no fence contained its yard. Beyond the house, the rain-deprived landscape sloped toward a band of lush native flora thriving along a creek. Smoke rose from the roof. Someone was home despite the lack of a car in the driveway.

I wiped damp palms on my thighs and pulled Val from his strap.

Twisted is far too simplistic, Val's first page said.

"What?"

Check the turbonis page. You'll see.

I flipped through the glowing pages, knee jiggling with suppressed nerves.

TURBONIS. Sometimes called an atrum *tornado, a turbonis is a vortex of pure evil. Usually they are created from* atrum *stirred to action by the continuous movement of evil creatures within a confined area. Once formed, a turbonis can evolve all* atrum *it encounters, including creatures. Unpredictable, these phenomena must be carefully unraveled. Use caution: New evil spins within the vortex and will emerge at random, fully formed, even as the funnel is unraveled.*

Beside the text was a sketch of a tornado, the base surrounded by imps. *Twisted.* I got it now.

"What do you mean, it 'evolves' *atrum*?" I asked, flipping back to Val's first page.

To put it crudely, a turbonis sucks in atrum—*pure or in sentient form—and spits out something stronger. It might consume an imp and spit out a hound.*

"A real, physical hound?"

It can't make anything physical, but a pure atrum *hound can cause as much, if not more, damage than a flesh-and-blood hound. However, creatures of pure* atrum *are rarely intelligent. A turbonis might devour a bunch of evil and spit out a demon no smarter than an imp.*

"Like the one Summer encountered while I was stuck at the mall? Rafi took out one yesterday, too. Could they have come from the turbonis?"

Brad said lux lucis *surrounded it. The only reason someone would do that is to control the turbonis and hold it in a location, if they were stupid. If there is something strong enough to disguise and hold a turbonis, it would be strong enough to eliminate anything the turbonis created.*

"Could someone harvest the creatures and transport them?"

It's possible.

The turbonis had been in Liam's territory, Liam's and Summer's. Why hang on to something so evil? Maybe Liam hadn't held on to it because he wanted it. Maybe he'd netted it like a hound and had been waiting until things died down before tasking his enforcers with taking care of it.

If so, why not tell Niko? Why keep it a secret? Out of shame that it formed in his region? Or for a more sinister reason? If he'd netted the turbonis before yesterday, Liam should have told Mr. Pitt about it when we took over that part of the territory. Maybe that was intentional. If a turbonis appeared in Mr. Pitt's region, it could be perceived as one more check mark on a long list of reasons to kick Mr. Pitt out. All of which assumed Liam had known of the turbonis's existence and didn't explain the second contained evil I was psyching myself up to face.

I circled back to my theory of Jacob being a rogue enforcer. Maybe he'd planted the turbonis and had been waiting to unleash it until he could step in and be the hero, and Jamie had mucked up those plans when he skewered the enforcer. But that didn't explain why Jacob would have planted it in Liam's region. Why not capture and contain the turbonis in his own territory? Even if he thought to discredit Mr. Pitt, Jacob hadn't known Mr. Pitt and I would take over that slice of Liam's territory. At the time, he'd been at the hospital.

"What are we waiting for?" Jamie asked.

Courage. I didn't say it out loud. Whatever lurked at the end of this driveway, it wasn't going to be fun or easy. Half of me hoped I'd find another turbonis. Then I could call Niko and wait for his assistance. Maybe I should wait for him anyway. I could exert caution, as Mr. Pitt wanted, and wait to have the big, bad optivus aegis at my back.

I blinked to Primordium. The landscape looked exactly as it should: gray house, gray dead weeds, white trees, black sky. No *atrum* coated the driveway. No demons lurked behind trees. Not even a single imp bounced our way. All was quiet and calm. It would be foolish to interrupt the peace, right?

A prajurit dropped to stand on the windshield in front of me. I jumped and hit the horn by accident. It—no, *he*—lifted on a blur of wings and zipped down the driveway, disappearing into the white oak tree canopy.

I undid my seat belt. With the exception of the night Jamie's wild energy had called a few prajurit—along with half the state's population of evil creatures—no one had seen a single prajurit in our troubled regions. Pinpointing the reason for their disappearance was almost as important as discovering the source of all the evil currently plaguing our region. I needed to catch that fellow; a prajurit appearing here, now, couldn't be a coincidence.

I took a deep breath and grabbed the door handle. It was time to prove I was the enforcer I claimed to be.

22

Betrayal Never Comes from Your Enemies

"STAY CLOSE." I WOULD HAVE told Jamie to stay in the car if I thought he'd obey, but his soul whirled with excitement, white and black swooping through his limbs in an endless riotous waterfall. I looked away before I became dizzy.

Jamie bounced out of the car. I stood and checked my arsenal. Val on the hip. Check. Pet wood and Medusa in my back pockets. Check. Knife at my belt. Tentative check. *Please don't make me need to stab anything.* Enough water and probiotics to kill a congress of salamanders. Check. One unpredictable pooka. Che—

Jamie lifted his nose to the air, scenting, then sprinted around the side of the house.

"Jamie!" I hissed. Growling, I jogged after him, but my footsteps slowed to a creeping tiptoe close to the house. I felt exposed and jittery. Heavy drapes shrouded the house's windows, and I strained to hear movement inside. A soft wind rustled the oaks' bare branches and pushed dried leaves across the gravel, but the interior remained eerily silent. Any second, the door was going to burst open and unfathomable evil would spill out.

When that didn't happen, I forced myself closer to the porch.

I hesitated at the sagging steps. The weathered wooden boards looked like they'd creak loud enough to rouse a slumbering demon. I set a foot softly on the first step and eased my weight onto it, leaping backward at the sudden raucous cry of a blue jay. It repeated its obnoxious call, then flew off through the trees. I waited, willing my heartbeat to slow, and strained to hear anything that might provide a clue about what lurked inside the house. The house and grounds remained quiet. Shouldn't I at least be hearing Jamie? Where was he and what was he getting into? What if he'd followed the prajurit and the danger wasn't in the house but somewhere near it? Cursing, I skulked around the side of the house, trying to look every direction at once.

"Jamie?" I pitched my voice low. "Prajurit?"

I checked and rechecked the curtained windows of the spooky charcoal house, unable to shake the hair-raising sensation of being watched. Nothing moved inside, and when I scanned the weed-studded pewter yard and the smattering of large white oaks, I didn't catch sight of Jamie, either. My footsteps on the gravel-strewn dirt crunched loudly as I minced down the side of the house, knife clutched in my right hand, pet wood in my left.

I reminded myself I was an enforcer. I had magical powers. Some had even called me a superhero.

A bright white lizard shot from the shade of the house past my feet, and I clamped a hand over my mouth to squelch a scream. The extended tip of pet wood grazed the siding, screeching like nails on a chalkboard. I jumped away from the wall, spinning to check for enemies sneaking up on me. My heart hammered against my ribs. No one materialized, including Jamie.

A whiff of decay hit my nose, then disappeared. I took another deep breath, catching a faint undercurrent of rot. On leaden feet, I sidled up to the back of the house, and the smell grew stronger. *Please, not a dead body.* I peeked around the corner.

A huge glass greenhouse easily twice as large as my apartment squatted in a bleak gray yard. The packed interior glowed with *lux lucis*, a radiant nature-made light box. Beyond the greenhouse, a barren charcoal hill sloped into dense vegetation growing along the creek, screening the backyard from neighbors.

A man-shaped swirl of *atrum* moved in the center of the greenhouse. Jamie. Without his dichotomous soul, it would have been easy to miss him amid the floor-to-ceiling jungle. In normal sight, he would have been invisible.

I rushed forward, remembering at the last second to check the back of the house. Like the front, all the windows were blanketed. My paranoia spiked. This was too easy, but I couldn't turn away, not with Jamie inside. Damn the pooka for rushing ahead!

Cold wind swirled across the greenhouse and I snorted. The foul odor emanated from the plant-packed enclosure. The rumble of Jamie's voice filtered out of the propped-open windows at the top of the glass walls, but I couldn't make out his words.

Bracing myself against a gruesome discovery, I tugged open the door. Moist heat spilled over me, carrying a coiling reek of decomposing manure. I rocked on my heels. Wall-to-wall plants pressed white limbs to the glass, searching for an escape. I considered calling Jamie to me, but I didn't want to bring attention to myself—from whatever was in the house or in the greenhouse.

Pushing enormous fronds aside, I squeezed into the mass of plants, unzipping my jacket as sweat instantly popped out on my forehead. The tight, humid confines amplified the odor, and I took shallow breaths, refusing to envision possible sources of the rotting odor coating my nose and tongue. I attempted to move stealthily through the tight path, but after slinking two feet, wincing at every scuffle and scrape of leaves against my clothing, I gave up on a secretive, quiet approach. Though I couldn't make out his words, Jamie sounded urgent, suggesting that I didn't have time to sneak. I embraced my inner rhino, barreling through aggressive vegetation and trampling thorny vines.

"There's something wrong with it," Jamie said, clear and close.

A higher-pitched voice answered him, the words inaudible above my racket. I strained to see Jamie. Was the greenhouse the *lux lucis* ring Mr. Pitt had felt, not the house? Plants this dense could hide a pack of hounds. Hounds who'd rolled in dirty diapers. The nauseating odor coiled in my throat. Did I really want to find the source?

Flies buzzed my face, and I brushed them aside, catching my arm on a sticky vine. I hacked myself free with the knife, raining tiny white petals atop my sweaty head. Through the last layer of foliage, I could see Jamie's liquid soul. I readied my weapons, heart hammering.

Pausing, I blinked to normal sight to make sense of the scene. Isolated in a small clearing of plants sat a knee-high black plastic pot. A single flower grew in it, but it was a flower unlike any I'd seen before. The base, thicker than my neck, sprouted into an enormous sturdy yellow-green petal easily three feet tall, like a pleated Easter lily petal on steroids. The top of the petal folded in a soft ruffled collar, revealing a velvety purple-maroon interior. Flies crawled into the heart of the flower, disappearing deep inside the enormous blossom. From the center of the flower, a grayish green, tonguelike column rose to the roof. The flower was too big for me to wrap my arms around, several feet taller than me, and smelled like death warmed over.

I blinked back to Primordium. The elephantine flower glowed with *lux lucis*. I glanced around in confusion. The carrion stench emanated from the flower, yet the flower wasn't evil. In fact, there wasn't a speck of *atrum* in the greenhouse, not counting Jamie. This couldn't have been what Mr. Pitt sensed.

Batting flies from my face, I stepped into the open and circled the stinky plant as I headed toward Jamie, hugging the jungle perimeter. I still couldn't understand the high-pitched voices, but I realized now it was because they weren't speaking English. However, the tones of an argument were universal.

I stopped beside Jamie. Tense lines bracketed his mouth, and he reached for my hand, settling on holding my shoulder when he saw I held a knife.

Two prajurit stood on the lip of the purple petal. Both were dressed in outfits similar to those worn by the prajurit who'd attended Jamie's hatching, though the fabric hung ragged on the woman. In Primordium, with them standing still, their wings stretched like gossamer kites behind them, almost too perfect and fragile to be believably functional. Neither acknowledged my existence. The man stared down into the flower, his face yearning, but the woman clung to his arms, pulling him back.

"What's happening?" I asked.

"He's ending," Jamie said.

"What?"

The woman screamed and slapped the man. He shoved her over the edge toward the floor with a harsh yell, then dove into the flower. The woman dropped a foot before catching herself. She fluttered drunkenly back to the petal's lip, tears dripping down her perfect triangular face. Her voice lifted in a broken song. I didn't understand the words or the reason for the woman's sorrow.

I glanced at Jamie. Grief hung heavy on his face.

The male prajurit climbed out of the flower on hands and knees, his luminous wings limp. Black flecks coated his shirt and pantaloons and smeared his face. He rolled to his back atop the petal, a blissful smile on his tiny face.

"That looks like *atrum* powder. We can't let—"

The prajurit spasmed, clutching his stomach and twisting into a ball. With a soft groan, he twisted and plummeted from the flower. I yelled and jumped to catch him, but his wings unfurled. For a moment, he coasted; then his body went limp. His wings folded back and he crashed the last two feet to the concrete floor.

"No!" I leapt forward, too late to catch him. He landed in a heap, his body already fading to gray. I crouched helplessly over the minuscule dead warrior, staring at his mangled corpse. I almost missed the body of another prajurit coated in *atrum* and crumpled atop a wide *lux lucis-*white leaf. This one hadn't fallen; she had curled up and died.

I blinked to normal sight. Yellow pollen replaced *atrum* powder on both prajurit. The flower had poisoned them.

Brushing aside tears, I rose.

"Wahyu, you've abandoned me," the female prajurit whispered. Then, louder, she announce, "Bereft of home and clan, I shall cast myself upon titan's mercy and drink its sun-drenched nectar one last time. Then to fair days' end I go, to be reunited under the eternal sun." She clung to Jamie's ear, wings flapping as she swayed on his shoulder despite his statue-still stance.

A jolt of surprise pinged through me. I knew this prajurit. She'd been the first to kiss my forehead after Jamie had supercharged me in the parking garage.

"Why did he kill himself?" I demanded. Anyone with a nose could tell this flower was toxic. "Was he forced?" I needed to be pointed in the right direction. I needed to take action.

The prajurit tilted her head back and released a shrill wail that bounced down octaves until it became a song, the foreign words interrupted by hiccups and sniffles.

Frustrated, I turned to the plant. Hoisting myself up to stand on the enormous pot, I grabbed hold of the purple petal. My fingers crushed a velvety fold five times thicker than a rose petal. Tugging, I pulled the petal wide open. Inside, a honeycomb of pollen stamens wrapped the thick stalk. Delicate veins of *atrum* overlaid the pollen, sifting down to sprinkle across strange bulbous tubers at the flower's base. I blinked to normal sight, unsurprised to find the tainted pollen a cheerful yellow. Death floated up my nose. I fell headfirst into the flower and caught myself with wobbly knees. The stuffy building continued to spin, and I planted a knee in the dirt, stabilizing myself with a hand on the rim of the pot.

"Remember me, Lestari Suryawijaya, last of the *Suku Dari Matahari*, unfit for this world."

"Sunan, no, you must stay," Jamie said.

Who was *Sunan*? Were the fumes muddling my hearing?

Lestari lifted from Jamie's shoulders, her wings beating barely fast enough to keep her aloft.

"Sweet, sweet poison, take me from this cursed existence." She angled for the lip of the flower. I spun, standing in a dizzy rush. Breathing shallowly through my mouth, I waved a hand in front of the prajurit.

"Wait. Lestari, please."

She veered out of reach. "I told them not to taste it. I ordered them." She planted fists on her hips, but her arms slid limp after a few seconds. "No one listened. Batari, Slamet, Mega. No one. I am unfit to rule. Unfit to live." Tears spilled from her large brown eyes. "Let me die. I don't want to be alone."

"You're not alone," I said.

"Never alone," Jamie said.

Lestari wobbled left as if to go around me, but I stepped into her flight path again. I couldn't grab her without hurting her, but I couldn't let her near the flower, either.

"Sunan Lestari. Rest on me awhile." Jamie waved a hand, and the prajurit turned, her eyes tracking his fingers like he held her under a spell. I blinked to Primordium. Jamie's hand radiated *lux lucis* so bright I could barely see the definition of his fingers. The rest of his soul clouded with *atrum*, but Lestari didn't seem to notice anything but his hand. She settled her feet on his palm, then sat, unhampered by her insectlike abdomen.

Jamie's eyes spun with angry energy. "The queen and I will be outside."

I swallowed and nodded. Had his face always been so angular? Jamie shoved through the path I'd carved, gently cradling the prajurit.

When the greenhouse door closed behind them, I jumped to the ground and opened Val.

"This plant is poison to the prajurit. How do I get rid of it? Will chopping it down be enough?"

Looping text spiraled around the page in an unfamiliar, ribbonlike font filled with long sweeps and diacritic notations above curved letters. Slowly, the words faded. *Long live the* Suku Dari Matahari. *I'd like a chance to speak privately to Sunan Lestari.*

"Why do you both keep calling her 'Sunan'?"

It's an honorific title for a revered queen. She is strong to have resisted the poison this long.

"I don't want to test her resolve any further. How do I destroy the flower?"

You shouldn't have to. This is a grievous crime against the prajurit. The flower, Amorphophallus titanum, *titan arum, corpse flower—whatever you call it—is sacred to the prajurit. A titan arum might bloom only once a decade, if that, but it turns the prajurit political system on its head every time. Blooms are times of celebration, and usually the only peaceful meetings between clans and the only time alliances shift without bloodshed.*

"Without bloodshed? They're all dead!"

The poison is not part of the flower. Prajurit cannot resist the siren scent of a titan arum.

"It smells like warm roadkill."

Not to the prajurit.

"So you're saying someone poisoned the flower knowing they were murdering prajurit."

Sadly, yes.

Bile churned in my gut. I dropped to the concrete beside the flower and lifted my sweater to breathe through its filter. This wasn't the big, bad enemy I'd expected; it was worse. How long had this plant been releasing its intoxicating scent, drawing prajurit to their deaths? How many more tiny bodies lay among the plants?

"Would a demon do this?"

Poison is seldom used by creatures of pure atrum. *It's too remote. It doesn't give power the same way feasting directly on a soul does.*

"This is an inside job, isn't it?"

More than likely.

My shoulders slumped and I gently closed and stored Val. It was no longer speculation. We had an evil rogue enforcer in our midst, and Jacob was the only enforcer who fit the profile. He had the characteristic meteoric rise in power and skill. His region sat four blocks and a freeway overpass to the west. His region was overrun with evil. He'd tried to kill Jamie.

My gaze fell on the crumpled body of Jacob's latest victim and I pushed to my feet with a cry of anger.

I pulsed *lux lucis* into the flower. It washed back into me. Good energy suffused the plant; the addition of mine made no difference. Grabbing my knife, I hacked at the base of the titan arum. The expensive blade wasn't the best saw, but I made it work. Sticky sap sprayed my hands and knife as I methodically decapitated the murderous flower.

The titan arum crashed to the concrete. A smell of carrion washed over me. Panting, I half fell from the pot and collapsed against its base, legs rubbery with insidious weakness. My hands fell limp on my thighs, the muscles in my fingers refusing to contract, and my knife clattered to the concrete. Lassitude sank into my limbs, drawing my head to my chest. If I closed my eyes, I could nap.

Tiny dots danced in my vision, settling to the floor, falling across my feet, the concrete, the tiny prajurit body. A cough racked my body. I tipped to my side and the plants bounced in my vision. Something was wrong with me.

Poison. I was poisoned. I needed fresh air.

I couldn't see the door or even tell which direction to look for it. I crawled to the closest plant, and with clumsy hands, I picked up a small ceramic pot and threw it high at the few feet of visible greenhouse wall beyond the jungle of plants. The pot bounced off the glass and shattered. I grabbed another pot, supporting myself on a sturdy stalk, and heaved it. This time, glass shattered. Sharp winter air whistled through the jagged opening, chasing poisoned pollen through the greenhouse. I sucked in crisp lungsful, holding on to the plant until my vision stabilized.

Marching to the collapsed flower, I tugged my sweater over my nose. The entire titan arum gleamed with hearty *lux lucis*; it was too soon for it to show the effect of being cut down. Slicing through the petal, I peeled it down to reveal the *atrum* and swiped a finger over the poisoned cluster of stamen, pushing *lux lucis* into it. The *atrum* disappeared. I smiled until I turned my finger over. The poison clung in a black smear to my fingertip. I shoved *lux lucis* against it, trying to erase it. My finger lit up twice as bright as the rest of my body, but the poison remained. Grimacing, I wiped my finger on the inside of the petal. The poison transferred to the more porous substance.

I opened Val. "Why can't I cleanse it?"

The poison is a physical substance. It has to be countered with a physical substance.

"That's not how it works. I remove *atrum* from physical things all the time."

That's different. You've cleaned the metaphysical elements of physical things—people's souls. This chemical's only purpose is to kill, making it evil, atrum, *on a molecular level.*

I paced away from the titan arum and back. I didn't need a biology lesson; I needed to take action. "How do I get rid of it?"

The same way you get rid of anything permanently. Burn it. The pages shivered.

I looked around for convenient lighter fluid or matches. Finding neither, I tucked Val back in his strap and picked up the base of the flower. I couldn't leave the flower unattended while I gathered flammable material. Until it burned, no prajurit in the area was safe.

I knew the titan arum was big, but its weight staggered me. Tugging it through the jungle left me sweaty and limp. When I pushed through the glass doors, Jamie waited near the house, Lestari in his hands, weeping heart-wrenching sobs. Tears tracked down the pooka's face, too.

Wind chilled the sweat on my scalp and neck and washed away the last of the poison's lethargic effects. With fresh strength, I jerked the enormous plant through the door and onto the dirt.

The house remained silent, the curtains undisturbed. We'd been here almost an hour. If someone were inside, they should have come out by now.

As if on cue, a car door slammed shut and an engine revved in the driveway. Someone had come home while I was in the greenhouse and was already leaving. Someone who grew a titan arum so he could poison prajurit. Someone who would leave rather than confront me and be exposed for a rogue.

Jacob was getting away.

I dropped the titan arum and sprinted for the front of the house. By the time I rounded the corner, the driveway and road beyond were empty.

"Damn it!"

I stomped back to the flower. Even in the open, the titan arum's powerful odor permeated the air. Lestari raised her tiny triangular face to the breeze, inhaling its moldy locker funk with bliss.

"Let's get her to the car," I said.

Jamie led the way, cradling the mourning queen. I huffed after him, the sticky stalk of the corpse flower tucked under my left armpit, the rest of the flower dragging behind me like a Christmas tree from bizarro land. When I reached the driveway, I expected to see Niko pull up. He'd tell me I'd rushed in without thinking, and I'd tell him I'd saved the day; then we'd figure out a place to set the titan arum on fire without igniting the dry grass around us.

Except Niko wasn't there. The turbonis proved a stronger foe than I reckoned if it kept the optivus aegis busy this long. Yet Mr. Pitt had sensed a similar level of evil here, and it'd turned out to be a poisoned flower. Or had it? The toxic pollen held less *atrum* than ten imps put together. As horrific as the poisoned flower was, it shouldn't have registered as such a large problem, even for a souped-up warden. Which meant the titan arum hadn't been what Mr. Pitt sensed.

The house loomed beside me, heavy curtains hiding the interior. The evil had to be inside. Or it had been. Jacob may have just absconded with whatever Mr. Pitt had sensed, but if I got lucky, he'd have left evidence behind.

"Wait in the car."

Jamie didn't protest. He hunched his body protectively around the weeping prajurit queen and continued toward the Civic.

I dropped the heavy stalk and pulled out my knife and pet wood. The blade stuck in the sheath, coming free with a suction of half-dried sap resin. I should have cleaned the blade before sheathing it, but I'd been too preoccupied with escaping the greenhouse.

I pushed *lux lucis* into the blade and another burst into the pet wood. Checking the road one last time for Niko's car, I faced the house.

The porch steps groaned and popped beneath my weight. I hunched, checking the windows. The curtains didn't twitch. Sidling up to the door, I blinked to Primordium. The house washed to gray. A black smear seeped over the threshold. I turned to get a better look, and it disappeared. Frowning, I checked the threshold from the corner of my eye. The *atrum* returned, barely visible in my periphery.

I leaned down to cleanse it but stopped myself before my fingers touched the porch. Just because Jacob had come and gone didn't guarantee the house was empty. In fact, if Jacob had an accomplice, he might still be on the premises. Heart pounding and muscles tense, I reached to test the door handle, only to realize both hands were full. I waffled between weapons. Pet wood was my tool of choice, since it was longer—but it was lethal only to pure-evil creatures. Reluctantly, I shoved it into my back pocket and kept the blade out.

The door handle turned soundlessly in my grip, and the door swung open. I jerked back, then peeked into the house. Three feet inside the door, the foyer ended in a wall of *lux lucis*. Thick rubber trees, hanging vines, bushy ferns, dwarf citrus trees, evergreens—from floor to ceiling, plants obstructed the entrance, so crowded I couldn't see through them.

A trace of *atrum* sprinkled the bare floorboards, giving support to my belief that this time, I'd found the barrier of *lux lucis* Mr. Pitt had sensed. Gathering a trickle of *lux lucis* in my palm, I looped it and set it free. It ate through the dark energy before feeding into frond tips brushing the floor.

I tiptoed over the clean threshold and blinked to normal sight. Harsh white light blinded me. Shading my eyes with cupped hands, I squinted into the glare. Grow lights hung from the ceiling, half obscured by a tangle of vines. On the other side of the verdant wall, bits of silver gleamed and refracted light. The plants had to be six feet deep, their intertwined branches speaking of months of growth. This house and whatever it held had been here awhile.

The door swung shut behind me. I jumped and lurched for the handle. It opened easily on an empty driveway. I patted my racing heart. This wasn't a trap; the natural cant of the door had swung it shut. I shivered, eyes bouncing hyper-fast to check my surroundings. As much as I longed to sprint from the house, I couldn't leave without investigating.

I let the door swing closed but stopped it when it rested against the handle's tongue. If this wasn't a trap, my best chance at escaping undetected, or at least maintaining some element of surprise if someone—Jacob—came back, would be to shut the door, but I couldn't bring myself to close off my escape completely.

I blinked to Primordium, pulling out the pet wood again. Unlike the greenhouse, the air smelled rich with wet soil and green life, and underneath it lay the faint aroma of smoke.

I crept up to the plants. What if the car I'd heard had been a neighbor's? I'd assumed Jacob had stopped by while I was occupied in the greenhouse and left again, but what if he'd been here all along? What if he was still here? I flashed on the rifle he'd brought to the pooka's rising, and tensed, primed to duck.

Think you're faster than a bullet?

I held my breath, listening. My heartbeat pounded louder. The rasp of my coat sleeve against my side filled the tiny room.

A path wound through the plants, hidden except for the crushed gray leaves previously trampled. Encouraged by the silence, I tiptoed forward. I'd take a look inside, see what Jacob was up to, then call Niko. A witness would be wise; then it wouldn't be Jacob's word against mine. Plus, it never hurt to have the optivus aegis at my back.

I blinked to normal sight. It'd be easier to spot Jacob in a world of color than to pick out his soul among all these plants. Beneath the hot lights, the air stagnated. Sweat collected along my spine. Each slither of plant leaves against my coat sounded as loud as sandpaper. The floorboard squeaked, and I froze, heart racing. Acrid smoke thickened the air, aggravating my lungs, and I swallowed hard to suppress a cough.

I'd pushed past enough plants to see the silver beyond was a metal wall bolted to the floor and ceiling. It curved out of sight left and right, following the arc of plant life and grow lights. If any normal interior walls remained in the house, they were lost in the jungle.

When no one rushed through the foliage to investigate my noises, I shoved aside a bamboo palm branch and stepped into the empty space between the wall and the plants. I stood in front of a cracked door. Before I could lose my nerve, I pocketed the pet wood and grabbed the handle.

Heat seared my fingers. Strangling a yelp of pain, I jerked my hand back. I started to stuff the scorched fingers into my mouth, but remembering everything I'd touched in the last hour, I settled on flapping my fingers and blowing on them. Hot, smoky air pushed through the widened opening. In fact, the whole metal wall simmered with heat.

Dread tightened my skin. I'd expected to find Jacob's lair. I figured a rogue would have problems keeping his home clean of *atrum*, so he'd need to use a barrier to disguise it from the wardens. But inside that barrier, it'd be normal. There'd be a couch, a TV, some food, maybe a nest of imps or a hound as a pet. This wall felt like it held the fires of hell within.

Now would be a good time to go back, call Niko, and wait in the car with Jamie.

No. I was an enforcer. Liam and Isabel thought I was too weak to hold a region, and cowering behind Niko would only prove it. This was my region, and no one was going to foster evil on my watch. Jacob's days as a rogue were over.

A blast of heat dried my sweat.

I knew opening a door on a room potentially already on fire was dangerous, but considering the door was already partially open, and untold evil lurked within, I couldn't wait for the fire department before investigating the inner room. Cautiously, I toed the door open another inch, and it swung wide on its own momentum.

The interior of the house was on fire. The metal wall wrapped around the entire hellish scene, amplifying the heat like an oven. Low wilting plants mounded the open floor, and flames guttered within their depths. Heavy gray smoke obscured the ceiling. Defying logic and air currents, all the ash collected in a mound at the center of the enclosure.

Flames burst out of nothing in the middle of a thick spider plant. I blinked to Primordium. *Atrum* coated the floor and spilled up the walls. Black flames ate through glowing plants, and the dark body of a salamander scurried through white plant fronds. It carried a smoldering piece of *lux lucis*–filled plant to the ash heap, climbing the obsidian mound to deposit its prize next to tiny glistening onyx spheres. Eggs. Handfuls of them. As I stared, a clutch of eggs wriggled and shivered, and a tiny triangular head cracked through one ebony shell, then another.

The dense ring of *lux lucis* plants, the gutted house filled with salamander eggs—this was definitely what Mr. Pitt had sensed, not the titan arum. Finding the poisoned flower had been a lucky break, though one that'd come far too late for the prajurit.

I eased back a step, pulling the door almost shut with the aid of my knife. Then I turned and ran. I burst from the house and tore down the driveway. My gaze went first to Jamie. He sat in the passenger seat of the Civic, face glum. Lestari lay curled on the dash, hopefully asleep. No BMW had arrived while I was inside. Where was Niko? Was he okay?

Jamie got out of the car and met me at the trunk. "You stink."

"Thanks. I need you to wait here and watch Lestari a little longer." I grabbed two jugs of water and balanced yogurt and probiotics on top. "How is she?"

"Hungry."

Suspecting it was really Jamie who was hungry, I shoved a grocery bag into his arms and raced back inside, slamming the front door behind me.

I considered calling Mr. Pitt, but he'd said to notify him only if I encountered something I'd never seen before. Salamanders fell within the scope of my limited experience, though not on this scale. All those eggs promised untold destruction. I had to kill them before they hatched.

I set the gallons on the foyer floor and poured two yogurts into each along with two opened capsules of probiotics. I gave each jug a vigorous shake, then checked them in Primordium. The water glowed faintly, like an afterimage of *lux lucis*. Knocking aside plants, I hurried to the fiery room. I sprinkled the threshold to prevent salamanders from escaping, then left a jug just outside and kicked open the door.

Plants clogged the floor in various states of combustion. Chasing down the salamanders in that tangle would be cumbersome and inefficient, not to mention dangerous. I needed to concentrate my attack on the easiest targets first: the unhatched eggs.

In fits and starts, and blinking back and forth between normal sight and Primordium, I threaded through flaming plants and fire-breathing salamanders alike, halting next to the nest at the center. I remained hunched almost in half to avoid the heavy smoke blanketing the top third of the room, even though I couldn't see it in Primordium. The entire room looked one good blaze away from complete collapse. Ragged holes pierced the ceiling, and through those, I could see holes in the roof, which from afar had looked like a chimney. The entire attic must be filled with smoke.

The salamanders ignored me until I poured *lux lucis*–enhanced water on the eggs. With the first sizzle of quenched coals, the salamanders charged. I spun, backpedaling to get to a wall. The plants writhed, lizardlike *atrum* bodies stampeding through their leaves and stalks, and bursts of black flames erupted throughout the room. There couldn't have been more than a handful of salamanders, but with the shaking plants and fiery explosions, it seemed like a hundred. I splashed any *atrum* that moved, cursing and hopping to avoid gouts of black flames.

As conservative as I tried to be, the first gallon didn't quench all the salamanders. With tears running from my stinging eyes, and each breath rasping in a painful fight against a coughing fit, I sprinted to the door, using normal sight to dodge flaming plants, then hopscotched back to the nest with the remaining jug.

Two more salamanders disappeared under the viscous yogurt water, and when nothing more charged from the depths of the burning plants, I turned on the nest. I dribbled water onto each glistening egg, stirring the ash with my knife to ensure each incubating salamander's death.

The room spun. A coughing fit brought me to my knees, and I remained on the ground, crawling around the nest until I'd killed everything there. Only then did I stagger to my feet and to the door.

The air outside the metal room slid cool across my skin despite the heat from the grow lights. A cloud of smoke exhaled from the front door as I stumbled down the porch steps, and I staggered a few extra steps to suck in delicious clean oxygen. Jamie bounced on his toes halfway between the car and the house, clearly torn between me and the prajurit queen still on the dash.

"I'm fine," I said, ruining my assurance by coughing until I gagged. Tears blinded me, but I waved him back. I had one last task. The poisoned titan arum needed to burned, and I wasn't going to waste this perfect opportunity.

Dragging the flower up the steps set me coughing again, but at least with my sinuses clogged with smoke, I couldn't smell the titan arum's noxious odor. The flower's bulk caught on the door frame. Holding the stalk tight in my armpit, I planted a foot on the wall behind me and shoved. The thick petal ripped, and I caught myself on a hand and knee before face-planting. Yanking the flower through the wall of plants taxed my strength, but I barreled on, determined.

The narrow metal door caught the enormous flower, too, and I turned to grab the huge stalk with both hands. The titan arum ripped free, stripping away most of the purple petal to reveal the poisoned center. The metal walls flexed, popping back into place with a thunderous reverberation. I jerked the toxic flower across the room to the embers of the ash nest.

Stumbling down the titan arum's length, I grabbed the long gray-green tongue and folded it into the flames. Heat swept up my side. I jerked back and blinked to normal sight. Flames leapt from the titan arum above my head, disappearing into the smoke blanketing the ceiling. The torn sides of the petal revealed the center of the flower where hundreds of poisoned pollen stamens blazed with an unnatural blue-white flame.

The fire spread along the titan arum's length, and I shielded my face from the heat with an arm, staggering toward the door. The ceiling crackled, and I glanced up in time to see the titan arum's column of flame touch the roof. Like a match touched to gunpowder, the ceiling combusted in a bright flare clearly visible through the dense smoke. With a hiss, the roof above the nest collapsed, blinding me with a spray of embers. When I spun to the doorway, the metal wall wobbled, canting inward as the ceiling sagged to trap me.

"Oh, crap." I squeezed through the bent metal doorway, flinching away from its searing frame. I tripped and clawed through the plants, blinded by tears and smoke. Heat built behind me, and the lights overhead flickered. A bulb deeper in the house burst, then one closer, as flames licked across the ceiling.

I burst from the house in a cloud of smoke and didn't stop running until I reached the Civic. Bracing a hand on the hood, I coughed until I thought my lungs would turn inside out. Jamie darted to the trunk and returned with a water jug. I swished and spit before gulping water. Through teary eyes, I watched flames shimmer across the roof.

"Are you okay?" Jamie asked.

I nodded. My cheeks stung as if I'd been sunburned, embers burned at the bottom of my lungs, and my ankle pulsed with pain, swelling against my tennis shoe, but I barely felt any of it. My mind raced to make sense of the day's findings.

I had answered the mystery of where all the salamanders were coming from, and it made the placement of the poisoned titan arum twice as sinister. Prajurit were natural predators of salamanders. Any prajurit who showed up to destroy the nest would have been overcome by the flower. And murdered.

The death of so many prajurit then freed up the rogue to plant salamanders around our regions without detection. With a nest under his control, he'd had two replacements for every salamander we killed.

I tried to muster exaltation or at least a measure of triumph. I'd demolished the nest. I'd destroyed the poisoned titan arum. Jacob wouldn't be able to distribute any more salamanders, and no more prajurit would die. So why was I unsatisfied?

"You're not going back in, are you?"

I blinked and looked away from the burning house. Jamie stood tense beside me. "No." The word scratched my throat. Once I could breathe, I needed to attempt to wipe out the *atrum*, but the fire made going back inside too dangerous.

A billow of smoke drew my eyes back to the house. The illogic of Jacob's actions gnawed at me. Why would he want to spread the salamanders around? Cheryl had used *atrum* to make herself look good. If Jacob followed the same pattern, he should have let a few salamanders loose in his region so he could sweep in and save the day. He could have destroyed the salamanders he didn't need rather than transplant them. In fact, from what I understood about being rogue, killing the extra salamanders would have benefited him, giving him more strength. So why set dozens of fires in all the local regions?

Maybe he had lost control. It would explain why evil had been increasing and spreading for weeks. After committing enough evil, there had to be a tipping point from which he couldn't come back and he'd stop being able to recover with *lux lucis*. At that point, maybe he'd have to conserve *lux lucis*. Or maybe he'd stopped caring about how much evil he unleashed. Yet, when I'd seen Jacob two days ago, his soul had been brighter than mine, and he'd had no problem fighting pooka-enhanced evil creatures.

If he hadn't lost control, the turbonis could explain the increasing evil. With it to supply him with unending evil, and with some means of transportation I still hadn't worked out, Jacob could transplant all manner of nasty surprises into all our regions—as we'd all seen in the last week.

But I kept coming back to the same question: Why? Why would Jacob put evil in *all* our regions? Spreading some around to cast aside suspicion would have been a good strategy, but bombarding all our regions was counterproductive to Jacob's advancement. With all the enforcers working together, he'd be less likely to shine and less likely to gain power.

Furthermore, why make *my* region the epicenter?

I dropped to sit on the bumper. Of course. Mr. Pitt and I had been thinking about this wrong. This wasn't about making someone look good; it was about making someone look bad: Mr. Pitt.

The wardens didn't like Mr. Pitt. Two in particular had been trying to force him out of his region, and their efforts had gained traction as more evil overran our region. What better way to make Mr. Pitt look like a horrible warden than to make it seem like he *cultivated* evil in his region? If Mr. Pitt hadn't found these hidden evils today, I could see how it would have played out. They'd "find" the salamander nest, swing around the back of the house, and "discover" the poisoned titan arum, and Mr. Pitt's career would be over. The turbonis was a bonus, a backup in case the nest wasn't enough.

We didn't have a rogue enforcer.

We had a rogue warden.

"Did anyone come by while I was inside?" I asked. It took two tries to get through the sentence between coughs.

"No. What's going on?"

Medusa played "Hail to the Chief" from my back pocket. I jumped, then bent forward to retrieve the cell phone.

"Mr. Pitt, I need—" My voice rasped and gave out. I cleared my throat, but Mr. Pitt talked over me.

"For the first time in your brief career, listen close and do *exactly* as I say. Get to the office. Now. Don't talk. Hang up. Drive. I need you."

I shoved to my feet. The house burned, flames licking across the roof. Inside, *atrum* flames ensured it would continue to burn down to ash. With the walls still standing, I couldn't see the black flames, but I should at least try to clear them before leaving. I took a step, then stopped.

I need you.

Mr. Pitt's words slid under my skin, tapping against my nerves.

"Get in the car," I said. Jamie darted to his door. I dialed 911. "I need to report a fire." The firefighters wouldn't be able to do anything about the flames fed by *atrum*, but they could prevent the natural fire from spreading. I slid behind the wheel, put the car in gear, and peeled out, abandoning the house to its unquenchable flames.

Jamie held Lestari in his hands while we careened around corners, then rocketed down the freeway, my imagination supplying ever-increasing horrors to rationalize Mr. Pitt's urgent call. When I reached the conclusion that something dreadful had happened to Niko, I shut down my thoughts, driving faster.

The queen woke up halfway to the office. Her enormous eyes were swollen from crying, but her tears had dried. She paced the dash, slashing the air with her sword, cursing her enemies and vowing revenge. I let her words wash over me and concentrated on dodging through traffic.

When I skidded into the handicapped parking spot by the lobby doors, my entourage spilled out of the car with me: a pooka, a prajurit, and a sentient book. I brushed my fingers across Val's soot-crusted cover as I got out. He deserved an apology; I'd forgotten about him when I'd rushed into the salamanders' nest. He must have been terrified.

I considered asking Jamie and Lestari to wait in the car, but it would have been a waste of breath. Jamie raced around the car to glue himself to my side, and I feared it wasn't safe to leave the queen alone. Grief and anger were a toxic combination.

"Stick close," I said. I didn't know what we were walking into. At the very least, I was going to get reamed by Mr. Pitt. More likely, it would be something worse. *Please let Niko be okay.*

I hardly recognized my reflection in the lobby's glass doors. It wasn't just the fresh-from-a-chimney look I sported, either. It was the way I walked, confident, like an illuminant enforcer, not a woman pretending to be one. When had that happened?

Warm air swirled through the hushed lobby. Chatter and the clack of keyboards drifted from open doors of offices I passed. A woman coming out of the bathroom stopped on the threshold to stare as I stalked past. In other words, business as normal.

The woman didn't notice Lestari, who flew along the ceiling tiles.

The prajurit were not like imps and vervet: I could see them clearly in normal sight, which meant everyone else should be able to see them, too. How they hadn't been discovered by normal humans was a puzzle for another day.

The closed doors to Illumination Studios gave me pause. I tapped the handle, half expecting it to be hot. The chilly metal jiggled. I blinked to Primordium. Nothing looked amiss.

Taking a firm grip, I thrust the door open. *Lux lucis* so thick it was opaque coated the doorway from top to bottom. I peered at the threshold. Powerful lichtwands built into the metal seam radiated *lux lucis*.

Dread chilled my stomach. Mr. Pitt would have put up a *lux lucis* barrier only if he were planning on keeping something fierce out.

I stepped through the sheet. Energy tingled through my body, jolting my senses.

I was wrong. Mr. Pitt wasn't trying to keep out anything. He was trying to keep raw *atrum* hell *in*.

23

We're Not in Kansas Anymore

L ESTARI ZIPPED PAST MY SHOULDER, loosing a high-pitched battle cry. Jamie stepped through the sheet, then gave himself a vigorous shake more suited for his Great Dane form, *atrum* painting the surface of his soul. If my feet hadn't been rooted in shock, I would have stepped away from him. The door latched softly behind us.

Atrum coated the industrial carpet, splattered across Sharon's desk, and slimed the wall behind it, shrouding the tall *Illumination Studios* letters. Like an oil stain, it saturated the walls in a slow, inexorable tide. Vervet clung to ceiling tiles and perched atop cubicles, razor claws and scorpion tails piercing our once-pristine office furniture. My eyes locked on Mr. Pitt. He stood at the center of the office, a white beacon amid a flurry of darkness. A gelatinous layer of *atrum* writhed on the floor in front of him, now-familiar bouts of inky flames bursting above the mass.

Blood drained from my head. What I'd mistaken for raw *atrum* was a seething pile of dozens of salamanders crawling over each other. More wriggled from a mound of eggs that dwarfed the nest I'd cleared at the house. *Atrum* flames licked across Will's and Joy's cubicles, invisible real flames burning holes into the fabric.

Holding back the swarm of destruction was Mr. Pitt's soul. Incredibly, it bubbled from his chest to encompass half the walkway and two cubicles. Salamanders clawed at his *lux lucis*, bathing it in black flames. I winced. Holding the tainted fire with his soul had to be agony.

I thought I'd pictured the worst-case scenarios, but this was unfathomable. Our headquarters had been attacked!

"Mr. Pitt!" I started forward, then leapt sideways to avoid colliding with a vortex of *atrum*. Thigh high, it spun like a top across the foyer, glittery onyx energy crackling across its surface. A turbonis. It looked exactly as Val had sketched. A vervet hurtled from its depths, fully formed, flying deep into the office. Shallow waves rippled across the smear of *atrum* beneath the turbonis, lapping against my toes, seeping into my soul.

"Twinkling tootsie toes! What was that for?"

Mr. Pitt's bellow jolted me into action. I hopped through the *atrum*, flaring *lux lucis* into my feet to cleanse the evil taint once I reached the clear strip of carpet left behind Mr. Pitt.

"Scum! Murderer!" Screaming, Lestari drove her sword into Mr. Pitt's neck. He jerked aside, and a bright line of *lux lucis* slashed across his throat, fading to gray. His barrier flickered. *Atrum* flames slipped past his boundary before the white sphere brightened and sliced through the encroaching flames.

"Traitor!" Lestari's bright sword slashed too fast to follow. Blood soaked into the torn fabric of Mr. Pitt's sleeves. The warden twitched with each strike, but rather than defend himself, he clamped his wrists to his sides. Sweat dripped down his chin.

I jumped between the prajurit and Mr. Pitt. "Lestari! Stop it!"

"He killed my clan. He dies! Move, spineless human."

I knocked into Mr. Pitt to avoid Lestari's dive. My boss grunted, but he still didn't move. Heat from the pile of salamanders permeated my jeans. As close as he stood, Mr. Pitt's legs had to feel burned.

"We don't have time for this, Madison," he growled. His eyes swiveled to mine, but otherwise he didn't move.

"Lestari, we were framed!" I shoved a hand between Lestari and Mr. Pitt's throat. The prajurit's sharp sword sliced into my forearm. I hissed and jerked back. The cut gouged deep but short. Blood welled to the surface, fading to gray as it ran down my arm. Jamie grabbed me by my shoulders and lifted me, setting me down behind him. I yelped in shock at his strength, but the pooka ignored me.

"Sunan, no. You cannot take your grief out on Madison." Jamie didn't yell, but Lestari responded as if he had. She flew to the ceiling, sword held before her. Jamie's soul frothed. I slid around him, closer to

Mr. Pitt in case I needed to intervene. My boss's wide eyes locked on Jamie, but his feet remained rooted.

"Taste him, Sunan. He's not responsible."

"Mr. Pitt would never harm a prajurit," I said, frowning at Jamie's weird wording.

Confusion furrowed Lestari's brow. She dipped down to touch Mr. Pitt's barrier, then licked her finger. Fresh tears shimmered in her eyes. "But . . . but it is his region."

"I can explain—"

"Why don't we save our chat until the office *isn't on fire*." Mr. Pitt's final words set my ears ringing. His soul flickered and shrank, releasing *atrum* flames beyond his barrier.

Two vervet dropped from the ceiling onto Mr. Pitt. He grimaced but did nothing while they gnawed on his soul. After a moment of shock, I grabbed the closest one, pulsing *lux lucis* into it. Lestari twirled past me, skewering the second before its stinger pierced her. Despite our size difference, her vervet disintegrated at the same time mine did. Whatever her sword was made out of, it was strong stuff. Or the prajurit was.

"I'll grab water," I said, turning to run around the burning cubicles.

"No!" Mr. Pitt's soul fluctuated. He clenched his fists, easing his breaths in and out until his bubble stabilized. "This takes everything I've got. You need to flatten the turbonis. It's making everything worse."

The plastic frame of the cubicle bubbled and melted. The bitter stench made my eyes water. I backed away from the heat.

"But the flames—" What was a few more vervet compared to the building burning down around us?

"Think like an enforcer, Madison. The sprinklers will take care of the fire. The more *atrum* that thing spits out, the harder this is."

"Can you defend yourself?"

"Stop hovering and get busy!"

He swiped a shaky arm across his forehead, wiping away sweat. His soul dimmed another milliwatt. I stopped arguing. I cleared all the vervet around Mr. Pitt with a sweep of pet wood, but more scampered from the break room and across Sharon's desk to take their place.

"Lestari, can you protect him?"

She raised the hand holding her sword to her chest in salute, then backflipped into a vervet clinging to the glass conference wall. Her sword slashed too fast to follow, and the vervet exploded in *atrum* dust. The prajurit zipped to a plant beside my desk just outside the circle of fire. Her feet barely touched the leaf before her soul gleamed twice as bright. The leaf fell brittle and gray to the desk under the back draft of her wings.

"This is for Bulan and her sweet laugh, never to be heard again." The tiny queen slashed through a vervet three times her size, then dropped through Mr. Pitt's soul into the seething mass of salamanders. Weaving through bursts of black flames, she sliced into several salamanders closest to him. They floundered but remained strong.

"This is for Suharto; the eternal sun is blessed with his beauty." Lestari shot straight up. Hovering, she rubbed her wings together in a blur, and a fine dust of *lux lucis* sifted onto the salamanders. The uninjured salamanders absorbed the minute traces of energy without effect, but when *lux lucis* contacted the wounded, they shrank as if doused with *lux lucis* water.

Flames flared around the queen, but she dove free, zipping back to the plant. Already, the empty spaces left by dead salamanders filled with fresh black bodies.

"Hurry, Madison."

The strain in Mr. Pitt's voice snapped me into action. I spun on my heel to face the encroaching line of *atrum*. I would do myself no favors by standing in *atrum* while fighting the turbonis. Plus, if I could wipe out the enormous pool, it might weaken or destroy the turbonis. Looping *lux lucis* over my fingertips, I whirled it up to blurry speeds, then released it across the floor. A clean line of carpet speared from where I crouched next to the conference room almost to the turbonis, then *atrum* closed in, erasing my efforts in seconds.

"Jamie, I need your help." The pooka hadn't reacted to our headquarters' transformation to a battle zone. If asked, he'd probably say he liked the office better now that it had a mix of *atrum*. But he *had* jumped in to protect me. "Just like last night."

"Together?" He crouched beside me, giving me his first smile since we'd found the poisoned titan arum. A tightness around my heart eased, soothing my panicky jitters.

"Together."

I rolled more *lux lucis* in my hands and released it. Another swath cut through the pitch-black pool. Jamie's *lux lucis* moved in a blur, sweeping through half the *atrum* while my weaker push succumbed to the tide of *atrum*. Side by side, we moved into the space Jamie had cleared and released *lux lucis* again. This time, I went through the motions but reserved my energy, letting Jamie do the work since his strength had an impact. In a few short sweeps, the floor and walls were clean.

"You're amazing! Thank you." I beamed with pride; I'd make a good creature of Jamie yet.

Jamie grinned and approached the turbonis at my side. Up close, it looked exactly like a miniature *atrum* tornado, complete with an erratic path and bulging sides. The top swayed and flopped, then spewed a fountain of imps in all directions. I jerked as they fell on me, tiny sharp teeth sinking into my soul from my neck to my knees. Rapid-fire, I pulsed *lux lucis* down my body, disintegrating imps like an exploding string of lights. Those that landed on Jamie bounced to the ground and rushed Mr. Pitt. I let them go. If Lestari could handle vervet, imps would be no problem.

Jamie leaned close to the funnel opening. Motes of *atrum* and *lux lucis* pulled from his soul into the cyclone. For a terrifying second, it looked like he was being torn apart and sucked in. The pooka jerked back.

"Twinkling tootsie toes!" Jamie exclaimed.

I gaped at him.

When a siren blared in the ceiling, I levitated with surprise. A monsoon opened above our heads, and Jamie shrieked like a scared goat, vaulting Sharon's desk and disappearing beneath it. I clapped my hands over my ears. Water pelted me, drenching me to the skin in seconds, and pain outlined the gash on my arm.

The turbonis spun, unaffected.

I splashed to Mr. Pitt. His sphere held, but it was smaller and weaker. The salamanders within didn't react to the water—without *lux lucis*, it fell harmlessly through their insubstantial bodies. The furniture hissed and smoked, and noxious fumes curled into the back of my mouth. Two vervet clung to Mr. Pitt's back. I swiped a hand through them, and their dust drifted to the floor on a gentle current incongruous with the deluge. Lestari was missing. I hoped the water had chased her away and she hadn't been injured.

"What do I do?" I shouted.

"Unravel it." He kept his hands clamped over his ears and paused for the alarm's piercing *BEEP.* "Find the end." *BEEP.* "Of the spiral." *BEEP.* "On top." *BEEP.* "Spin *lux lucis.*" *BEEP.* "Through it."

Water funneled through his thick brows down the sides of his face and ran in twin streams off his elbows. I envied his meaty hands. Mine barely blocked the upper vibrations of the shrill alarm.

"Hurry!"

I ran back to the turbonis. He didn't have to spell out the urgency. The carpet and cubicle wall in the center of his soul's bubble burned unchecked beneath the water. Coated in *atrum* flames, it would burn until nothing but ash remained, no matter how much water fell from the sprinklers. If Mr. Pitt lost control of all the salamanders, we'd face disaster.

I killed four vervet that scrambled up my legs. A few ducked around me, heading for Mr. Pitt. I spun to catch them as a fresh spout of imps catapulted from the turbonis. Gritting my teeth, I turned my back on my boss and focused on the source generating fresh evil.

The shape of the turbonis reminded me of a wraith, only more volatile and without the creepy faces. Reluctantly removing a hand from an ear, I swirled *lux lucis* into a perfect spiral on the first attempt. Who knew deafening alarms could be motivational?

Unlike a wraith, with a solid, unmoving anchor, the funnel's mouth danced erratically. I darted forward and jabbed my hand into the center, loosing a spiral of *lux lucis.* Whirling *atrum* latched on to my fingers and guzzled energy from my soul. I yanked my hand free, breaking the connection and backpedaling a few steps when the turbonis shifted to follow me. It remained unchanged despite the heap of my *lux lucis* it'd consumed. Swiping water from my eyes, I prepped my energy again. It moved sluggishly.

Find the end of the spiral.

The next time the turbonis closed in, I let my hand hover above the rim, but I didn't loose my energy. The vortex passively vacuumed *lux lucis* from my hand and arm in a dizzying pull as it had from Jamie. I gritted my teeth and used my left hand to steady my right. The alarm drilled into my head, shattering my concentration. I shimmied out of the turbonis's path, then reached for the top again.

A piece of the rim felt different. I swung my hand above the tornado twice to be sure, then pressed my fingers into what felt like a loose strand and gave my spinning *lux lucis* a jolt. As before, the turbonis sucked down my whirling energy, but this time *lux lucis* spiraled down, eating away *atrum* like fire on a wound fuse. The turbonis jerked away, now barely ten inches tall.

My knees collapsed, and I splashed into a cold puddle, bracing myself with a hand. The walls spun at the edges of my vision. It could have been an afterimage of staring into the spinning turbonis, but I was pretty sure I was dizzy from *lux lucis* loss. My soul glowed weaker than a 10-watt bulb.

I tipped my head forward until water ran like a river of tears down my cheeks and off the point of my nose. The deafening alarm pounded my willpower. The turbonis wobbled toward me, *atrum* smearing beneath it. A tiny imp popped out the top and hopped around in a circle before latching on to me. I trickled *lux lucis* into it, then turned my head to check Mr. Pitt. His once-sturdy soul flickered alarmingly around the salamanders, black flames eating away his immense strength. Vervet clung to his legs, leaching more energy from him. He needed me to be a strong enforcer, and I didn't have it in me. We needed Niko, and Niko wasn't coming; he had a turbonis the size of a car to unravel.

A turbonis the size of a car. My heart clenched. This one had been the size of a filing cabinet, and it'd sapped my strength. I should have gone with Niko. We should have stuck together, not divided our resources.

I sagged over my knees. I *needed* Niko right now. Our office was under siege, and I couldn't handle it by myself.

"Finish it," Mr. Pitt shouted between alarms.

I shook my head. Couldn't he see there was too much *atrum*? Couldn't he see our souls? The tiny turbonis had almost done me in, and the salamanders surged against his weak cage. We needed to run.

"Madison!" The deluge shadowed the air between us. "Prove them wrong."

I couldn't fight it all. The salamanders would escape and set fire to the rest of the building, then the whole block. The whole city. The vervet would be loosed on innocent souls. The turbonis would unleash untold evil in our region. Mr. Pitt would look guilty and a rogue warden would escape and continue to spread evil.

Mr. Pitt drew himself up, the sphere of his soul strengthening. He was a good person, a good warden. This should never have happened in his region.

I held his fierce gaze. Despite the odds, he wasn't wavering. Neither could I.

Fatigue weighted my body, but I pushed through it. Straightening, I reached for the turbonis again. I wasn't in this fight alone. I was teamed with my warden, and we had a job to do, one more important than cleansing our offices. We had a rogue warden to stop.

More of my precious energy sucked into the vortex, pulled from my outstretched arm in a gossamer of shimmery *lux lucis* particulates. Dark spots edged out my vision, but I locked my hand over the pint-size turbonis. Twice more, I released a spiral of energy into the wrong spot and jerked free weaker. Finally, I found the loose end and hit it with my remaining strength.

Lux lucis raced through the turbonis, then spiraled into the floor, clearing a small pad beneath the negated vortex.

I wobbled on all fours, fighting the urge to lie down.

Jamie peeked over the rim of Sharon's desk. The sprinklers plastered his dark hair to his scalp, and his eyes were perfect round vortices. I smiled tremulously and staggered to the closed doors, collapsing in the lichtwand's steady energy. *Lux lucis* soaked into my depleted soul with a kick more potent than an energy drink, and my awareness unfurled beyond the tunnel it had shrunk to. Keeping a foot in the lichtwand's stream, I planted my hands in the fresh layer of *atrum* on the carpet. I rolled *lux lucis* from my fingertips, using the lichtwand as I had the tree in the park after the fire. Unlike the tree's passive energy transfer, the lichtwand used *me*, turning me into conduit. *Lux lucis* burst through me and flooded out my fingertips in a solid, uncontrolled stream. It didn't roll; it simply spread. Gleaming white energy ate through the *atrum* like water through tissue, racing from me in an all-consuming rush deeper into the office.

Jamie yelped and ducked behind the desk. The wave of *lux lucis* blasted out of sight around the conference room wall. My teeth chattered; my bones vibrated. The room bounced. I closed myself to the *lux lucis*, but I couldn't find an off switch. In desperation, I kicked out, using the closed door to shove myself free of the lichtwand, then collapsed to my side, panting. Slowly my vision refocused and my shuddering limbs stilled. I closed my mouth against the downpour and examined myself.

Maybe that hadn't been the brightest idea, but at least my soul glistened. I picked myself up and hobbled down the hall. *Lux lucis* blanketed the carpet all the way to Mr. Pitt's feet, and his soul held steady again. I swiped vervet from his shoulders. Close to the salamanders, the air became muggy with steam.

"What did you." *BEEP.* "Do?" Mr. Pitt demanded, glaring from my shining soul to the *lux lucis* carpet.

"Lichtwand!" I yelled.

My boss's eyes bulged. He opened his mouth, closed it, then, frowning, bellowed for yogurt. I ran to comply, my tennis shoes splashing through an inch of standing water in the break room. I pulled down the largest mugs from the cupboard, raided Mr. Pitt's stash of yogurt in the fridge, and returned to my boss.

"Give it here." *BEEP.* "Help Sharon."

I followed the line of his finger. An orthopedic shoe stuck out from Mr. Pitt's office doorway. Something black and thorny twisted around the receptionist's motionless leg. Her gritty white soul was barely distinguishable from the gray carpet. *Oh, crap!*

I shoved my supplies into Mr. Pitt's outstretched hands. Backtracking around the pocket of water-resistant evil flames, I sprinted to the office.

Sharon's tiny body lay unconscious in a suspended spasm on her side in front of Mr. Pitt's desk. She was lucky; if she'd fallen facedown or on her back, the deluge of water or the puddle collecting beneath her could have drowned her. My weak relief to find her breathing faded to horror. A broken pot spilled soil onto the carpet near her knees, as if it'd been thrown at her feet. Swelling from the mud, a matte-black vine snaked across the carpet and coiled around Sharon's thighs and torso. Separate tendrils webbed her hands and throat, twisting into her flesh. Thorns longer than my fingers spiked the nefarious plant, piercing Sharon's soul a hundred times over. Where the vine touched the floor, dark roots tunneled into the carpet.

Sharon's contorted position mirrored the murdered prajurit's death pose, but a faint pulse of life throbbed through her soul. Fresh fury surged through me. Whoever did this was going to pay.

I swiped a hand through the thorny plant, pulsing *lux lucis* into its stalk. A spike the size of an ice pick shot from the vine, piercing straight through my palm and my soul to protrude from the back side of my hand. I cried out in agony. Gravity bloomed beneath my palm, pulling me to the Earth's surface. New sprouts burst from the stalk, twisting through the air to wrap around my wrist.

I jerked back, falling onto my tailbone. The plant retreated, feigning dormancy. Lifting my hand, I stared at the thorny black weapon puncturing my soul. My fingers tingled, and when I flexed them, they responded sluggishly while pain sawed my palm. Frantic, I pushed *lux lucis* into the thorn. It melted from the ends inward, and I didn't let up until I'd erased the last twinge of lethargy and the pain faded to a dull ache.

I examined my palm, finding the flesh unblemished where I'd expected a giant bloody hole. I blinked to normal vision. Remarkably, my stinging hand remained wound-free.

Emergency lights flashed in a frantic strobe, adding an instant ocular ache to the headache pounding in rhythm to the blasting alarm. The solid-feeling evil carnivorous plant was invisible. Sharon's brown polyester skirt and coat clung to her, outlining stout thighs and biceps. Mud smeared the floor around her, making it appear as if her clothing had melted onto the thin carpet. Falling water distorted a fringe of red around the soil. Blood?

I leaned close, and the unmistakable metallic odor of blood filled my nostrils. Dizzy from the strobe lighting, I blinked back to Primordium and ran my eyes over the small woman. Despite the thorns, no *lux lucis* leaked from her. In fact, black *atrum* slicked the floor where I thought I'd seen blood.

I pulled out my pet wood, wishing I could open Val for advice. He was probably already waterlogged, but I couldn't risk exposing him to the downpour. I didn't know if a sentient book could drown, and I didn't want to chance it. I jabbed the base of the soul-sucking plant with the tip of the pet wood. *Lux lucis* flared through the wand, building up without releasing. Frustrated, I jammed the tip into the soil and *lux lucis* shot in a line across the *atrum* in the dirt. The pencil-thin neutral line slowly disappeared, and the thorny plant remained unaffected.

With a jab, I collapsed the pet wood against the floor, then shoved it into my back pocket. A quick loop of *lux lucis* released from my palm cleared the puddle of *atrum* around the soil but did nothing to the sinister vine.

I grabbed the knife, tearing a belt loop when the sap-coated blade stuck in the sheath again. Channeling *lux lucis* into the blade, I sliced through the main stalk. The vine resisted, then snapped in two. Sharon twitched. The base of the plant shriveled back to the soil and disappeared, but the rest of the vine pulsed with dark energy.

Kneeling, I hacked through the roots anchoring Sharon's legs. Each cut severed a piece of the vine, and it shrank away from the blade. The remaining plant squeezed tighter into Sharon, and her soul fluttered weakly. I sliced with frenzied haste.

"Hang on, you weird little woman."

When I cut the last of the vine away from Sharon, the roots disappeared into an ooze of *atrum*. A final push of *lux lucis* cleared the carpet. Without assistance, Sharon's soul strengthened, the pulse steadying to a dim, gritty white. I fell back on my heels, relieved.

Wishing I could lie down with Sharon, I floundered back to Mr. Pitt's side. His soul's bubble held only a handful of salamanders, and yogurt smeared the floor around him. While I watched, he dolloped yogurt into a cup, held it out to fill it with water from the sprinklers, gave it a stir with his finger, then dashed it across the sea of squirming black bodies. The salamanders died by the handful. I crouched and rolled *lux lucis* through a patch of *atrum* fire near Mr. Pitt's feet. Steam hissed as the sprinklers extinguished flames no longer fed by evil, unquenchable energy. With a final toss of *lux lucis* water to kill the last of the salamanders, Mr. Pitt's bubble guttered and winked out. He wobbled, then slid down the glass wall. His soul had lost its regional dimensions, and he looked like a normal person, or at least a normal enforcer who'd been overworked.

I dropped to the soaked floor beside him. The remaining unnatural flames continued to burn despite the deluge, and air thick with smoke and steam clung to my lungs. Blinking water out of my eyes, I rolled another handful of *lux lucis* through *atrum* flames. Mr. Pitt slouched forward, and a feeble wave of *lux lucis* trickled from his fingers across the closest black flames, extinguishing a few square inches. He'd told me he'd been an enforcer once, but I hadn't quite believed him until now.

Jamie knelt beside me, and *lux lucis* burst from the pooka through the remaining *atrum*. Mr. Pitt listed against the wall. I patted Jamie's knee, my gratitude too immense to express between alarm bursts.

The sprinklers extinguished the last of the flames and turned off. The alarm squawked to silence, though my ears filled the void with a high-pitched ringing. I braced a filthy hand against the floor. We'd done it. We'd saved the office. Joy's desk crashed to the floor, bringing down Will's and Rose's in a cacophony, spraying gritty water into our faces. I swiped my face with a filthy coat sleeve and looked around. Across the walkway, my cubicle and the spare Niko sometimes used were both scorched through. Soggy papers wilted in puddles beneath the desks, and drywall bulged and bubbled from water damage. Blackened concrete circled by charred carpet and coated with slimy yogurt spread around us, and smoke hung heavy against the ceiling. I amended my thought. We'd saved the city from destruction. The office hadn't survived.

"I found the one I want to bring home," Jamie said. He raised his *atrum*-black cupped hands to reveal a salamander trapped between his fingers.

Oh no. I scrambled to my feet. "Put it down, Jamie." We were both yelling, our eardrums shot. "We can't keep a salamander."

"Why not? You have a pet. I should have a pet."

"My pet doesn't set things on fire."

"I'm sure we could ask him not to." Jamie leaned close to the squirming lizardlike creature. "Will you promise not to spit fire in the apartment?" The salamander opened its tiny mouth. A gout of flame speared through Jamie's fingers. "Taffy turds!" he squealed, dropping the salamander.

In his pain, Jamie's fluctuating soul expanded. The salamander fell through a bubble of pure *atrum* and landed the size of a Komodo dragon.

I grabbed a carton of yogurt, ripped off the top, and dumped it over the salamander. Swiping my hand through the standing water, I sent a spray over the dairy-coated salamander. It shrank out of existence.

"Quick. Thinking." Mr. Pitt closed his eyes and passed out.

Jamie sucked on singed fingers, expression contrite. I swallowed my reprimand. But *taffy turds*? As of tomorrow, I was teaching the pooka how to cuss properly.

24

NEVER GO TO BED ANGRY; STAY UP AND PLOT REVENGE

WE EXITED INTO CHAOS. I carted out Sharon, who'd miraculously recovered enough to walk with support. The receptionist's dowdy outfit must have absorbed fifty pounds of water: It was the only explanation for the tiny woman's disproportional weight. Jamie carried Mr. Pitt, who lapsed in and out of consciousness, and Lestari flew near his shoulder. Everyone except the prajurit queen looked like a drowned kitten, drenched clothing plastered to our bodies, hair in sticky straggles around our faces. Mr. Pitt's white shirt had become transparent, and I averted my eyes from his nipples puckering beneath the thin material. A few vervet bounded out with us, but even if my hands had been free, I wouldn't have had the energy to chase them.

Firefighters intercepted us near the back door and hustled us to waiting paramedics. Between the turbonis, the soul-eating vine, and the salamanders, the battle in our office had felt like it'd lasted a lifetime, but hardly enough time had lapsed for the emergency crews to arrive. In the strobing lights of the fire trucks, the parking lot looked like a kicked ant hill: Firefighters swarmed from gigantic red trucks, some rushing into the building, others herding the milling, confused people expelled from neighboring offices. The scene washed over me, my eyes refusing to focus on any one thing, the world muffled behind deafened ears. A paramedic took Sharon from me and laid her on a stretcher. She looked like an ill-dressed child on the long bed.

My teeth chattered. For all the protection my drenched clothing provided from the winter wind, I might as well have been naked. I squeezed water out of my ponytail, then shoved numb fingers into wet armpits. A paramedic draped a thick blanket over my shoulders and I burrowed into it. Warmth woke up my sluggish thoughts, and I looked around for Jamie.

The pooka sat on the tailgate of an ambulance, looking lost. He'd gotten a blanket of his own, and a paramedic dabbed ointment on his burned fingers. She tried to get Jamie to talk, but he didn't seem to hear her. When I approached, he jerked to his feet, startling the small woman, and rushed to my side. I smiled to reassure her, then enfolded the pooka in my blanket. She must have thought us lovers, or maybe siblings, with the way Jamie fused to me, cradling his hurt hands to his chest. It would have been more accurate to view us as mother and son.

Nope. That's too weird.

"Are you okay?" I asked.

"Are you?"

I hugged him tighter. "Yes."

"Okay. Me too."

Mr. Pitt lay on a stretcher, an oxygen mask over his face. His soul flickered too weak, but he refused to let the paramedic load him into the ambulance and gestured me closer, yanking the mask free with his other hand.

"I'm fine. I need to talk with my employee." The paramedic stepped back, his face set in disapproving lines.

"You should let him take care of you, Mr. Pitt."

He waved aside my good advice. "You just saved my Abba-Zaba, Madison—call me Brad."

His Abba-Zaba? Best not to ask for clarification. "Where's everyone else . . . Brad?" His name felt strange on my tongue.

"Rose is at Margaret's office. The Illuminea are at the hotel. I couldn't chance them once I realized our region was sabotaged."

Knees weak with relief, I sagged into Jamie. Everyone was safe.

"Why not send Sharon away, too?"

Mr. Pitt—*Brad*—glanced toward the prone woman and snorted. "I'd sooner argue with a rock. What did you find today?"

I glanced at the paramedic, unsure if it was okay to speak in front of him. Gray and a few blotches of black marred his soul, proving he wasn't CIA. I chose my words carefully. "A salamander nest, though with fewer eggs than you were holding back. And a poisoned titan arum."

Brad tried to whistle and coughed instead. The paramedic forced the oxygen mask back over his mouth. My boss shoved it aside after a few breaths. "That explains Lestari."

"This wasn't Jacob, Mr., ah, Brad." Using his first name was going to take some getting used to. "We don't have a rogue enforcer in our midst. We have a rogue warden."

"I know."

"You do?"

"Who do you think planted all that *atrum* in our office?"

"Excuse me. Hey, Jim. I'll take over." Gavin barreled up to Brad's side, black doctor's bag in hand. Kathleen, Margaret, Isabel, and Liam trailed in his wake. Well, wasn't their arrival a shocking coincidence. *Not.* I rested a hand on Brad's stretcher and watched the wardens warily.

The paramedic, Jim, spoke medical jargon to Gavin. The two men obviously knew each other. How often had Gavin taken over a scene involving a CIA employee? From his confidence and Jim's reaction, this wasn't the first time, which perversely pleased me, since it meant I wasn't the only person who messed up on the job and got hurt. From the way everyone had talked about my incompetence, it'd seemed as if other enforcers mastered every problem without a hitch.

Brad waved away Gavin as he had Jim, but the medical enforcer ignored him. He gave my boss a mundane check, then probed him in several places with *lux lucis* and set Brad up with an IV and butterfly bandages for the cuts Lestari had inflicted on his neck. The other wardens ringed the stretcher, and I made sure none stood behind me. Jamie pressed tight to my side.

"You'll live," Gavin said. He turned to me, but his eyes slid to Jamie. I checked the pooka. He was behaving, his soul gleaming white where it pressed against me and swirling thunderously on his other side. "You're next."

"Stand down, Gavin," Liam said. "We can see she's not about to collapse and I'm done delaying. I evoke council and propose we revoke Brad's powers as a warden until a formal trial can be formed."

"I recognize," Isabel said.

"I recognize," Kathleen and Margaret echoed.

Disgruntled, Gavin turned to tend to Sharon, helping wheel her into an ambulance.

"Unless anyone disagrees, I disband Brad's region and place his enforcer under custody," Liam said.

I wiggled my jaw to pop my ears, but I knew I'd heard correctly. I wasn't surprised. This was all part of the rogue warden's plan. There wouldn't be a better moment to pull Brad down. No one spoke up in protest, either.

"On what grounds?" I demanded.

"On the most offensive of charges, and don't pretend ignorance," Isabel said. "Brad's done it again. He's making a rogue army. Look at you: a brand-new enforcer who takes out a demon. That's too fast to be normal. You poached a pooka—"

"I did not—"

"—and we all know pookas are attracted to two types of enforcers— those who are likely to be corrupted or those very strong. We can rule out strong. More damning is all the evil centered here, in your territory. Evil goes where it's invited, and Brad rolled out the welcome mat. If we needed further proof, all we have to do is look at your office. We all sensed the evil."

"A rogue army?" I sputtered.

"Again?" Brad asked.

"Don't feign innocence, you monster." Isabel lurched toward Brad with snarl. "You corrupted my sister. Cheryl was a good enforcer until you got your hands on her."

I reeled back, startled by the abrupt change in the motherly warden. I could see from Brad's expression he was just as surprised. He studied Isabel's rage-contorted face, eyes widening. The other wardens looked confused.

"Who is Cheryl?" Kathleen asked.

"A rogue enforcer who worked under me years ago," Brad said.

"My sister wasn't rogue!" Isabel said.

My shock faded quickly, Isabel's accusation filling in the final piece of the puzzle. Up until this moment, I hadn't been sure if Liam or Isabel was our culprit. Both made no secret of their dislike of Brad. Both stood to gain territory if they kicked Brad out. But only Isabel had a personal vendetta, and it provided the link that illuminated a pattern. Isabel hadn't been satisfied with stealing Jacob from Brad; she'd tried to plant doubts in my mind about my boss, too. I would bet my Civic Isabel was behind all of Brad's problems keeping enforcers.

Brad struggled to sit up. "Bubble gum on a cream puff! You're a *warden*; you should know better. I had nothing to do with Cheryl's choices. She nearly killed me. *She killed Lupe!* And now you tried to kill a pooka, got your own enforcer injured, and almost killed Madison and Sharon because you blame *me*? You're insane! You're—" Brad started coughing, and Gavin forced the oxygen mask over his mouth, easing him back against the stretcher.

Kathleen and Margaret shared a look over Brad's prone form, their faces unreadable.

"He's the insane one," Isabel said. Her voice shook, but next to Brad's outraged outburst, she was the model of righteous anger. "He did this once before and got away with it. I won't let him get away with it again."

Liam glanced back and forth between Isabel and Brad, clearly conflicted. Like Kathleen and Margaret, he didn't look convinced of Brad's innocence. I wanted to yell at them all to wake up and see the facts, but screaming wasn't going to persuade anyone. I needed to be the voice of reason.

"Mr. Pitt—Brad—has done nothing but protect those who work under him. He sent the Illuminea and Rose away today because he feared for them."

"More likely he didn't want witnesses," Isabel said.

"If he was rogue, could he have fooled the Illuminea as long as they've worked for him? Would he have sent me and Niko to combat evil he discovered hidden in his region?"

"'Discovered hidden'? More likely he realized he was about to be unmasked for the despicable human he is, and he sent you to get rid of the evidence."

I squeezed the blanket in my fists, stretching it tight around Jamie and myself. The pooka shifted. I didn't have to look to know he mirrored my agitation. I willed him to remain calm. Isabel had the perfect response to every argument, and the wardens were far from convinced. Brad glared over the oxygen mask, but he didn't try to speak. It was up to me to prove his innocence.

"If Brad was rogue and using *atrum* to increase his power, why would he spread it all over?" I asked. I'd realized Jacob wasn't rogue when I'd applied this same logic to him. "Why not accelerate just our region? And why would he make himself look incompetent at a time when his job is already on the line? If anything, he would have undermined Liam and Isabel since they both openly oppose him. He would have used his strength to discredit them." I appealed to Kathleen and Margaret, but neither appeared swayed by my logic.

"You're deflecting, and it's pathetic. We're standing outside your headquarters. Both your souls are weak from cleaning up the evidence before we arrived." Isabel turned to the other wardens. "We've decided to disband the region. Let's get on with it."

Liam frowned at me, but he stepped forward, his soul rotating to float around his waist. "We can sort out the details after this region is under proper protection once more."

Kathleen nodded, brow furrowed. Margaret crossed her arms, but she didn't protest.

"What about the giant turbonis?" I asked, desperate.

"Explain," Margaret said. Was it my imagination, or was she eager to slow the proceedings?

"The turbonis I spent the morning unraveling," Niko said. He strode from between parked cars, his soul gleaming like a coat of armor. I couldn't take my eyes from him. He was safe. I'd been silly to worry. The man probably ate a turbonis for breakfast each morning and walked on fire to warm his toes.

Niko took in the scene in one sweeping glance, lingering momentarily on my wet hair and Jamie plastered to my side under our shared blanket. He rested a hand on the stretcher near Brad's head.

"Brad discovered it last night, thanks to Madison." None of Niko's earlier censure at the unsafe method Brad had used to gain his insights bled into his tone. "It was in Brad's new region, contained by powerful lichtwands, and it'd been there awhile. Far longer than Brad had the region."

"Are you accusing me of something, Niko?" Liam demanded.

"Whoever put the turbonis there—and there is no question it was intentionally placed—planned to unleash the turbonis across Liam's territory."

"I certainly wouldn't do that," Liam said.

"But Brad would," Isabel said. "Everyone knows you two don't get along. It would have made you look bad, Liam, and Brad would have gotten off scot-free."

"Not with such an obvious trail pointing straight back to Brad," Niko said. "He would have implicated himself."

"No one is accusing Brad of being smart," Isabel said.

The wardens turned thoughtful eyes on Brad, but I didn't look away from Isabel. She'd had years to plan this day, and she had considered every angle. She met my eyes with a small smile. She thought she'd won. Despite everything we'd discovered, we didn't have proof. I needed more.

"Brad told Niko about the turbonis first thing this morning, right when he discovered it." All eyes focused on me, but I maintained my staring contest with Isabel. "He never lied about evil in his region, unlike you. I found a huge clump of *atrum*, vervet, and imps in Isabel's region last night." According to Val, wardens lost their edge as a by-product of using too much *lux lucis*, and a warden trying to hide her interactions with *atrum* would have to use a lot of *lux lucis* to cover up. Jacob's comment about Isabel's scattered nature seemed a lot more sinister now.

"I didn't have time to report it," Isabel said. "If you recall, my enforcer was hospitalized by *that* pooka. We were scrambling to cover the region."

"Maybe you were scrambling because you were losing control. Maybe you didn't report it because you were so busy distributing evil, you couldn't keep track of your own region. Your soul's corrupted, just like your sister's."

"My sister was a saint." Her calm facade cracked. I drove my next words into her like a knife.

"Your sister was a murderer."

"Don't talk about her! You didn't know her." Isabel stepped around the foot of Brad's stretcher, fists clenched. My heart hammered, but I clutched Jamie's arm when he shifted to step in front of me. This was my chance. Isabel had manipulated events with masterful skill, but her control over her emotions was her weakness. I pressed my advantage.

"I know Cheryl almost brought Brad to ruin, and I'm not going to let you do the same. You need to answer for killing the prajurit."

"I didn't kill the prajurit. Brad did."

"You're a murderer. Just. Like. Your. Sister." The chill in my voice almost frightened me.

"Brad is a murderer! He poisoned them! You want proof? I'll show you the titan arum he used as bait."

For one moment of silence, Isabel held her dramatic pose, arm outstretched to point at Brad. Then her face crumpled when she realized she'd incriminated herself—I had never mentioned the titan arum, only that the prajurit had been killed.

She lunged for me. I shoved Jamie aside, and he fell, tangled in the blanket. Isabel's fingers closed around my throat and squeezed.

"It's all your fault!" she screamed. *Atrum* gushed into her hands, then speckled down her soul. "Why couldn't you see Brad's evil?" Her eyes flared with insanity, fingers curling into bruising claws. I grabbed her wrists and tried to tear her hands free, but she clung to me with freakish strength. Gasping for air, I jerked a knee into her pelvis, but Isabel fell back with a cry before I connected.

"Die, murderer!" Lestari shrieked, swirling around Isabel's neck, slashing a dozen cuts into the rogue warden's flesh. Isabel released me to clamp her hands over the wounds, wailing.

Wheezing, I stumbled into Jamie. He sprang to his feet, eyes locked on Isabel. A deep dog's growl rumbled in his human throat, lifting the hairs on my neck.

"No," I croaked. Tension corded his forearm into steel bands beneath my shaking fingers. Everyone was shouting, trying to grab Isabel and block Lestari's blows. No one paid Jamie and me any attention. I tried to force the pooka to meet my eyes to break his focus on Isabel, but he'd turned to stone.

Giving up, I stretched my free hand to brace against a tree, holding my body ready to intercede if Jamie pulled free. *Lux lucis* seeped into me from the tree, and I used the energy to banish the cold taint of *atrum* Isabel had wrapped around my throat.

The rogue warden swerved closer to us in an effort to use Liam as a shield against the enraged prajurit. In a blink, Jamie pinned me to the tree, using his body to shield me.

"Oof!" The same strength that had lifted me earlier when Lestari had mistakenly attacked me held me squished against the rough trunk. Jamie fixated on Isabel with unnerving intensity. My ribs creaked under the pressure, and I fought once more to breathe.

I shoved Jamie's back, and when that didn't work, I reversed tactics. Lifting a hand to the nape of Jamie's neck, I gently stroked his exposed skin. The impact with the tree had jarred me back to normal sight, and his pale neck was shockingly warm against my icy pink fingers. The pooka turned to me, startled, and I sucked in an unrestricted breath.

"We'll make sure she gets what she deserves, but the human way, okay?"

Jamie blinked, golden eyes shifting from hound to human. I shivered, and not from the cold December wind chilling my wet clothes.

Lestari buzzed Isabel, screaming in a language I didn't know. Her wings glistened in the overcast light, but her dark clothing almost blended into the background, making her hard to track—and harder for Isabel to dodge.

"It wasn't supposed to kill so many," Isabel said, now cowering behind Liam. "I swear. The flower wasn't supposed to be so strong."

Niko stepped into the warden riot and clamped a hand on Isabel's bicep. With his usual aplomb, the optivus aegis took control of the situation, convincing Lestari to land on his shoulder and directing Gavin to tend Isabel's wounds. The rogue warden quieted in Niko's grip. Glaring at Brad, hatred twisting her expression, Isabel appeared oblivious to Gavin's ministrations and the blood seeping into her periwinkle sweater's soft collar. No trace of the kind schoolteacher-like warden remained. Even her previously pristine soul had altered, the rigid delineation of her region now a distorted blob murky with *atrum*.

"I'll collect Jacob and Grace," Niko said before escorting Isabel from the parking lot. Lestari went with them to preside over Isabel's detainment.

I waited until they were out of earshot before I asked, "Why?"

"Jacob and Grace trained under a rogue warden," Margaret explained. The events had clearly shaken her, and she huddled close to Kathleen, pulling her coat snug around her slender frame. "Their actions and loyalties are questionable, especially Jacob's with how fast he learned. They'll be interviewed by an inspector and face a Triumvirate hearing. If they're lucky, they'll be allowed to work again."

Which meant Jacob possibly was rogue. Even if he was pure, he wasn't a wunderkind, just an enforcer presented with more opportunity for speedy growth than was healthy. Or maybe he was special. After all, he'd handled all Isabel's evil by himself for two years. He'd gone through the experiences and gained strength, regardless of the origin of the evil he'd fought. Yet, even if he was Isabel's victim, I couldn't bring myself to root for him to work again. Not every decision he'd made had been good. He *had* shot Jamie.

The solemn wardens matched up souls—Brad from his stretcher—and divvied up Isabel's region. The new boundaries were temporary, until the Triumvirate sent another warden, but it meant that for the time being, Brad and I gained more territory than we had when we'd taken a piece of Liam's region.

Despite being exonerated and expanding our region's borders, Brad expressed no joy. I understood. I thought bringing down the rogue would be satisfying, but the victory rang hollow. Grief had warped an otherwise good warden into a monster. It gave me no pleasure to take part in her defeat.

I retrieved my blanket, and Jamie and I huddled together until the paramedics left with Brad and Sharon. Our offices were destroyed, but we'd recover, as would my coworkers. So would our region, now that Isabel was no longer poisoning it.

Once I finished cleaning up the mess she'd left, maybe I'd finally get to experience a normal week as an enforcer—no demon, no rogue warden.

My gaze slid to the pooka shivering beside me, his soul a swirl of good and evil energy except where our bodies touched. With Jamie tethered to me, I had a feeling normal would remain elusive.

Then again, normal was overrated.

25

DOGS HAVE OWNERS, CATS HAVE STAFF

IT WAS DATE NIGHT, FOR me and my pooka. Jamie was having his first friend date, though I'd cautioned him against calling it that in front of Sam. I owed Rose my firstborn and any other boon she requested for not only coming up with the idea but also volunteering to chaperone the outing. Jamie had left twenty minutes earlier, dressed head to toe in his brand-new clothes—including much-praised boxers—for an evening with Sam playing miniature golf and arcade games at Golfland-Sunsplash, one of the few teen-friendly locations within Jamie's tether range of the restaurant Alex was taking me to. Right now, they were still close to my apartment at Chipotle, the first meal of a dozen I was sure Jamie would charge to my credit card tonight.

As fond as I was of the pooka, and as much as he'd become an integral part of my life in four short days, I reveled in tonight's freedom. For a few hours, I wouldn't be enforcer Madison or moral referee Madison; I would just be me—excited, nervous, and horny.

I took another look around my apartment, double-checking my bedroom—which was silly, because nothing was going to happen in there, not tonight. Jamie's enormous dog bed peeked out from beneath my bed's skirt, and I scooted it in with my foot. The pooka liked sleeping in the nude as much as I did, and we'd compromised: nudity was permissible in Great Dane form only, hence the dog bed. I would continue to sleep in my pajamas.

Everything else in the room looked good. I paced back to the front room, trailed by Mr. Bond.

"It's date night!" I said, hefting the cat and spinning in a circle before plopping him into the recliner. He sprang to the floor and licked the ruffled fur on his side. Over the last two days—my first days off since I'd become an enforcer—I'd followed up on my promise to lavish attention on Mr. Bond, and he seemed to have forgiven my recent neglectfulness. I grabbed a fake mouse from his toy bin and tossed it to him. Mr. Bond leapt into the air, catching it between his paws before landing. He batted it back to me, and I tossed it again. The tubby cat enjoyed the takedown more than the chase.

I twirled to pick up the mouse, then twirled again, enjoying the flare of my skirt. Come vervet or salamanders, wraiths or turbonis, I was going on my date with Alex. I'd more than earned it, and the man had been beyond patient.

My cell phone rang, blaring out a tinny "Hail to the Chief," and I abandoned my game of mouse with Mr. Bond, my heart sinking. I stared at my boss's number on Medusa's screen, half of me demanding I bury the phone under a pillow and carry on with my date, the other half fretting that I might be needed.

Though I'd more than earned a few days off—and Gavin had insisted I'd overworked my *lux lucis* and needed to rest it to fully recover— guilt had whispered in the back of my head the last two days. While I recouped, Margaret's, Ron's, and Liam's enforcers worked overtime to clean up their regions, Isabel's former region, *and* my region.

No. I'd be back in action tomorrow, and it was foolish to think the neighboring experienced enforcers couldn't handle the diminishing evil without me.

Unless something new had cropped up.

I answered the phone with a forceful flick and growled a hello.

"Madison, how are you feeling?" my boss asked.

"Fine, Brad." Using his first name still felt foreign on my tongue, but I was getting used to it. I didn't care if I sounded clipped, either. If he said I was needed right now, a few curt words would be the least of Brad's problem.

"Good. Gavin thought two days would be plenty of recovery time, but if you need more, let me know."

"Really?" My fingers relaxed around the phone.

"You're linked to a pooka, and we can't afford for you to be vulnerable now. And speaking of the pooka, Rose told me about your arrangement for tonight. It should work out okay, but I expect a call from you as soon as the pooka's back under your care. Until then, keep your phone near you; I'll call you if he does anything that requires your attention."

"Ooo-kay?" Brad would be waiting by the phone until the end of my date? That was awkward, to say the least.

"Also, in the . . . excitement, I forgot to mention your bonuses came through."

"My what?"

It turned out there was no such thing as a pooka budget, but imprinting one qualified me for a hazard bonus. Combined with a belated bonus for taking out the demon, my checking account had an unheard-of five-figure balance. Not long ago, that would have made me feel secure for months, but between the necessary detailing of my car to get rid of ash stains and the smoke odor, feeding and clothing Jamie, replacing all the clothes I'd ruined, and paying down my credit card, part of me hoped I'd find myself in another perilous situation soon to augment my paychecks.

"How are you doing?" I asked, remembering my manners now that I knew my date wasn't on the line.

"Fine. Gavin made a big deal out of nothing. He gets too excited when he gets to take one of us to the hospital."

I hadn't gotten that impression from the ME, but rather than ruffle my boss's pride, I changed the subject. "There's one thing I haven't been able to figure out: How did Isabel get the salamanders and turbonis and that wicked plant into the office at all?"

"The element of surprise," Brad said. "She struck with a blast of *atrum* first. I think she thought she'd scare Sharon."

I snorted at the idea of *anything* scaring Sharon, and Brad chuckled in agreement before continuing. "When Sharon ran to my office to warn me, Isabel threw the goat snare—the thing you call a 'wicked plant'— across my office threshold. With us trapped, she was free to loose whatever sour ball taffy she wanted into our office. If Sharon hadn't thrown herself on the goat snare, we both would have been trapped, and Isabel would have gotten away with everything."

It was easier to picture Sharon's act of bravery than to envision the stoic receptionist running through the office. My respect for the woman increased, too; one spike through my palm had been agony, yet Sharon had knowingly embraced the pain of an entire plant's thorns to let Brad escape.

"Is she okay now?"

"She was released from the hospital before me. Sharon's made of tough stuff."

"Good. And Lestari? How's she doing?" The prajurit queen's losses weighed heavily on my mind and heart, and I wished there was something I could do for her.

"She's spending some time with a Grass Valley clan. They are the closest clan with whom Lestari doesn't have a blood feud. Or a current blood feud, I should say."

Val had said the prajurit were territorial and usually only came together peacefully over a titan arum, but Grass Valley? That was over forty miles away.

"Will she come back to our region?"

"Maybe, unless she decides to usurp the ruler of the Grass Valley clan and take over up there."

I hoped she'd decide to return to our region. I liked Lestari, and I wanted a chance to work with more prajurit.

When I hung up the phone, I checked the clock: I still had ten minutes before Alex was due. Returning to the bedroom, I checked my reflection in the full-length mirror. The orange and cream dress's ruffled skirt fluttered when I walked, emphasizing my curves and exposing my legs to just above the knee. With its square neck and empire cut, it hinted at cleavage, which was a miracle in itself, and the colors in the dress offset my skin's natural paleness. I'd left my hair down and loose, though I'd tweaked the ends to give them a bit of a curl. Makeup had never been my specialty, so I kept it simple, with concealer disguising the fading bruises on my throat, a hint of eye shadow, pale lipstick, and dark mascara to enhance my eyes. I batted my eyelashes at myself. Objective achieved: I looked kissable.

The soft murmur of a woman's voice drifted from my closet where Val rested. It'd taken three hours to get him completely clean. Afterward, I'd left him in the sun on the balcony until his pages dried. He claimed to be fully recovered and ready for more action, but it had been his suggestion to sit out my date and listen to Robin McKinley's *Sunshine* instead. Since I wasn't going to wear his strap on my date, and he didn't like being inside purses, it worked out for the best.

A rhythmic knock at the door set my heart racing. I smoothed nervous fingers down my skirt and sprinted down the hall. Mr. Bond raced across the front room and sat to one side of the door. I halfheartedly shooed him back a few steps, took a deep breath, and opened the door.

Dr. Love stood on the threshold. *Alex,* I reminded myself. He wore slim gray slacks and a long-sleeve blue button-up with a faint pinstripe. The shirt molded itself briefly to his chest when the breeze hit it, and my mouth went dry. He'd spiked his thick brown hair, and my fingers twitched to run through it.

I returned Alex's smile. "Hi."

"Hi."

He stepped inside, and I shut the door behind him, releasing my death grip on the doorknob.

"You look amazing," he said. His gaze started to slide down my body, then bounced back to my face. My entire body warmed with delight, especially when a faint blush stained his cheeks.

"Thank you. So do you."

Mr. Bond head-butted Alex's leg, then threw his body's weight against him. Alex chuckled and bent over to pet my cat.

"I see Mr. Bond is as sizable as ever."

I guiltily jerked my gaze from admiring Alex's butt to his face. Fortunately, he was looking at Mr. Bond, not me. "Oh, yes. He's still in need of a diet. And more attention. With my new job keeping me so busy, I haven't had as much time for him as I'd like."

"So I'm not the only one," Alex said, straightening, his eyes teasing.

"I'm afraid Mr. Bond has suffered worse than you," I flirted back.

Alex looked around my apartment curiously while I rooted through a blank brain for an intelligent thought.

"Have you given any more thought to the kitten? Sometimes having a companion can help relieve a cat's boredom or loneliness."

"Actually, I can't stop thinking about her," I said. The tabby kitten had been curled up in the back of my thoughts since I'd visited Alex almost a week ago. She needed a home, Mr. Bond needed a companion, and Jamie wanted a pet of his own. I wasn't sure it would work out that easily, though, which is why I hadn't mentioned it to Jamie yet. "I think I fell in love when I was in your office."

I realized it sounded like I'd confessed my love for Alex, and my tongue cleaved to the roof of my mouth. Any attempt to backpedal would make me sound like a complete basket case. The words hung between us, heating my skin until I was sure I looked sunburned.

Alex's blue eyes shone with delight. "I was hoping you'd say that."

His soft tease released me, and I stammered, "I . . . I didn't know if Mr. Bond would approve. I don't want to make his life worse."

"He seems pretty easygoing to me." Alex suffered another head-butt and body rub from my twenty-two-pound cat. "Most cats do just fine if the newest addition to the family is younger."

"Sold. We'll take her." I couldn't suppress a wriggle of anticipation. Maybe everything would work out as fantastically as I hoped.

Alex rewarded me with a grin that crinkled the corners of his eyes and made my heart flutter.

"You want to pick her up after dinner?"

"You wouldn't mind?"

"Of course not." Alex brushed hairs from his hands. I held out the lint roller, and he swiped his pants.

Jamie was happy. Val was happy. I was leaving for a date with the sweet and sexy vet I'd had a crush on for the last three years; I was beyond happy. And now Mr. Bond would have a companion.

"This is the best first date ever." I'd meant to keep those words internal, and another blush crested my cheeks. Dear God, what was with me and handsome men?

Rather than laugh off my words, Alex gave me a shy smile. "I agree."

Alex followed me down the stairs, and when we reached the sidewalk, he casually took my hand and placed it in the crook of his arm, pulling me close against the warmth of his body.

"I'm really glad we can finally do this," he said, his handsome face close to mine.

"Me too."

My body tingled from head to toe as if touched by raw *lux lucis*. I blinked and checked our souls. Alex's was white and gray, a normal human soul. Mine glistened with steady strength. The electric sizzle originated from a commonplace yet extraordinary source—pure joy singing through my veins.

Whatever catastrophes my future held, whatever disasters Jamie's dual nature orchestrated, whatever complications cropped up in my expanded region, I'd be ready to deal with them. Tomorrow. Tonight I had a date, and nothing was standing in my way.

Acknowledgments

A Fistful of Fire would not exist without you. Thank you for reading—and liking!—*A Fistful of Evil*, and giving me a reason to spend more time playing in Madison's world. I've enjoyed myself immensely, and I hope you have, too. Also, to those of you who are wonderful newsletter subscribers, thank you for voting on Madison's middle name: your responses were overwhelming and almost unanimous, and now I can't imagine Madison's middle name as anything but Amelia.

Without my editors, this book would have been a paltry shadow of itself. Thank you, Laura Anne Gilman, for your superb edits and suggestions for ways to strengthen this novel—and for calling me on it when I phoned in a major scene.

Carrie Andrews and Brooke N. Hall, thank you for making the final draft shine and for allowing me to publish with confidence.

Kate Abbott, thank you for being available for support and advice at the drop of a text. I continue to be inspired by you—your writing, your bravery, your pursuit and achievement of so many wonderful things— and consider myself amazingly fortunate to have you in my corner.

For your patience with my plot rambling and enthusiastic marketing idea monologues, thank you, Sara. You're a wonderful friend and a better sister.

Thank you, Mom, for all your support and encouragement. You're the captain of my cheering squad and my secret publicity weapon all rolled into one, and I couldn't have found the strength to achieve my dream without you.

Dad, thank you for being proud of me, even though my novels are neither scary nor about golf.

For your pep talks and sanity support, for plot analysis and brainstorming sessions, for endless hours of Photoshop work on my "quick and easy" ideas, for all the gentle reminders that my entire life is not my writing, for being my best friend, and for trusting me with your heart—I can never thank you enough, Cody, but I'll spend every day trying.

REBECCA CHASTAIN'S NOVELS ARE "A GREAT MIXTURE OF ACTION, DANGER, FANTASY, AND HUMOR."*

THE ADVENTURES OF MADISON FOX

A Fistful of Evil

Madison just learned that her ability to see souls is more than a sight:
It's a weapon for fighting evil. The only problem is she doesn't
have a clue what she's doing.

A Fistful of Fire

In the midst of an uncharacteristic flare-up of evil and with fire-breathing
salamanders blazing unchecked across the city, Madison must determine who
she can trust before her region and career go up in flames.

"Rebecca Chastain has a hit series here, one full of humor,
danger and amazingly awesome characters!" *–Tome Tender*

GARGOYLE GUARDIAN CHRONICLES

Magic of the Gargoyles

In a race to save the lives of helpless baby gargoyles, Mika must jeopardize
everything she holds dear, including her life.

Curse of the Gargoyles

Rescuing a gargoyle from a sadistic invention should have been simple for
Mika, until it ignites a chain reaction set to destroy the city, the world, and
magic itself.

Secret of the Gargoyles

In her brief career as a gargoyle healer, Mika has faced some daunting
challenges, but none have stumped her—until now.

"I loved every minute of this series." *–Feeling Fictional*

Tiny Glitches

Dealing with her electricity-killing curse makes living in modern-day
Los Angeles complicated for Eva—and that was before she was blackmailed
into hiding a stolen baby elephant and on the run with Hudson, a sexy
electrical engineer she just met.

"I laughed out loud too many times to count." *–Pure Textuality*

**Books That Hook*
www.rebeccachastain.com

About the Author

REBECCA CHASTAIN is the international bestselling author of the Madison Fox, Illuminant Enforcer series and the Gargoyle Guardian Chronicles, among other works. She has found seven four-leaf clovers to date, won a purebred Arabian horse in a drawing, and once tamed a blackbird for a day. Writing stories designed to amuse and entertain has been her passion since she was eleven years old. She lives in Northern California with her wonderful husband and three bossy cats.

Visit RebeccaChastain.com
for updates, extras, and so much more!

Join Rebecca on Facebook and Twitter
https://www.facebook.com/rebeccachastainnovels
@Author_Rebecca

www.ingramcontent.com/pod-product-compliance
Lightning Source LLC
Chambersburg PA
CBHW020324140726
47905CB00012B/234